THE DROUHIN OF SHADDIMUR

THE DROUHIN OF SHADDIMUR

A murder mystery in the Power of Pain series

ACM PRIOR

Langdown Press

Cover and Seven City map design
GA Roberts

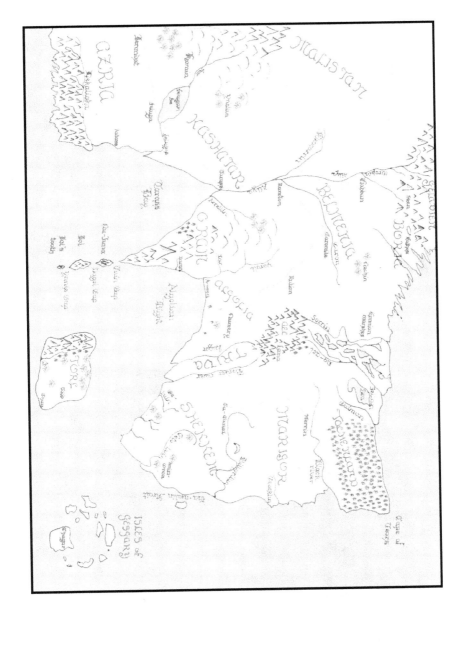

Allecundo

Palemur

Hethrin

Crab Island

Bruel

Shaddumur

moon palace

Glasts

Tartenia

Pollomol

Chersen

Correburon

Gallendia

The Seven Cities

The Land of Shekkem

Where towers grown from ancient stones
Are raised and razed again.
Dreaming mists cloak schemes and fists
And shroud the priestly chants.
Great armies march on shifting paths
Carve names in History's bark
And kings arise, their treasures pile
In shadow-haunted dark.
Whole cityscapes of minarets
Are razed and raised anew.

Prologue

Strammon spilled coins towards the rickshaw driver, then fell out onto the wet cobbles of the street. The driver was shouting something about cleaning but Strammon curled up with a moan, seeming unaware. Keen to escape the industrial area and return to where another fare was likely, the rickshaw bounced away trailing curses, jaunty lamps swinging to the beat of footsteps. Alone, Strammon staggered to his feet. The motion inside the rickshaw had been torment as it juddered over the rough stones. He retched miserably, producing little but a drool of something black in the dimness of the night. Still doubled up, he half-ran to a portal in a large double door.

Every breath marked with an 'Ah' of pain, Strammon fumbled a key from his pouch. His hands were shaking so much he had to use both of them to guide the key to the lock. He spat to clear his mouth, staggered inside and relocked the door, leaning against it blindly.

With a whimpering effort, he turned. Half-running, half-stumbling, he made it to a flight of rough wooden stairs and crawled up them. Palsied hands tearing at the fastenings of his finest clothes, he waddled to his privy, eyes nearly closed, groaning louder.

Later, he staggered from the privy, one hand holding up his breeches. He tottered as far as his bedroom but had no strength left to climb onto the bed. Strammon lay on the floor, unaware of anyone else until a voice spoke.

"I'd better clear up after you, I suppose. Business before pleasure."

Strammon twitched his head to look but his eyes were filmed. The voice was masculine. The man held a sword, which he put down on the bed. A callused hand rested on Strammon's neck for a moment, a heavy touch.

Strammon tried to turn his groans into speech. "Ha... ha... help. War ... water."

"Of course. You have nothing more to worry about."

Then the man patted Strammon's head as a sculptor might pat a block of marble and walked away. After a while, he returned with another lamp and water in a bucket. There was a strong smell of lavender. The man cleaned the floor under Strammon's face. When Strammon reached feebly towards the bucket, the man trod delicately on Strammon's sleeve to keep the hand out of his way. Then he worked back to the privy, wiping the floor with a rag. There was a stream of disgusted noises as he worked in the privy but Strammon could no longer hear them.

Finally, the man returned to Strammon.

"What a vile mess you made. Still, we can't have anyone knowing you've been puking half your innards onto the floor, can we?" He pulled Strammon's pouch from beneath his unmoving body and emptied it into his palm. Leaving only the key to the door downstairs, he slipped coins into a bag and took a second key to a strongbox under Strammon's bed. When he had rifled that to his satisfaction, he tucked more things into his bag.

The man kicked the strongbox out of his way. He collected the sword from the bed, looked down at Strammon and smiled.

"Now the fun begins... By the Tooth, you're not dead already?" He bent down and poked Strammon's eye with a thick finger. There was not the least reaction. The man stood back, wiping a hand over his bald head.

"Ghulsk! Doubly unfortunate!" In a burst of rage, he stabbed the sword right through the body at his feet and left the hilt standing like a monument while black blood crept across the boards to kiss his feet.

The man yanked the sword free. He inspected the scant smears of blood on the steel and frowned. Then he crouched and dipped both sides of the blade in the dark puddle.

"Still," he said softly, "Who's going to know?"

The Last Apprentice?

"With these murders spread before you like a banquet, you said you needed a new apprentice, Kalainen. Lord Berrin's boy Mardenifol is the right age. Smart lad, I'm told."

"Berrin's third boy? You mean he's clumsy, can't fight and has no affinity for the gods. What is Lord Berrin to do with number three, eh? Still less, me - you know I've already found a girl from Meiling Square. Why him, Quern?" Kalainen's slight drawl and his habit of accenting words marked him as not only a stranger in Shaddimur, but from beyond the Seven Cities.

"He's had the best tutors. Clever as a weasel, I expect, Kalainen. All books and cleric things." Sprawled across a chair, Quern smiled coaxingly, strong teeth showing through his beard. At best, the sight was alarming.

"He may have mastered his letters but..."

"Then shall I arrange it?"

"By the Bell of Mirrin's Tower, Quern, why do you want me to take him? Have you taken a wager?" Kalainen turned from the window, the skin crinkling round his eyes as he tried not to smile. In his middle years, he had a solid warmth about him, but he seemed small compared with Quern.

Opening hands the size of bucklers, Quern tried for an expression of wounded innocence. "Certainly not!"

"Is there a woman involved at all?"

"How could you possibly think...?"

"Who is she this time?" Kalainen sounded more resigned than reproving.

Quern shrugged shoulders as wide as the sea and grinned. "Well, this boy Mardenifol, it's his older sister, Rallamela, pretty girl, she may have sort of suggested..."

"I see. I should've known. It's not just that I have a duty to preserve Rallamela from your attentions; I don't want to coddle some noble brat." The smile faded from Kalainen's round face and he sighed, staring out of the window. He gestured outside. "What do you see?"

"Out there? Nothing to see. Hills, trees. You've rented a house on the rump of Shaddimur. What am I supposed to be looking at?" Stifling a yawn, Quern leaned back, stretching his arms. His olive-green shirt strained at the lacings and the chair creaked a complaint.

"I wouldn't know where to begin to tell you." Kalainen's lips twitched in a wistful smile as he gazed out. A hefty man in a smock was trudging along behind a handcart from which he sold milk from a copper-bound churn by the stoup or half stoup. Trailing autumn's mist of flies, he was heading home for the next milking. Beyond the edge of Shaddimur, two plump Correbaran cobs with a wagon of lumber from the sawmill paused in the Battafell Brook while the horses cooled their legs in the stream. In the low ground to the west, water-oaks and softbark trees enmeshed in vines marked the edge of a swamp.

"You've lived here all your life. All this is just Shaddimur to you.

I'm from Drouhin; a stranger here. I've seen many towns and learned to read them."

"I've travelled a bit," said Quern, sounding hurt.

"Really? Quern, I've known you almost all the two years I've been in Shaddimur and you've never said. Where've you been?"

"Bruel."

"Bruel," said Kalainen after a pause. "That's it? You live in a little group of cities in a forgotten corner of Shekkem, itself but one country in the vast lands of Kassa and you have only been to Bruel? That isn't even one of the Seven Cities proper, just a large port that split off from Hethrin about thirty years ago!"

"Is it?"

"Yes. Have you never wondered why the Seven Cities had eight cities in it?"

Quern's gaze drifted sideways as he did some counting. He shrugged. "Well, since you've had me watching your back, I've earned a bit of coin and cracked a few heads here. Lots of fun! Why travel? Anyway, I still went there."

"What impression did it make?"

"They talked strangely and laughed at *me* for having an accent."

"Outrageous," Kalainen chuckled. "Quern, I have walked the lanes of Marigor, crossed the great rivers of Triva and even been on part of the Golden Road as far as Caronile in Belmenia. I have visited four of the Seven Cities – and Bruel. When I look through the window, the fields speak of what Shaddimur does to feed itself; wheat, goats and apricots. The tracks tell me how much trade there is and in which direction, the very colour of the stream speaks of minerals in the hills. You know this and don't need to see, for the dust of Shaddimur has grown into your bones. Look, is there a wind blowing?"

"Yes, I suppose so; a light one. From the south." Quern sounded rather triumphant with that.

"Indeed. But see that drift of old mimosa seeds curling and eddying this way and that; the cat's paws of wind dipping the grasses in waves? Nothing's constant, is it? That column of kites spirals upwards on a gyre hidden to our eyes. Within the wind there are a thousand variations of flow and speed. I need someone who can see the city like that. Who is drifting with the current, who is fighting against it; who rising and who falling."

"I don't think watching a few social mimosa seeds is going to help your imp from the rat holes of Meiling Square spot the assassin that haunts Shaddimur, until a blade digs her between the ribs. You won't get a better lookout than Imber."

"It's different. Nobody sees Imber because he makes himself near invisible. Nobody sees street children because nobody notices them, any more than they notice pigeons."

"But why take on some gutter urchin rather than a boy with a fine education? It's not decent!"

"Perhaps not, Quern. Decency doesn't come high on the list of virtues in the underbelly of a city. And on that matter, my urchin Yanni is small for her age, but she's growing into a woman. You know what her future's likely to be if she stays where she is. And yes, I do think a girl from the streets will pick up a lot more than some noble's son raised with his nose in the air. Just to survive, she's had to be alert to these nuances. However, we'll conduct a little test and see. You'd better meet Yanni. She's in my workroom now."

There was a faint scrape and a rustle from behind the door, which Kalainen opened to reveal a room with shelves of books. Lamps surrounded a battered leather chair near the window. A pair of discarded boots sagged beside it. The skull of some sharp-tined beast was twisted sideways by the weight of a chainmail hauberk carelessly slung over one prong. Scrolls, papers and maps had no doubt once been nicely ordered before time and Kalainen's enthusiastic riffling had toppled the piles. A girl, all spiky hair and huge eyes, was sitting in a chair behind the desk. She gave her head a tiny shake as though drawn back from some deep introspection and looked up. She saw Kalainen's eyes flick over a pile of half a dozen florins on the desk, almost hidden by papers.

"Was they the test then? I ain't touched nothin'." She pulled a bright red wrap Kalainen had lent her more tightly round her bony shoulders.

Then Quern ducked inside. Yanni took one look at the massive warrior, his tousled mound of hair and wide beard making him look even huger, and almost slid under the table.

"Girls who make such a fine job of pretending they were not eavesdropping at the door shouldn't give themselves away with the first thing they say. Do you think that was the test?"

Kalainen's voice was so kindly and Quern's grin so full of humour that Yanni found the courage to reply.

"Some wouldn't be able to stop themselves and swipe the lot. Some clever ones would tickle one, maybe two coins. Maybe some would be too a-feared to take any."

"So why didn't you?"

"You'd notice. You want summat but I don't think it's a thief or a runner. If I can pretend I have it, I can escape Meiling Square."

"You don't mind telling me you might pretend to something?" asked Kalainen, trying not to laugh.

Yanni shrugged. "Pretend or be: no difference. Pretend to be confident or be confident, what's the odds to everyone else? Pretend to have a hidden blade convincingly enough and there's no need to draw it. People think you have back-up, you don't need to call on them. Or double bluff, pretend badly to be weaker than you are and they worry about what you're hiding. All that matters is someone believes your version and that makes it same as true."

"How could you pretend to be weaker than you are?" Quern

chuckled, then became suddenly serious. "You might not be better off working for Kalainen, you know."

"You think it's easy living on the street? Finding something to eat takes all day or doesn't happen at all and the best night I can remember was spent on a donkey's breakfast where the conkin' dogs couldn't reach me."

Quern made a harrumphing noise. "Yes, well. What's your full name anyway?"

"Yanni ... Smowt."

Kalainen smiled with amusement. "Well then, Dame Smowt, perhaps you would accompany Sir Quern here to the Levanine Market, where you can meet Lord Mardenifol Berrin. Just have a look round and bring me back a report of anything that seems to you to be worth mentioning."

"Can't go to the Levanine." Yanni's head sank into her thin shoulders.

"There is a killer in Shaddimur, but they're killing rich, powerful people, Yanni. You're safe enough."

"You think anywhere's safe for people like me in Shaddimur? Quern said you needed a new apprentice. What happened to the last one?"

Quern gave a sour snort. "She's sharper than you might like, Kalainen. But what's wrong with the Levanine Market?"

"Run by the Owlers. Won't let me hang around there."

"What Owlers? Place is peaceful as a nunnery." Quern looked suddenly thoughtful.

Kalainen flicked a glance at him, suspecting that rather than considering a life of quiet contemplation, Quern would be thinking how he could disturb the nunnery's peace. "The Owlers are a group of petty thieves and beggars that operate in the Levanine," he said. "They wouldn't tolerate anyone horning in on their patch. But don't worry, Yanni. You're now wearing a proper blouse and tunic rather than..." He waved vaguely in the direction of a pile of unidentifiable scraps reeking quietly in a corner. "You'll just be a kitchen girl stocking up with provisions."

"I'll do it," blurted Yanni, "but don't know what you want from me."

"I need someone who can listen just like you listened at my workroom door, but not get caught. I need eyes in the city that can see without being seen; ears that overhear unnoticed. I need to know if you can tell what to see and what to hear – and whether you can remain inconspicuous. We'll meet back at Coromal – that's this house, Yanni - at sundown. You should be all right at the Levanine, unless you try to filch something." He made to toss one of the florins to the girl, changed his mind and slipped it into his pouch with the rest of the coins. He handed Yanni a few copper coins. "No good asking you to blend in and then giving you a big silver coin to spend, eh?" Kalainen shot a questioning look at Quern and received a nod. "Don't worry. Quern will go with you. It's on his way to Berrin's."

The Levanine market was in a square under plane trees, speckled with sunlight. The place buzzed with chatter as folk browsed, haggled or sat in the sun with glasses of beer. Old women filled baskets with nuts and radishes or pecked over trays of sea urchins with disapproving clucks. Aubergines and peppers glistened, wrinkled tubers and roots still clung to crumbs of soil. Jerryn the knifeseller sharpened old blades while hopefully pointing out new ones to women in shawls, or fingered daggers and rapiers while nodding to bravos, who leaned against trees, bare arms folded. Rich smells beckoned from ham sliced off the bone or cheeses, from tiny dollops of goat's cheese up to half-barrel monsters with rhinoceros skins. A couple with a viol and triangle played and sang while puppets aped their actions by their feet. Children stared with round eyes while their parents cruised past hawkers of elixirs and potions, racks of artichokes and apples, jars of oil, honey and jam.

The atmosphere was as different from Meiling Square as it could be. A smile tickled Quern as he watched Yanni gawping. The smile widened as he spotted flagons of cider under an awning. He shooed Yanni away and decided to refresh himself in case he met Rallamela.

The Drouhin was lighting lamps in his snug when Quern returned to Coromal, two youngsters in his wake. Mardenifol was in his late middle teens; nearly as tall as Quern but gangling and slight with a sharp nose and pointed chin. His adam's apple looked as though he had swallowed an arrowhead and it bobbed up and down as though held by a terrified bowman as Quern introduced him to Kalainen.

Kalainen frowned for a second at Mardenifol's strangely lop-sided arrangement of straight hair, then smiled a welcome and motioned them towards a platter of shortbread and a jug of water flavoured with citrons. Yanni looked at the water as though it concealed scorpions.

"Mother Yellern made the shortbread for you this afternoon. The water is from my own rainwater cistern; the fruit just makes it taste nice. Mardenifol, what can you tell me of the Levanine Market?"

"Just a typical market; busy, noisy, dirty." Mardenifol's eyes flicked sideways to Quern's meaningful expression and he lowered his piece of shortbread with a sigh. "I saw lettuce and olives and stuff being sold. The baker's boy was minding the baker's stall for him and judging by how red-faced he was, I think he was struggling to work out the change. No good for more than humping sacks of flour, that one." Mardenifol relaxed at the smile from Quern. "There were loads of material stuffs on offer. The Preacher's Stand was occupied most of the time. Two, maybe three different preachers, all spouting about gods and prayers and punishments."

Kalainen nodded encouragingly, thinking that while Mardenifol's accent was from Shaddimur, it marked him as from an aristocractic family as clearly as the fine weave of his clothes or the delicate tooling on his broad belt. "And how would you interpret what you saw? What did it mean?"

"Oh. Well, it was just what you'd expect. The market was full of traders trading. The commerce continues, nobody fomenting sedition. All seemed well." Mardenifol turned back to the shortbread, but the plate was miraculously empty.

"Excellent. And what about you, Yanni? Anything to add?"

"Nobody doing what?" Yanni tried to talk normally round an enormous mouthful and wiped away crumbs with a quick gesture.

"Fomenting sed... oh, encouraging rebellion against the Queen."

"What sort of half-wit would be doing that in the middle of the Levanine Market? Unless it was agents of the queen looking to arrest anyone what agreed with them. But he spoke right. Right about the baker's boy too, but he was flustered because he'd been left in charge of the last bit of stock and some rolls got pilfered – it weren't me - and he couldn't chase the lifters without losing more and he'll likely get blamed for the loss.

"There was a Lady Gotha and she made a great fuss at finding nothing to please her in the silks of O-Ram, and finally bought one expensive Tia feather after much flouncing. There was a trader from Palemin but he never bought nor sold nor flapped his cape about. There was also a group from Gallendia going from stall to stall asking for purple dyes. There was a Captain Maiban came from the saddlers. He ordered several pairs of new boots and bought dried fruit; dates, figs and apricots, as well as hard biscuits and Modrella cheeses."

"Well, there you have it," said Quern. "Just a normal market." He glanced at the crestfallen Mardenifol. "We don't learn anything from your test."

"No? Clearly Lady Gotha is out of money and trying to show otherwise. If she owed me a large sum, I'd be more than concerned.

We can tell that Captain Maiban is off on another expedition somewhere. Important? It all depends."

"Ridiculous guesswork, Kalainen. Am I supposed to infer some
plot against the crown just because someone stole half a dozen rolls
from the baker?" Quern rolled his eyes theatrically. "They bought
seven buns! Aha, a secret code proving the wife of the Bruelan ambassador consorts with camels!"

"Everyone needs breakfast," admitted Kalainen with a chuckle.
"But suppose they were buying marzipan rolls topped with nuts and
honey, then what?"

"Then they have a sweet tooth. What of it?"

"With such rolls, they would be devotees of Schren celebrating
the feast of the blessed Arlia – making them schismatic or heretical
to some."

"Perhaps," said Quern after a long pause. "I see what you're tilting
at. And you just have to ignore pointless information like the
traders from Palemin and Gallendia?"

"They were the most interesting. Quern, you know the political
situation is a tinderbox; all the Seven Cities on edge, treaties on
the point of being signed, alliances shifting, the Tarlenian military
machine building. Not everyone is sitting waiting to see what happens. Everywhere agents are jockeying for an advantage; ferreting
secrets, sniffing out fears, planning for contingencies. A trader from
Palemin who neither trades nor twirls his cape is neither a trader
nor from Palemin. So who is he and what's he trying to learn? The
group with long belted coats and tall hats may be from Gallendia.
But asking for purple dyes is likely a cover. Purple dyes are hideously
expensive. But it's a great story for talking to many merchants and
collecting news and views. Don't you think?"

"Bah. You'd best keep your urchin, Kalainen." Quern's face was
glum, his thoughts on the retreating form of Rallamela.

Where Quern was down, Yanni was buoyant and chirped up again.

"There was a trader that I never saw do no trading. What about him? Never saw no buyers. Not sure what he was selling and he made no effort to hawk it. Looked like yellow spice and hard honey and bottles of black stuff and a flask of water. He was a bit fat and old, his cloak was all stained and he'd no money pouch on him."

"I saw him," said Mardenifol, his wide mouth drooping at the corners as he thought. "Don't remember what he looked like. I think he was an alchemist."

"Really? Why?"

"All those things burn. It was sulphur, resin and black oil. The flask wasn't water, it was naphtha. The smell is unmistakeable, of course."

Kalainen was looking at Mardenifol with a quizzical expression. "How would you know that?"

"I love that stuff. I've got all sorts of glassware and stuff at home. I love working out how things work, you know, fire and stuff. That's what happened to my hair. The stuff burned a bit friskier than I expected."

"You saying you're a magician," asked Yanni doubtfully.

"Not sorcery; alchemy," said Kalainen.

"What's the difference?"

"Sorcery is a formidable but rare phenomenon, though there are loremasters even in Shaddimur who may have that ability. These people can use their own pain to power arcane spells."

"I read about them," said Mardenifol. "People who drink pain and vomit fire! Sounds fabulous."

"Perhaps it is, until you feel the pain, which I am told is severe. It takes a strange person to provoke that much agony for magic, but they are frighteningly powerful. Not in the Seven Cities, but I have seen..." Kalainen paused, his face twisted by memory. "Horrors, or wonders." He cast the memory aside with an effort and brightened for Yanni and Mardenifol's benefit. "Alchemy covers a range of skills. Some say alchemists can extend life or create gold. Mostly it is shaping natural matter for various ends; creating explosions or potent toxins."

"But mostly bad smells," said Mardenifol with a grin. "Particularly with sulphur. Really bad smells."

"I think," said Kalainen, "I might be able to manage two apprentices."

Why kill a dead man?

"Captain Traid of the Shaddimur Watch," announced Mardeni-fol. With a much-practised bow that was considerably more than the occasion warranted, he ushered in a heavily built man with impressive whiskers. Despite the warmth of the day, Captain Traid was wearing a coat of blue leather with brass buttons, together with one of the wide belts favoured in Shaddimur. He looked powerful but his sprinting days were long gone.

"Kallanan," muttered the captain.

Kalainen managed to give a respectful nod, rather than wince at the mispronunciation of his name. Few in Shaddimur got it right.

Traid sucked in his cheeks and looked at Kalainen with an air of magisterial disapproval. The investigator smiled seraphically and raised his eyebrows. Traid chewed on his whiskers for a moment and then made an announcement.

"The forces of the Watch are fully engaged with matters of state." He glared round but it wasn't clear whether he thought they should be impressed or whether he feared some might argue the point.

Kalainen's expression remained entirely unchanged. "Yes, well, given the shortage of resources while prosecuting these duties, a matter has cropped up requiring tact, diplomacy and skill."

"My middle names," murmured Kalainen.

"Hmf. Be that as it may, I'm short-handed ... look, are you sure these imps should be listening?" Traid suddenly broke out, waving with distaste at Mardenifol and Yanni, who sat demurely enough but stared at the Captain with what looked like impudence to Traid.

"Quite sure," said Kalainen, and waited for Traid to continue.

"Anyway, I have been directed by the highest authority – the *highest* authority - that you be required to deal with this issue, despite.... well." Traid waved vaguely at Kalainen's clothing; soft charcoal breeches and paler grey shirt, which revealed nothing of his affiliations in the Seven Cities.

"Me? I am flattered the Queen would know my name."

"I'm sure she does not. But someone demonstrably neutral is required. And quickly. You're from Drouhin – wherever in Balgrim's name that is - with a reputation for solving problems. Best we can do."

Kalainen made a tiny movement of resignation. "So, what do you have?"

"A trader was killed last night. It's complicated because he is – was - a Tarlenian. The Tarlenian ambassador has already alleged that no action has been taken because of the trader's Tarlenian identity. The Tarlenians even had the audacity to impugn the impartiality of the Watch! They tried to insist that their own agents should be empowered to investigate, as there were no unbiased organisations. That's when your name cropped up. You have been of some assistance in the past – for a fee – and owe no direct allegiance to any of the city states. Drouhin, of course, doesn't qualify as anything."

Kalainen rubbed his temples with the thumb and middle two fingers of his right hand, then drew a deep breath. "You want me to investigate the death of some minor trader? I'm sure every death is equally significant in the eyes of the Lady Lessan, but what about whoever is killing the richest and most powerful nobles of Shaddimur?"

"The full weight of the Watch is endeavouring to bring that matter to a close without interference from nit-picking outsiders. However, we are further stretched as I'm also in charge of security in the matter of the tournament. You will be aware that this event, designed to promote peace, harmony and fraternal union between the Seven Cities, is extremely important. Your role is to settle these carking local difficulties that might chafe at the bonds of amity."

"Chafe?"

"Look, they're all itching to get at each other's throats, Kallinum. Tarlenia wants war. Nobody trusts Allecando in the east or Gallendia in the south because they're hiding behind buffer cities between them and Tarlenia. The rest are only united in fearing Tarlenia, bleating for allies to help them but refusing to commit their own forces or antagonise the Tarlenians. The least excuse will be a flame to burn half the city states. Including Shaddimur. It must be prevented."

"And the fee?"

"Fee? If an excuse to use military might is offered to Tarlenia, the Queen, you and every last ragamuffin in Shaddimur is under extreme threat. You have a civic duty!" rejoined Traid hotly.

"No doubt. However, a man must eat. My fee?"

"Do you eat nothing but quails' eggs and larks' tongues?"

"I may have quirks but better a flawed diamond than a perfect pebble."

"Bah, in truth the Queen herself has insisted you be well rewarded – on success."

"Very well. My associates will have costs during the investigation."

"What associates? The whole point is that you have no ties in Shaddimur!"

"Nor do I. You may know Quern..."

"Quern? Marked as a Shaddimur man and hardly subtle! If you compromise this investigation..."

"... and Imber."

"Imber? That scoundrel?"

"I've never seen him do anything untoward." Kalainen gave an innocent smile.

"No-one ever sees him do anything. Nobody *sees* him at all!"

"Perhaps even Chelidor the Wanderer may happen this way."

"A crew of disreputable wastrels! Fortunately, at least Chelidor has wandered off." With a sigh, Traid waved his hands at Kalainen. "Oh, very well, a reasonable sum can be found. You've employed Quern before, but Imber? Well, if you fail for any reason... that responsibility will have repercussions, I warn you. The fate of one Drouhin won't cause ructions with any state or faction. Now, may we proceed?"

"What details do you have?"

Traid assumed a pose, hands behind his back, and declaimed, "The trader is one Strammon. He has a business and warehouse on Butsun Causeway and there he was found this morning by his staff, stabbed to death. We have established that the only keys were held by Strammon and the members of his staff. A vital clue! Only two men working for him, Tastan and Ythil. As Strammon's key has been identified and is accounted for, both men have been arrested and are held while we establish which of the two killed him."

"The case seems as good as solved," murmured Kalainen. "But since I am compelled by a sense of duty, was the place actually locked?"

"Well, of course Tastan and Ythil *said* they found it open, but they would, wouldn't they? Strammon just forgot to lock it yesterday evening with all his trade goods there? Highly unlikely!"

"What did Strammon trade in?"

"Stone and stonework. Marble, soapstone, alabaster and malachite. Just rock. Worked and even allegedly imbued with nebulous qualities such as 'luck' at his warehouse. Ha! Tarlenian charlatan. Anyway, you will understand that speed is critical here. The matter needs to be settled swiftly. Were the workers not also Tarlenian, it would already have been done. Even a confession..." Glowering darkly, Traid thumped one meaty hand into the other.

"Would not be credible," finished Kalainen.

"No. So we need proof. And so do you if you want to be paid."

"Have you done anything to stop the queue of sightseers, gawpers and quidnuncs trampling over the place?"

"I have indeed detailed a man to wait down there. The place is locked and my man has Strammon's key. Now, I have much to do and suggest you hurry off and sniff about like a good doggie." Captain Traid marched to the door, which Mardenifol opened for him, sweeping a low bow. The Captain growled audibly.

"Traid," called Kalainen. "The leading citizens who've been murdered in Shaddimur are all..."

"We're on the verge of a breakthrough there, without your help."

"Oh, not the Dancing Goddess."

"Kallerin, there are sigils of the Dancing Goddess at every murder scene! We have but to identify..."

"The Dancing Goddess is a Shaddimur cult. They might well attack any outsider but why would they kill the most powerful in Shaddimur? It doesn't make sense!"

"Scrawls of the Dancing Goddess every time. What am I supposed to think?"

"You are supposed to think – not think what they want you to think!"

"You and your words! It may not make sense to you but I'm not ignoring images of the Dancing Goddess at each murder scene, always drawn in white with red on one hand. I've pulled in cult members. There are hints of shady deals, selling out to other cities, conspiracies..."

"When aren't there, Traid? It doesn't matter how many people you punch, there isn't any evidence because it's just misdirection. A few wispy emblems of the Dancing Goddess pirouetting over blood stains and you're chasing rainbows. Can't you see that all the dead are people concerned with the defence of Shaddi..."

"We're dealing with it. Keep your nose out, doggie! You deal with Strammon." Traid banged the door behind him.

As the front door slammed, the workroom door opened and Quern hopped out, grinning. "He really doesn't like you!"

"Xenophobic antipathy."

"Or a resentment of the amount of money you were paid in that matter of the Moon Palace!"

"You feed the duck that lays the egg."

"Meaning what?"

"I get results where he has failed."

"Ah yes, another good reason why he hates you."

"Perhaps. We have a different approach to solving a crime. Traid relies entirely on grabbing some unfortunate and beating them until they admit they did it. I try to follow reason to establish who is actually guilty."

"And he doesn't mind whether they're guilty or not?"

"Not really. Providing someone is caught and punished, he's seen to be doing his job and the populace sees that punishment follows crime."

"Even if it's the wrong person?" Quern needled cheerfully.

"Nobody knows – well, except the real malefactor and they can't say. Traid would argue that good knowledge of the city meant nabbing the right villain in the first place. He'd say if they hadn't done it, they would have done if they'd thought of it. But this time, it isn't good enough. He has a Tarlenian victim, Tarlenian suspects and orders to be nice to Tarlenians. No wonder he's unhappy!"

"He doesn't seem to know you've worked with Imber before."

"No, well, Imber is easy to miss. Anyway, I said Traid'd come to me eventually."

"You said Traid would come to you about the assassin killing the rich and powerful in Shaddimur. You've pumped everyone in the Watch you know for every detail, you've got all your notes and diagrams on every murder and he gets you to waste time on some minor mason."

"The brook would stop singing without a few stones in it."

"Would it? Not the sort of thing said by the person who's just stubbed their toe on the rock."

Kalainen laughed. "Perhaps. But you saddle on the horse you're holding. The mason was Tarlenian; it is a start. Now we just have to see whose hole the mouse runs into."

"Can you only talk in sayings?"

"A saying to a Drouhin is as natural as song to a thrush. But now a man's been killed and if we don't solve the murder, war looms between the states. The stakes could hardly be higher." Kalainen sounded delighted.

"But why is war looming? A stone mason is killed. There were three bodies in a heap behind The Strangler's Arms on Balgrim's Eve and nobody was talking about Traid panicking or wars between the city states. But a war...!" Quern's head came up. There was a grin on his face and his right hand clenched into a fist.

"Quern! Wars are bad, particularly for Shaddimur and everyone in it."

"Yes, yes, I know." Quern completely failed to look abashed.

"No, you don't. You've been in more fights than all the cats in the fish market, but not a war. Battles are being caught in a crush of men running blindly towards an enemy or running blindly from no-one knows what; or being hit by impersonal arrows from archers you never saw or being stabbed in a melee by the wild blade of friend or foe."

"Wars change everything..."

"Wars change nothing. The conscripted smith returns to being a smith. His forge may be smashed or his body broken but he remains a smith. Perhaps a different name sits on a throne. Perhaps a priest in a robe of different hue urges you to bow in a new direction when the vesper bells ring."

"Didn't know you'd ever been in a battle!" Quern assessed the Drouhin as though seeing him for the first time; the hair and beard were cut very short but perhaps prematurely greyed, the frame was stocky, the fingers thickened. The big man frowned thoughtfully.

"A long time ago and I don't want to see another."

"All right, all right. But these killings seem to get more important every time you talk of them."

"Because that is exactly what's happening. When the first city notable was killed, it was a shock but seemed just a bungled robbery. Then the second and third murders happened and each time something important was stolen, but just one thing from some of the richest houses. It began to look like someone stealing to order. But after the next murder and the next it hinted at a much deeper plan; a plan to weaken Shaddimur itself by killing those who would orchestrate the defence."

"But why all this talk of war, Kalainen?"

"Tarlenia is a military nation and the economy needs expansion. I've seen their expansion first-hand. My road here passed through Cherisen, a sweet little town on the Correbaran side of the Gattan Ridge near Tarlenia. Tarlenia now claims the gutted bodies and burned ruins they left of it. Cherisen was not the only town. The

Tarlenians will need more; the only question people ask is whether the Tarlenians will go on attacking isolated towns or whether they will gobble up Bruel; it's the smallest city and it would give Tarlenia access to a good port. But the Seven Cities are a mess. Bruel is split with some fearing a war and some happy to provoke it while their alliances with Correbaran and Gallendia hold and they are near a new one with Shaddimur. Of course, Bruel's nearest neighbour, Hethrin, still maintains an empty claim to Bruel and some in Hethrin may intrigue with Tarlenia hoping to get it back."

"Fools," snorted Quern. He pushed fingers through the lacings of his shirt and scratched pensively. "What would you say? If you're made of meat, don't throw titbits to a pack of wolves?"

"Something like that," smiled the Drouhin. "Generally, outlying lands with limited resources are eager for war and plunder. Those nearer to Tarlenia fear to be the first victims of the same thing. Logic suggests that Tarlenia will work to weaken the alliances and stop new ones. Or perhaps go for the big target and plan to take Shaddimur."

"Ha. Shaddimur's too strong for them," Quern laughed, clenching a huge fist.

Kalainen sighed. "Nobody sees it – yet. You all love this place, this charming, sprawling chaos of a city on the bay with its tree-lined squares and ridiculous divisions of Loremasters, Neers and Sunsunnis, but you won't see it is under threat! The best response I've had was an admission that the murders might inconveniently reduce Shaddimur's effective response time if Bruel were invaded. Suggest Shaddimur might be attacked and all I get is a complacent laugh, or a pat on the head and someone asking, 'where is it you come from again?' as if that meant I was obviously ignorant of the invulnerability of Shaddimur."

"You think Shaddimur might be under threat?" asked Mardeni-fol, worry rumpling his face. "Why don't we just sign the treaty with

Bruel then? I mean, why haven't we got one already?" His voice was getting higher as though Tarlenian thugs were beating at the door.

"There's time to stop it, if people act," Kalainen reassured him. "There was a treaty with Bruel that died with the old king. A new one is complicated. Too generous to Bruel and relations with Hethrin are soured. How should Shaddimur be compensated for sending troops to Bruel? And Bruel doesn't want to swap the over-lordship of Hethrin for Shaddimur, just for trying to dodge Tar-lenia."

Mardenifol grimaced as the simple treaty dissolved into a roiling knot of difficulties. But at least Kalainen had responded to his questions without making him feel a fool, rather than the humiliating comments he would have received at home.

Quern rolled backwards and scratched a bit lower. "But this tournament is supposed to be all about friendship between the states and the Tarlenians are taking part in that. They even started the whole thing off!"

"Yes. Strange, that. Quern..."

"I know that face. What do you want me to do?"

"No point in running until we know where the lion waits. Could you take part in the tournament?"

"Not a hope. Only one contestant from each of the eight cities. And for Shaddimur it is of course Shen of the Sunsunni. In any case, the lists have long been drawn up and the first bouts start today."

"Hm," said Kalainen, scrawling a note. "Well, get this message to Imber for me, then do some digging while we look at the stone ma-son's place."

After Kalainen had spent a while studying maps of the city around Butsun Causeway, they walked there, both youngsters com-fortable in his company after a week at Coromal. For a time, they followed a wide-wheeled brewer's dray which cleared their path down a bustling street. There were few wagons or carts in Shaddimur and they were supposed to stay on the cobbled or paved roads. It kept the streets fairly clear of horse dung and prevented damage to streets of packed earth. Even then, the cobbles of one road from the docks had been inadequately underpinned. After laden wagons had broken it into stony waves, the locals called it Jumblegut Lane and made sure not to cross it.

A rickshaw came slapping up behind them. Balked by the dray, the runner showered the dray driver with original invective, probably for the benefit of whoever sat in the curtained box. It had no effect on the drayman but caused many bystanders to laugh. Yanni merely scowled and stamped along angrily. Eventually she snapped out, "So who is Shen of the Sussnis?"

"The Sunsunnis. Sunsunni is the warrior god," said Kalainen with calm patience. "The devotees form one of the three main factions in Shaddimur and the best warrior among them wears the beaded cape and headdress as the Avatar of Sunsunni. At the moment, the avatar is Shen."

"Never heard of him."

Mardenifol laughed. "No, but anyone in a faction in Meiling Square would be a Neer; those with a flexible attitude to laws."

"All right, oh fount of knowledge," said Kalainen. "What is the third faction then?"

"The Loremasters."

"So why are we ruled by a Queen from the House of Khaad and not one of the factions?"

Mardenifol blushed. Kalainen's tone immediately softened. "Don't mock anyone for what they don't know. Even the eagle only flies so high. You shouldn't feel bad about not knowing things, Yanni. Ask your questions. Just as we're doing about this murder. You've worked hard to stay alive, not worry about political manoeuvrings in Shekkem or the Seven Cities or even Shaddimur. You know a lot more about Meiling Square and surviving with nothing than I do."

There was a long pause before Mardenifol mumbled, "Sorry, Yanni." Just the way he said it made Kalainen think apologising for failure was normal for Mardenifol.

Yanni brightened. "Well," she asked, "why are we ruled by Queen Nylla then?"

"Ah, so I am punished! I know little of it except there is some Shaddimur traditional ceremony out in the old Moon Palace to pick a new monarch. Normally the selection made miraculously accords very neatly with the powers of the different three factions at that time. But no doubt it is all very mystical."

"Why aren't we ruled by Shen as king then?" asked Mardenifol.

"Because it is a bit more complicated than that. If ever one of the big three rises too high, the other two find their interests running parallel and the leading faction is brought down again. A bit like a three-legged stool; to keep it flat, it needs all three legs the same length. Queen Nylla has little power of her own and must tread more carefully than a lily-hopper in a lake of crocodiles. But now we are near Strammon's warehouse and must be even more careful ourselves. Watch where you put every single foot lest you smudge some print."

Traid's man was playing dice with a couple of wild-haired locals dressed in stained hessian trousers. In-between frequent pulls at a skin of small beer to wash down their lunch of sardines and wheat cakes, they joked and gybed over the dice rolls like gulls over a scrap. Kalainen walked quietly over to them and greeted them, causing them to jump, the watchman toppling a tower of pennies on top of the barrel they were using as a table. Kalainen introduced himself, established that the two were both workers from the saddlery on a break and exchanged the usual bland comments on what a bad business the murder was. The watchman sensed that his dedication to his allotted task had been slighted. He refused to lend the warehouse key to Kalainen and swaggered off to unlock it himself.

"This where you normally take your break?" Kalainen asked the saddlers.

"Often as not, aye."

"You'd know Strammon's lads well, then. What are they like?"

"Tastan, he's no more'n a bullock for shiftin' stone. Big lad but not much of a dice player neither," answered one with a grin. "And he never seems to learn!"

"Oh. Was he down much money then?"

"Naw. Never play for more than pennies. Still, reckon we 'ad a drink or two off him."

"Ythil and Strammon not play?"

"Strammon were the boss. Good boss, fair enough, but a boss and he don't play dice with the likes of us. And Ythil, he's a shaman or something, like. Would you play with a shaman? Dice probably roll whatever he tells 'em to be!"

"Strammon have any family? Partners?"

"Don't think. Came from Tarlenia to make his fortune, s'pose."

The watchman called impatiently to Kalainen. The Drouhin smiled with a friendly wave to the leather-workers and headed to the warehouse.

Strammon's building was solidly constructed with large double doors; a smaller portal was set into the right-hand door. This had been opened by the watchman, who returned to his game, still gripping the key. The main doors were of dark oak studded with iron and were big enough to admit a wagon for deliveries of stone. The front of the warehouse was set up as display area and shop: sections of ashlar, carvings and polished stonework were laid out for viewing. Talismans and amulets on silver chains were pinned up in an iron cabinet with fretwork doors. Kalainen frowned thoughtfully at them and fingered the simple lock before moving into the larger rear area, partitioned off with wooden screens. A hoist leaned over the centre of the wagon area with pulleys and chains to unload large blocks. Sturdy shelving on the left-hand side held a collection of heavy slabs. Lighter shelving on the right held a petrified autumn of jasper, carnelian and malachite. Some blocks showed signs of work in progress.

"Should we check these to see what he was working on? Might've been done in by an unhappy customer." Yanni and Mardenifol were both staring about excitedly, thrilled to be involved.

"Unhappy indeed, Yanni. Let's look at everything and then plan our next step."

Further back were work benches with reciprocating saws and lathes powered by a water wheel dipping its toes in the Battafell Brook. The axle beam came through the wall. Various cogs and gears produced different driving speeds for the tools. A hose dangling from a waterskin provided a means of cooling the saws. There was a strange air of unaccustomed quiet, a hint of the forlorn about the disused machinery. There were more double doors on the back wall but no personnel port. Both double doors were secured with heavy beams.

Kalainen moved quietly up the stairs up to an upper floor, shadowed by Mardenifol and Yanni. The air reeked from an infusion of lavender in alcohol used in cleaning stone. The smell had a sickly edge. A draughtsman's table was covered in pictures of carving details and scale plans, held down by a metalpoint stylus, a pen tray and some ink pots. Finally, there was Strammon's private quarters including a kitchen with a tiny larder stocked with onions, a wedge of cheese and pickled eggs in a jar. There was a table with four chairs for dining, Strammon's bedroom and a spare room with three truckle beds. Kalainen tested the stove for warmth, then sifted the cold ashes for any hints of burned paper.

Strammon was on his bedroom floor. He had been stabbed right through the body with a brutal thrust. A small puddle of blackening blood had pooled under the corpse. Mardenifol stood back, his shirt pulled up over the lower part of his face, eyes wide with horror and revulsion. Kalainen studied the body for a while, noting that Strammon's money pouch was still on his belt but open and empty. Yanni stood beside him, a sleeve over her nose.

"Conkin' pongs, don't he?"

"Dead bodies do. It's perfectly natural and he's not too bad yet," said Kalainen, face determinedly blank. "And if we're with clients, try not to use language like that. Could cost a commission – or give us another body with some of the more sensitive sorts." He put out a hand to stop Yanni getting too close and pointed to where the blood was scuffed where a slippered toe had touched it. Once they started looking, Yanni and Mardenifol could see a half-moon blot of blood left where the footprint had turned from the body and moved with long strides to the stairs. The prints faded at the foot of the stairs but could still be seen heading towards the door.

The strongbox was under Strammon's bed. The key was in the lock and the box was only half-pushed under the bed. Kalainen lifted the lid and glanced inside; papers but no money. He looked into the privy, where the stench was offensive despite even more of the lavender reek. There was a simple bucket under a seat. The bucket was empty but splashes suggested the contents had been recently tossed out of the window.

Returning to Strammon, Kalainen put his fingers on the corpse's neck, assessing warmth. He poked his fingers through the cut. He heaved the body over. It was stiff and awkward, an outstretched hand thudding into the boards. Ignorning retching noises and muttered prayers from Mardenifol, Kalainen looked into Strammon's unseeing eyes, sniffed his open mouth. Then he unlaced the silk shirt and cut the sleeves to pull it off, using a sharp blade no longer than his finger. The heavy red marks of lividity showed where blood had pooled inside the body. Kalainen stripped the body entirely while Mardenifol turned the same colour as the dark marks on the corpse. He was reduced to swallowing and blowing like a fish when Yanni observed,

"Them breeches was undone. Probably had a whore up here and she yerked him for the money or when he couldn't do the business."

"Possibly, possibly," Kalainen murmured distractedly as he checked Strammon's clothes. They were damp, muddy and soiled but he found nothing odd, no jewels or scraps of parchment sewn into them. Kalainen wiped the blood from the corpse and examined everything; nails, every flake of skin, even the soiled anus. At last he sat back on his haunches, rose with a sigh and cleaned his hands with water from a jug in the kitchen. As he wiped them on a rag, he pointed to the smudged puddle of dark blood. There was a deep gouge on the floor beneath where Strammon had lain. The blade had passed right through the body.

Kalainen turned back to the strongbox. "Money is often the simplest reason for a murder. Let's see what we have." He riffled through a few drawings of carvings and some technical details on the best speeds for running the machinery in the workshop. There were two documents with wax seals at the bottom, one with a stylised eye and teardrop, the other with a hare leaping over a hound. Finally, there was half a porphyry token with a tag attached. The tag read Capt. Portis Maegre of the *Cormorant*.

"What are those?" asked Mardenifol, returning from the window where he had been gulping fresh air.

"It seems sometimes Strammon took favours for work rather than getting paid directly. This one is from the Chapel of the Weeping Eye and the token is from Portis Maegre, I think he must be the captain of a ship, the *Cormorant*."

"I know the Chapel of the Weeping Eye," said Mardenifol. "Just off the Long Wyrm. They do healing there – maybe he thought he might need their services. He was right too, but never got the chance to call in the debt."

For a moment, Kalainen held the scroll from the Chapel of the Weeping Eye, locked in some indecision. "I can't. It was his," he murmured to himself. Then his voice became firm. "When we're finished here, take this to the Chapel. They will take appropriate care of Strammon's body." Kalainen handed the scroll to Mardenifol.

"These are the favour tokens still in the strongbox. Maybe we should be looking for one that was removed," put in Yanni.

"That's a very good thought. And Captain Maegre? Could he be a smuggler? Was Strammon planning an escape route? He might tell us something of Strammon in return for the favour token." Kalainen stared at a third favour for a while. Impassively, he scrunched the document into a ball. He took flint and steel from beside the range and struck sparks into a charcloth, then tossed cloth and parchment into the range firebox, where they flamed briefly and died.

"What are you doing?"

"Repaying an old debt."

"Who was it to?"

"It's rather the point that I don't say."

"Well, you'll have to tell them you burnt whatever it was."

"Not at all."

"What's the point if they don't know you've paid the debt?"

"I will know. And you mean a good deed is only a good deed if someone knows you've done it! You are a rascal! See if you can glean anything from those foot marks, eh?"

The apprentices scampered off on the trail like children searching for hidden honey treats. They were excitedly pointing to each new print, measuring distances by bounding alongside the dots of blood.

"Look, we came in the middle of the door, but there's a smudge of blood here on the right-hand side and then those slippered prints go round in a big curve where there are no other footprints. Why do that?"

"We've got to think like Kalainen! He – or she, but there's a whole print in the mud here, big feet for a woman – accidentally trod in a bit of blood. Then they ran. Maybe they were surprised by someone. Seem to be running, anyway. But instead of running directly up Butsun, they ran across the road towards that bit of shrubbery between the brook and Harleon's saddlery. Then they turned up the road and the prints are lost in the general traffic. Was there someone in the road? Or in the shrubbery?"

"If so, we'd have a witness!"

"Yes! Then our villain would look obvious carrying loot. Maybe they tossed it in the bushes?"

To their amazement, after a cursory search, Yanni found a short but elegant little sword, stained with blood. They went tearing back to Kalainen with their find.

"Well done indeed!" Kalainen admired the sword, his eyes narrowing as he studied the bloodstains. "So then, what do you think happened here?"

"The killer, he or she, were off on their toes straight from the body. So the robbery must have been done first," said Yanni. "So Strammon comes back and finds the robber. The robber draws a sword – swish! Strammon begs for his life on the floor but gets stabbed anyway. The robber panics, runs and ditches the sword."

"The killer may have simply gone back to the body to check Strammon was dead before leaving, and put his foot in the blood then," suggested Mardenifol.

"Oh. Yes, I s'pose. But the finished talismans weren't taken neither."

"But they're traceable. Money's not."

"Well anyway, we don't know why yet, but someone stabbed him. Then they left in a hurry and chucked the sword in the bushes. We've found a bloody sword. It's not any old sword, it's got runes and etchings and things! All we have to do is find out whose sword and we have the killer!"

"Very good. But why so little blood and why didn't Strammon writhe in agony after being stabbed, not even a twitch?" Kalainen paused, then continued with the air of a conjurer. "Because he was already lying dead on the floor. The question is, why kill a dead man?

The question hung in a heavy silence in the stilled workroom.

"Make sure he's really dead?" offered Yanni.

"Plague! He had the plague and was killed to stop him spreading it!" Mardenifol was looking round fearfully as though the plague were a shadowy figure clutching at him.

"Stabbing someone who's died with the plague wouldn't help. I've seen the plague. This isn't it."

"These talismans he makes and sells. Do you think they could have brought him back from the dead?" Mardenifol's speech was accelerated by the rush of ideas. "Did he need killing twice? Or there was little blood - Vampires! Perhaps he'd been ex-sang-guin-ated! He was stabbed through the heart to stop him turning into one!"

"Yes, I'm not sure all your stories are going to prove helpful, Mardenifol. But for that matter, the stab wound cut the liver and the diaphragm but was not that close to the heart."

"Killer might not be an expert in anatomy," muttered Mardenifol darkly.

Kalainen hooked a chair forward and perched on it, steepling his fingers. "The key to the strongbox was taken from Strammon's pouch and money - or a mystery favour document as Yanni suggested – may have been removed from the strongbox before the stab, judging by footprints, or not, as Mardenifol pointed out. The strongbox may have been opened purely to make it look like a robbery. We don't know. But we do know that the last thing our swordsman did was deliberately step in blood and leave a trail –

successfully followed by two youths without tracking skills. And he threw the sword into the shrubbery, where it was easily found, rather than the handy brook."

"Deliberately? You mean we were meant to find the sword?" Yanni sounded crushed.

"The Watch was meant to find it. But they didn't – and you did."

"I was watching to see who came back for it," said a new voice.

Mardenifol leapt in the air with a gasp and was backing away rapidly as he asked, "Who are you?"

"This is Imber," said Kalainen, smiling at a man with a flat, weathered face, of middle height and dressed in soft brown leathers pulled in with the wide belt that marked him as a man of Shad-dimur. Imber now stood immobile as though he was a wooden carving which had always been there. "I asked him to look over the place before we arrived. He's better at that sort of thing."

"But it was locked!" said Mardenifol, sounding shocked. He kept Kalainen between himself and the stranger, and peeked out past the Drouhin's shoulder.

Imber gave a small shrug. His hooded eyes gave nothing away as he studied first Mardenifol and then Yanni when she mastered her fright sufficiently to creep back from Strammon's bedroom where she had bolted on his appearance.

"You never made no sound at all," she breathed. He gave her a crooked little smile as she looked up at him distrustfully.

"Good idea to watch the sword, Imber, but nobody was going to come. It was supposed to be found."

Imber looked at Kalainen. "No mark of the Dancing Goddess here. Nothing to do with the other murders then?"

"Hm. I'm not so sure, but not done by the same person, perhaps."

"What are you sure of?"

"Strammon's been dead perhaps twelve hours. Lividity consistent with him not being moved after death. Poisoned – but then some- one stabbed him and left us to find an identifiable sword."

"This is all much too fast," said Mardenifol. "We don't really know he was dead before he was stabbed. You can't know he was poisoned. He might have died of apopolyexy like my uncle."

"And then be stabbed on the floor? I am sorry your uncle had apoplexy. But let us think," Kalainen beamed like a gourmet hearing a dinner gong. "The lavender smell was strong upstairs, but the in- fusion would normally have been used downstairs. Someone cleaned up the mess and did their best to conceal the stench of diarrhoea and vomit, traces of which stained his clothing. The unmoving body was hacked on the floor. Could Strammon have been knocked down, even rendered unconscious? There were no signs of other injury. Could he have been supine and pleading for his life? Although there was some blood, it was hardly splattered about where someone died thrashing in agony from a massive stab wound. The blade passed through the liver, cut the diaphragm, passed just beside the spine. There was too little blood altogether; there was no beating heart when that cut was made. You might also have noticed a little foam from Strammon's lips. His eyes were glassy and the pupils fully di- lated. The question is indeed who would kill a dead man? For Stram- mon was poisoned and lying freshly dead upon the floor when the sword was thrust through him.

"He was stabbed simply to conceal the fact that he had been poisoned. I could see no puncture wound for the poison. Normally there is a raised and reddened area round such a puncture, some- times white.

"Normally?" squeaked Mardenifol. "This is normal?"

"Perhaps the stab wound was done to hide the puncture wound?"

"Good idea, Yanni. But I saw no sign of that. He ingested it."

"What?"

"He ate it. Probably not deliberately for if this were suicide, there would be no need for all this pretence. Most poisons have quite identifiable tastes, so someone laced spicy food, or strong drink perhaps, with their toxin. So, what we need to know is where Master Strammon has been recently."

"Well, he can't tell us. Do we have to talk to all his acquaintances?"

"Come now, Master Strammon was a stone mason. Look at his clothes. I doubt he habitually wore a silk shirt nor breeches with slashed thighs showing a vermilion lining. He was wearing the best he owned. He must have attended some celebration. I doubt it was a religious affair as there are no emblems or icons. So, who was throwing a party in the stone mason's world? Perhaps a patron, a big guild event?

"Seems an easy trail to follow."

"Of course, Imber. Because we're still on the trail that was left for us to find."

"So what do we do?" asked Yanni.

"I think we may allow ourselves to be drawn along the path. Of course, we must satisfy Captain Traid's commission. That might be to say who killed Strammon the first time. Or who killed him the second time! For the first time, he was poisoned. Perhaps by the Assassins. Imber?"

"There's a contact point: Leavy's Gate. But can't just ask. They're notoriously close-mouthed."

"Indeed. And I have known that particular door shut by someone paying the assassins to work their skills on anyone asking questions." Kalainen paused, running a hand over the greying stubble of his hair. "First, we must find out where the poison was administered and tread the trail we are given. The goat follows the rope, but the tiger follows the goat. At the same time, we must consider who killed Strammon the second time. It's true they didn't commit murder but they have tried to obfuscate the case and are guilty of collusion at least. Let us consider what we know.

"It was someone who didn't trouble with the sale items downstairs but did take money from Strammon's pouch, money and perhaps more from the strongbox. Someone wearing light shoes. Someone who knew what was going on and either agreed with or was paid to cover up the poisoning and attempt to frame our mystery sword-owner.

"I have very strong suspicions who that might be, but we need proof. Ythil and Tastan had keys to the door, but that clue doesn't help us as given the state Strammon would have been in by the time he made it home, it is more than likely that he left the door wide open, never mind locking it."

"Locked doors merely an indication," put in Imber.

"Yes, true enough, my friend. Now, to work! There is the matter of poor Strammon's body to settle. Mardenifol, away to the Chapel of the Weeping Eye with the scroll, then to the lapidarist at the Duke's end of the Long Wyrm. See what you can learn about meetings or celebrations recently for stone workers. Yanni, do you know the mason by the Goose Walk?"

"Goose walk, where there's them pits of tar and sand? Yes, I've seen the place. Does headstones and the like? I can't ask him anything! He'd never talk to me."

"He has teams of youngsters cleaning and cutting. I'm sure you can listen to them. They'll know where their master was last night if he was out partying! Subtlety and patience – always better to get no information than tip your hand. If you need to talk, you can say you have a commission for your mistress who has a fancy for a yellow jacinth ring. If they have one, she will come and look. Mardenifol has his own background, you must invent some prosperous merchant, perhaps with a family, but never volunteer more information than is requested."

As the apprentices left, Imber raised an eyebrow at Kalainen. The Drouhin smiled. "Of course they'll hear something but let the fledgling flutter! Whoever went to all this trouble must be furious the Watch didn't find the sword. They will be trying to get the investigation back onto their version. Keep an eye on Mardenifol, I'll shadow Yanni."

Imber nodded, and was gone.

The Amulet.

They made a cheerful group at Coromal, ripping chunks from loaves of dark bread Mother Yellern shovelled from the range with a flat-bladed peel, then dipping sausages in a green sauce that ignited the mouth with spices. Yanni first recoiled suspiciously, then laughed with delight at the new flavours and sucked her fingers noisily. Imber joined them as the old woman left and Kalainen told them all to eat, saying the hungry man could only see the stew-pot. The two youngsters were vying to tell the most details round mouthfuls of sausage while Quern was trying to share his enthusiasm for the tournament.

"Allamee's. You heard Strammon went to Allamee's, right?" Mardenifol was hopeful.

"Course! Kalainen, can I cook tonight?"

"Know where it is?" Mardenifol went on.

"What, Talley's Yard? Course I do. Everyone does. Can I, Kalainen?" Yanni's face shone with enthusiasm, plus a helping of grease from the sausages. She turned back to Mardenifol. "And they

45

said the whole of Talley's Yard was lit up with lamps and candles like on Lessan's Day! And it was all the masons in Shaddimur invited."

"Yes, and the lapididarists."

"The what?" Yanni glowered at Mardenifol, fierce as a terrier, though her over-sized tunic emphasized the thinness of her arms.

"Lappy didarists. People working stones and jewels and stuff." Mardenifol's eyes sidled across towards Kalainen to see if he would be corrected but the Drouhin had been talking to Quern.

"All right, Yanni, I'll ask Mistress Yellern to help you tomorrow." Kalainen's kindly smile faded as he turned back to the warrior. "Quern, did you see any bouts at the tournament? Hear anything interesting?"

"You wanted me in one of these bouts? Any of these champions would have pounded me into the dirt and used me to clean their boots in the first minute. I'd collect a lot of bruises and very few amulets!"

"You saw the actual morning bouts then?"

"I did. Got to see three. Shen is through so far – and either fighting on the sands or standing with the sun glittering off the cape and headdress, he truly seems the avatar of Sunsunni! Just staggering!"

"What about the Tarlenian? Did you see him?" Kalainen bit at his lip in worry he might have missed something important.

"Yes. Unbelievable fight."

"What about the money?" burst in Mardenifol to Yanni. "You hear about the money?"

"What money?"

"Allamee didn't have the kind of money to pay for that sort of party and stuff."

"What about the Tarlenian's fight?" asked Kalainen over the din. "Who is he?"

"Astelin."

"Never heard of him."

"You will now after his fight with the Gallendian, Nisbah. Could have won that fight about four times over. Disarmed Nisbah twice – and let him collect his weapon both times!"

"Strike you as strange?"

"Well, the crowd loved it. Cheering, stamping and roaring. Nisbah's good. Nobody gets that many chances against him as a rule. Even at the end, Astelin held Nisbah's own blade to his throat and Nisbah had to submit but hardly a scratch on him. Then Astelin had Nisbah join him for the salute."

"How magnanimous," murmured Kalainen thoughtfully.

"Well, did you hear Strammon was trying to sell his whole business?" asked Yanni, waggling a sausage at Mardenifol.

Kalainen held up a hand and the tableau froze into silence. His head spun round to stare at Yanni.

"Are you sure about that?"

Yanni shrugged. "The people what said it was conkin' sure enough."

"Yanni, don't use words like that. If Strammon was trying to sell up, he knew he was under mortal threat in Shaddimur. But from whom and why?"

"Whoever it was, they were just lying in wait for him. Set it all up to get him, you think?" Yanni was demonstrating her remarkable ability to talk and eat simultaneously, but it wasn't pretty.

"Strammon probably thought he'd have been safe in a large gathering. And miraculously there was one, with all the people he needed to talk to in the same place. All provided by someone who couldn't afford it. Yes, what a set-up. You've both done well but I sense we are going to need to hurry more. This isn't a simple killing."

"Simple?" asked Yanni.

"The simplest murder to solve is usually done by a man. He strikes in a sudden rage, then looks down and wonders what to do with the body at his feet. A woman kills more rarely, but if she does, it may be planned all the way through."

"You saying this was done by a woman?"

"No, Yanni. But it is carefully planned and executed with lots of people involved – even if they each only know a tiny part of the whole plan. This speaks of money and power behind it. Far from the simple matter suggested by Traid." The Drouhin grinned and waved his hands upwards. "We must climb the chain faster! Quern, back to the afternoon bouts. And try to talk to people rather than just admire technique. Yanni, head to Allamee's and listen; pick up what you can. Mardenifol, down to the docks and see what you can turn up about Portis Maegre and his ship, then meet us at Talley's Yard."

"The *Cormorant*, wasn't it? Right. I'll just finish..." Mardenifol reached for the dish of sausages, but there was only a smear of grease left on the plate. Yanni smiled at him, her hands behind her back.

Kalainen strolled into Talley's Yard. A single huge plane tree covered the entire yard and would have sheltered the booths from the squalls that swept in from the bay. Today, the leaves broke the sunlight into a million dancing fireflies. Amid the jumbled houses and businesses was a down-at-heel establishment selling cheap bangles and necklaces to locals or curios to the wealthy daring to visit the poorer quarters. A man, with a thin moustache and tightly curled hair bulging out beneath a greasy cap, was poised under an awning before his shack. With his thumbs stuck behind a belt with a brassy, triple-clipped clasp, he scanned passers-by for anyone that might be cajoled into a purchase. His gaze met Kalainen's, a smile oiled across his face and he beckoned the Drouhin over.

"See here, Master! You have come to Allamee's; storehouse of wonders! Treasures from every land from here to Kathos! Note this brooch of garnets, charged with spells to ward against demons. Or perhaps here, a stone rose guaranteed to melt the heart of any maiden! Just glance at this workmanship, tourmalines from Gelavien..."

Kalainen put his hand over the offerings and his steady gaze deflated Allamee into silence. "I may buy - but I think we'll leave out these magical appurtenances, shall we?"

Allamee made a resigned motion, then waved his hand at his stock, raising his eyebrows hopefully.

After a thoughtful browse, Kalainen's lips quirked up. "Show me that stiletto."

"Aha. You have a discerning eye! Felugan steel with an aquamarine pommel stud carved by Hijaro himself! These runes guide a strike with the accuracy of Sunsunni!" Allamee's eyes took in Kalainen's expression and he gave another little shrug. "It's a nice blade," he said in a different voice, pulling his great belt up across his belly.

"It is," admitted Kalainen. A token negotiation later, Kalainen handed over a few silver coins and slipped the sheathed stiletto into a pocket. After some bland exchanges, Kalainen looked round the yard. "Strange place for a party."

"Had the whole yard cleared! Tents and lights there was. The beer flowed and even up-town wine. Some had proper beakers to drink from an' all!"

"You know how to throw a party!"

"You'd have to have been here, an' nearly everyone was - what was in the business, leastways. They all know the name of Allamee!"

"The drink ran like rain in the gutters of Clatch?"

"Ha, an' one or two was fair blathered, I tell you!"

"Really?"

"Lots of 'em singin' happy! There was that uppty chap from Butsun Causeway, Strammon. Never said owt to me but he was offering his business to anyone with cash to pay. But after he'd seen the bottom of a few beakers he were heels up and away! Never thought he'd be the sort, but he could hardly stand! Had to get a rickshaw home and redecorated the inside with most of my excellent feast. Runner came all the way back to demand extra! But o' course, he just wanted another ride and the only tip I gave him was not to pick someone so weltered. Strammon got in a towering tizzy with that fellow from Hethrin, you know, Tessavian! I allow there were a few what was egging them on a bit but the row were that fiery, it's a wonder there weren't blood spilled."

"People egging them on? Who were they?"

"Don't rightly recall who it was, now. Folks I didn't recognise but there was plenty of those – all the best was here."

"You provided food too, then?"

"Did, by Rashen Akru! Whole trestles of top stuff. Geese an' all manner of fowlses. There was even girls here dressed up like sprites or summat just to hand the stuff round! Some of them girls," Allamee whistled softly. "If my old woman din' have eyes like a conkin' eagle, I'd 've ... well. Probably got me face slapped, tell the truth."

Kalainen laughed. "The stone rose not entirely infallible? And where did these delightful damsels come from?"

Allamee looked deeply regretful. "Don't know, I didn't do the details. Don't see many girls like that in a long spit from Talley's Yard."

"Forgive me for saying, but you did well to pay for such a glorious event on the profits from ..." Kalainen made a gesture to encompass Allamee's little patch of Talley's Yard.

"How I pay for things is me own affair."

"Of course! I meant no disrespect."

"Well, it were a bit of a gamble. You know, try and get some real business. The big one, you know?"

"Oh yes. Did it work?"

"Well. Nothin' sort of def'nite, as yet. But maybe, maybe."

"No other shadows on the evening?"

"No. Well, Tessavian came back the next morning a-roaring and a-bawling that he'd left without his sword and wanted it back. There was nowt left here and he could only skulk off with nothing more than what he brought; a foul temper and a head you could almost see throbbing. The girl what ran the booth taking hats and swords and cloaks was here, part of the clean-up. She said most particular she remembered him taking it. Too much in his cups to remember, the fool."

"The girl isn't about, is she?"

"Sadly no. She were one of them..." Allamee waved his hands in an hourglass shape. "They never came like that in my day," he said regretfully. "I tell you, they moved like priestesses of the Dancing Goddess herself."

Kalainen glanced sharply at the trader, but Allamee was drifting in reverie. "If I wanted to throw a party, the man who set yours up might be good to know."

"You'd have to be a brother of the stone, I reckon." Allamee spoke softly, his mind full of swaying hips.

"Not to worry," said Kalainen and wandered into the yard as Yanni trotted past, an unidentifiable sack slung over a shoulder. She paused near him to resettle the sack and muttered, "Imber says Allamee's is watched. I've been in the kitchens; party was all paid for by a Tarlenian." She hurried off, lugging the sack awkwardly.

Kalainen paused, tapping his teeth. He nodded abruptly to himself and straightened. At that moment, a voice called, "Kalainen! Kalainen!" and Quern strode across Talley's Yard towards him, swatting at stray branches from the plane tree.

For a moment, Kalainen's eyes clamped shut at the unfortunate timing. Not much chance of any watcher missing that. "The open mouth always catches flies."

"What? Look, I haven't time for your riddles now. I have big news for you from the tournament. Talking to the chap who drew up all the lists, I was telling him that I was a bit confused because this minor stone worker Strammon gets killed and the whole City Watch is talking of war! Strammon, he says to me? What, Strammon from Butsun Causeway? That's the fellow, I told him. Strammon's dead? Yes, I says, double dead. Well, he says, that is a coincidence. Did I know Strammon made the amulet that'll be awarded to the winner of the tournament! There! How about that?"

"Even a blind singer catches a coin sometimes." Kalainen spoke automatically, his mind busy calculating. "By the bell of Mirrin's Tower, Quern! If there's a connection... They may not wait. We must hurry!"

"Who's not going to wait? Wait for what? I'm lost!"

But Kalainen had already turned away. He made a subtle signal for Imber, then another to Yanni before marching away. Just as they were leaving, he watched her intercept Mardenifol as the gangly youth came from the docks.

"Did you find out whose sword it was?" asked Quern.

"Oh yes. Belonged to another lapidarist called Tessavian, who was goaded into a fight with Strammon."

"Aha! Did you ask whether this Tessavian had his sword with him when he left?"

"A definite yes from the girl who kept such things."

"So it was Tessavian after all! We have our man."

"No, Quern. The girl was one of the same group that poisoned Strammon. She lied. Quern, I am getting the strongest feeling the quarry is outrunning us. We need to hurry. Any chance of a rickshaw here?"

"Very little. We could head up to the Long Wyrm – but where does Tessavian live or work?"

"Kerola's Run, near the corn-market."

"Quicker walking then. Imber will be quicker still over the rooftops. But what's the rush?"

"This wasn't just a set up for Strammon. Some swords have two edges. Quickly now!"

They arrived at Tessavian's shop as two men swaggered in before them. Both were broad with shaven heads, their bare arms tattooed with blue waves and a shark fin motif. One was armed with half a dozen daggers on crossed leather straps, the other had a war hammer across his back.

"Shop elsewhere, this is closed!" snarled the man with the daggers, giving a hefty shove to Quern, who was coming through the doorway. He might as well have pushed the building. Quern remained blocking the entrance, grinning at him. The dagger man found himself looking up at Quern and did a comical double take suddenly noticing one of his own daggers in Quern's left hand, just before the right hand half-lifted him by the belt. While Kalainen stepped neatly out of the way, Quern turned and hurled the dagger man back out onto the street in a clatter of metalwork.

The other tattooed man gaped for a moment in astonishment, then scrabbled to release his hammer from its fastening. Dropping the dagger, Quern reached him in two strides, seized him with both hands, spun round as though they were partners at some wild dance and tossed him out on top of his colleague. The man's scream turned from a bellow of rage, through a cry of horror to a thudding silence.

Kalainen slid in and closed the door. He looked round at the other people in the shop. Swathed in black, a priest hunched his shoulders, clutching a money bag to his chest. The fingers of his other hand were already curled possessively over a reliquary set with dark stones that flickered with inner fire. The priest's eyes sidled across the newcomers, fear pulling at his mouth. A woman in long skirts was appraising some heavy necklaces, be-ringed fingers clutching vainly after her middle-years. Standing demurely behind her was Yanni, carrying a basket with a few small loaves. On the other side of the counter was a dapper man with a neatly trimmed beard, his jacket, shirt and breeches all in the black and white typical of Hethrin. Wide-eyed with alarm and making "What ... what..." noises, he was reaching for something under the counter, his hands flapping like netted fish while his eyes twitched between the bag of coins and Quern.

Quern rolled his shoulders and waited by the door, predatory and hopeful. Outside, a hushed but vehement argument could be heard.

"Sir priest, complete your transaction and depart in safety. Madam, you too must go. We are co-opted onto the City Watch and must insist!" Kalainen's voice was commanding and would have been clearly audible outside. In the quiet that followed, the priest dropped fat gold coins onto the counter, the thuds of the coins sounding loud and hollow, like hammer blows on a coffin nail. Receiving an angry wave of acceptance from the man behind the counter, now spluttering in rage, the priest scooped the reliquary into his robes and scuttled to the door, trailing a reek of sweat. The woman gave no more reaction than a sniff and drifted out with her head high as though that was precisely what she had intended. Nobody seemed to notice that her serving girl had unaccountably remained behind.

The door opened again. Quern nearly fell over trying to stop himself in the middle of an attack as Mardenifol wandered in, as oblivious to Quern as he was to the tattooed men outside. Mardenifol had acquired a square cap and a long list, which he consulted with thespian concentration.

Quern recovered his balance. "That makes our association with the Watch clear for anyone with ears. I thought you liked working in the shadows," he said, ignoring Tessavian's outraged squawkings.

"No choice. Not if Tessavian is to have any chance of living out the day. And I think the people I would have hidden it from already know."

As Mardenifol entered, Tessavian shovelled the coins to rattle down a tube. Spitting with fury, the bearded man lifted a short rod out from behind the counter and held it before him. The multi-faceted head of obsidian seemed to bulge and ooze out of focus. "By the seven bells, what is the meaning of this? Who are you to order good folk from my shop! How dare..." he began, before the import of Kalainen's words hit him and his voice faded in confusion.

"We could have just got Traid to take him in," said Quern.

"And if Traid has Tessavian and the evidence, he will hang him. Even if we were able to convince him not to, Tessavian would be a straw target in jail if killers need to silence him."

"This is preposterous!" roared Tessavian. "I've done nothing! Are you even from the Watch? I see no sign! Call them and prove it!"

"Didn't you listen? If I call the Watch, you will be arrested. I do not think you will survive that. Those fellows Quern asked to leave? They didn't come to buy. We have a little time to talk while they decide they need fresh instructions. Perhaps lower that rod?"

"And perhaps not! You sense its puissance – when artefacts are imbued by Tessavian, their power is bewildering!"

"Master Tessavian, we have little time. Have you worked for any Tarlenians recently?"

"I have not!"

"No?"

"I've had nothing to do with them! I am a man of high principle!"

"You didn't have anything to do with the amulet for the tournament..."

"I tell you I had nothing to do with the Tarlenians nor their vile amulet."

Kalainen made a non-committal grunt. "Did you wear a sword to Allamee's event?"

"Yes, I had my dress sword with me; cut quite a figure, I must say. I even wore two tassels of cerulean blue! The sword has gone now. I went back the next morning – Iol's Light, what a cesspool that place is when you can see it! Do you know, they denied having the sword? Tried to tell me I took it home, which I did not. I don't clearly remember coming back, true, but I don't have the sword now. I can only have left it there. The bandits robbed me!"

"You had an argument with Strammon at the party?"

"Not my fault! You would not believe some of the things that villain accused me of! I am without question the finest imbuer of periapts in Shaddimur. Trinkets, he called them! And then, the gall of it, then he tries to sell me his business. Angry? I was furious and rightly so!"

"These insults heaped upon you, did you hear them from Strammon?"

"Of course," shouted Tellavian, thrusting the rod forwards. Then he paused, his head rocking sideways. "Well, no. Not as such, but that's hardly important. All the people I was with had all heard the calumnies – it was common knowledge."

"You knew these people, the ones with their ears so attuned to the jeweller's hammer that they had all heard rumours you had not?"

Tessavian frowned. "They, they seemed to know me. Fame, you know... I didn't remember, well, don't remember any of them exactly."

"How did the argument happen?"

"I had drunk too much, I admit it. The girls poured with a liberal hand! Perhaps Strammon had too – he could barely get his words out. He offered me his business, at a fair rate, I concede. Then, I don't know quite how it happened. The people I'd been talking to earlier were suddenly all around us. Someone told him I had aspersed his concern – I had not! Someone else piped in that he'd said the only woman that would buy adornments from my shop would have to be happy with a millstone carved by a bullock. Strammon didn't deny it! I reacted badly, and well, lots of people seemed to pick sides and, well, no doubt we both said things we regret."

"Tessavian, you do know Strammon is dead, don't you?"

Tessavian looked shifty for a moment, then clenched the rod anew. "I had heard. But it had nothing to do with me. After abusing me to all, this man comes stammering and blurting offers..."

"He was desperate and poisoned," said Kalainen quietly.

Tessavian looked at him sideways. "I heard he was stabbed. How do I know you are not the ones who killed him, now sent to murder me?" He pushed the rod forwards with both hands.

"Mostly because you are alive. You must see the plot. You were to be arrested by the Watch and executed."

"For what?" screeched Tessavian, the rod carving sludgy runes of dark light in the air.

"Murder. Consider the evidence. You had a very public and furious row with Strammon. You were drunk. He was found dead with a stab wound. Your sword was found near the body with blood slathering the blade. It is enough. All your denials would have been swept out of the door of expedience. You must flee Shaddimur."

"And look guilty! I have a good business here and have done nothing wrong! Must I be hounded from my home by innuendo? As for those thugs..." Tessavian waved the rod, the head bubbling slow winks of light of such dark red it was almost black.

Kalainen watched with compassion as the fear built in Tessavian's eyes. The jeweller was no warrior, however powerful the strange rod he wielded. "The only way out of here is for you to be arrested. If those men outside think you are going to be executed by the law, they may not strike."

"But you said that if I'm arrested, I'll still be killed!"

"And those outside wait for you to flee."

"Then there is no way out!"

"He's right, Kalainen," put in Quern. "If the Watch take Tessavian, they'll have him for Strammon's murder. If we arrest Tessavian, we have to take him to Traid or the ticks outside will know; same result. If we don't arrest him, they'll kill him anyway!"

Kalainen's lips tightened in a flicker of exasperation. "If Tessavian will consent to my protection, we may have a chance."

"My family..."

"I strongly suggest they visit friends in Hethrin - immediately."

"I cannot leave them!"

"Good. If all goes to plan you will be with them."

"There is my business! This has taken years to establish."

"Then I hope you can leave a foreman in charge for a short while? You should be able to return when this issue is cleared up."

"My reputation will be ruined!"

"And that is less important than your life. The shattered glass cannot be cleaned."

Tessavian put the rod down, opened a locker and removed a pendant. He held it up in front of Kalainen. "You speak true and mean me no harm, then?"

Kalainen looked at the pendant. A gold ring inlaid with lapis lazuli with a deep sapphire in the centre. "I speak true and mean no harm. Fine work. If you die, I won't get paid."

Tessavian looked from the pendant to Kalainen and back again. "Bah," he said, and tossed it back in the locker. "Well, I can't see a way out. If I am to trust you, what is your great plan?"

"You have a black and white cloak. Do you have a spare?"

"Certainly not! I'm an artisan, not some palace fop!"

"Perhaps your wife has a similar garment? Good. We'll need to borrow it. We will arrest you in the name of the Watch and escort you to Traid. We'll pass through the Levanine market. While there, you will be pushed down as we pass a stall. Fall to the ground, drop your cloak and slip on the one you will find there, a hooded cloak of yellow and green."

"I am neither in mourning, nor courting a new wife!"

"I understand the importance of colours in Hethrin. However, you need to disappear and without that cloak your wife is very likely to be both in mourning and in need of a new husband. You will wear the cloak you are given. Mardenifol will be wearing your wife's and stand up in your stead. We'll take Mardenifol to Traid and explain matters to him. You should use every minute you have to leave Shaddimur. Head for the port; you will have a token for Captain Maegre of the *Cormorant*. He will take you to whatever port you like in Hethrin."

"But my family...?"

"Will join you on the *Cormorant* and you go together."

There was a long quiet while Tessavian looked round him miserably. "How did this happen? I have done nothing! Except to refuse to act for the Tarlenians. Do they kill anyone who gainsays them?"

"Perhaps not. But someone has gone to a lot of trouble to make sure you are dead. In a roundabout way, the skill of the Watch has made sure you are alive so far. But those hired bully boys outside are waiting."

Tessavian cast a sharp glance outside where one of the men could be seen leaning against a wooden wall opposite. Perhaps the other had gone for reinforcements. He sighed. "Very well, it will be as you say."

"Mardenifol, take the spare cloak. Hurry back to Coromal – here's the key – and collect the yellow and green hooded cloak. Put on the chain mail shirt and the black and white cloak over the top. Make yourself inconspicuous by Jerryn's stand in the Levanine. Tell him you're with me and he won't be surprised at anything you do."

"You want me to wear the chain mail?"

"Yes. When we come past, I'll push Tessavian down behind Jerryn's booth by my cloak. You stand up in the black and white cloak and take Tessavian's place with Quern and me. It has to be quick; in the busy market, it should work. Understand?"

"Well, yes, I suppose so."

"Hurry then – and leave the half token for Captain Maegre in the pocket of the coloured cloak. Go." Kalainen turned to Tessavian. "We have a little time while the set-up is made."

"I, I need a few moments to talk to my wife. She will not be happy. Then I must collect some things; a money belt and whatever magical contrivances for our protection I can find. Then I must speak to my foreman."

"Of course. And if you have a back way out and prefer to flee on your own, I will not stand in your way. I advise against."

When Tessavian had gone, Kalainen drummed his fingers, frowning at Quern's back. The burly man was checking outside for about the tenth time. "I know what you're thinking," he began at last.

"Doubt it," growled Quern absently.

"Well, you must be wondering why – "

"Not really."

Irritably, Kalainen turned to Yanni, who was munching on one of the loaves from the stolen basket. "Yanni, repeat the plan to me, then tell it to Imber. He'll know what to do. And in the short term, he might warn us if more of those wharf rats are coming."

"Enough of them come, we're in a bad place," Quern put in, toying thoughtfully with his newly-acquired dagger. "Wonder what that rod thing of Tessavian's actually does, if anything."

"Might not be Tarlenians," Yanni blurted.

"Aha, excellent! Always good to question our assumptions, Yanni. What are you thinking?"

"You're saying Tarlenians poisoned Strammon, then fingered Tessavian to cover up the murder."

"Yes."

"But why? Why kill Strammon when he made the amulet for them, and only set-up Tessavian when he didn't."

Kalainen smiled. "You mean they should have killed Tessavian and implicated Strammon?"

"Why would they kill Strammon at all? Perhaps it isn't the Tarlenians and we have all the motives wrong. Could be another group stirring up hatred of Tarlenia! Maybe the cult of the Dancing Goddess?"

"Very good, Yanni, you hold the key that unlocks the puzzle. A lot of effort went into the death of both men."

"Was Tessavian just some convenient mark with a recognisable sword and a short temper?"

"When bulls fight, the grass gets torn!"

"What's that mean? Tessavian is just a sacrificial goat to throw off suspicion from the poisoner?" put in Quern, dragged into the discussion.

"No, no. Too much time was spent setting it up for that. They were both marked for death."

"If they did want Strammon and Tessavian dead, why not just poison both of them? Look like bad oysters or something," said Yanni.

"I wondered if it were pure panache. But not at all. The only way to cover the crime with just the poison would be to kill a whole slew of people at the party and even the assassins would jib at doing that. You see, if there were just two deaths and someone finds the connection between them, it points to who was behind the whole thing. And there is a connection."

"But what then? The whole party was jewellers and such."

Kalainen smiled happily. "I assumed Tessavian didn't work for the Tarlenians because he didn't like them. It wasn't that. He said he hadn't worked for the Tarlenians nor their vile amulet. Not vile Tarlenians nor their amulet, as he'd have said if he just hated Tarlenians.

So it was something about the amulet. Something they asked him to do that he refused. Why is the amulet vile when made of simple stone? The link is not that Tessavian and Strammon could make it, but they could both imbue it with power. Tessavian must have had some knowledge of what they wanted, and for that he had to be silenced. And if someone did spot the link, it would look like simple jealousy after Strammon was selected to make it and not Tessavian. Makes him a more likely suspect."

"Strammon actually made it. He knew exactly what it would do! There's still no reason to kill him!"

"Not quite, Yanni. Strammon made the amulet that will be awarded to the champion of the tournament. But he was only the stone artisan. The person who imbued it with some quality is Ythil. Ythil the Shaman. Strammon became aware that something very wrong had been imparted to the amulet. He was a decent man by nature and likely agonised over what to do next. If he spoke up, repudiating Tarlenia, he would incur the wrath of his own people, which would be bad for business. Even worse, he could hardly say anything without turning in Ythil who was his most important employee, countryman and perhaps even friend. But even if he stayed quiet, and ignored the affront to his scruples, if something awful happened to the winner which could be traced back to the amulet, there is no doubt that someone would come knocking at his door; even worse for business and him.

"Strammon had to attend the event at Allamee's, where he could try to sell his business to all of the possible buyers and thrash out a deal in one night where he was safe in a public environment. Whether or not he was going to reveal what he knew, he was going to run. His decision had been made and it cost him his life.

"That was why they killed Strammon. He knew what Ythil had done and could not countenance it. And why Tessavian was a lesser target, but equally destined for the long walk into the sun. He knew that the amulet was to have been doctored, and perhaps who wanted it done."

"You can ask him what the amulet will do!"

"He won't know, Yanni. Off you go now."

"He doesn't know," said Tessavian, coming back into the shop as Yanni trotted out with her basket. "As soon as it became clear that they wanted me to imbue the amulet with power to injure the wearer, I threw them out. It would hurt the wearer and the effect had to be delayed. That's all I know. And I don't know who. Some oily weasel with a Tarlenian accent. If I had done it, they would have betrayed me the moment the effect hit the winner. Neither I nor my business would have survived. I am ready."

Kalainen nodded. "Good. What did the Tarlenian look like?"

"I don't know. Just ordinary-looking, obviously thought he was hard as corundum. Wore a mess of dull colours like goat hide on brick dust. Long, oily hair. Are we going?"

"Just give Yanni a moment."

"Hammer man's still waiting," said Quern. "He's bound to follow, which could be a problem."

"We want him to. Just need to keep him far enough back." Kalainen gestured at the rod. "Did you imbue that yourself?"

"It's complicated. I use a partner; a sorcerer."

"To provide the power – and take the pain." Kalainen's drawl was mild but Tessavian seemed to sense criticism.

"She's crippled, unable to walk. She suffered a broken leg years back. For some reason, the slightest touch on the leg can cause agony. Healers are baffled. She says releasing the power as magic deadens the pain. I guide the power to imbue the artefact; a skill rarer than being a magician!"

"Let's go. Remember, when I push, get low, drop this cloak and put on the green and yellow one. Kick the other under Jerryn's stand."

"I'll want it back."

They moved off, shadowed by the tattooed man with the hammer. At one time, Quern thought he was getting too close and stopped to look back. The man took one glance at Quern's face and turned to a nearby stall, where he evinced great interest in lace shawls and headscarves of magenta silk. Kalainen kept close by Tessavian, scanning passing folk worriedly, watching for the glint of a blade, a knife in a throng or a toppling beam.

When they reached the Levanine market, Kalainen was relieved to find it crowded with evening shoppers but concerned at the opportunities it afforded any attacker. As they passed the stall of the knife grinder, Tessavian appeared to trip, but bobbed up almost instantaneously. Without looking, Kalainen's peripheral vision picked up Tessavian slipping on the coloured cloak and sliding away, moving faster than he should have done to be inconspicuous. Kalainen shrugged and kept scanning for trouble. "Well done," he breathed to Mardenifol, squeezing his arm through the black and white cloak. "Head for the Watch House."

When they turned onto Steeple, Quern murmured in his ear, "Is Imber shadowing us still – or Tessavian?"

"No idea. Is our friendly tick still stuck to us?"

Quern looked back. A tattooed arm, a bald head, glimpsed through a moving curtain of ochre cloth and preoccupied faces. "Still there."

"This is for Strammon, you murdering dog," roared a figure from the roof top, barely fifteen paces from where they stood. The man swung a crossbow towards them. It was an easy shot, with Mardenifol stopping and gaping upwards at the sound instead of diving for cover. Quern roared a warning and hurled the dagger which smacked into the wall below the eaves. Even as Kalainen wrapped his arms round Mardenifol and bundled him to the ground, his own broad back turned to the quarrel, the crossbowman hunched in a sudden spasm, his bow firing with a slapping noise. The bolt clattered excitedly down the street, a yelping cry marking its progress. The figure on the roof half-turned, a leg buckled, and the crossbow fell from his hands. He collapsed prone, clung to the edge of the roof for a moment, then slithered over and landed in the street like a sack of wet beans.

Kalainen picked himself up and pulled Mardenifol back to his feet. Quern and Kalainen were looking in all directions for a second threat, Mardenifol was staring at the fallen crossbowman. Around them, passers-by were all making the same noises as they first edged away from the rumpus, then craned forward curiously when the danger seemed to have passed.

"Make way!" roared Kalainen, "Make way there. An arrest has been made on behalf of the City Watch. Make way!" He hurried Mardenifol forwards.

"Aren't you going to check on the bowman?"

"I am not. He had one of Imber's bolts near buried just under his right armpit. Look up and around, not down!"

After some rapid progress, Quern said, "Nobody could have thrown accurately with all those people round us."

"No, I imagine not."

"It wasn't a throwing knife, anyway. Impossible shot with just a dagger."

"Yes, quite." Kalainen was still hunting round with his eyes, but he was grinning broadly.

Quern made a few awkward noises, and finally said, "In the end, you think this was all about the amulet?"

"Yes. Tarlenia paid for the tournament. They provided the amulet as a prize. Strammon made it. Tessavian refused to. They are both dead or fled. The Tarlenians organised the party at Allamee's too."

"Here's something you haven't thought of, Kalainen. Astelin the

Tarlenian might well win the amulet back for them at the tournament."

"Astelin winning would ruin my whole theory. But I am sure this is part of the plot to weaken the defenders of Shaddimur. Shen is a likely winner and how else to get at him? Even if our murderer is a top warrior, tackling Shen in the Sunsunni barracks must be suicide. Semi-finals next? I hate to encourage you in the evil of gambling, but I would take a wager that he loses. If he's that good a fighter, perhaps he could be our killer?"

"No, wrong again! He only came from Tarlenia for the tournament."

Kalainen's tone turned waspish. "Look Quern, the tournament has three functions. One, to hide Tarlenian aggression behind a show of friendliness; nation states working together. Two, Astelin has been extraordinarily sporting. Allowing fallen opposition to re-gather their arms and so on. Shows Tarlenia not as bad as painted. And three, Astelin will have no intention of winning. The aim is to give the false amulet to the winner, hoping to disable the best in Shaddimur and destabilise the city, robbing Shaddimur of her best warrior leader."

"Right, right." While still keeping watch, Quern flicked his glance over the Drouhin. "When you're cross, there is an alarming edge to you, you know? Come on, tell me how you knew about the roof man?"

"Obvious, wasn't it? A couple of wharf-rats were never going to do anything to Tessavian and risk his magical defences. Their role was to frighten him into the open. By the Bell of Mirrin's Tower, one of those rats had a war hammer! Fine choice against heavy armour, but if he met anyone in plate mail he'd run bleating like a goat. I suppose he only used it to threaten shop-keepers or impress dock-side whores, so it wouldn't matter much."

"But we're ahead of them now, aren't we?"

"Sadly not. If Tessavian gets away, then that's the first thing that has crossed their plan. But we can't use him for evidence or they'll kill him. And now they know they face Kalainen the Douhin and we still don't know who is behind it; just some shady Tarlenian figure. However, when you think about how carefully they planned to kill Strammon and Tessavian, suddenly falling back on a group of dock-side thugs shows they are rattled." A smile returned to the Drouhin's face.

"And now?"

"Traid. I must get him to send a few men asking questions."

"Thought he was best out of the way."

"He is. But I don't like being so visible. Someone is on to us already and they won't like what we're doing."

"But we've completed Traid's mission now."

"We know who stabbed him, which was what we were asked."

"We do. Who was it?"

"Ythil, of course. Ythil the Tarlenian shaman. Strammon would have spoken to him about the amulet. They probably had a heated discussion about it – after all, Strammon could see what a position it would leave him in. Ythil would have reported to his true masters and they put the whole plot in place."

"We're back where we started then. Traid will have to beat it out of him and the Tarlenians won't accept that."

"It won't matter what Traid does now. It has all been about delay. This is part of the big murder issue in Shaddimur."

"That's just what you want to think."

"No, no, there is more to this. Just look at the number of people involved, the cost of the whole thing. This is part of it. Think, Quern! One of the foremost bankers, the leader of the militia, the owner of the largest private guard, one of the Queen's own counsellors..."

"Rich and powerful people in Shaddimur. I imagine those are

the people with the money and possessions that attract robbers and murderers."

"But those are all the leaders in the city. And if Shen the Avatar of Sunsunni is killed or debilitated by the amulet... Don't you see the whole defence network of the city is compromised? Tarlenia aims to take Shaddimur! There is going to be at least one more murder, Quern. We have to get to Traid!"

They hurried to the Watch House. Holding the door to usher Mardenifol inside, Kalainen watched a man with tattooed arms nodding to himself. The man patted the head of his war hammer proudly, then swaggered off in the direction of the docks.

Hunting a name

Quern joined Kalainen as he emerged from the Watch House after his appointment with Captain Traid. Kalainen was stepping gently as if he feared a jolt might cause him to explode.

"Didn't go well?"

"No."

"How did he take the news of what happened to Strammon?"

"Uninterested."

"So long as we got paid."

"We didn't."

"Why not?" Heavy brows lowering, Quern almost stopped for a moment, but Kalainen marched on and he had to stride out to catch up.

"No first-hand proof that Ythil did the stabbing," said Kalainen, jabbing fingers into his palm with each point. "No proof as to who ordered the poisoning and the one suspect Traid could have nailed with the crime we helped escape. No, it didn't go well."

"So, what did he say when you explained about the reason for the murders – ?"

"He'd no time for guesswork."

"– and said there would be an even bigger one coming?"

"He said he had enough trouble with murders that had been committed to worry about ones that hadn't."

"What about the amulet?"

"He said he'd mention my concerns, if he had time."

"What do we do? Imber could swap the magic amulet for a fake one."

Kalainen sighed. "Yes, except for the inconveniences that we have no idea where the Tarlenians have stashed the amulet and we won't see it until they present it, we can't afford to have one made and there isn't time to do so. I suppose we'll just have to get a message to both finalists that on no account should they put the amulet round their necks."

"I'll do that. Unless one of them is Astelin."

"If Shen wins, you should tell him to clap it on the nearest Tarlenian!"

"It'll be presented by Guzarin, the Tarlenian ambassador. That's a convenient neck. Wait, that's perfect. Shen could make a speech," – Quern assumed a silly voice that Shen at least would have found offensive – "'For brotherly unity, I donate this excellent amulet to the generous giver!' Then if Guzarin panicked, we'd know he knew about its powers!"

"Yes, and if he didn't, we might have colluded in the murder of an innocent man. We don't know that the ambassador is personally guilty of anything. Come on, I said we'd meet the lads from Harleon's Saddlery for a drink at the Pink Pilgrim."

"Funny name for the place."

"I don't think they overpaid the sign artist and now no-one knows the original name."

"Perhaps some lady?"

"A sign the artist should change career. There's the Tavern of the Holy Saint Sipahni in Ispanitur and everyone calls it the Fuddled Friar. Customers evidently share enthusiasms for wine and alliteration."

"Still, happy to come if you're paying. Why do we always meet at an inn if you're short of coin?"

"Alcohol preserves many things, secrets are not among them."

"Nor dignity," said Quern cheerfully, forcing the door to the Pink Pilgrim to squall open on bent hinges.

The saddlers were already there, nursing thimbles of small beer. They brightened when Kalainen ordered two jugs of ale and sat at their table. After a while, two lads with long hair and thin fingers stood near them by a wall and kept up an enthusiastic playing on recorders, first one tooting a slow melody while the other extemporised a fluting accompaniment, then swapping roles with easy familiarity.

Quern went to get more beer but was waylaid by a girl and ended up at her table. The remaining three chattered companionably, their conversation lost in the skirling of the recorders. Kalainen probed with innocent questions, hoping to get something on the oily-haired Tarlenian or other visitors.

A man in soft leather trousers and a leather jerkin laced over a linen shirt called over the pot boy and held out coins. "I've a fine ear and love of music, myself. Buy these stalwart boys a quart of Old Dimity apiece! The only condition being that they finish the beer before they play again, eh?"

There was a comfortable ripple of laughter. The musicians fell silent with a flourish as the beer arrived. Kalainen appeared not to notice but just continued talking, telling a tale of how he had once ordered a saddle for a donkey. He tapped his head at his own fool-ishness in wanting a back rest and the saddlers chuckled.

Shortly afterwards, Kalainen signalled to Quern and left. He was nearly back at Coromal before Quern caught up with him, looking suspiciously satisfied.

"She was probably a set-up, you know?"

Quern's rolling bass laugh was like the purring of a monstrous lion. "Sourpuss! Well, if she is, I might learn something, you never know! You organised the musicians to block eavesdroppers, then?"

"Of course. And because they were stopped, we know we're being shadowed."

When they reached Coromal, Yanni was happily gnawing on a carrot while stirring a vegetable stew to Mother Yellern's vaguely re-membered instructions. Imber worked on some metal device at the table. Mardenifol had returned home to spend the evening with his parents and then collect more of his glassware and reagents. Appar-ently Kalainen had proved more tolerant of his experiments than Lady Berrin.

While sploshing the stew into wooden bowls, Yanni told them that Tessavian and his family had escaped safely on the *Cormorant*. Captain Maegre had accepted the token without question, only re-gretting the demise of Strammon, whom he thought a good man.

"You've done really well, Yanni. Thank you." After trying the stew, Kalainen rolled a lump round his mouth for a moment. "Yanni, do you like cooking?"

"Best thing ever! All this food, different stuffs, tastes I never dreamt of. Def'nite!"

"Hm. I think some bits need a bit more cooking than others." Kalainen chewed the unidentified gobbet diligently. "And perhaps not all of the store cupboard should go into one pot."

"Old mother Yellern makes a fine pie," said Quern. "Perhaps she's a bit chary with her tips for Yanni."

"Hm. Was this really what Yellern said to do, Yanni?"

"Yes, well, sort of. She said things a bit quickly."

"I see. Oh, I almost forgot; this is for you." Kalainen took out the stiletto and passed it to Yanni. The girl took it gingerly as if she thought it would turn into a wasp. She turned it over gently a few times, then drew the blade. She slid the steel needle back into its sheath and looked at Kalainen with huge eyes.

"You mean I can keep it? It's mine?"

"Yes."

Yanni tried to say a couple of things, then ran from the room, leaving her stew uneaten.

They ate in silence for a while. Then Kalainen said, "Mother Yellern's all right for us but could you take Yanni round to the Iron Eye when you can? If she's really keen, Mistress Lassith can show her everything she needs. If not, well, the hard work won't hurt. Best to choose the direction before the journey is half walked."

"I've eaten at the Iron Eye. It's good. Might stop Yanni poisoning the lot of us. By the way, did you learn anything from the saddlers?"

"Only that we are being watched. I should have got you to trail that chap that bought the beer for my musicians, Imber. People watching us means this is still on-going, whether Traid realises it or not. They're still worried, even if we aren't sure who 'they' are. If Shen isn't going to be the end of this, then who on earth is it going to be? The Queen herself? She is well-protected, I think, but would it be enough?" mused Kalainen.

"Everyone killed was well protected," rumbled Quern, "and they all thought it would be enough, no doubt."

Kalainen stared at Quern until the big man waved his fingers before the Drouhin's face. "Anyone in there?"

"That's brilliant, Quern. That may be it."

"Good! Very good. What may be what?"

But Kalainen was on another tack. "Imber, can you make Coro-mal safe?"

"Safe? With you four blundering about? No. I can make it more interesting. Particularly if there are doors and windows you do not ever use."

"Thanks. Get it done. Yanni can help and then she'll know what to avoid. May help her elsewhere. I need to think."

Kalainen spent most of his time closeted in his work-room and when household duties called him out, he was distracted and un-communicative. Quern spent his time at the bouts. He made no mention of a wager against Astelin, but after the Tarlenian lost in the semi-final, reports dribbled in later of an uproarious evening with the girl from the Pink Pilgrim. However, he made time to take Yanni to an eatery near the Slatch called the Iron Eye after a huge ellipse nailed over the door with a blob of paint in the centre. The place was a volcano of noise and colour, with patrons queue-ing for food, or sitting on benches at rough tables. On the left there was a massive stove where the cook was tipping fried onions from a pan into a cauldron. She glugged oil into the pan and scraped in some cubes of something coated in flour. Almost hidden, an-other girl peeled vegetables beside her. At the cooler end of the range were three cauldrons of stew, lentils and vegetables spitting coloured flecks. A sweaty woman with greasy hair dumped ladles of food onto over-baked discs of flour paste for customers and tossed coins into a wooden box. To the right, behind another counter, two potboys tapped barrels or squirted wine from skins into jugs. Sev-eral well-dressed people joined the queues or elbowed cheerfully at the tables, though there were none of the customary money bags on view. A bearded giant with a quarterstaff leaned against the door frame. His sleepy eyes drifted constantly over the diners. The eyes stopped on Quern, but Quern just grinned at him.

Everywhere people were talking or clicking beakers or shovelling food with bits of bread roll. A fastidious few tied napkins about their necks and ate with their own cutlery brought for the occasion. Left-over trenchers were tossed into a crate near the door for anyone to help themselves without charge.

Half-stupefied by the rolling din and the savoury smells, Yanni stood entranced until Quern's grip on her shoulder propelled her over towards the cook.

"Mistress Lassith! Kalainen was hoping you might teach Yanni here about cooking."

"Kalainen the Drouhin? Well, I owes him a favour. More'n a favour really. She'll have to be useful though. Come on, Yanni, get over here."

"Thanks," said Quern. "Would the favour run to a free..."

But the cook had already turned her attention back to her pans. "Start by chopping them mushrooms. Quarters'll do."

"Mushrooms! I thought they was deadly!"

Lassith laughed with a crackling sound like someone crunching up dried hogweed stalks. "Some of them is. Some of them kill you..." she clacked her knife down on a board, "... like that! You have to know what's which. I've been over everyone one of those, don't you worry. All good! Can never get enough of them." She turned to the other girl present, who was humming to herself as though the cacophony of the room didn't touch her. "Come on, Saphin, you should've done them! I need six fat cloves of garlic, quickly now!"

Quern shook his head and bought his own meal. By the time he left, Yanni looked happy, greasy and full.

Once she did get back to Coromal, Yanni spent hours with Imber, installing wires and traps, spring-loaded devices and alarms. She was an apt pupil. Mardenifol busied himself with his chemicals in his own little workroom. The apprentices were surprised when Kalainen roused himself sufficiently to visit a local place for their provisions, rather than just sending them. It seemed strange to walk without a steady stream of explanations and apothegms.

Mardenifol endured being hushed by Kalainen in the shop, but when they emerged with their groceries, the young man stood in front of the Drouhin.

"They've over-charged us!"

"I am sure they have not. Come now, try some honeyed fruit while we're here."

"No, I checked. A helm on the breads and..."

"Not now, Mardenifol."

"But they've cheated you!"

"No, no, they, ah, they have no doubt included a few items that were on credit from last week. Yes, they helped me out when I foolishly left my pouch behind. Think no more on it."

They walked to Coromal in silence. Once Kalainen had shut the door to his workroom, Mardenifol turned to Yanni in outrage.

"They cheated him!"

"No. He lied to you." Yanni stared across the table at Mardenifol.

"There may have been a credit, but nobody mentioned it when they totted up the bill. And I had already done it, of course."

"Course you had. But there weren't no credit from last week. Nor any other week neither."

"Then what?"

"They made up a basket. Eggs and olives and bread and beans. That's gone to be delivered elsewhere."

"Really? You sure?"

"Def'nite. You reckon he's got a lover or what?"

Mardenifol went scarlet.

Yanni pulled a lemon from their provisions, scraped a nail over the skin and sniffed ecstatically. She grinned at him over the lemon. "Tell you what, next time he does that, one of us should follow the basket!"

Mardenifol nodded slowly. "Yes. Or – or we could make friends with whoever does their deliveries. Just see if it could come out in chatter, eh?"

"That's better. It's only what he's teaching us to do, ain't it? I can imagine – Poor you, how far do you have to carry that basket? What sort of person doesn't come and fetch their own vittles."

"All that stuff, yes." Mardenifol grinned back.

"Tell you another thing; all the money what he gets paid by Traid; what's happened to it, eh? Got a woman for sure."

While they plotted, Kalainen sat on the porch at Coromal watching the lightning play over the hills west of Shaddimur. The thunder was sometimes so loud that young goats leapt into the air and galloped to nowhere better. He heard the pattering hiss of the rain striking the leaves before the first drops clattered down. The air was filled with the scent of the lavender and the wet earth. Then the purring of the rain eased, the sky lightened and the little shower was gone.

Kalainen leapt to his feet. "Imber!" he bellowed, bursting back into the house. "Find Imber!" The apprentices scattered like sparrows before a hawk.

When Quern hurried in, Kalainen was pacing the kitchen. Quern took one look and beamed. "Action, then!"

After a moment, Kalainen's face softened with sympathy. "You don't catch a moth in a mousetrap."

Quern's outburst was cut short by Imber.

"What've we got?"

"Don't ask me! Apparently, we are trying to catch a moth and Kalainen thinks I'm a mousetrap. Or something."

Imber gave a little snort. He was breathing harder than normal and trying not to let it show. He arched his eyebrows at the Drouhin.

"We have a lead. It is tenuous, and it will be hard – but it's there, I can feel it. What do we know of the killer?"

"Works on his – or her – own. Better than handy in a straight-up fight. Guards have been killed, good ones too. And not all taken by surprise."

"Very good. Someone who can face off against the best guards in Shaddimur, some of them armoured as well. No sign the intruder has ever been injured. And they weren't creeping round at night in armour."

"Nothing new," said Imber.

"Quite," said Quern, still not mollified. "One lone warrior. Doesn't narrow the field all that much. You've told us this before from all your quill-scratchings."

Kalainen smiled. "But as you said, Quern, all the people that have been killed have been well guarded. And yet one warrior has breached all those defences. A warrior has taken the optimal route, every time. We seem to be investing every skill in one person, eh?"

"A demon, perhaps?"

"Possibly. But let's assume mundane and human while we can."

"So someone has done a very thorough research job before one warrior goes in against professional defences. That's not a warrior's work. They've used a spy."

"Exactly. And if we are right and the Tarlenians are behind it...?"

"Then they'll have needed a local and hired one."

"As they have done with other matters, yes. And with your contacts in the Neers, Imber, you have to find the spy."

"Spies are good at not being found, Kalainen. Rather the point."

Quern butted in again. "Tarlenians hired assassins to kill Strammon. They may have done that every time. Assassins are spies and swordsmen!" He bit the words off in distaste, flexing his fingers to promise a proper grapple with any assassin he found.

"No. If you're an assassin, how do you work?"

Imber coloured slightly, "You poison their wine, or shoot them in the back with a crossbow, slide a knife between their ribs in a crowded market or ..."

"Exactly. Why expose yourself to danger? All of the deaths we know about are brought about by a single swordsman in the home of the deceased. Not assassins' work."

"So we have to hire a spy to catch a spy? I hate all this skulduggery. Stand up and fight toe to toe!" Quern was waving his arms about as though to catch an invisible interloper.

"We don't need to hire one. You're right, Imber. Spies can be hard to find. But this one was contactable to get work. First we must discover who we're looking for."

"Too many possibilities if we're in a hurry."

"No so many. They'll have used the best spy all their gold can buy."

"Best is matter of opinion." Imber's flat face gave little away, but his tone suggested the line of inquiry was dead.

"Can't be that many at the top, Imber. You must know them all in Shaddimur."

"Top of what? Nyrudin can open any lock, Mabs of Leavy's Gate has no peer in disguise. There are specialists in shadowing and tracking, experts in assay, hunters of arcane equipment..." Imber blew out his cheeks.

"Infiltration specialist. Someone has been doing the spying for the killer. If they have done their last reconnaissance, whoever it is has just lost their usefulness and they are the one loose end that could lead us to the killer."

"Could be many cutouts between the spy and the killer."

"True. But even the knotted rope can be coiled." When Imber looked doubtful, Kalainen went on. "They are Tarlenian. You know far more about spies in Shaddimur than they do. You have to follow the line they will have used to find the best spy. That will be our man."

Imber paused, immobile. Eventually he nodded. "I see. Yes. They would almost inevitably have spoken to Drogulus. Have we anything to offer him? He's not the sort to hand out free information."

"I knew him before he called himself Drogulus," said Quern. "And I didn't like him then. We could lean on him a bit," he added, cracking his knuckles hopefully.

"We're not thugs. I can talk to him," said Kalainen. "He may let something slip."

Imber shook his head. "I know Drogulus. You really don't talk the same language. It has to be me." While Kalainen fretted, Imber gave the tiniest wink to Quern.

Imber pushed into the wine shop on Fellows. The wood of the door was oiled to a sheen and it opened noiselessly. Light trickled down from somewhere overhead. There were no windows. Two thirds of the room were taken up with wine racks running from floor to ceiling, uncomfortably close together. Each passage ended against wainscoting with multiple facets. Imagining myriad traps and knowing imagination was not required, Imber almost flinched as he walked past them towards a counter, where he could hear a steady clicking noise.

"Here to browse?" asked a woman, glancing up from her knitting. She was middle-aged and puffy-fleshed, her lips a thin slash across a round face. The eyes assessing Imber were like frozen glass.

"Something more ... discriminating." The light from above slid over Imber's face.

Sudden recognition jolted her mouth open. "Imber!" She stood up and carefully arranged the knitting on the counter. She knocked on a door at the end of the room, then opened a panel on a box attached to the door, giving Imber a brief glimpse of a matrix of rods.

Standing firmly in front of them, she pushed in a number of rods to make a pattern that would be replicated on the other side of the door. Then she closed the box.

"Do go in," she said sweetly, returning to the knitting.

Imber exhaled softly, then walked to the door.

There was a rattle as the rods were reset inside the box, then the door opened. A swarthy man in well-worn leather took one look and three rapid steps backwards. The small crossbow in his right hand didn't quite point at Imber.

"Imber!"

"Imber? Imber!" Drogulus had been sitting at a table with three other men. He was thickset with a protuberant belly and hair that looked as though the sweepings from the barber's floor had been dumped on his head. Drogulus leapt to his feet, hands held wide in greeting, he came forward with a smile. He stood too close to Imber for comfort but made no move to grip hands. Bulbous eyes assessed his visitor.

"What could have kept you away all this time?"

Imber gave half a shrug. "Business."

"Business. Of course, what else? And what now leads you here?"

The other half. "Business."

Drogulus grunted. "Then before we are overwhelmed by your unstoppable social chattering, perhaps we should see if we have things to discuss. What light can you shed on the shadowed corners of your business?"

"I have a job on. Slide in, ghost away. Don't know what I face in there. I need eyes on the inside."

"Very sensible. Even a lion sends a rat down a hole. And you want me to point you in the direction of a suitable rat?"

"They'll need to be good. Won't need teeth. But the best you know for this."

"Hm, complications." Drogulus chewed his lip for a moment,

then brightened. "I can do that. Of course, I can – who else but me? And there would be no charge for an old friend. But then I know you would feel an imbalance, perhaps even that you owed me a favour. Naturally I would deny it, but the obligation would be there just the same. So, you do me a little service and the matter is resolved at once." Drogulus smiled more widely.

"A service." If Imber's voice had been flatter, it could have slid under the door.

"A small matter, but one that requires swift resolution, which you will be more impelled to do if your own issue speaks of urgency. So, find a girl for me. A young woman, goes by the name of Kari Witchet." Drogulus watched closely as he said it. Imber merely gave another tiny shrug, lifting one eyebrow with it. Drogulus snorted. "Well, if you are looking for a rat, this is a mouse. Understand?"

Imber nodded a morose assent. "You want her found or brought – alive."

"Of course alive, what are you thinking? Still, found would do, if confirmed. Brought would..." Drogulus smiled but it had a sickly edge, "... incur a bonus. Can't tell you much. She lives with some woman of no consequence. And by live together, I mean..." Drogulus leered with an obscene gesture. "You find her, I'll tell you what you need. Now, give me a moment – I must select a suitable vintage to celebrate so auspicious an occasion!"

"Time presses."

"I insist! Time will press little harder after a glass from the Riddiphir Hills! Azeer! A hand if you please. Those aisles are too narrow for me!"

The smallest of the trio remaining at the table rose. Azeer kept his eyes on Imber as he sidled past to join Drogulus in the wine store. Imber waited in silence. The man with the little crossbow watched him steadily. Attempting to look relaxed, the two men still at the table tried a few snide digs but when Imber turned an unblinking stare at them, they too lapsed into quiet. One of them pulled his shirt closed to hide a medallion showing a shark's fin on a blue enamelled background. Imber remained standing, turning his head slowly to look round the room. It was a creation, a work of art designed to show Drogulus as he wished to be perceived. There were pictures of libraries with open books, a chest with a raised lid and glowing treasures, a triangle with a pentagram lined with runes. Elsewhere, a trio of daggers in a stand, mounted medals and awards. On the back wall, a black marble niche with a statue of Belshaz, goddess of the night. None of it meant anything; this was merely Drogulus's shop window. There was also a bitter scent in the air, only partially smothered by the aroma of wine. Imber glanced at the men at the table, looking for some hint of glassiness in their eyes, but they were fully alert. Perhaps they had been concocting something? The table was bare but there had been plenty of time to put whatever must have been on it in a cupboard. Imber's face remained expressionless.

Finally, Drogulus waddled back without Azeer. He still made no effort to introduce the others at the table. Still prattling inconsequentially, he took an unbroken wax seal off a small clay bottle, brought four glasses and poured. Only the man with the crossbow remained apart. Drogulus frowned at Imber, who was watching the full glasses impassively.

"Really? Come now, that is foolish. You choose your glass."

"Just being polite." Imber took the glass furthest left and they all sipped.

There was an awkward period during which Drogulus maintained almost a monologue of bonhomie. Imber offered occasional monosyllabic responses to direct questions and the other two laughed where Drogulus paused for it. Finally, Drogulus seemed to tire of his games. He tossed back the last of the wine. Moving too close to Imber again, he said, "It's just business. Find me the girl and you will have the name you want. Fare well." He waved his hands towards the door and allowed Imber to leave.

After only a few paces from the wine shop, Imber seemed to notice a loose thread on the stitching of one boot. He took out a knife and trimmed it carefully. He made a show at his hip but the blade did not return to its sheath.

Early evening; light still good. Imber reflexively looked at a low wall, a window above it, easy access to the rooftops. Not this time. Several people on the street; heading home, heading out. Time and again, Imber subtly changed course so he didn't pass too close to anyone. The direction didn't matter so much. Imber headed for the streets he knew best, watching all the time for that jarring movement, the eye contact, the twitch of a weapon.

Imber walked on, moving quickly. At that pace, anyone coming up behind him would be obvious doing so. He turned sharply at a harsh laugh; a couple of field hands, big men and tough-looking, but they were aiming for the nearest tavern. As they went in, Imber caught the flash of a sleeve, the same colour that Azeer had worn.

Imber turned back to the road. He so nearly missed it. It was always the boots that gave it away. Three men looked like timber-workers, one still carrying a length of wood, perhaps a pick helve. They were carefully not looking at him. But it was the boots. Not right for timber-workers. They turned on him, fast as falling stones, the first swinging the pick helve at his head. Imber twisted away, thrusting his knife at the enemy's wrist. A leather guard turned the blade but it sliced into the hand at the base of the thumb. Imber dodged a punch and kicked the next man in the thigh, missing his knee. Then the third assailant half-caught him in a clumsy grapple, enough to pull him off balance. The man he had kicked grabbed him and the next moment Imber found himself sitting on the ground, the man behind him had his knees in Imber's back while he pinioned Imber's elbows.

The man with the pick helve was clutching his injured hand. "Message for you. Wherever you're sticking your nose, don't. Or next time, it'll be a lot worse." He looked at the blood pouring from his thumb and hefted the helve. "Or maybe not."

Imber looked up. Two men loomed over him, one lifting the helve, the other aiming a kick. This was going to be bad, he thought.

There was a rending thud of impact on bone, a grunt of effort and a sound like a carthorse stamping on hard ground followed by the retching, whooping noise of someone trying unsuccessfully to breathe. A curse from behind Imber and the pressure on his arms disappeared. The curse changed to a shrill scream as Quern lifted the man up by the ears. As he came down, Quern hit him under the chin with the heel of his hand. The man landed on his back, made a soft groan and lay still.

The big fighter glared round at them. Two apparently unconscious and one first red, then white in the face, curled up and spasming for air.

"Come on, make an effort!" Quern roared, hands balled into fists.

"They look tired out." Imber stretched his shoulders back, making a face.

"Want me to beat something out of them?" He seized the nearest by the shirt in his left hand and lifted him towards the fist that waited by his ear.

"Just message boys. They delivered it. Drink and a chat across the road looks favourite." Imber indicated Yanni, waiting by the inn door. She pointed inside and to the left.

"You know, that little girl terrifies me," murmured Quern, regretfully dropping the false timber worker and forgetting all about him.

"She's great, isn't she? Got you to the right place. And thanks."

"Didn't last long after I knocked their heads together. Let's see what she's got before he legs it."

Inside the tavern, Azeer was standing at the bar, laughing at some toff way out of his area getting ragged by locals. Imber suddenly appeared next to Drogulus's man.

"Glad you're buying."

Azeer shot backwards in a stumbling flail of arms and legs and turned to run. One of Quern's hands dropped round his neck and half-propelled, half-lifted him back beside Imber.

"I'm happy to drink and talk," said Imber, who hadn't moved. "There are other options. Your choice."

Praying under his breath, Azeer fumbled over coins for the jug of beer he had ordered for different company and pulled his lips back in an attempt at an ingratiating smile. "I can't, Imber. You know I can't." Sweat began to bubble on his face.

Quern drew the sign of the teardrop over his beer, tapped a finger on the surface and touched it to his forehead. He had just taken a swig when his eyes were drawn by a nasty guffaw from the locals. "Just a minute," he said. Quern strode over to where Mardenifol was standing defensively against a wall before a ring of grinning locals.

"I don't have an accent! Just leave me in peace, you..."

"Lord Berrin," said Quern. "I've been meaning to thank you for showing me that arm lock."

"What arm lock can 'e do?" said a local, eyeing the skinny boy. "Ow!"

"That would be this one. Any more questions? Thought not." Quern bared his teeth at the locals in a way that someone with really poor sight might have thought was a grin, then gave a wink to Mardenifol. "Come and join us."

"That's all right," said Mardenifol quietly, much to Quern's surprise. "They meant no harm. I'll buy a jug of beer and we'll have a chat."

Quern nodded and went back to loom over Azeer, who looked ill.

"You can talk to me and it could work out for you." Imber's voice was unchanged. "Or you can talk to him, and it won't. He's already had words with the three you sent after me."

"Imber, please..."

Imber took a slow swallow of beer. "Expect they would prefer to have had a drink. If they were able to."

"Iol's Tooth!"

"It's all right. Just tell me what Drogulus said to you in the wine shop."

"Nothing of interest, honest. He just said you were a terrible actor. Sorry, that's what he said!"

"Fair enough. What else?"

"Said you'd never want help on a job like that – wouldn't trust anyone to do it better than you even if your pride allowed it. There were a few other words in there, but that was it. Then he just told me to take a message to the Tarlenian embassy. Just to the door. I had to say, 'Kites are dropping to your carcase.' The Tarlenians told me to collect them ..." Azeer waved outside, where quite a crowd had gathered round the three assailants, "and point you out."

"You did that. Just business. Anything else?"

"Nothing. I did ask if he wanted me to set up protection for the spy but he said no need, they've finished with her now, and she's gone."

Imber remained staring at Azeer. The words were crashing round his head. Her. The spy was a woman.

He twitched when Azeer said, "There wasn't another syllable, honestly!"

Imber drew a knife and laid it on the bar.

"Ghulsk, Imber, I've told you everything, please..."

"Best go then."

Azeer gaped at Imber for a moment. He shuddered as Quern

growled behind him, then began backing away. "Thanks. Thank you, Imber. I won't forget it."

Imber put out a hand as Azeer began to sidle away. "I've got lots of these. All throwing blades, sharp and true. You don't want to see any of them at night, Azeer. Might want to think about that."

Nodding like a woodpecker, Azeer was gone. Quern shrugged and addressed himself to the jug of beer. Imber was gazing sightlessly across the room. Yanni came scampering in and rushed up to them.

"Quick! Want me to follow him? He's going fast!"

"No, we're done with him, Yanni. Good work there!" Quern rumpled her hair and gave a beery grin.

Imber snapped back into focus. "We have to get back to Coromal. I must talk this through with Kalainen!"

"I'll get Mar... What *is* he doing?"

Mardenifol was sitting at a table with half a dozen of the locals. More crowded round watching him. He seemed to be holding a ball of fire which he rolled from one hand to another. The locals had faces of horrified fascination, some nearly hidden behind their hands. Some made the sign of the Lady or half-laughed in nervous gasps. Mardenifol waved the ball of flame round, his face lit with delight. He taunted the most truculent of his earlier tormentors and dared him to take the firey globe. Reluctantly, the man was shamed by his friends into holding out a trembling palm. Mardenifol made a few more passes with his own hands, then dropped the ball onto the man's hand. Almost immediately, the man yelped in pain, shot backwards off his bench onto the floor, the burning material landing on his smock. The crowd exploded with laughter, someone's boot finally extinguishing the ball of fire. The injured man showed his burnt hand and a scorched patch in his smock. Mardenifol showed his own undamaged hands.

The crowd were all talking and grinning, even the burnt man was accepting defeat with a shake of his head, but they called Mardenifol Master and touched their foreheads as he rose in response to Yanni's beckonings.

Outside, Yanni was frantic with questions.

"That was magic! You was doing magic, wasn't you?"

"No, of course not."

"But the fire didn't burn you!"

"It's a scrap of cloth soaked in light naphtha. It burns cool enough to hold."

"So why did it burn him, then, eh?"

"Three reasons. One, he expected it to hurt. Two, I always kept it moving so it doesn't get time to burn any one spot. He held it still. And three, the naphtha was almost all burnt out and the cotton was burning. I could tell because it started smoking. Burns a lot hotter then. I learned that with a few blisters myself!"

"Trick went well. Another day they might think you were a demon and decide to lynch you. You want to be careful." Imber eyed him as though unconvinced on the matter of demons. "If you want to pretend to be a mage, better have a staff, at least."

Back at Coromal, Kalainen was waiting for them. He made them tell their stories chronologically and then rested back in his chair, steepling his fingers. He looked at Imber.

"So, you think you know more, and you want to see if I come to the same conclusions? Hm. Our spy is female. The list of top infiltration experts that are female must be short."

"One. Tertius Orbis."

"Excellent. But she's gone."

"Yes. And if she doesn't want to be found, she won't be."

Kalainen nodded. "I see. The Tarlenians paid for Tertius's name from Drogulus, but they also then paid him to rough up anyone following their tracks. And you guessed that would happen."

Imber shrugged. "Seemed reasonable."

Kalainen's glance took in Quern, who gave a smug grin. Tapping his fingers together and then putting them to his chin, Kalainen continued as though reeling in a fish. "Tertius Orbis has vanished and the Tarlenians have finished with her. She's done her last job for them and is now a liability they want to erase. They probably tried and she's fled. That's not the end though. What's the other snippet you have?"

"Drogulus wants me to find a girl called Kari Witchet; a trainee spy who lives with a woman."

For a moment, Kalainen's eyes were blanked with thought, then his lips twitched up with a little snort. His shoulders shook a couple of times and then a laugh burst out of him. Imber's face was suddenly lit up by a rare boyish smile. Kalainen burst into an unrestrained peal of laughter that had everyone joining in.

Quern, still laughing, shook his head. "What in the Lady's name has got into you?"

Clapping Quern on the shoulder, Kalainen said, "Drogulus has contrived to outsmart himself!" He turned back to Imber.

"The Tarlenians want to get rid of Tertius, but they've lost her. Drogulus is now looking for another girl, this Kari Witchet. You think Tertius has a lover, a girl, and Tertius is the woman of no importance who lived with Kari? So Drogulus has tried to get you to find Kari to locate Tertius. Then he'll tell you Tertius is the spy after he has sold the information to the Tarlenians."

"His style."

"Twisty snake," grumbled Quern. "Should have let me talk to him. Well, except we have the name now and Drogulus doesn't know where she is anyway."

Kalainen was tapping his teeth, deep in thought. "Tertius and Kari are probably not together because as a twosome they would either have left Shaddimur or be in a bolt hole so secure they were safe. The Tarlenians must have split them up. Now the Tarlenians and Drogulus – and Balgrim knows how many more - want to use Kari to get to Tertius! Drogulus is looking for Kari Witchet, the apprentice spy. So we have to find the mouse first."

"If they're, you know, lovers," put in Mardenifol, turning red, "Wouldn't they have fled together?"

"Yes, if they could, but not necessarily if Tertius Orbis were panicked into flight. There would be no way for Tertius to know it was the last job. Imagine a sudden attack by Tarlenians, perhaps the women fled in different directions in the confusion, perhaps only one of them was home or they tried to assassinate Tertius Orbis at a meeting. Imagine Kari Witchet coming back to a wrecked home, where does she go?"

"I've heard of Kari Witchet before. It's an assumed name. But the girl who called herself Kari Witchet led the children of Green Worm tower until she had to leave."

"Not Green Worm tower," said Mardenifol. "That place at Coign where the walls of the Cornmarket loom over the Slatch? It collapsed and was abandoned years ago."

"It was. But for many years the ruin has been taken over by a band of feral children. They don't let anyone stay once they become adult. If Kari was their last leader, she'll have had to leave. They won't let her back."

"She's got nowhere else to go. Not if she came from there."

"They will not deal with any adults. Ever. Not even those who try to help them," said Kalainen. "They do not trust any adult."

"It's one place I would fear to go," said Imber. "Could not go."

"Doesn't matter. They only allow children in and there are no exceptions. Ever. They won't let Kari Witchet in either."

"Nothing else to be said," announced Yanni. "She was their leader. She has nowhere else. And it's the only lead we have. I'll go and look. Nobody else can." As they all began to voice objections, Yanni overrode them. "You know it's true. Now, we have a fish and Mistress Lasith told me a way to cook it. It should be nearly done, so wait, and don't say anything else on this." And with that she marched off to busy herself at the range.

The rest of them were almost silenced, but eventually they set about their evening chores and conversation resumed. Mardenifol sewed a scrap of cloth into another ball and demonstrated his trick with the burning ball of cotton. They all had to have a go, rolling the little ball of fire from one hand to the other. Kalainen shook his head in wonder and debated with Mardenifol how one flame could be hotter than another.

"Imber, how did you know you'd be attacked?" asked Quern.

"We were following a wide road and they'd trapped it. It's what I'd have done."

"Still don't see how you knew it was going to be an immediate affair."

"Drogulus held me back deliberately and sent Azeer to get the thugs and point me out to them. Drogulus said it was business. He'd already taken gold to pass on a message if someone asked after the spy so they would be warned off."

"If he isn't a friend, why warn you?"

"Because he doesn't want me coming after him. And I won't. He did his job whether the attack on me succeeded or failed. Perhaps he also hopes I'll give Kari Witchet to him. He doesn't know he has carefully confirmed Tertius Orbis's name to us. By the way, Kalainen, I don't think his sight is good. Could be useful."

"It might. But he sees some things clearly. He knows you're working with me. What an insultingly clumsy effort at a metaphor. Lions sending rats down holes!"

Yanni produced a parcel from the range. The fish had been wrapped in a wet cloth, which was now dry and charred on the outside. Inside the fish was baked in fennel and garlic. Succulent flakes pulled easily from the bones.

"Ghulsk! It worked!" said Yanni.

After the meal, Imber looked at her with a shy smile. "That was really nice, thank you."

Kari Witchet

Yanni looked up at the remains of the tower. It had partly fallen long ago, but a section of the original tower remained upright, still capped with a copper roof embossed with a stylistic dragon. The doorways had all been lost when the tower subsided. A couple of giant tree trunks had been wedged against what was left to stop it toppling into the Slatch. Yanni suspected that had the tower been likely to fall onto the Cornmarket, it would have been carefully dismantled long ago, for there was wealth. Corn trading had been moved nearer the edge of the city long ago and the old centre had been taken over by expensive shops and imposing houses of yellow stone with painted shutters, three storeys high.

The tower was sliced with arrow slits in places, some marked pale with bird excrement. There were also cracks and crevices where a small person might creep in. Yanni perched on a tilted monolith near the base and waited.

After a while, a stone clattered down near her. Yanni ignored it. A second pebble pinged off the slab she was sitting on. Looking up, Yanni saw the flicker of a face through a slit. A hand waved her away. She shook her head and remained sitting. Another stone hit her on the shoulder. She flinched at the sting but refused to rub it. She stayed where she was. It went quiet for a long time.

"What're you doing here?" The speaker was a girl, perhaps twelve years old. She wore a shirt that would have fitted a lumberjack and perhaps once had. Yanni had not seen her coming.

"I need to talk."

"Any reason we should talk to you?"

Yanni held out a small money pouch. The girl took it and looked at the coins inside. She sat down a couple of strides from Yanni but didn't look at her.

"You trying to buy your way in?"

"No. Just need to talk."

"You're talking."

"Yes. But I need to talk to someone else."

"I'm the best you're going to get."

"Lifted that purse this morning. If I'd wanted, he would've noticed me and chased me. Maybe if I'd come with him pounding after me, you'd have let me in; kept the bad man out. But I didn't. Don't think you want attention drawn to Green Worm tower."

"True. No reason to let you in, though. Where're you from?"

"Meiling Square."

"Oh? You know Bellhopper then, and Leggy and Flour-duff."

"Leggy's still lame, Flour-duff's still an idiot. There's no Bellhopper."

The girl grunted. "Who d'you want to talk to anyway; someone from Meiling?"

"She's known as Kari Witchet now."

Finally, the girl turned to stare at Yanni. The right side of her jaw was furrowed by a scar. "Not here. Not for a long time."

"But she's here now. You don't want her no more, and I know somewhere safe if she wants to go there. No pressure, just an offer. And you really don't want her here. A lot of people are hunting her and they'd pull this whole conkin' stack down without a thought to get her."

"So what's it to you?"

Yanni stared back. "Does it matter in the end? I'm trying to help her. It may help me. It will help you."

"Where's the safe place?"

"How many people know before it ain't safe no more? I'm only offering. If Kari says no, that's it."

"World ain't right," muttered the girl, fingering her jaw.

"No. It's how it is."

The girl rubbed her jaw again and sighed. "Rain coming."

"Yes." Yanni sat still. As the first drops pattered down, she hunched her shoulders and glared defiantly forwards.

The girl turned back to look over the Slatch. They were just a couple of urchins perched on the mossy tumbled wreckage of old glory. No-one was paying them the least attention. "Come on then. But if she says a word, or you do something we don't like, there's no coming out again."

Yanni followed the girl as they hopped over the great stone blocks like weasels. They dropped into a roofless chamber where they would be invisible to all. The stones were black and slippery with rain, gullies green with alga. Valerian and navelwort somehow found footholds and clung on grimly, much like the children. Yanni moved towards a long gap at floor level she could easily have slid through. There were marks on the stone clearly showing where things had been dragged that way. The girl gave a soft snort of laughter.

"Not that way. Definitely not that way."

The girl led Yanni to a smaller cleft they had to wiggle through. They crawled along a short tunnel and wormed through a trapdoor. As Yanni squeezed up, she looked into the fierce eyes of a boy of perhaps ten summers. His spear looked home-made, but the spear point was very real and lovingly sharpened. The boy thrust it at her warningly until the girl pushed it down and called him a donkey.

"Conkin' clod! Come on then, both of you." The girl led Yanni through a room and up a spiral staircase, all on a slight slant that made Yanni feel disorientated and unsure of her footing. Yanni's guide jerked her head at a door. "Wait here while I have a quick word. Keep an eye on her, Bry."

The girl slipped through the unlocked door. It had perhaps once fitted perfectly, but the movement of the tower had ruined it. Someone with poor carpentry skills had hacked off various bits until it functioned without catching. Yanni was more concerned with what Bry might do with his spear and was relieved when the girl emerged a few moments later.

"Not long, right? And it's my neck as well as yours stretched under the axe."

Yanni nodded at her and went in. The room was little more than a monk's cell. Given the twisted walls and the cracked and bowing roof, a few prayers might have been appropriate. Yanni forced herself to ignore the ruination and concentrate on the young woman sitting on a paillasse. Even in the grey light, Yanni could see that she had been crying but she was calm now.

"Are you Kari Witchet?"

"Yes. Today."

"Oh." Yanni's mouth opened and closed a few times. "This your old room?"

"Hardly. It's where I kept my birds." Kari waved vaguely at disused perches. "They were free to fly but they always came back to me. I hoped they would be still here. Everything's gone."

Yanni looked at her. Kari Witchet may have been desperate but she remained self-possessed, in control of herself. Yanni was the one out of her depth. She hadn't thought what to do once she found Kari and just blurted,

"We know about you and Tertius Orbis. Ghulsk, that sounds like a threat. I mean the opposite. Look, we know about the work for the Tarlenians and that they turned on her." Yanni searched Kari's face for some clue as to her response, but the face was schooled into an expression of polite interest. "Look, we're trying to stop the Tarlenians and..." she ran out of words.

Kari gave a tight smile. "You really don't look like a negotiator on behalf of Shaddimur."

"Ghulsk, no! I mean, no, obviously not. But everyone's going to be trying to find Tertius. Including you. And they're all trying to find you to get to her. All I'm saying is that I think there is somewhere you can go in safety. Somewhere safe."

"On the other hand, you could well be someone trying to flush me out of here."

Yanni's face crumpled. "Reckon those people will just knock the tower down. Look, Kari, if you had some way of finding Tertius that easily, you'd be with her, not here. We want to find Tertius before the Tarlenians kill her. We need to know who she spied on last to stop them being killed too. You know you can't stay here and they can't afford to let you."

"So you just want to help me?"

"Give you a chance anyway."

"Despite the fact that Tertius' work allowed those other murders to happen?"

"I don't know," said Yanni miserably. "She didn't kill anyone. Perhaps she had her reasons."

"Who has a hold on you, forcing you to do this?" Again, Kari's expression only showed mild interest.

Yanni shook her head. "Nobody. Just wanted to make one thing better."

Kari Witchet looked at her as though reading her future on knucklebones. "Pruny said you're from Meiling Square. Is that where this safe place is then?"

Yanni sniffed. "That's a conkin' laugh. Everyone knows everyone there. You'd stand out like a turd on a cake stall. Oh! I don't mean..."

"Quite. So where, then?"

"I don't actually know. No, listen. You can go to Kalainen."

"Kalainen the Drouhin?"

"Yes. You know him then?"

"Yes, Tertius told me - and Ruffin was one of ours, back when I was here."

"Ruffin?"

"But Kalainen's at Coromal. Hardly secure."

"I know. But he's got a safe house. Don't know where it is, or even who's in it but he has. Kalainen'll look after you."

Kari Witchet sat as still as a moonbeam. Then she nodded. "If there is anyone to trust... I will come."

"Come with me now!"

"I'm better alone."

"Alone you are Kari Witchet. Together we're just nobodies."

She snorted. "No. For your safety and mine, I go alone."

Yanni grinned happily. "Just use the front door at Coromal. Imber's put a lot of discouragement on other entries."

Kari almost laughed, intelligent eyes crinkling. "Is that a challenge? Go on, you've done your bit."

When Yanni slipped out, the two children were waiting for her, Bry still keen to use his spear. The girl slipped her head in to check on Kari, then led Yanni back to the exit, where two more youngsters were guarding the trapdoor.

"You've got a lot of dark rooms," said Yanni thoughtfully. "Reckon you could grow mushrooms."

"Mushrooms?"

"They're not all poisonous, you know. Some are good to eat - Mistress Lassith at the Iron Eye done them yesterday in butter with samphire and garlic." Yanni licked her lips. "She always wants more. Pay in food or maybe even coin."

"Reckon?"

"Could even sell some from a barrow in the Levanine market."

"Like the Owlers'd let us."

"Dress up nice. Be a trader, not a lifter. Why'd they worry?"

The girl looked at her shirt. "I'll tell the girl what dresses me to open me wardrobe of special frocks. Dunno nothing about mushrooms or growing 'em."

"Nor me. Come to the Iron Eye, middle of the day tomorrow. I'll get a name from Mistress Lassith. Someone you can ask. Could work."

The girl gave Yanni a long, calculating look, her fingers going back to the scar on her jaw. "I'm Pruny. Maybe see you tomorrow."

Yanni nodded. It was never more than a maybe, not for the children of Green Worm tower.

Yanni picked her way back down towards the Slatch, shafts of evening light drifting over the stones like lanterns. She glanced behind her where the falling sun blackened the Cornmarket walls, shadows of the battlements ranked like sentries. Her breath clawed in her throat as she spotted a silhouette slouching against a crenellation of the old battlement. For all the studied ease of the figure's position, Yanni knew she was being watched. But then the dark shape raised a finger to its hat. As she recognised Imber, a grin tightened her whole body and she skipped onwards with a lighter heart.

A scrivener tinkled past, his shaker, ink horn and pen pot dangling from his belt. Yanni narrowed her eyes, looking again. Was that age that weighed on his shoulders and bent his knees, or was it a carefully copied gait from some grandfatherly figure? Was it even a man? Had she been fooled simply by a pair of baggy breeches? But no, even if the ink stains were faked, those hands were bulged and knotty from long years. She looked for other unlikely suspects. Perhaps she could be the one to find Tertius Orbis herself! She imagined yanking off Tertius's disguise in triumph... but if Tertius were unmasked, the spy would be more likely to react with steel and venom than congratulations. Yanni shrugged away the daydream.

Being so close to the Iron Eye, she couldn't resist slipping in to see what Lassith was doing for the evening meal. She disappeared into the fug; scrubbed pans, boiled lentils and beans and fried shavings of pungent sausage while Mistress Lassith talked of ginger, hyssop and saffron, or demonstrated how to fillet mullet and fry them until the soft flakes of flesh were just cooked, succulent and tender. It was full dark when Yanni left. Too late for her to be abroad and she knew it. This wasn't Meiling Square where she knew every ramshackle timber post. Yanni touched the little stiletto like a talisman. If she got into trouble, it would only be useful for bravado. Imber would make himself part of the night, take to the roofs on paths he knew in darkness. She wondered what Kari Witchet would do and whether she was creeping the streets even now, dodging the killers that hunted her.

The night seemed full of menace. Everything creaked in the wind like hatches opened by stealthy fingers. The breeze shook the blackest clots of shadow into masked faces, hunched shoulders pressed into hiding. A distant screech might have been a bird, or a child's cry choked off by a tightening fist. Yanni slid along darkened buildings. She knew she looked like a thief, liable to be collared by the Watch or the owner of any of the premises she passed. But if she were more visible, she might be more likely to be accosted. There were still people abroad in knots or wandering alone; pack hunters or lone child-snatchers. Mardenifol's tales of long-fingered ghouls, so easy to deride in the light, came back into her mind. As she sidled past a narrow gap between two shops, she startled a small dog, which yipped and fled. Yanni leapt vertically in fright, imagining some tentacled horror grasping from the darkness. She began running.

Once she started, it was impossible to stop. The faster she ran, the less she could hear any pursuit; the quicker she needed to be to outrun it. She hurtled past a group of half-a-dozen figures, two of whom carried torches. They were perhaps chatting after a day's work. Yanni only saw sinister shapes plotting torture. There was a shout — it could have been a man surprised as someone sped from the darkness into shadow. Yanni heard the cry, saw an uplifted arm, fingers stretching for her, imagined pursuit, thrown knives. Gasping round the pain thudding in her chest, she sped ever faster for the safety of Coromal.

Almost blind with terror, she crashed into the door. She scrabbled wildly with the catch. But the door was bolted against her. She was sobbing hysterically when the door was suddenly flung open. Quern was there; massive, fierce-eyed and bristling for combat. There was a naked sword in his right hand. He snatched her up with his left hand and put his shoulder to the door.

"Who? How many?" he roared at her.

Imber landed beside them, dropping down almost silently from his eyrie with its mirrors and spyholes. He shook his head and shrugged.

Yanni clung to Quern as he shoved heavy bolts into iron rings. The warm sense of home and safety sank into her. Very slowly, her breathing began to ease round her throat which felt like constricted metal. She was able to croak out that nobody was following. Then suddenly she burst into sobs again. In her whole life, she had never had anyone prepared to fight for her, as Quern and Imber had been. The realisation was more profound than all the overwhelming terror of her flight. She was so overcome, she allowed Quern to swing her up and carry her into the snug.

Kari Witchet was already there. She sat prim and upright, her hands folded in her lap. She was speaking in a matter-of-fact tone.

"Banging on the door like that is bad. Advertising that it was unexpectedly locked is like shouting that there is something – or someone – to hide. What's your phrase, Drouhin? The locked chest draws the thief?"

Yanni shrivelled but Quern just held her tight and Kalainen remained imperturbable.

"True. But sometimes the hare runs in wisdom, sometimes just in fear. Children get frightened in the dark, Kari. We all have fears, some more firmly grounded than others and few as well as yours. And I already have good reason for bolting the door."

The Drouhin flicked a kindly glance at his apprentice, still shivering and trying to master her breathing. He returned his full attention to Kari Witchet, whose petite frame was perching on a chair like a queen on a throne. Her face was so still it might have been painted on pottery, her eyes were locked on the Drouhin.

"Kari, this is really important. Whoever Tertius was investigating last may be robbed and murdered in the next few nights. It could destabilise the whole balance between the seven cities! We have very little time. Please Kari, who was Tertius Orbis investigating?"

"I don't know."

Kalainen's gentle smile was rich with understanding. "I will protect you as best I can whether you speak or not. But I should like you to trust us."

Kari Witchet sat upright, a picture of poise and elegance. But she seemed fragile as a sugar rose in the confectioner's shop. Kalainen's voice was as calming as he could pitch it.

"You know we won't harm her. She's sought by many who cannot claim the same. As are you, for you are the best link to her. And you do have some way of contacting her, I think."

"You're just using me to get to her. Then you'd turn her over to the Watch."

"She could hardly complain!" said Quern. "She's set up murders over half Shaddimur!"

"Quern! Kari, tell me, did Tertius Orbis approve of these murders? Did it matter to her?"

"She hated it! They said the first was a terrible accident; a failing of her research. She felt obliged to do another exploration. When there were more deaths, she refused to do a third. But by then she was implicated. They forced her to go on. The more she did, the more tied she was."

Kalainen nodded. "And has she been paid?"

"They were always spilling coins about, more lavish still with promises. The fee was added to their debt which they were always going to pay."

"Of course. And had the mongoose decided to bite the snake? Had she talked of blackmailing them to get the money?"

Kari's answer was whispered. "She's been collecting provable evidence. Yes."

"I will not give her to the Watch. I want to prevent murder; the murder of some high official in Shaddimur, yes, but her murder also."

Kari just looked at them. She was swallowing hard, tears welling in her eyes. When she could speak, she asked, "Why do people tell you their secrets?"

"Secrets always want to be told. People don't like holding them."

Kari's voice was slowed by a weight of sadness. "You ask where she was working. It's what I need to know to find her. But I have no idea."

"I don't understand," said the Drouhin.

Kari hung her head for a while. She spoke to the floor now. "They attacked her when she thought she was getting another commission. We have a ... she contrived to warn me. I think she was hurt. But because of her warning, I evaded the attack, ran before they came. We have a secret place to leave messages in case of something like this."

"Then you do know where she is!"

"Wait a minute," interrupted Imber. "Tertius Orbis is one of the best. She'll have bolt holes and hideaways all over Shaddimur. I don't believe you don't know one of them."

Kari Witchet nodded. "But I daren't use any of them. I went to find the message. You know Tinker's Bridge? On the outer face of one of the stone piers there's a loose rock with a space behind it. When I went there to check for the message, there was a civic work team checking the safety of the bridge, moving along it, tapping at every stone with hammers. As if a city team would work by torchlight! Somehow, they knew the cache was near - and they would find it. If there was a message, I had to get it before they did. I just reacted. Mama Shoddy was taking her cart across the bridge which gave me some cover. I jumped over the parapet to the ledge, pulled out the stone and a scrap of parchment. There was a shout. The work's team ran towards me. Men at either side of the bridge each whirled a bolas – they wanted to catch me alive! My first thought was to jump into the Pollomol; but there were boats up and down stream with lights. I tossed my cape and pack into the river. They heard the splash and thought it was me. The boats converged. People ran up the bridge to where I'd been. But I climbed along the wooden crossmembers on the underside of the bridge."

Imber gave an involuntary huff of appreciation.

"I escaped, but only just," shrugged Kari. "I cannot imagine how they knew roughly where the dead drop was. I can't risk any other hiding place."

"They have every resource money can buy, perhaps including magic."

"Why wouldn't they just stake out the bridge?" asked Quern. "When Kari went there, without the work team to warn her, they'd have taken her easily."

"They'd have no idea how long it would be before she appeared, or whether Kari had gone elsewhere and was safe. If they had found the loose stone, they could have found the trail to Tertius. Even if not, by leaving disinformation there, they might win another chance to find Kari. And they were well prepared if she tried to reach the drop before them. She did well to evade them."

"But who're *they*?" asked Mardenifol. "Are they Drogulus's men?"

"Not Drogulus's style at all. Hurl men with hammers at a problem needing a light touch? The Tarlenian approach!" Imber sounded offended.

"They had Tarlenian accents – although they could have been put on," said Kari.

Kalainen turned to Kari. "I doubt it. Now, I know Mama Shoddy well. Her wanderings for old clothes and rags takes her all over Shaddimur. She has sharp eyes and a keen mind under that ridiculous hat."

Kari gave a tilt to her head. "She'll confirm what happened."

"What was in the cache?" chirped Yanni, too excited to stay quiet.

"She left me a note."

"You can read?" asked Quern incredulously.

"Yes. But not this."

"I see. Perhaps she knew the secret cache might be compromised. Is it a code?" asked Kalainen, intrigued. "Do you have a key for it?"

Kari shook her head. "The words don't make sense."

"Ah! Perhaps you should only read some of the words. The fifth, then the seventh and so on, something like that? Is there any number of significance to you?"

"No. And the message is too short."

"Will you show me the note?"

Kari remained still for another moment. Then she reached into her boot and passed over a scrap of parchment. "I have to. It means nothing to me. You are my only hope. The writing is hers."

Kalainen took the little note, his eyes alight with excitement.

> Go to where I work.
> Look at the picture behind this one
> So you will recognise me
> I will be when and where I am.

"The message must be for you. You must know where she was working!"

"But I do not. She was very careful never to tell me. She said it was for my protection."

Kalainen frowned. He smoothed out the parchment and turned it over.

> A cob spins
> By a brown cob
> In a cob
> Carried by a cob
> On a cob.
> Over a cob wall
> A cob
> Swimming under a cob
> Cobs another cob
> Cob that!

Kalainen sat immobile, staring through the parchment. Smiling slightly, he looked almost radiant. Quern broke the silence.

"Cob, cob, cob! Load of cobblers. What's it supposed to mean?" The others all were silent in thought. "Go to where I work! She worked all over the city, from Meiling Square to the palace!"

"Not Meiling Square, nor anywhere else amidst the slaughter-houses, tanneries and parchmenters of the south. Only rich places," said Imber. "Perhaps if we marked them all on a map, that might produce some clue, a rune perhaps? Could c-o-b be part of a key, some gramarye puzzle?" he mused. "Could this be a forgery? Perhaps they had already found the cache? The work party just more misdirection?"

"Then no need for the work party. But the note is not what I was expecting."

"Expect? What did you *expect*?" Kari's tone was rising towards a screech.

"Something highly specific to you that would mean nothing to anyone else. Perhaps, 'go to place we went after we ate crab watching the sunset'. Something you would find easy to understand without bringing to me. Even more surprising that you don't know where she worked."

"Well, I don't. Got that? I don't know!"

"If Tertius had any idea her hideaways were known, this must be somewhere else," suggested Imber. "Perhaps somewhere they have never been?"

"Imber! You have to get Kari to safety. As soon as possible. Now."

"Wait," cried Kari, "You can interpret this! What does it mean?"

"I can't tell you – yet. But it is an assignation; a time, a place and a recognition code. She's very clever, your Tertius Orbis."

"I'm not going until I know what this means! You know more than you've said."

"This is serious, Kari. Drogulus has people looking for you. He might hold you to blackmail the Tarlenians. More likely he will just sell you to them or silence you for money. The Tarlenians will have their own agents searching. Who knows who else? Every minute you are here..."

"I will not go before you tell me."

Kalainen looked at the floor for a moment and sighed. "All right. Look, this was written on a scrap of parchment with a stylus. That suggests she was somewhere safe, somewhere such materials could be found. Maybe we could guess at where she was; the fact this is parchment rather than paper, the type of ink, the nib. But look at the writing; this was done hurriedly, very fast. She was probably just passing through somewhere. She didn't have much time for thinking. So either it is simple or entirely pre-planned." Kalainen sat back and steepled his fingers. "Note she says to look at the picture *behind* this one. Where would you have one picture behind another? They are displayed above, below, left or right. But behind?

"An artist's garret, perhaps?"

"Wonderful," said Quern. "Must we search every attic where some closet dauber splashes paint about?"

Imber scratched his head. "It was where she worked. Didn't work in a garret. We don't know where she worked *last* but we do know several places where she worked because we know where people were robbed and killed. Were any of the victims noted art collectors? Perhaps one of the rich houses had so many pictures they had spares stacked somewhere?"

"Ah," smiled Kalainen. "And what happens when those rich houses aren't quite so rich as they pretend?"

Imber chuckled. "They take their fancy paintings and intricate tapestries down to the pawnbroker – where they are stacked in long lines awaiting redemption."

"And the sign of the pawnbroker? It's her name: three balls. Tertius Orbis. Where she works."

"So we have to go to the pawnbroker, find a stack of pictures and look at the one behind the one with all the cobs?"

"Exactly!" Kalainen's smile was tarnished by smugness.

"But what is the cobby picture?"

"That was a child's game in Drouhin."

"Really? My childhood games revolved round whacking other boys with a stick. Good times! Give me a stick and I'll demonstrate," grumbled Quern.

Kalainen ignored him. "What's a cob?"

"A sort of horse," said Imber.

"I believe the male swan is called a cob," offered Mardenifol.

"They was selling cob loaves in the Levanine," said Yanni. "And cob nuts too!"

"All these and more," said Kalainen, dipping a pen with a flourish. "Our spy weaves a maze just like the cob spins a cobweb. I think I've got something that might do. Try this."

> A spider spins
> By a brown loaf
> In a basket
> Carried by a horse
> On a pier
> Over a wall of round stones
> A swan, swimming
> Under a nut tree
> Hits another swan
> Top that!

Kalainen sat back with the air of one waiting for congratulations. In a silence notable for a complete absence of positive remarks, Mother Yellern stumped in.

"I can't manage the door. You'll have to let me out."

"Sorry, Yellern. I didn't know you were still here."

"That imp's been in the larder again," said Mother Yellern, waving a disapproving arm at Yanni. "Whole place had to be cleaned and sorted. You'll have to pay extra this week."

"That's fine, thank you. Quern'll see you out."

After she had gone, Kari spoke.

"We go to the pawnbrokers and look for that picture. Or the one behind it, anyway, which tells us how to recognise Tertius – which I can already do. That just leaves the last line. 'I will be when and where I am.' That is obviously true but doesn't help. What does she mean?"

"That will be clearer when we've seen the picture," said Kalainen, piqued by the lack of appreciation. "The picture behind the cobs one may show some disguise where you would not recognise her. And 'we' does not include you. Do you not understand? There are a thousand uses the Tarlenians can put you to just to winkle Tertius out of cover and you really won't like any of them. If you don't keep out of sight you will get yourself and Tertius killed."

"You have to promise to tell me what you find."

Kalainen glared at Kari Witchet, but she was quivering with passion, her fingers white on the carved wood of the chair. "Very well. I give you my word. Now, we must destroy any bits of writing."

"Suppose the whole bit of writing is just a ruse and there is some hidden text..."

"She was in a hurry. You open the oyster to find the pearl, not crush the pearl looking for a diamond. We have already deduced the meaning of most of it. Try to be too clever and you are the snake that hypnotises itself! Now, Imber, take Kari to join Ruffin. And you two prod-noses," he indicated his apprentices, "away to bed."

Kalainen turned back to the scrap of parchment. Imber and Quern were moving for the door, Mardenifol was clumping upstairs.

Kari's head was down but, just for a fleeting moment, Yanni saw a sly smile of triumph cross her face.

The Ball

The moment Imber appeared, Kalainen leapt up from sharpening a quill and began firing questions at him about Kari Witchet; whether she was safe, had they been spotted, how did Ruffin take it? Imber, keeping clear of Kalainen's wild gesticulations with knife and quill, gave short replies; yes, probably not and Ruffin hadn't reacted much. Imber looked at the fine rolls in the bread crock and then at the lumpy tiles of bread by the range which he presumed were Yanni's attempt. Hearing that she was moving about elsewhere in the house, he heroically selected one of Yanni's and chewed it morosely.

"So, she's safe? Will she stay there?" fretted Kalainen.

Imber shrugged. "She's not suicidal. But if I don't take news to her daily, she might do anything. Without Ruffin, she'd probably go mad."

"She's young and frightened but I agree, talking to Ruffin will be an anchor and she must be kept abreast of developments. And to get in and out undetected, it has to be you. Now, where is Quern? I wanted him here early! Actually, I wanted him to sleep here but he was off cavorting with a strumpet from some acting troupe. That man would walk from here to Kathos for a girl."

"She's a fine girl," said Quern, shouldering his way through the door. "And sleep would be a rare thing with you banging about here like a man beating a boar from a thicket – and starting at an hour when only murderers and vagabonds are about."

"The murderer and vagabond has only just arrived," muttered Kalainen darkly, "so that would be a late start for me."

"You're in a sour humour. Perhaps a night of singing and dancing would lighten your soul." Quern helped himself to a roll, scraped it through a dish of honey and stuffed half of it in his mouth.

"Cloud my mind and empty my wallet, more likely." Kalainen made a cut with the knife to make the quill finer and sliced his thumb.

Quern gave a sudden snort, spitting crumbs from the roll. "I know what it is. You want to hurry round to the pawnbroker as soon as he unchains the door and you want to see the final bout and you don't think you can do both!"

"By the bell of Mirrin's tower, it's not seeing the bout! Why would I want to watch two grown men beating each other senseless? It's somehow getting to see both combatants beforehand and convincing them that neither of them must put on that amulet! There'll be little chance after the bout." As he stood with his head bowed and a finger-whitening grip on the table, the two apprentices came in. From their subdued appearance, it was clear they had already suffered from Kalainen's temper. Seeing Yanni, Imber picked up her grey brick of bread again and took another chew at it, pretending enjoyment with great heart but limited success. Kalainen tossed down the knife and the bloody quill with a sigh. "But yes, you're right. The dog that hunts two hares, catches neither. I cannot do both."

"I thought the bout was this afternoon," Mardenifol whispered to Quern. "Surely there is enough time?"

"The pawnbroker keeps late hours," snapped Kalainen, "when no doubt he does his best business with drunken gamblers trying to prevent their wives discovering how much they've lost, but he won't open his door this side of the noon bell."

"The Queen has declared a holiday today for the final bout. Perhaps he won't open at all?"

"Quite the reverse, according to Mama Shoddy. Strangely enough, the more people with time on their hands and their wits washed away with wine, the more ridiculous bets send business straight to the pawnbroker. He will open with longer hours."

"Oh, you spoke to Mama Shoddy? Last night? Did she...?"

"Confirm what Kari Witchet said? Yes. Now, Quern, the amulet..."

"I spoke to Shen himself! What more can I do?"

"I've sent messages to Shen, to Kadren of Palemin, to the Queen, to Traid, the Master of Ceremonies and the ostler's uncle's pot boy but none of us has had any assurances! That amulet must not be worn."

"Shen's a mite touchy..."

"He'll probably be a mite dead if he wears that thing!" Kalainen swept his hands over his stubbly hair. Mind inwards, he spoke to himself. "Hmf. Don't look for a better horse until you're sitting on one. We have only one way to go, might as well start walking."

"You're muttering again," said Quern. "What do we do?"

"Your task is to ensure that amulet isn't worn. Take Mardenifol. It's possible he may open doors shut to you."

"If the effect of the amulet is delayed, why not just have Shen wear it for a moment to put the Tarlenians at their ease, and then take it off before the effect happens?"

"Wonderful. And if the effect is immediate? Or suppose whatever magic there is passes directly to the wearer and then expresses its evil intent later? Suppose it cannot be removed?"

"What do you want me to do? Run up there and snatch it off the winner while ignoring a couple of spears and a volley of arrows from the Queen's guards?"

"I'm sure he'll listen to reason."

"Met Shen, have you? Winner of the Queen's award for gentle discussion and compromise?"

"Just make sure nobody puts on the amulet. Imber, do what you can to track the amulet. If you get a chance to steal it, do."

"Oh good," Quern rumbled on. "You want him killed too? That's fair, then."

"Yanni, you're to come with me and we'll follow the riddle set by Tertius Orbis." Kalainen clapped his hands to encourage movement but the front door was already closing on Quern and Mardenifol. Imber was nowhere to be seen.

Dressed in a woollen coat that looked as though it was older and had travelled further than he had, much of it through challenging conditions, an unrecognisable Kalainen wheezed into the pawnbroker's, leaning on a knobbly stick. He tugged a faded cap from his head, allowing long oily ringlets to wriggle to his shoulders. Peering out from under enormous eyebrows, he blew through a grimy beard as he assessed the stock. He suddenly lashed with the stick at Yanni, dressed in her rags once more.

"Don't crowd Astreya, girl."

Yanni skittered back, hunching in expectation of another blow. Kalainen returned to his study of the goods on the other side of the metal grille. One wall was largely taken up by stringed instruments, in the middle of which was the stuffed head of some horned monster. The glassy eyes stared in different directions and the mouth drooped, giving it a plaintive air. Weapons adorned another wall, mostly gilded, bejewelled and engraved swords better suited to a court than a battlefield. The dusty air of the place made the most fantastic embellishments look tawdry. The pawnbroker hurried over to his counter and eyed them suspiciously through the grille. Beneath a plush beret with golden tassels, his hatchet face had a pocked complexion. His spare frame was hung with an ill-matched assortment of costly materials, topped with a brocade cape with a fur collar. Every thin finger had a ring and his waistcoast was spotted with brooches, but somehow he retained a dilapidated air as though he spawned a miasma of dust.

"Astreya has a commission from a noble lord," began Kalainen, drawing himself up importantly as though he wore chancellor's robes. "I, the incomparable Astreya, have been specifically entrusted with very particular details. And, ah, Astreya has a few items that he might be able to part with, terms being suitable."

"Yes, Guv'nor." The pawnbroker seemed entirely disinterested but his gaze flicked to Yanni periodically, trying to catch her in some act of pilferage. "Do you actually want to look at something or shall we go directly to these old family heirlooms of yours?"

"Ah, perhaps," said Kalainen, fishing out a bag about the size of his head. "But no, no, Astreya must look for the picture first."

"Picture? What sort?"

Kalainen narrowed his eyes. "You trying to steal my commission? Astreya will say nothing! I must search with diligence for a rare quality, the ineffable!"

The pawnbroker made a noise that wasn't quite rude, but not quite a sigh either. "Very well. One moment." He struck a couple of notes on a line of tubular bells. After a pause, a woman joined them. Kalainen noted her solidity, the easy balance of her movements and the entirely utilitarian blade hung from her belt of worn leather. He made a lackadaisical gesture of respect.

She assessed him thoughtfully for a moment. "All right," she said. "Just him. Not the girl."

While the pawnbroker unlocked a door in the thick bars, Kalainen jabbed his stick at Yanni. "You disgrace Astreya, girl! My kind heart will be the end of me, one day."

"One day, no doubt," said the pawnbroker. "Before you enter, show me some coin."

Kalainen hunched over, hiding what he did from Yanni with his cloak. He shook a few silver testoons and helms into his palm. The pawnbroker raised an eyebrow and made a disapproving face. Kalainen wobbled his head from side to side and tipped more coins from the pouch. A couple of double-leopards and two or three gold ryals were visible. The pawnbroker sniffed and let him in.

"The best pictures are displayed over here. Note this fine hunting party! Here is an avatar of Sunsunni from centuries past!"

"Indeed. Still, Astreya's commission is precise! My skills are boundless!"

"Perhaps. Your time is limited, however."

Kalainen hopped to a long line of pictures standing one against the other; uneven numbers of them between upright wooden posts. He began at the start, studying some carefully, flipping past others.

"Those aren't ready to go yet," said the pawnbroker.

"Nonetheless, I must be methodical. Astreya takes pains! He accepts patience may be required!"

The pawnbroker rolled his eyes. He jerked his head at his guard to ensure she watched Kalainen while he dealt with other customers, still continually firing mistrustful glances at Yanni. There was a stout woman smelling of old wine with her head covered in a thick headscarf. She stared resolutely at a spot some handspan above the pawnbroker's head as she pushed a glittering brooch over the counter. The pawnbroker wrote in a ledger, then counted coins towards her with a coloured token of carved wood. She took them without comment and left. Her place was taken by a man in a hat with a wide, drooping brim. Yanni stood too close to him for his comfort, first one side, then the other, and he kept flapping her away with irritated gestures. He was unable to concentrate on the pawnbroker, still less on Kalainen, clacking his way through the rank of pictures.

The Drouhin was looking at an exceptionally detailed picture of a sturdy pony crossing a bridge. A basket on its back was filled with bread rolls. Amongst them lurked a spider of enormous size. Kalainen glanced at a nut tree and two swans and reached for the next picture. He found himself staring at a striking green bird. It was superbly realised, its eye gleaming, beak half yellow, half a reddish orange, bright bars of blue on the front edge of the wings, a darker blue tail bright with yellow markings. Only its claws were an ashy grey. Kalainen guessed it was painted by the same hand that had done the previous picture and then had the nagging thought that both might even have been done by Tertius Orbis herself. They were talented works but involving them in this charade was remarkable. Hugely impressed, Kalainen moved on through the paintings.

"Astreya searches with assiduity and finds!" he finally called to the pawnbroker. Kalainen held up the picture of the parrot. "Fine work!"

"But not available until Mid-winter."

"Perhaps some additional sum might smear the dates?"

"No. It wouldn't. I said I'd hold it until mid-winter and so I will do. This business runs on trust."

"Such a pretty thing. Perhaps Astreya could borrow it for a while?" The pawnbroker's stare was flinty. "Ah well, possibly something similar can be found elsewhere."

Kalainen slid the picture in two behind the picture of the swans and the bridge.

"Don't rearrange the pictures," said the guard. "Carefully ordered, see. All done by availability and date."

The Drouhin placed the parrot correctly and waved at the picture of the bridge and the swans. "Call me quirky if you must, but Astreya has taken quite a shine to this picture too. Calls to mind something of me youth! Is this available?"

"No, Guv'nor. Mid-winter. Not before.

Kalainen moved to a third picture. "This now. A trifle. We could come to an arrangement regarding...

"It will be available on Collyon's Day." The pawnbroker's tones were becoming clipped.

"If Astreya found another picture like this, you would lose business! Is this not madness? What price could begin a negotiation?"

"Not a price, Guv'nor. A time. Collyon's Day. Not Collyon's Eve neither. Now as you clearly don't want a picture, show me what you've got or out."

Kalainen seemed reluctant to put down the last picture. He glanced at the door from the storeroom, flickered his eyes over the guard, even looked at his coat as though measuring its capacity. Then he dropped it back with a show of disinterest. "It was merely a whimsy, nothing more. Now, as to these other treasures Astreya can lay before you..."

The pawnbroker glanced at the last picture and frowned at Kalainen thoughtfully for a moment, but he would look at none of Kalainen's gewgaws until the Drouhin had been ushered outside the grille. Once the door was locked, he consented to assay a few trinkets. Kalainen bargained and cajoled and dithered but finally left a few items with the pawnbroker, collected a similar number of tokens and a few coins.

When they left, Yanni trailing behind out of reach of the stick,

Kalainen headed directly towards the tilt yard where the bouts were held; a valley outside the city. It would be easy to lose any pursuers in the crush of spectators there and Kalainen was desperate to see what happened at the end when the amulet was awarded. However, he was still in the guise of Astreya and he suddenly realised that there would be no talking to anyone of note dressed as he was. Furthermore, as Astreya, he would be the one pushed furthest to the back. He would be too late by now anyway. The bout would be safely out of the way, the amulet bestowed and the serious businesses of selling food and drinks, music, dancing and crafty robbery would begin. The brew of beer, rigged games and pickpockets would send some to the pawnbroker. Kalainen cursed, waved an automatic poke at Yanni with the stick, which, as always, failed to connect, and scuttled down a side street.

After a while, he slipped into a livery yard providing temporary stabling for anyone riding into Shaddimur. The place was busy and most of the stalls were taken by the horses of folk coming for the final of the tournament. As Kalainen neither rode a horse in nor led one out, nobody took any notice of Astreya, another customer among many checking their horses had been properly wiped down and provided with hay and water. Nor did he evoke any interest a short while later, when he marched out looking very different, leaving the stick in a corner.

As Kalainen turned in, Yanni pattered away in the light rain, unremarkable and unremarked by anyone. She slipped round a corner and huddled by some barrels in a lean-to, just another piece of human flotsam in a city, taking shelter while she could. When Kalainen strode past later, he was barely recognisable. The beard had shrunk to normal, the cap and ringlets had gone along with the enormous eyebrows. Now he wore just trousers and a shirt, the open front revealing a brindled matting of chest hair. A straw hat, whose brim was already sagging under the weight of water, was wedged on his head. He carried the inverted coat on his shoulder as a bag and seemed like any other workman about his business in town with the few merchants not on holiday. Yanni waited patiently to see if anyone was following him. The coast seemed clear. Her eyes flickered briefly to the rooftops. She frowned. Imber was peerless on overwatch. But he wasn't here. Still, Kalainen was moving fast. No doubt he would cross open areas and wider streets to foil aerial pursuit, unless he were too preoccupied. Yanni sighed. She was starting to grow now and would soon look like a brandy-soaked derelict rather than a convincing urchin. She needed a new role. Yanni looked up at the rooftops again, then set off after Kalainen.

Back at Coromal, they barely had time to change before Quern and Mardenifol were crashing in, laughing happily, retelling each other parts of the bout, and smelling of beer. Kalainen burst back into the kitchen with half his shirt on.

"Well? What happened?"

"It was fantastic! Shen's incredible – they both were!"

"It was like watching the fastest dance you ever saw. When Kadren did that leap…"

"The amulet!" roared Kalainen. "What happened with the amulet? Did Shen win? Did you talk to him again?"

"Yes, Shen won. I talked to, well, I think it'll be all right."

"Stop!" Kalainen made an effort to push his shoulders down. "Everyone sit down. Then just tell me what happened. After the bout, that is. I do not need to hear who broke which bits off whom."

They sat. Imber was suddenly there too, pulling up his own chair. Yanni quietly pushed a kettle onto the range for tea. Then she began gradually beating goat's milk into flour.

"So," began Kalainen. "Shen won. Then what?"

"Yes, Shen …" Quern managed to stop himself, then looked at Mardenifol. They grinned at each other while Kalainen sighed and stared at the ceiling. "Ah, yes. Well, after the fight, Shen went to collect his award. Kadren couldn't, because, well, obviously, he couldn't. So Shen puts on the cape of the Avatar and goes up there."

"You had warned him of the power of the amulet and he agreed not to wear it?"

"Ah. I spoke to him again this morning. He recognised me!"

"He said, 'Not you again,'" put in Mardenifol.

Quern made a rueful face. "Yes, well. I did talk to him. Shen said that when he won it, he'd ignore childish yarns of curses and wear it to show that he was the best fighter in the seven cities."

"Stupid bravado. Was he angry about something?"

Mardenifol gave a bark of laughter. "Shen has a face designed for anger; furious bulging eyes, reddened skin and spiky hair and stuff. When he just looks at you, your bones turn to water and your lungs to mud!"

"What did you do, Quern?"

"I spoke to one of the clerics of Sunsunni who I hoped might have some influence on their Avatar. She said she'd check the amulet and do what was appropriate."

"Very reassuring. Then what?"

"Well, then we sampled some beer and went to find a good place to watch the fight."

Kalainen closed his eyes, thinking of all the things he might have done. But Quern was Quern. He looked at Imber. "I don't suppose...?"

Imber gave his head a brief shake.

Quern continued. "So, the Tarlenian ambassador, Guzarin, gets up and says a bit while Shen just stands there swatting flies. Then..."

"What? What did he say?"

Quern shrugged. "Usual guff." He looked hopefully at Mardenifol.

"He talked of the noble competitors, particularly Astelin, the Tarlenian. He said something like, 'Astelin was perhaps not the best in Tarlenia and just happened to be passing, but I feel his honour and prowess have not disgraced his home city. It is clear that Tarlenia is not as some present her and should not be blamed for all ills. Let this fine amulet, made by the Tarlenian artist Strammon, sadly stabbed to death by a robber in this city of Shaddimur...' and stuff like that."

"Clever speech. He makes us all feel guilty by association!"

"He had a wizard with him. Maybe the sorcerer had something to do with the speech."

"What wizard? Tarlenians normally employ wizards with all the enthusiasm of someone paying to get their cess pit emptied."

"He was there," shrugged Mardenifol. "Staff and a robe covered with eye symbols and stuff. Not a Shaddimur loremaster."

"And a patch over one eye. Pfff." Quern dismissed the magician and returned to his story. "Anyway, finally he stops yapping and gets the amulet ready to put on Shen. Shen hops up in his full regalia as the Avatar and takes the roars from the crowd, then he takes off the headdress and bends his neck for the amulet. And at that moment, the Queen stands up."

"You saw the Queen? The real Queen? What's she like?" burst in Yanni.

"She's very, well, beautiful."

"Yes, obviously," said Yanni, "but what was she wearing? Did she have a crown and all?"

"She had a sort of silver thing on her head, I think. "

"Her diadem was a silver circlet studded with pearls and a single emerald," said Imber. "She wore a simple pale dress, full skirt of a light material and a close-fitting bodice stitched with lines of pearls. Her arms and shoulders were bare but she had a stole with a brilliant green lining. She did indeed look wonderful."

"Charming. Now by the Great God Rashen-Akru, will you please tell me what happened!"

"The Queen commended Shen and all the heroic fighters," said Mardenifol. "She said, 'Shen has shown his supremacy and done much for the glory of the Sunsunnis – praise to him and to them all! However, the Tarlenians have given this amulet for friendship between all the city states. I have here commissioned a bust of the ideal warrior – admitting that today it should wear the face of noble Shen. Shen himself bears the cape of the Avatar of Sunsunni and needs neither monument nor jewels to augment his glory. However, his name shall be inscribed upon this statue as a lasting testament to his superlative powers. Now we shall have this tourney as an annual tradition. (There were screams of approval from the crowd for this idea.) Shen's name shall always be first. Guzarin has praised all the warriors, so let him honour the great warriors from every city state and begin the tradition of the Tarlenian Tournament by placing the amulet upon this bust.' But it was better than that. She basically made it so Shen would look mean and grasping if he took the amulet and Guzarin would dishonour the other fighters and repudiate the Tarlenian Tournament if he didn't put the amulet on the statue."

"Bust of the ideal warrior, indeed. We were next to an old man who was once a palace guard. He said it was a statue of the Queen's grandfather from the House of Khaad, dragged out of the palace back rooms! Specially commissioned? Might have been specially dusted."

"Never mind what she looks like. That was the act of a true Queen! The amulet was placed on the statue?"

"Yes. Shen was hustled away by clerics of Sunsunni, looking baffled and rebellious, but he liked the cheering of the crowd. Then the crowd surged forwards, Shen and the priests were engulfed and there was quite a scuffle. Shen was roaring like a bear with the headdress all askew and there were a few thumps before the crowd went back. The priests were reacting as though someone had tried to assassinate the Avatar and fussing over some tear in the cape as though the walls of the temple were breached. Back on the stand, Guzarin was grinning like a skull biting a lemon. I think he knew about the amulet well enough."

"Guzarin knew? This goes all the way up to the ambassador?" Kalainen spoke aloud but was talking to himself. He was swiftly roused from his reverie as the others demanded to know whether he had found what he needed at the pawnbrokers. Kalainen told the story and gave a detailed description of the bird.

"A green parrot? Doesn't really matter how many blue bars or yellow dots it has. It's a parrot! Has someone muddled up the pictures then? Or is she hiding in an aviary? You've gone wrong, Kalainen!" said Quern, wagging a finger at the Drouhin.

"No. I don't think so. It's a brilliant set-up. Nobody can buy either of the pictures because their time has not expired and nobody but Tertius Orbis can redeem them because she will certainly have the tokens – and I think she painted them herself. I tried to muddle them up and couldn't because the pawnbroker keeps them very carefully ordered for his business."

"Is the parrot some sort of pointer then, or are we really looking for someone dressed as a parrot. Should stand out pretty well wandering through the Levanine!"

"She can hardly draw attention to herself by meandering round with a parrot on her shoulder. But either that or she will be dressed as a parrot. The question is where would such a one not stand out?"

"Your friends in that acting troupe, Quern," said Imber. "Could they make someone up as a bird? Great place for Tertius Orbis to hide out!"

"Is there some bird cult in Shaddimur?" asked Mardenifol. "Perhaps a festival where everyone dresses as a bird? Actually, I suppose Tertius Orbis might mean Third Ball. The Third Ball of the social calendar is always a masked ball. Lots of people there dressed as parrots and stuff," he said off-handedly.

Kalainen rolled his eyes. "Tertius Orbis - Third Ball. 'I will be when and where I am.' That is our assignation! I'd no idea there was a First Ball, never mind a Third. Well done, Mardenifol! Do you know where and when this might occur?"

"Of course. It's tonight."

"Tonight! By the bell... How do we get in?"

"Well, you'd need a personal invitation from Earl Fechlan and a costume, I suppose."

"Got as much chance of growing the feathers ourselves as we have of getting those," said Quern.

"Not really. The Earl's a great friend of my uncle's. Expect he could sort the stuff out for you."

"For us? Weren't you going anyway?" asked Quern. "You know about what we're supposed to do; manners and food and dancing. I'm, well, a bit out of place. And I don't think I'll make a good parrot."

"Some people, especially women, go to amazing lengths with make-up and feathers and furs and stuff. Most of the men just dress well and wear masks."

"Me, going to a conkin' nobs' party! Ha!"

"Not you."

"I'd be in disguise. Nobody'd know nothing!"

"I'm not going either. Never let anyone underage in. There's lots of alcoves which get curtained off. Supposed to be for sensitive discussions or quiet withdrawal from the hurly burly of the ball, but everyone knows there are assignations. There's stuff goes on," said Mardenifol with disapproval. He stared at the floor but still reddened.

Mother Yellern poked her head round the door. "I'll be going now. So wore out with resorting and cleaning in the larder, had to shut me eyes in the chair. I've left you two pies. Can't come for a couple of days. Don't know whether you still want me if your uppity little piece is going to do the cooking now."

"Oh. Thank you, Mother. We'll see what we need when you can come back."

"What you'll need is a physic. And a maid with two brooms," muttered Yellern, heading to the door. "One to sweep up the mess and the other to warm up a certain madam's backside."

"We have to run!" said Kalainen, his head snapping up. "I must see Traid. Mardenifol, get to your family, organise what we need for entry and costume. Include Kari. Quern, go with him; there may be trouble and you'll need to be there to be fitted. Nothing normal size will fit you. Imber, tell Kari about tonight. She'll need a costume, she has nothing of her own. Take Yanni. She'll need to go back with clothes for Kari Witchet or may need to collect something from one of Tertius's bolt holes. You'll be busy at the Fechlan Estate."

"Outside the Shaddimur wall. Not my home ground," muttered Imber.

"And Yanni, you'll see Ruffin. I will explain later."

Yanni's mutinous expression faded a little at the prospect of a roof-top run with Imber and seeing the mysterious Ruffin. But Imber was already moving and she had to scamper to catch up with him.

He led her on a swift walk through busy streets. They ducked into a quiet courtyard, then dropped down beside one of the water conduits that ran under the city.

"Thought we was going on the roofs."

Imber didn't reply, but touched a finger to his lips, then tapped his ear. Yanni understood and crept along as quietly as she could, breathing through her mouth and listening for any footfalls behind them. A short walk along a stone edging led them to an opening on their left to what had once been a wide underground chamber ringed with fireplaces. The ceiling had partly collapsed long ago into a mound of damp masonry but a couple of fireplaces still gaped. Imber ducked into the one on the left.

"Can you climb it?"

"Course!"

"Take it steady."

Imber boosted her into the chimney. Yanni wedged one foot behind her bottom and pushed the other into the stonework in front of her. She straightened her legs, braced herself with her arms and brought her legs to their start position. In no time, she was halfway up.

"There's a grating across it!" she whispered.

"Yes. See all the wires on your right? Pull the third one from the wall you are facing. That will pull the grating up."

"And the others?"

"Any other wire would let the grating fall – and all the fire bombs. Try not to do that."

"Thought a chimney would be full of soot!"

"What use a secret chimney if you leave a trail of soot and reek of smoke?"

They hurried over tiles and catwalks, made short leaps over narrow streets where buildings leaned towards each other like overcrowded plants and finally vaulted a parapet into a valley between two steep pitches. There was a shuttered window under a gable. Imber showed Yanni a little wire to unhitch and moved a safety plate over a small hole. Then he opened the shutters with a knife and they slid into Kalainen's safe house.

"Is this the only way in?"

"Of course not. But it is the way we can get in and out without attracting attention or letting anyone make connections."

When they found Kari Witchet, she was sitting well back from an open window but staring at the wheel and curl of gulls over the docks. Further out to sea, gannets turned and arrowed into blue water.

"I love birds," she said softly. She turned and focussed on them. "Tell me everything!"

While Yanni stared at Ruffin, Imber told Kari of the artwork at the pawnbroker's.

"She loved to paint. What exactly did the parrot look like?"

Imber described it just as Kalainen had. "Is that significant?

Kari shrugged. "Just a green parrot, I suppose. Wondered if I'd ever seen that picture. Don't think I have. Go on."

"Tertius Orbis's name means Third Ball. That is a masked ball held at the Fechlan Estate tonight. Tertius will be there dressed as a green parrot. Kalainen didn't think you'd stay here, so Mard is going to get us all in. Do you have a costume anywhere?"

"No. I have nothing."

"Well, he'll sort out something for you as well. I'll bring it to you and take you there from here. Just wait for me." Imber turned to where Ruffin was lying on a bed. "Hey, Ruffin. This is for you. Few more inks and brushes." He winked at the boy and slipped him a package, then jerked his head at Yanni and they left.

"What happened to Ruffin?" Yanni demanded as Imber reset the traps on the window.

"Accident."

"But his legs ... his throat! Ghulsk!"

"Run over by a coach. Should've been dead."

"But he ... shines."

"Kalainen's paying a fortune for magical healing. Maybe working but slow."

That gave Yanni a lot to think about. She was quiet as Imber led her back to the chimney and went down in front of her. Once back on the street, she turned for Coromal. Before heading off to the Fechlan Estate, Imber said, "Best not talk about it," and gave her a tight smile.

"Oh. By the bell of Mirrin's Tower... the naïve fool!" Kalainen suddenly stopped his pacing round the kitchen table.

Quern was poking some stodgy grey things on the side of the range. He turned one over thoughtfully and discovered it had a black side. Yanni had been using words like crisp and golden. Perhaps there was something else. He was squatting down and optimistically checking inside the range when disturbed by Kalainen's outburst. "What? Who?"

"Tertius Orbis," cried Kalainen, resuming his pacing. "The whole message for Kari Witchet was far too complex and relied on too many props to be something dashed off while she was fleeing into hiding. She had it planned in advance, either as her main strategy or a back-up, but definitely planned in advance."

"So it wasn't just for Kari Witchet?"

"Good question. But there's money owing and Tertius has been collecting evidence against the killer. She thinks the masked ball will be a public place where she's relatively safe. She's set up a meet with Tarlenians to get her money. The fool thinks they'll hand it over to stop her blackmail and she'll get away. She wants Kari there so they can go together."

"But the Tarlenians'll just kill her."

"Yes. If they can find out she's the green parrot. She must have a plan for collecting the gold and escaping. But there's something too pat about this, Quern. We're being pushed too fast to consider everything."

"Too much consideration is overrated. Make a plan and just boof!" Quern scrunched up his face and swung a fist in a satisfying clonk on an imaginary foe.

Kalainen rolled his eyes. "Well, we have no choice. If Tertius Orbis has collected evidence to implicate the killer, for her life and the information, we must get to her before the Tarlenians do!"

"If she gives it to us."

"Why wouldn't she? She's more at risk from the Tarlenians than anyone. By all the bells, where are Mardenifol and the costumes! We should have met at the Fechlan Estate! The girl will be dead before we arrive!" Kalainen's march round the table became even quicker but the more imminently they expected Mardenifol to return, the less sense it made to rush off without costumes.

The rain had set in hard, churning the ruts of Jumblegut Lane to porridge. Imber and Yanni were back and dry before Mardenifol finally rolled up with a carriage. Imber double-checked that he had the right bundles of clothes for Kari and himself and then sped off into the drenching darkness.

Kalainen grabbed his bundle and dragged on charcoal hose with a silver-grey undershirt and a doublet of pale grey stitched with little downward-pointing chevrons. Jumping up and down to haul the hose into place, he commended Mardenifol on finding a carriage.

"Was a bit difficult to get but most of the guests have their own conveyances and stuff. The driver's Modliss; used to work for the Earl years ago. He's just helping out while they're busy but he's not the quickest."

Quern was already dressed in breeches of gold thread cinched below his knees, yellow stockings and a matching jacket. "Give the boy his due, these clothes nearly fit," he complained. "I can barely move my arms and if the waist was any bigger, there'd be room for all of us in here." He showed Yanni his bear mask and roared at her for good effect. By then Kalainen was half-dressed and they ran out to the carriage, shouting to Modliss to make his best speed.

"Are you sure it's Clatch where it rains all the time? Seems like Shaddimur holds its own," grumbled Kalainen. He looked at the ground moving by the squelching carriage, bushes of whin splattered with mud from the road, then back to Quern. "I could walk quicker!" He stuck his head out in the rain. "Modliss! Can't you drive this any faster?"

The horses came to a stop as Modliss slowly turned to reply. "Sir, there is a danger of slithering off the track."

"Drive it faster?" said Quern, "I could pull it quicker!"

"The Earl would not appreciate guests arriving covered in mud with the horses blown." Modliss turned forward and gently wagged the reins. The horses gingerly plodded onward at the same stately pace.

"The Earl won't appreciate the Third Ball turning into a bloodbath either," fumed Kalainen impotently.

"Can you drive a two-horse carriage?" Quern asked the Drouhin. "No."

"Neither can I. Still, good time to learn, eh?" Quern shrugged back into his cloak, opened the door and swung up beside the old man, his weight almost upsetting the light vehicle. Modliss shrieked as the carriage lurched over onto one wheel. Quern snatched the reins in one hand and gave them a savage clack. He caught Modliss with the other hand and stopped him being catapulted off the carriage by his arrival. He regretted this generous impulse as the old man wailed in a protest that sounded like sheer terror. Quern gave a bear-like roar, one of the horses whinnied and the carriage shot forwards in a welter of mud.

Finally abandoning an almost catatonic Modliss sitting rigid on a carriage bogged in a flower bed, they hurried towards the mansion. Leaping up a broad flight of steps, glistening in the rain, they entered a rainbow world. Lamps sparkled and glittered, a gallery of players brushed music from strings, silk hangings trembled. Brilliant costumes of scintillating colour eddied past as dances and conversations mingled the guests.

While Quern stood gulping, almost stunned by the kaleidoscope of colour and light, Kalainen breezed in as though he was the Earl's brother. He waved across the hall as though spotting an old friend. Collecting a drink from a table, he sipped for a moment, allowing his gaze to sweep over the guests. There was no mistaking a trio of Tarlenians, wearing gaudy uniform jackets with small domino masks as a nod towards the requirements for a costume. Kalainen assumed Ambassador Guzarin was the broad-shouldered man dominating the group. His hose showed the powerful legs of a dancer but he held himself rigidly aloof. He was being addressed by a puffy-faced, sweating man with a stork headdress. The disdain on the ambassador's face was not a mask.

If Guzarin was here, Kalainen expected the other ambassadors would be as well. He scanned round, but he knew few of the ambassadors by sight and the costumes concealed much. He thought one might have been from Hethrin, but then he noticed Sarrepo. The Bruelan ambassador was dancing with a graceful woman of his own age. Both were clearly enjoying themselves, chuckling and swaying, quite wrapped up in each other's company.

Everywhere there were flickers of green and he had been still too long. With a smile and a gallant little bow, Kalainen proffered his arm to a slim woman in a shimmering blue dress and a peacock mask.

"Do I know you?" she murmured, putting her fingers on his arm and allowing herself to be drawn away.

"I certainly hope not. I'm supposed to be in disguise! I knew I'd forget something. I hope it wasn't my mask."

"My husband may say something about me being whisked from his side," she said archly.

"That mouse was your husband? How could any man have that much luck?"

She laughed. "Perhaps if we danced rather than whispered together like plotters in a play?"

"There is a single flaw in your brilliant plan. My dancing..."

"Another who cannot dance? I'll not have my slippers ruined, thank you!"

"Not at all! But Drouhin dances are boisterous."

"I've not heard of your city, this Drouhin. Are you a Drou from Drouhin or a Drouhin from Drou? And why does that mean you can't dance?"

"I'm a Drouhin from Drouhin - perhaps somewhat less than a city - and the steps I know may not be appropriate to your dances. However, this music will suffice to explore possibilities – if you will take the risk?"

"How alluring!"

Kalainen glanced back at the peacock's husband, but he was talking to a woman in green. Kalainen's snapped back for a clear view of the woman. A jewelled lizard face glanced idly at him and away again.

They began slow circuits of the dance floor, negotiated with elegance by the peacock and fitful enthusiasm from the Drouhin as he was distractedly looking at women in green. They passed a sideboard with a bronze statue of the Dancing Goddess in a graceful pose. Someone had daubed a smear of red fruits over one hand, which slowly dripped from the fingers. Kalainen almost froze with shock when he saw it, causing his partner to move off the floor. She inclined her head gracefully. "Your feet, sir, are as wayward as your eyes, which ogle every female in the room. Am I to be grateful that at least your hands were controlled?"

Kalainen's head sank. "Your pardon, madam. In truth, there is a young woman here in grave danger. It is imperative I find her before ..." Kalainen's voice faded.

"You're going to have to tell me more than that. I hope you're better at intrigue than dalliance!"

"And I hope you're not an assassin. Madam, there is a girl dressed as a green parrot who may be killed at this ball."

"Hm. And have you warned the Earl? Or the girl?" The peacock remained poised and graceful, her voice unaltered, but it was as though a nodding rose proved itself fashioned of iron and adamant

"I hoped to deal with the matter quietly with no disturbance. I don't know the Earl."

"My husband, the Earl, is the mouse you nearly met on the way in. Perhaps it is not customary for Drouhins to greet their guests – even very late-comers? You will meet him now." The peacock's fingers held firmly to Kalainen's forearm and he was steered towards Earl Fechlan, wincing at every step.

"We have an owl from some place called Drouhin here," she murmured to her husband. "Not wise to normal customs but he has an interesting tale of a death threat to one of our guests."

The Earl turned to look at Kalainen. He wore a doublet of carmine silk and gold thread in the tiniest of stitches. Despite a bearing of command, some quirk had caused the Earl to select the mask of a vole with little rounded ears and delicate whiskers.

"Be welcome. But to hear your tale, I see the third alcove is untenanted. Perhaps you would accompany me."

There was no hint of a question in the Earl's tone and Kalainen felt his elbow taken by another man wearing black clothes and a panther mask. A curtain of green velvet closed behind them, muting sound like a heavy snowfall. The Earl and Kalainen pushed up their masks.

"So, you have evidence of a threatened murder on my estate. Yet you meander here to arrive when the ball is half over. You didn't think to send warning?"

"I spoke with Inspector Traid of the Watch. He sent a runner this afternoon, requesting that you protect the girl."

The Earl cocked an eye at the panther.

"We did receive a Watch runner, my lord. His message was that a person or persons unknown for unknown reasons might attack an unknown person dressed as a parrot. I asked him how credible he thought this threat was and he said very uncredible indeed."

"Uncredible?"

The panther shrugged.

"And yet," said Kalainen, "Traid sent the runner." He regarded the Earl steadily. "If the message has been ignored, the threat is definite, real and immediate."

The Earl stared back at the Drouhin standing squarely before him. Then, his decision made, he wasted no time in recriminations. His eyes flicked to the panther. "I don't remember a green parrot – perhaps someone else who neglected to pay their respects – but if there is one, find her. Now. Code amethyst." The panther slipped out. "You too, Drouhin. But before I permit you to go, you will bear in mind this is my estate. You have more to tell me."

Quern was standing as though on guard duty. After a while, he spotted a drinks table and lurched towards it, nearly knocking down an elderly fox doddering beside a stately hen. He took a glass, waved a cursory teardrop over it and dotted his forehead. He refilled it after it had miraculously emptied itself and resumed his impersonation of a pillar, looking at the women as they glided past, some wearing remarkably daring dresses, scandalously tight or low-cut. One or two sent him coquettish glances and he began to feel better. He even huffed at one girl with a mock snarl and a swing of his mighty paws. He grinned as she skittered away in terror, then looked over her shoulder at him. He regretted she was wearing white with a red headscarf and a long crane's bill instead of a mask. Had it been green she would have merited much more attention. He dragged his eyes away to look for a parrot.

His attention was drawn to his right by roars of laughter and shouts of "Do it again, Telas! Again!" Telas was a bearded chubby man of jovial disposition with the mask of a grinning frog pushed back on his head. He was playing Find the Lady with three drinking cups. He paused to down a large bumper of wine, then set his cups up again as a woman was calling, "My turn, my turn!" She had a square face and thick white hair drawn up into a pair of wings that flapped gently as she nodded her head enthusiastically and clapped fat fingers together in girlish excitement.

Telas obligingly rolled a white ball beneath one cup, hitched up his sleeves and gave the three cups a few lazy sweeps.

"There, there!" the woman cried, tapping a cup. "I'd stake my life on it."

"Oh, just your honour, I hope," grinned Telas. He lifted the indicated cup. Instead of a white ball, the lady's brooch sparkled from beneath the cup. The woman did a comical double-take and then squealed, "My brooch, that's my brooch!". As she shrieked a counterpoint to Telas's mirth, Quern found himself grinning too; Telas's laugh was ridiculously infectious. So involved, he failed to spot Imber and Kari coming in and didn't recognise Kari as she walked past him. The girl was dressed in black with wide sleeves. She had yellow slippers and a crow mask.

"Thought you were a stuffed bear."

Quern started at Imber's voice beside him. Imber was lean and sinuous in tight leather of mottled black and wore a snake mask.

"Don't see you getting a dance tonight, unless the girl is very weird indeed," guffawed Quern.

The snake turned unblinking eyes on him as Kari sidled away in the crowd. "Put your mask back down. We're looking for a green parrot. Thought you'd find looking for a girl easy. I was going to try the minstrel's gallery - but who's up there by the musicians? Could be our assassin!"

"No, I asked who he was. It's Mati, the chief steward. Watches everything; sends minions to replenish drinks and pastries as trestles empty, makes sure the curtains are open when alcoves are available."

"And you haven't asked him if he's seen a green parrot?" But then Imber put out a hand and nodded forward. A black panther had slipped from a curtained alcove and signalled to another. They were both moving with purpose. "Something happening. I'll get up there, talk to him. Best view anyway." And Imber was gone.

Seeing a flash of green, Quern surged forward, demolishing an echelon of dancers trying a new measure from Belmenia. The green turned out to be a high choker on a girl. She laughed with everyone else, imagining how badly he had misinterpreted the steps. Grateful for his mask, Quern plunged on into the lines of people chatting at the side of the floor. Growling apologies, he hurried through them towards stairs at the back of the enormous hall, hunting from side to side for the green parrot.

Suddenly he spotted a panther-masked figure emerging from a different curtained alcove. The panther made quick come-hither gestures to a second black figure and disappeared back into the alcove. Only careering into two people on his way, Quern was there even as the second marshal let the curtain fall behind him. Quern burst in, surprised to find Kari Witchet beside him. A woman lay on a divan. She wore a high-necked dress of shimmering green, the sides split to the hips. One bare brown leg was bent at the knee. Her head was tilted back, face covered by an exquisite parrot mask, yellow beak sticking up like a handle. The grey-blue silk of the divan was stained by blood that still trickled from a hole just below her ear.

Just as Quern cursed, Kari gave a gasp and a single, shuddering scream. "Tertius!"

"Get them out," snarled one marshal. "And nobody else comes in."

As a marshal bundled them through the curtain, Kari cried at Quern, "You failed! The Drouhin's failed! You might as well have killed her!"

Then the marshal was trying to ask questions, Quern was still swearing, nearby revellers were craning curiously and more marshals were convening. They wanted to detain Quern quietly but he was in no mood to be stopped and certainly not quietly.

"Release him," said the Earl in tones of steel. He dropped a hand on the shoulder of the senior marshal and spoke quietly. "Mati will likely have seen who went into this alcove with the parrot. He always does. Find out how long ago. Get the description and find them if they are still here."

Away from the hubbub of the party, Kalainen sat alone in a long gallery leading to double doors into the garden. There were four great windows paned with glass and the gallery was full of flowering plants towering towards the ceiling, swathes of dark leaves spangled with stars of jasmine. There was a small table and wooden seating at the centre of the gallery, but Kalainen settled well back from the garden doorway which was brightly lit with twin sconces. He perched on the side of a stone trough between phlox and wisps of night-scented stocks and stared moodily into the garden. He could see no more than a few isolated lamps marking a path with swaying puddles of light. The rain had stopped and a thin moon occasionally peeped past heavy clouds. Candles wavered and dribbled on the table and light bulged outward from sconces by the pillars between the windows, but Kalainen was hardly noticeable, silent and still under the foliage.

The deserted gallery was quiet but for the merest tremor of music and a faint bee-like murmur from the hall. Suddenly a woman was padding noiselessly along it. Patches of light revealed a short-sleeved shrug in purple over a flamboyant dress of red feathers, the skirt panelled with blue at the front. The woman's face was hidden behind a parrot mask with a dark beak. Just before she reached him, Kalainen moved forwards.

"Hello, Tertius Orbis."

The woman flowed into a fighting crouch, a curved glint of steel like a claw in her right hand, the left holding a small bag. The beak raked the gallery before and behind her, but there was nobody but Kalainen, who spread his hands to show they were empty. Shoving the mask aside, Tertius measured the distance to the doors. She relaxed slightly.

"Kalainen? You didn't know. How could you possibly know?"

"Your message had to have something only Kari Witchet would know. She loved birds. She kept parrots in Green Worm Tower. And your picture was so perfect. The exact image of an Eclectus parrot. But the Eclectus parrot is noted for the different plumage of the sexes. It's the male that is mainly green with a yellow beak. Kari would know that you would dress as the female; red and purple with blue underparts and a black beak."

Tertius snorted softly, edging closer to the door. "Knew you'd work out the riddle and get Kari here. Never thought you'd get that close. But you're too late. You can't stop me now."

"No, I can't." Kalainen rubbed his head and sighed. "The Tarlenians are trying to kill you, you know?"

"Of course, I was counting on that. They wanted to, and now they think they have. I wanted that sweet little parrot dead and they did it for me. All I had to do was send her the costume. Teach her to try to steal Kari from me."

Kalainen stared into the young woman's eyes. Then he shook his head. "No, that's not the truth. Perhaps she was one of your informers. Did she get greedy? Threaten to sell you out?" When Tertius volunteered nothing, he sighed. "Well, I failed to save her, either way."

"Save her? A bitch on the make. She went scuttling off to an alcove with her killer thinking she'd found the one who'd sent her the clothes. Still wondering how to twist the situation to make more gold when the needle slammed through her head. Won't threaten me again – and the Tarlenians think they've killed me."

"As Kari will have no doubt confirmed. There is a clever, cold neatness to it," Kalainen said regretfully. "But what if others had also come as green parrots?"

Tertius shrugged. "Bad luck them. Life's a chancy thing. Everyone, including you, followed the path I set them, like sheep on a track. And while the Tarlenians were killing that weasel and thinking it was me, I didn't ask them for my payment like a little lamb, I stole it and more from them. Now they think I'm dead and that's the end. Pfft! We birds fly off into the night." She waved her arms gracefully and edged a step closer to the door.

The Drouhin watched the delicate movements, then noticed the four red rings on her right hand, bright as a line of blood. "You drew the Dancing Goddesses. I should have recognised the style from the pawnbroker's pictures."

Tertius made a derisive noise even as she struck the Goddess's pose. "People believe any rubbish, and it sent the Watch spinning away from me."

"Kari spun a good tale." Kalainen looked sad. "I had to give you a chance, see if you'd been lured in by the Tarlenians and trapped into doing it as she said. But you enjoyed it."

"I couldn't give a dung ball how many of them were killed. But if I'm implicated in murder, so are you, Mr. Pious. I told the Tarlenians you were investigating them. I even got them to hire a magician. They know every conkin' thing said in Coromal and laughed at your flounderings. I knew you'd talk of the green parrot. And because you're so clever, the Tarlenians thought they had me and that's why our darling green parrot in there has her little beak turned to the ceiling and her brains stirred to mush. Without you, she'd be alive."

The Drouhin regarded her impassively for a moment. "Mother Yellern," he said at length.

"You knew?"

"I wondered if Yanni was talking too much or whether a girl had trapped Mardenifol, or even Quern. But it was Mother Yellern. How much did you pay her?"

"Nobody paid her anything. The magician just talked to her; sad, lonely, bitter thing that she is."

"What if I'd mentioned the Eclectus parrot and said you would be in red with purple shoulders?"

"Then I would've switched costumes. You think I didn't know what that magician reported?" Tertius dismissed the matter; past history. She moved nearer the doors, forcing Kalainen to turn to keep facing her, his back towards the hall. "How did you know I'd come this way?"

"I know you would have preferred the hubris of walking, un-marked, from the main doors. But there might have been panic when the body was found. You could have been blocked there. And too many of us might stop Kari Witchet, and then what? This was always going to be the easiest way."

"Lucky guess then."

"As you said, life is chancy."

"Yours, particularly," sneered Tertius.

"Want me to kill him?" breathed a voice behind the Drouhin. A knife pricked through his clothes and dug between his ribs.

"Kari ..." began Kalainen.

"You dismissed me as a little girl, easily broken. Fool! I led the children of Green Worm for nearly four years! Did Tertius or I care for the rich and so-noble marks he killed? Not one spit. Had they spared a thought for us, let alone a single ryal? Nothing. I hope their souls are eaten!" Kari looked back to Tertius. "Does he live or die?"

"He can't tell anyone without admitting how he's been used, out-thought and out-manoeuvred every step of the way. It's better he goes back to his dead apprentices and the smoking shell of Coromal." She laughed at the sudden horror smearing Kalainen's face. "Didn't expect that, did you? Comes of always poking your nose where it's not wanted. If I'd had time, you'd have found a picture of the Dancing Goddess on your door. Come on, my crow, let's fly."

Kari whipped her knife away, but still sliced through the material and nicked Kalainen's back, drawing a line of blood. She laughed. Arm in arm, the two young women stepped through the bright doors from the gallery into the dark garden, pinpricked with distant lamps. The door shut firmly behind them, leaving Kalainen standing alone with his face buried in one hand, the other pressed to his back.

"There's something wrong about all this," said Yanni. She slid a pancake onto a platter but didn't tip any more batter on to the skillet.

"What?" Mardenifol was perched at the kitchen table, swirling water through white crystals in a glass beaker. He waved the beaker through a candle flame and sniffed at the bubbles coming up.

"You know I went to convince Kari Witchet to come to Kalainen?"

"Hm, yes, you did well," he said distractedly, clearly much more interested in the bubbles, but then, they might have been poisonous. Eyes rolling high, he sniffed again.

"But I didn't. I bungled everything. It was like she was sitting there thinking how she could worm her way into Kalainen's confidence."

"You think all the puzzle stuff's a fraud?" Lighting a spill from a candle, Mardenifol dipped the flame into the beaker, ducking slightly. However, instead of anything exciting, the flame died. He frowned at the blackened spill.

"Don't know. But it's a great hook for Kalainen; can't resist it, can he? And Kari let slip that Tertius had mentioned Kalainen to her." She waved a wooden spatula at him for emphasis.

Mardenifol gave a last sniff and put the beaker down with a sigh. "What could they gain from having him involved?"

"Don't know that either. But Ruffin knows something. He's smashed to bits, Mard. An' Kalainen's got no money 'cause he's paying it all to some magician to heal Ruffin, giving him a place to live and all. But Ruffin was trying to signal something to me. I was too busy looking at the mess he was. He knows something about Kari Witchet what we don't. He drew something and showed it to me when Imber was telling Kari about the parrot picture. I think it was proper writing but I can't conkin' read! I need to go back."

"Can you remember what the writing marks were? If you could reproduce them, I could read it to you!"

Yanni gave him a blank look. "Course I can't. Scribbles meant nothing to me."

At that moment, there was a little click and a length of fabric unrolled by the range. Mardenifol looked at it in surprise. "What's that?" he said crossly.

Yanni touched a finger to her lips and whispered. "Someone climbing the house."

"What?" Mardenifol's eyes were round as eggs. "What do we do? There's nobody here! What if they get in?"

Yanni tapped her finger to her lips again, listening and frowning furiously. After a moment, there was a sharp clicking noise, a cry, then brief wild scrabbling from the roof tiles followed by a heavy thump on the ground outside. Muffled voices; some in anger, at least one in considerable pain. A solid thump on the door, scratching noises, perhaps someone trying to lever a blade through to the bar. Another thump.

"Bet nobody told 'em Coromal's been trapped by Imber!"

"I shouldn't be here!" Mardenifol was white-faced, his head jerking from side to side as though hunting for a way to run.

Yanni glared at him. The little stiletto had appeared in her hand. Her eyes were afire with rage. "This is our home now." She looked round at the cosy kitchen; the stack of copper pots, the wooden table worn smooth by a generation of pastry cooks, the once-white walls now a thousand shades of cream. "And they're not having nothing."

"The Lady save us," cried Mardenifol as the window shutters creaked under heavy pressure.

"Lady won't do nothing, never does. Hush and listen." They could hear voices outside but not what was said. "Bet they reckon the trap's sprung on that easy window. Going to try it again. See about that!"

"Don't leave me! I'm no good at this, Yanni!" Mardenifol clutched at Yanni's thin arm.

"Then do what you are good at." Yanking her arm free, Yanni spoke in a whisper but her ferocity might have been a shout.

"I'm no good at anything," squeaked Mardenifol, echoing a litany heard from his father.

"Do something with fire. Pretend to be a wizard."

"I can't ... I ..." He stopped. Suddenly Mardenifol leapt to his feet, muttering as he hurtled round Coromal, from the kitchen supplies to the workroom. "Any sugar and that stuff you use in baking and that alcohol liniment that Kalainen rubs on and the light naphtha and spare lamp oil and bowls and..." A few moments later, he was feverishly mixing sugar and soda into a large pile of white powder. He towed the table out of the way, legs squealing objections on the flagstones, then dumped out Yanni's precious herbs from their pot and made a base of the sandy soil in the middle of the floor. He drenched that in alcohol and naphtha and made a great heap of the powder on top. The candle gave life to a spill and Mardenifol managed to shake fire onto the oils. They burst into blue and yellow flame. A moment later, black bobbles appeared on the powder. Mardenifol grinned and began filling bowls with oils.

Up-stairs, there was a fierce scream from Yanni, a man's hoarse yell, then clattering from the tiles while Yanni's banshee wailing scraped across Coromal. Someone was shouting curses outside. As Yanni ran back into the kitchen, they heard a shout, "They're only two conkin' children!" Then there was a terrific crash as something heavy thudded into the shutters. Then again, and again.

"Two fallen off the roof. Think there's only one left!" cried Yanni, then, "Ghulsk!" when she looked at what Mardenifol was doing. The boy was crouched behind a fiery mound, the black coalescing into a rearing snake lapped with flame. Mardenifol was grinning like a demon as the light from fire and candle washed his face from beneath.

"Anyone comes in, throw that over them." He jabbed a finger at the large bowl of oils. Then his voice changed and he boomed out,

"Come Nephutar, Fire Demon of Laksklammir, come Azdrugor, Dragon-Lord of the Flame Pits!"

There was a brief pause in the crashing impacts on the shutter, then the pounding was renewed, louder than ever, with heavy grunts accompanying each house-shaking thump. Yanni was snarling like a wild cat, the stiletto still clutched before her. Still Mardenifol roared out his summons.

"Come Nephutar! Come Fire Demon! Azdrugor the Dragon Lord! Come!"

Another black snake head lifted, curled and grew above the burning oil. Then there was a cracking noise, another blow and the shutters burst inwards. A man tossed down a heavy fencepost and rested for a moment on the sill. There was a flicker of light on a length of steel, then the man climbed heavily into Coromal. Panting, he looked straight into the kitchen and his face contorted in a whirl of rage and fear.

"Rise Nephutar! Rise Azdrugor!" roared Mardenifol, still crouched behind the hazy screen rising from the burning coils of black. Even as he shouted, they grew still further, curling towards the interloper. Mardenifol lifted the small cup to his lip.

First stepping back, the man pushed his sword before him and bellowed as he moved forwards towards the indistinct figures writhing behind a screen of flame and smoke. Yanni screamed, long and piercing, while hurling the bowl of alcohol and lamp oil over him. The snake-like columns of black reared anew, swelling from their flaming bed. The man looked up in horror just as Mardenifol drew in a mighty breath and suddenly blew a mouthful of oil and alcohol over the candle. A fireball of burning gases exploded forwards, the oils already soaking the man's clothes burst into flame and his battle cry rose into a scream of terror and pain. Mardenifol rose up, screaming wildly as Yanni rushed forwards, poking with the wicked stiletto. Blinded inside a sheet of fire, the man dropped his sword and fled. He fell through the open window with Yanni slashing wildly at him with the stiletto, still howling madly.

Mardenifol slammed the shutters closed again but the bar was ruined beyond use. He stood with his hands holding them closed, yelling for Yanni to fetch a fresh timber. Yanni had run to Imber's little nook and was checking spy holes and mirrors. She watched their enemy rolling weakly outside but failing to extinguish the burning oil. She saw him tear his clothes off while his hair burned and finally crawl out of sight.

Yanni checked round all Imber's devices again before she finally came down to find Mardenifol still clamped onto the shutters. She triumphantly showed him a severed finger she had found by the top window and wondered why he was nearly sick. They finally located some odd lengths of planking and inefficiently nailed them over the damaged shutters. Yanni reset the warning wires and reloaded the trap at the window. Then they stood grinning at each other in disbelief at their victory.

Unsure what else to do, Yanni gravitated to the stove and started stirring the pancake batter again. Mardenifol trod out a few blobs of burning oil on the stone floor, then collapsed into a chair. He was very pale and shook as though he were freezing.

"You used all my sugar!" Yanni protested.

"I can buy you some more if we're still alive," stammered Mardenifol, half-choking on bile.

"We ARE alive." Yanni spilled a drift of flour and clenched her fists to hold them still.

"If there aren't more of them or they don't come back."

"Think there was only three. How many men would you have sent? Anyway, two fell off the roof, one missing half his hand -" Yanni gave a cacking parody of a laugh "- and you burned the other one like a straw doll." She jumped suddenly as a coil of black lurched across the floor. "What happens if the demon you were calling turns up?"

"Don't ask me!" Mardenifol laughed weakly. It turned into a dry retch. "I just made up all the names."

"Really? Funny if it turned out to be a real name." Yanni gave up with the bowl of batter and collapsed onto a chair next to Mardenifol, wrapping her arms round herself. "Or maybe not." They sat by the pancakes she had made earlier, but neither of them actually took one. "What is that stuff," she asked, prodding dubiously at one of the black snakes, still growing and curling.

"Just ash. Of a sort."

"And you're saying it wasn't magic? But you breathed fire. I saw it! Like a conkin' dragon!"

"It's just alchemy."

"How did you get into all this stuff?"

"I had a Natural Philosophy teacher, but he was rubbish. He told me of the different states of matter; stone and fire and air and water. How they were immutably different and immiscible."

"Talk normal."

"You can change a stone to sand or build a great wall, but it is still stone. Fire is just fire, you can't make a brick of it and so on."

"Seems obvious."

"So I was told. But I had questions. Why can't fire burn without air? How is it that if you chip two flints together, they produce an exciting smell and sparks of fire?"

"What did he say?"

"His answer was a good clip round the ear, telling me I should learn from my betters and not ask silly questions."

"So why can you get fire from flint?"

It was the perfect question for Mardenifol and his enthusiasm dampened the shock of the battle. "I think flintstone was condensed from unimaginable fires aeons ago. Some of that heat is somehow trapped in their substance. Cracking them together rattles their essence and some of that latent fire leaks out. Just imagine if I could find a way to release lots of the energy at one time." Mardenifol made an expansive gesture of waving arms and waggling fingers with a whoof noise.

"Sand soaks up water. Maybe flint soaks up fire and let's a bit out when you squeeze it! How can you ever find out?"

"Don't know," Mardenifol grinned at her. Don't even know what question to start with – but that won't stop me asking!"

Madam Vermoil

Yanni and Mardenifol were sitting at the kitchen table poking the cold pancakes when Kalainen and Quern thundered in. Imber sealed the door and grimaced over the baulks of timber nailed across the broken shutters. Yanni tried not to let anyone see her cry. Mardenifol was very pale, his eyes rounded with shock, his voice still wobbling uncertainly. But slowly the terror faded and then there were hugs and back-slappings and Yanni endangering everyone demonstrating with the stiletto and too many people talking at once as they tried to get over how close a call it had been.

"We came as fast as we could. Quern had to borrow transport. The driver tried to say no, but apparently Quern is hard to turn down when he smiles in that way that suggests he could bite your head off. I begged the Earl for the use of a carriage but he merely caustically observed that he thought there was one in a flower bed. Sees more than he should, that man. Then I asked Traid, but his were fully occupied..."

"Never thought Traid would get invited," said Mardenifol. "What did he dress as?"

"While we're talking, perhaps a smear of honey on some of those pancakes, Yanni?"

Kalainen busied himself brewing a tisane, to which they added various amounts of an apricot brandy which smelt of summer and warmed like a winter fire. Mardenifol sipped his while tilting the mug on the table and everyone pretended not to see how much he was shaking. Imber quietly joined Yanni at the range, whisked the mixture she was slopping out of the bowl and gently poured even puddles of batter onto the griddle.

"Traid was not invited," said Kalainen. "But he was waiting where I told him, outside the gallery, for Tertius and Kari. They walked straight out into a Watch detachment and were both taken before their eyes adjusted to the dark."

"Traid was waiting for them? How did you persuade him to do that?"

"Life is chancy indeed. Had that not worked, I would have been drummed out of Shaddimur! It was all complicated. I'm sure some of you guessed Mother Yellern was spying on us."

"Mother Yellern spying on us?" Quern's beard bristled as he clenched a fist. "The rancid old bat! I'll tie her ankles round her neck and hang her up in the larder!"

"Don't worry, Quern. She meant no real harm and best if she knows nothing of this. We could use her to send disinformation, but I doubt they'll bother with her again. But now is the time for the telling of tales. What have you two scamps been doing in my kitchen?"

"It was like real magic," cooed Yanni. "You should have seen Mard blowing a fireball!"

"What fireball? And what IS this on the floor?"

"Just a minute, I don't understand," said Mardenifol. "Tertius Orbis was a top Neer spy, locating people and defences and stuff. But if the Tarlenians have a magician, why couldn't he just use some sort of scrying spell to look into other people's houses? What did they need Tertius for?"

"She's an infiltration expert, Mard," said Imber. "It isn't just looking at a floor plan. There are guard rosters, movement patterns, view angles, traps and wards. You need to know where you can show a light, where you can't. These things cannot be done by remote viewing. Maybe richer places have magical defences that would either block the scrying or warn the defenders – or even launch a counter-spell against the scryer."

"Truth is, nobody who isn't a magician seems to know quite what a magician can do, if anything," said Kalainen. "I wonder if Mard with his alchemical tricks or Imber with his disappearings are not more magical than anything the wizard can do."

The chatter went on long after Quern and Imber had departed. They hoped for congratulations and payment from Traid and it was very late before they sought their beds. Kalainen sat with each of them for a little while and made sure both were asleep before he left.

It was, however, in the dark before dawn when they were rousted out again by a pounding on the door. One of the two men was Traid, but neither congratulations nor payment were on his mind.

"Who's dead?" asked Kalainen after one glance at Traid's face.

"Kallernin, this whole thing's a disaster! A debacle, a d... calamity. The entire city's in uproar. There's been butchery at the Bruelan embassy. Sarrepo, the ambassador, is slaughtered, along with others. The bust of the Ideal Warrior lies decapitated before the palace, a shrunken amulet beside it. So much for amity between the cities!" Traid slumped into a chair.

The second man tired of Traid's litany and rapped a long staff on the floor with heavy thuds. Tall and heavy of shoulder, broad of girth, with short hair and a large beard, he looked like one accustomed to dominating any group. He introduced himself. "I am Aldarilen, the Queen's loremaster. May I recap in a less hysterical fashion? Over the past weeks, a number of deaths of high-ranking members of society have occurred with associated robberies."

"And each of the deaths weakens Shaddimur's ability to organise it's defence," put in Kalainen.

Aldarilen's mouth tightened with irritation at the interruption, but then he accepted the point with a nod and continued. "There is general unrest between the various states of the Seven Cities. The failure of the authorities of Shaddimur to arrest culprits is unfortunate. Rumours abound that the murders are state-sanctioned and that the Watch are deliberately bungling their investigations."

Traid made an inarticulate gargling sound and his heavy fists bunched.

"Sarrepo, the Bruelan ambassador, has been murdered while under the protection of Shaddimur. While this would be grim enough on its own, there is more. Bruel and Shaddimur enjoy good relations and were on the verge of signing a treaty that would have advanced mutual trade and defence, the first part of a series of treaties for mutual defence between cities. However, this event will preclude the rapid adoption of the treaty.

"Now the Tarlenian ambassador, Guzarin, is taking ship to leave Shaddimur, claiming the city is unsafe and fails to protect foreign dignitaries. He has publicly urged the ambassadors from Allecando, Correbaran, Palemin and Hethrin to follow suit. The thinly veiled threat is that if they do not, Tarlenia may consider them part of some Shaddimur plot and take action accordingly."

"Guzarin," said Kalainen softly. "Our researches reveal that he knows about all the plots and all these killings only benefit Tarlenia."

"Correct. My agents had suggested that Tarlenia plans to take Bruel by force, splitting the other states and giving themselves access to a port - one reason for the haste to complete the treaty. Tar-lenian agents will foment opposition in Bruel using this death to drive a wedge between our two city states."

"*Had* suggested?"

"Indeed. It is true these deaths have affected our ability to wage war; the Lady's Fortune alone has preserved the Avatar of Sunsunni – and perhaps the intervention of our Queen. Is Tarlenia preventing us going to the aid of Bruel, or could they even be planning the bigger coup of taking Shaddimur itself?"

"Finally, someone sees it!" cried Kalainen, flicking his fingers skywards. "Is there word of troop movements on the borders?"

"On the border?" scowled Aldarilen. "What border? Tarlenia treats the Correbaran southern slopes of the Gatten Ridge as a parade ground to flaunt their squadron of cavalry and cross the Thrail into Palemin with impunity. My agents have reported that Guzarin himself is known as a swordsman of great renown in Tarlenia. I believe he and his coterie of agents and assassins are responsible for the murders. We have rumours and guesswork; frankly we have cold certainty but we have no evidence!" Aldarilen shouted, thumping his fist on the table.

"But you can hardly forcibly detain an ambassador – let alone accuse him of orchestrating murder – without making matters worse," observed Kalainen.

Aldarilen nodded sour agreement. "Quite. Unless there were proof incontrovertible."

"And as before, a confession would mean nothing. But this was the last murder."

"What do you mean?" Aldarilen glared at the Drouhin as though he were responsible.

"The Tarlenian ambassador is leaving. They've weakened this city badly. They've proved Shaddimur can't protect foreign dignitaries, the alliance looks likely to fail and the Tarlenians have their excuse for war. This is the end of their gambit!"

"Doesn't help us," said Traid. "Sarrepo, the Bruelan ambassador is dead."

"Another death I failed to prevent, true. But there is a loose end. The spy the killer has been using. That spy is now a liability to Tarlenia and the killer. That was Tertius Orbis. They think they killed her, but you have her in custody! She knows the killer and can give us the proof we need!"

"I thought after we apprehended those two dire witches last night, things were turning for the better," groaned Traid. "But no, it's the worst. The Watch House is wrecked, the spies are gone."

Kalainen shut his eyes, then exhaled deeply. "Did someone free them or kill them?"

"Piecing through the rubble makes it hard to tell." Traid's voice suggested that the idea had not occurred to him and had it done so, it would have been slightly lower on his priority list than polishing his buttons.

"But they knew who the murderer was. Kari said 'he'."

"Perfect. That narrows it down by half the population of Shaddimur. Keep going, you'll have it down to the last couple of thousand possibilities in no time," growled Traid.

"They could have given us the proof we needed! Had you, er, interviewed them?"

"I was letting them sweat a bit first in separate cells. It's good technique. Or would have been if some group hadn't stormed the place. They're gone and that's that."

"But who stormed the building? The Tarlenians thought Tertius was dead. Did Tertius get word out to friends?"

"We... well, some of the lads, you know... They were pleased with the arrest. May have let something slip..." Traid screwed up his face and pinched the bridge of his nose.

"You mean they trumpeted it in half the taverns of Shaddimur."

Traid winced. There was a long silence before Ardarilen spoke again.

"Sareppo was a fine man and a personal friend of mine. He will not be unavenged. I don't know what proof there can be. But find it you must and it must absolve Shaddimur. At worst, Shaddimur itself may be friendless before the Tarlenian tiger."

"How long do we have?"

Aldarilen's snort was discouraging. "Until the first Tarlenian ship puts in."

"Why would he go by ship?"

"Ha. He says he fears treachery on the roads. I suspect he has an itinerary taking him to other coastal cities to work mischief. Until a ship arrives, we have a matter of days at best. Perhaps only hours. Captain Traid has all the details. Don't let the Queen down." With that, the loremaster turned to go.

"Aldarilen, a couple of questions. Is there any way of disabling a ship at a distance? It might come in handy."

Aldarilen sniffed. "I'll look into it."

"Was the embassy magically warded?"

"Of course. The wards still hold – but of course they only prevent magical incursion."

"Could they have been circumvented?"

"Only with the collaboration of the spell-caster. In this case, me. Any other questions?"

"Just one. What is the minimum outcome you need?"

"Do I have to spell it out? At the very least, you must find a killer and prove he or she committed this murder, and demonstrate that person was not representing Shaddimur in any way. The who is less vital, though Nylla feels it important that the treaty is ratified if possible, uniting what cities we can against Tarlenia, so don't kick dirt up that sticks to that."

Aldarilen grunted significantly and walked from the kitchen, pausing long enough to scrape the end of his staff through the blackened sand on the floor like a bloodhound snuffling a trail. He glanced significantly at the hastily sealed shutters then turned and looked at the Drouhin over his shoulder.

"You should remember there are factions within Bruel, perhaps some favouring or fearing Tarlenia. They may have reasons of their own for killing Sarrepo and could have taken advantage of circumstances when our concentration is elsewhere. Changing the ambassador may have far-reaching effects. The Tarlenians represent but one suspect amongst many – but Guzarin will leave and this must be settled before he does." His gaze on Kalainen became very direct. "You might notice you fit my requirements perfectly – and you have been poking around each of the murders. Eh?" Aldarilen made a meaningful expression suggesting where scapegoats could be found, and left.

Kalainen pointed at Mardenifol, saying, "Get Imber. Hurry." As he turned to Yanni his voice clouded with doubt. "Can you go out again?"

"Course I can."

Kalainen looked at the fierce little face and shook his head. "I don't think you should. I can ..."

But Yanni had already called, "I'll get Quern," and was gone after Mardenifol. As they ran, Kalainen winced in resignation and turned to the Watch Captain, waving a vague hand towards the kettle. "Do you want...?"

"Might as well."

Unsettled and worried over the apprentices, Kalainen busied himself at the range, pushing logs onto the embers. He opened the base to get the fire drawing and slid the kettle over the firebox. "Don't suppose you've heard anything of Chelidor the wanderer? Not back in Shaddimur?"

"No, happily." The Captain stuck his feet out and slumped lower in his chair.

The Drouhin spoke carefully. "You can't really falsely accuse me of these murders."

"No? Why not? It would suit everyone."

"It would certainly suit the killer."

Traid ignored him. "Plenty of evidence of you, the killer, returning to the scene of the crime. I assure you Aldarilen will do it if necessary. As a loremaster, who knows what proof he could achieve with magic? You are expendable."

"What possible motive could I have?"

"Who knows what Drouhin plots to achieve? You know, I've never met another Drouhin."

"For a long time, neither have I," said Kalainen softly.

Traid missed the pain in Kalainen's voice and blundered on, "What's Drouhin like?"

"Drouhin; the town is set into a chine, funnelling cool breezes off the water – there's always a zephyr in Drouhin. The sound of the bell in Mirrin's Tower reverberates from the cliffs as the sun touches the water. To sit on the warm rocks over the sail-speckled sea, surrounded by birdsong over the stuttering buzz of carpenter bees, awash with the scents of pine and angelica..."

"City man myself. Beats me why you don't go back there."

"I would have gone last winter. I was going to head up north of Allecando. The Tarlenians had just crossed the Thrail river and looted and burnt Alaste between Palemin and Hethrin. Whole place was a war zone. Anyway, I can't. Not yet. I still have a promise to keep."

"Don't really care. If this goes wrong, Kallernin, you won't have a choice. That's a promise I will keep."

Kalainen sighed, trying to wipe away his irritation with a slow blink. "Tell me what you can then."

Traid scratched his whiskers with thick fingers. "Don't look possible. There's only one way into the Bruelan residency which isn't firmly locked and bolted."

"Locks can be picked. Inside men can open bolts."

"Yes. But it didn't happen. There were two guards, both provided by Shaddimur, outside the main door. Both were killed; no alarm, no struggle. They must have known their killer or killers well and suspected nothing." He raised his hands skywards, shaking his head in bafflement. "Bruel organised their own two guards on the inside who patrolled at night. Again, both killed without a fight. Sarrepo was killed in his bed. The other casualty was Telas, Sarrepo's brother and a more or less permanent guest at the embassy."

"Telas? Why would anyone kill him? Did he surprise the killer?"

"Doubt it. Telas was also killed in his own bed. No sign that either he or Sarrepo were moved – and with that much blood it would have been clear enough. No other staff were injured, neither were Gwyan, Telas's son and therefore Sarrepo's nephew, nor his female companion, a girl called Esferle from O-Ram."

The Drouhin frowned into his cup and said nothing.

"I don't mind telling you, I'm baffled, Kallyan. It's going to be rough. That thing with the Dancing Goddess has focussed resentment on foreigners. Shaddimur bubbles with trouble and we'll be hard-pressed to keep a lid on it. Even Vermoil was killed yesterday, for Lessan's sake! You knew her, didn't you?"

"Madam Vermoil, the apothecary at the Herbiary?" When Traid merely grunted affirmatively, Kalainen continued, "Of course I knew her. She was a good woman. What happened?"

"Vermoil was killed by an opportunist robber. No chance of finding the killer and it won't bring her back. I've left a good man there, Corporal Vallis. Told him you'd want to take a look anyway. Now, I have to get every Watchman onto the street and keep a city at peace, or what passes for it. I've got locals beaten up by Bruel sympathisers, lynch mobs looking for stray Tarlenians and it won't be long before shops get smashed and looted. And you better get on with your job." With a burst of energy, Traid slapped his thighs and stood to go. "Bring me word as soon as possible."

Imber sat on a balcony overlooking the darkened streets of Shaddimur. The sky was lightening in the east and a few lights burned in upper windows but the pre-dawn was quiet. The morning sea breeze had yet to waft its familiar sharpness over a city still waiting for the first competitive cries of gulls and hawkers. An empty goblet stood on a table of pale wood beside him. Beside it, a decanter held something that looked black in the moonlight. A tiny watch lantern left Imber in the dark but shed a pool of yellow light on a sheet of parchment with a schematic diagram, a reel of wire, some lengths of metal and a couple of thick springs. Imber's head turned slightly, his lips parted for a second of listening. The moonlight caught the flicker of his eyes as he checked around the balcony. There was a whisper of sound and Imber vanished in the shadow to one side of the window, knife in hand. There was a soft knock on his chamber door.

"Come in."

Someone entered, their every move betraying nervousness. A head turned left and right, peering into the apparently empty room. "Um, Imber?"

Imber glanced at the adam's apple popping up and down like a displaying sand grouse and moved into a part of the room greyed with reflected moonlight. "Speak, Mardenifol."

"Something urgent. Kalainen asks that you join him as soon as possible."

Imber seemed to blend back into the shadow. There was a movement of air and suddenly the room was empty in truth. Whether Imber had left by window or door, Mardenifol had no idea.

Yanni tapped on the door. Noises were audible from the inside. It did not sound like someone sleeping, nor coming to the door to open it. And that was a giggle. She rapped louder, then put her ear to the door.

"Sh! Someone's here. Stop doing that. Oh, no don't stop! Yes, you'd better."

This time, Yanni put some shoulder behind it and pounded the door.

"Oh, what is it?"

"Quern? Are you, er, alone?"

"Of course. One moment."

There was a soft snickering, a disappointed moan and the sound of a slapped rump. Running footsteps clopped over towards an adjoining privy.

"Do come in."

Yanni opened the door and took a couple of steps inside. Quern was in bed, smiling in the most innocent fashion. It was enough to sound warnings from here to Kathos. Only his left hand was visible. Snorting giggles were not quite stifled in the privy.

"Quern? Kalainen needs you. As soon as possible."

"Very well," says Quern gravely. A slight spasm crossed his face and the bed clothes moved. For an instant, a shapely bare leg was visible. It certainly did not belong to Quern. Seeing the direction of Yanni's gaze, he gave a tiny shrug.

"There's been another conkin' murder!" snapped Yanni.

"Another mur...? Oh." Quern sighed and wiped a hand over his face, squeezing his eyes. "Kalainen'll be pleased as a crow on a battlefield. All right, on my way."

Yanni left, face determinedly blank.

Imber reached Coromal before the apprentices; Quern somewhat afterwards. Kalainen was pacing when the big man finally arrived. A few concise sentences conveyed Traid's details. Then Kalainen sent Imber to get to the Bruelan embassy as soon as he could.

"I need to know as much as possible of what happened last night, Imber. I don't think this is where it gets dangerous but the Tarlenians might do anything. Quern, watch his back."

"Will do," said Quern, trying to sound decisive while looking like a man seriously sleep-deprived with a crushing hangover.

"We'll join you shortly. Just need to stop off at Madam Vermoil's on the way."

"Tea would be..."

"Obviously out of the question. Drink water and go."

The morose wave of a finger would have been unrecognisable as a teardrop, and Quern nearly poked himself in the eye trying to tap his forehead, but then he glugged his way through an entire jug of water, tried to hide a bleary belch, and shambled after Imber. Kalainen was collecting scraps of paper and charcoal from his study and thrusting them into a small satchel when Mardenifol asked,

"What is it with Imber? He's an ascetic crossed with a lemon. What does he do for fun?"

Kalainen sighed. "He was on overwatch when Ruffin was nearly killed. He hasn't forgiven himself."

"If Imber couldn't prevent it, nobody could," cried Yanni.

"No. The fault was mine. And I repeat it every day I put you and Mardenifol in danger."

"If I died tomorrow, it'd still have been better than rotting in Meiling Square. And if Imber was on overwatch, it wouldn't happen." Yanni suddenly threw her apron on the floor and ran from the kitchen.

"What is that about?" asked Mardenifol, his lip curled like a salted slug.

Kalainen opened his mouth to answer, but sighed instead. "You'll learn. Maybe. But you at least should go back to your family until this is over. It really isn't safe. You'd best grab your things now, Mard."

Mardenifol just stood in the doorway. "I'm not going."

Kalainen stopped what he was doing and looked at the boy. "No, Mardenifol, you must. For your safety and my conscience, you must."

Mardenifol hung his head and swallowed a couple of times. "I can't do anything my father wants. I can't fight, I can't hunt. Can't preach. Don't have the ability to command respect and loyalty and stuff. No good with dogs or horses, or people for that matter. Father says I should be a man and make my own choices and then allows me none. But there are things I can do. And it can make a difference here, I know it can. I don't have Yanni's courage, but she's right. I don't care if I do get killed, it's still better than crawling back home."

"Brave words spoken by day sound hollow in the darkness." Kalainen's voice was gentle.

"I mean it. I won't go."

"Mard..."

"Don't make me go, Kalainen. Please. Don't make this something else I can't do."

Kalainen sighed and pushed blunt hands through the short spikes of his hair. He turned bright eyes on Mardenifol until the lad managed to meet his gaze. "Best get Yanni then."

Madam Vermoil's shop was on the Hallow, a street running up to the Fane of The Lady. By local ordinance, neither draught animals nor wheeled vehicles larger than a rickshaw were permitted on the uncobbled road. The Herbiary was tucked between a chandler's and a little place selling cakes and tartlets from an open window. Tubs of flowers outside might have been decorative, but they served to keep the rickshaws and their attendant sprays of mud away from the shop fronts.

The scented oils from the chandler perfumed the morning, but they were trumped by the waft from the cake shop. Yanni was transfixed by the blobs of gleaming colour and swirls of icing just within her reach on a wooden stand. Kalainen's touch on her shoulder stilled her twitching fingers as he murmured, "Perhaps when we have finished here."

A man was leaning against the door jamb of the Herbiary, gazing vacantly across the street. Tufts of white hair bulged from under his cap. He was of less than average height but greater than average paunch. His uniform was a compromise; too tight in the belly, too long in the limbs.

"Corporal Vallis?"

Watery eyes drifted round to Kalainen, then Vallis suddenly straightened himself, huffing like a walrus. He even gave some form of salute.

"Yes, sir! You are the Drouhin, then. I was ordered to await your arrival, sir."

"Well, what have we got?"

"Madam Vermoil, herbalist and apothecary of Shaddimur, was foully murdered by person or persons yet unknown."

"And how goes your investigation?"

Vallis's eyes swam a lap or two before he replied. "I was instructed to watch the premises after initial enquiries were completed by the Watch. Did you wish to inspect the scene?"

Kalainen nodded and was conducted inside the apothecary's shop. He was met by a complex aroma of dried herbs mixed with green scents coming through a large open window to the herbalist's garden. The shop was lined with shelves of bottles and jars, all neatly labelled and ordered. Creams for joints, draughts for shortness of breath or ulceration of the throat, tonics for maladies of the liver and salves for chapped skin. Behind the counter were racks of ingredients; dried herbs, spices and aromatic oils together with alcohol and water solvents, flour and lard for making up tablets. The jars were muddled with gaps obvious as missing teeth.

"I have maintained my watch," said Vallis stiffly. "No-one has interfered with the scene of the murder."

"Indeed, you are to be commended," said Kalainen. "A similar stalwart guards the rear window? The roof?"

"Hm. Manpower is regrettably limited. However, observe! The robber was clearly ransacking the place when he was disturbed by Madam Vermoil. To protect his, or her," Vallis tapped his nose significantly, "identity, Madam Vermoil was killed." Vallis picked up the petty cash box, which was empty and turned it over to emphasize the point. "The money has been purloined, you will observe."

"I do. However, Madam Vermoil's herbal is on the counter with her mortar and pestle and if the petty cash box were also out, it would suggest that Madam Vermoil was working. A curious time for a robbery, perhaps. I also note that the strongbox, hidden with limited subtlety under this counter, is undamaged."

"The burglar was surprised in his villainy, I should not wonder!"

"Perhaps, but by whom, for then we'd have a witness? And speaking of things behind the counter, why all these herbs and ingredients strewn on the floor?"

"Signs of a struggle, sir. Vermoil must have put up a fight! Notice how many jars are disarranged at haphazard!"

"However strong her potions, Madam Vermoil was a wisp of a woman in her sixties. Was the window open?"

"Yes. Or it may have been opened by the Watch for better light and fresh air."

"Thank you, Corporal. Tell me, have you searched the garden?"

"The dire murder was committed in this room. However, I recall someone looking for footprints by the window and saying there were none. I can also confirm that the door to the garden was bolted on the inside. Nobody left by that way."

"Thank you. If this were done during her working hours, have you spoken to the neighbouring shopkeepers who might have seen or heard something, or tried to find customers who were close by at the time?"

"I'm sure anyone with information appertaining to the case would have come forward, sir."

"I see. No doubt. Exactly how was she killed?"

Vallis shrugged. "Stabbed. I think someone said half her chest had been hacked open."

"Hm, perhaps a sword rather than a dagger, then. Interesting. Where's the body?"

"Conveyed away for funerary rites after the Watch completed its investigation, sir."

"Well, thank you, you have been most hel... er, very civil. Perhaps you could resume your surveillance outside while we look about a little more?"

After Vallis had assumed his post outside, Kalainen looked down at the drifts of herbs split on the floor. He recognised lavender and bay leaves amongst the litter but there were other things he could not identify. He rubbed sweet lavender between his fingers, inhaling its summery fragrance and looked sadly at the bloodstain on the floor.

"These plants are commonly used in scents, aren't they? Could they be needed to mask a smell? Confuse a tracking dog?" Mardenifol was hunting round like a hound himself.

"Lot of effort for that. Although people have died for less."

"All this business with the herbs and stuff," said Mardenifol slowly, "Only makes sense if the killer took some. I mean, a robber would have grabbed the cash box and be gone. If they came when Madam Vermoil was working, they must have come for something.

They couldn't afford it, or for some other reason she wouldn't do it for them. They killed her and took stuff to make it themselves."

"I like that," said Kalainen.

"Shame Madam Vermoil's herbal wasn't still open, or we'd know what they wanted." Mardenifol held the herbal by the spine and let it fall open, hoping it might reveal the last page used but the parchment showed no such helpful inclination. "Look! There's a page torn out! That's what the killer's going to make!"

"Maybe Vermoil got the recipe wrong or that potion turned everyone green and she tore it out herself," said Yanni.

"Not this time," said Kalainen. "There is only one page removed. Nowhere else is there a single crossing out. Everything is beautifully neat. All written in the same hand. She would never roughly tear a page out. Is there an index?"

"No. But if they're alphabetically sorted..." began Mardenifol excitedly, then groaned with disappointment.

"She probably wrote the recipes in the order she happened upon them. Notice the herbal is not yet full."

"So other than that the killer wanted something, the missing page tells us nothing."

"Except the killer can read," put in Yanni, leaning out of the window. She turned her hand over, looked at dried leaves stuck to her palm and then at the woodwork. "There's herbs on the windowsill," she said. She hopped through the window and crouched down. "And more outside."

"Are there now?" murmured Kalainen thoughtfully.

"Suggests the killer went that way then," said Mardenifol.

"Maybe," replied Yanni. "Reckon it'd be possible to sneak out without leaving footprints in the soil. But if they was in that much of a hurry that there's a trail of herbs, likely would've left marks. Unless they flew, of course. And Imber would have climbed the house."

"Sound thinking."

Mardenifol also climbed through the window and immediately left a footprint, and then another one as he nearly fell over trying not to. While Yanni tried to follow a trail of dried herbs, he went further into the garden. The herb trails rapidly petered out, but Mardenifol gave a triumphant cry.

"There's a jar here! And another!"

The apprentices searched thoroughly while Kalainen looked round at potential exit routes from the garden. None showed any sign of use. Nor were there any signs beyond where Madam Vermoil had shuffled along sandy paths, tending and snipping. By the time the apprentices had finished, four jars had been found and a great deal of damage had been done to the carefully tended plants.

Back inside, Mardenifol arranged their discovered jars on the worktop. There was one labelled bay, a broken one labelled elecampane root and two more; galbanum and lavender.

"So, someone tries to get Madam Vermoil to make them some tincture or potion or stuff. She won't. So they kill her. They find – or possibly Madam Vermoil had already opened her herbal at the page – the recipe and tear it out. They take these ingredients, spilling some in their hurry and tossing jars into the garden. If we can find out what can be made from these four things, we will have a big clue to the killer."

Kalainen was frowning at the disordered jars on the rack behind the counter. "It could be. But the person who could tell us is dodging the issue by being dead. And now we must get to the embassy."

"Kalainen, can I ... I know where there's another herbalist. Can I take these to him and find out what they were trying to make?"

When the Drouhin paused, looking at his enthusiastic face, Mardenifol went on. "All this stuff, it isn't alchemy, but it's sort of like alchemy on a person."

Kalainen gave a half nod. "All right. You take over here. But keep careful notes of everything. Meet us at midday at the Silver Hart near the embassy. Good luck."

Yanni looked from Kalainen to Mardenifol, wondering whether she should stay or go. She followed the Drouhin, perhaps because he was going closest to the cake shop. As they passed Corporal Vallis, the old Watchman came to attention, half-blocking them.

"Sir, Captain Traid mentioned you might want me to continue my watch. Under your command. Sir." Vallis' red-veined nose was pointed at Kalainen but his eyes stared over the Drouhin's shoulder.

Kalainen looked at the man standing stiffly beside him, ridiculous in his ill-fitting uniform. "Corporal Vallis, are you on active duty?"

"Yes, sir." There was a pause while Vallis licked his lips, his eyes blinking like diving swimmers. "That is to say, I was retired, sir, but Captain Traid asked me to return to duty, sir. On account of the current crisis."

"And he wants me to be responsible for your pay, do you think?"

Vallis was redder in the face than before. "I believe that was his intention, yes, sir."

Kalainen paused for a moment, then continued in his gentle drawl. "I would be glad to have an experienced officer to advise in this case. Your pay will be the same as a Corporal in the Watch and will continue from today until the case ends. For the time being, maintain watch here, Corporal. The boy may come and go. I will expect you to protect him, of course."

The old man dropped one hand to his short sword and stood straighter. "Yes, sir!" As Kalainen and Yanni left, Vallis looked fiercely left and right to deter unseen looters.

It was not far to the embassy district, but Kalainen was in a hurry and moved fast. However, just as Yanni was about to sigh as loudly as she could, he tossed her a groat and told her to catch up. She caught the coin and spun to hold it up to the woman in the window, her eyes already raking the glistening sweetmeats.

On the other side of the Herbiary, Mardenifol held up his hand to attract a rickshaw. Leaping aboard, he urged the lad to best speed, calling an address. He couldn't stop his lips tightening into a maniacal grin as they hurried along. He was in charge of this part of the investigation! His head filled with images of himself delivering the killer to Traid, receiving congratulations from Kalainen and even his father. Then they hurtled across the deep ruts of Jumblegut Lane and he was flung into the canvas top of the rickshaw. He smacked onto the floor just in time for a repeat performance as the rickshaw was yanked over the next rut and the dignity of the moment was lost.

His enthusiasm remained undimmed as he marched into Longyle's apothecary, which had a pleasantly earthy, aniseed smell. After the regimented order of Madam Vermoil's Herbiary, the assortment of boxes and drawers and jars seemed haphazard. Mardenifol looked longingly at an extensive jumble of glass vessels, tubes and pipettes. Longyle had just been heading into the back regions and heaved himself back to his counter with a sigh, sweeping his thick gown round him. Longyle was heavy-set with no neck and a big head with thin strands of fine dark hair and looked like a vulture shuffling back to a corpse. He planted large and hairy hands either side of his herbal and looked at Mardenifol with irritation in eyes so dark they looked black.

"What can you tell me of these plants?" asked Mardenifol, hauling himself away from the glassware and putting his three and a half jars on the counter.

"Thought you'd want a cream for spots or a particularly optimistic love potion," rumbled Longyle as he held up the first jar at arm's length, squinting at the label. "Bay: a noble plant! Versatile and puissant, particularly in protective concoctions against magic, bolstering resistance to all manner of malignancies. The berries are also good against poison."

"I didn't see any berries. Just the leaves, I think."

Longyle sighed and selected the next jar. "Elecampane: I use it to treat coughs, consumption and other pulmonary complaints as well as the colic. Also known as Elf Dock or Horse Heal. Galbanum: a herb used in perfume, just a touch to add depth and mystery to incense, though I suspect its bitterness is to remind worshippers of their sinful natures. It's also used in tonics and, together with oil of spondylium, makes a sovereign snakebane. Lavender: a plant with virtues particularly against maladies of the head, though it is unsafe to use on a body slaked with blood and humours." Longyle became loquacious on its uses, such as a decoction made with flowers of lavender, horehound, fennel, asparagus root and a little cinnamon which was paramount against falling sickness and all giddiness. He warned that oil of lavender was so fierce and piercing that its use should be restricted.

"Hm, yes and so," Mardenifol interrupted the disquisition, "but does any potion use all of them together?"

"Not that I can think of," said Longyle airily, "Without going through my entire herbal. Now, I have other duties. The fee for the consultation is two testoons."

There was a long pause while Mardenifol drummed his fingers and fixed Longyle with an unwavering stare. "Know that I am," the son of Lord Berrin paused, "working on assignment for the Drouhin of Shaddimur. This is a matter of vital importance for the whole city. Your cooperation will be appreciated."

After a brief contest of wills, Longyle bent grumpily to his task. He checked through every recipe in his herbal, keeping up a steady grumble in which a keen ear might have discerned a number of unflattering references to his client. He finally shut the herbal with a snap. "As I said, there is nothing using all four ingredients. Or even three."

"Oh. Could there be something you don't know of?"

"By definition, yes. The herbs are not antithetical but they are disparate. I can't imagine what would call for all four of them."

"Thank you for your time and expertise," said Mardenifol, working hard to keep his voice steady to hide his disappointment. Swallowing hard, he pushed two testoons across the counter before the apothecary increased the fee. He took a rickshaw back to the Herbiary, getting out to walk and help keep the rickshaw vertical when they bounced across the ruts of Jumblegut Lane.

"I don't understand this, Vallis. Why would someone tip herbs on the floor and throw jars from the window?"

"Ah..." Vallis raised his eyes, perhaps suggesting that the ways of burglars were inscrutable.

"Why do the herbs not make something useful?"

"Hm," murmured Vallis.

Mardenifol looked sharply at the Corporal. "You're thinking it must be some form of misdirection, aren't you?"

"Well, I ..."

"Yes! Everything in here is perfectly ordered. Except the jars of ingredients. So, they were organised, but the killer disarranged them. He must've been in a hurry to get out before his crime was discovered. So why waste time shuffling jars? Surely because if they had been in order, we might have known what had been taken.

"But we found the jars, we know what was taken and it doesn't make anything. And if he'd just taken a bit from the jars and put them back where they were, we would have no idea. No. I have to work through this logically!" Mardenifol banged the heels of his hands against his temples, screwing his face up as though he could wring the answers from his brain. Vallis's eyes wobbled round to watch him. He looked worried, as though concerned for Mardeni-fol's mental stability.

"We know Madam Vermoil was working because her balance, her mortar and pestle, cash box, herbal and stuff were on the counter," Mardenifol continued, waving his hands to punctuate his points. "Therefore, this wasn't a planned robbery but someone coming in to ask for something. Plainly, Madam Vermoil refused to give it to our murderer or he or she would merely have left with their potion or unguent. There was an argument, and Madam Vermoil was slain.

"What does our customer do now? A potion is needed and the potion-maker is dead. But here on the counter is her herbal! So, the killer takes the page from the herbal with the recipe he needs. Then the villain collects the ingredients required and switches jars, no, takes samples of... no, remember, Vallis, he's just killed Madam Vermoil and will be flustered, desperate to leave. He's no time for weighing! He might not take enough of something – or the herbs might be vitiated by contact with each other – or the air. He takes the whole jars!

"But, just as I tried to work out what potion could be made from the herbs on the floor, one could deduce what potion was being sought from what jars are missing - and Madam Vermoil's shelves are so neatly arranged and labelled! In a terrific rush then, our mur-derer shuffles jars, opens some at random, dumps contents on the floor and tosses the empties out of the window. Yes!

"Now, all I have to do is identify the missing jars, then perhaps Longyle will be able to tell me what potion was being sought! This must be important, or the killer wouldn't have gone to such lengths to conceal it."

Mardenifol paced about the workroom, his hands on his head. He took all the jars of ingredients and arranged them all alphabet-ically. The jars didn't fill the shelves, and it didn't tell him what wasn't there. He turned to Vallis. "How can we tell what's missing?"

Vallis started guiltily as a schoolboy caught daydreaming, but Mardenifol had spun back to Vermoil's herbal and opened it to the first page; a gargle for sore throats. Ingredients were listed as coneflower, elderberry, sage, ginger, honey and brandy.

"Of course! I go through the whole herbal. If I find an ingredient without a corresponding jar, I have found something the thief took!"

At once, Mardenifol sat down and began working through the recipes in Vermoil's herbal one by one.

"What if the ingredient didn't come in a jar?" asked Vallis.

Mardenifol glared at him as if he had just deliberately sabotaged the investigation. But then he sighed. "You're right. I'll have to check against everything else I can find too."

"She could have run out of something," suggested Vallis.

"Yes, possibly. But there'd be an empty jar still."

"Unless she put it elsewhere to remind her to fill it. Perhaps the missing recipe had an ingredient used in no other concoction in the whole book." Vallis smiled helpfully.

Mardenifol faced the old Watchman, his lips compressed. "I accept this is not fool-proof. Do you have any positive suggestions?"

"I will follow the Drouhin's recommendations and pursue enquires with the neighbouring enterprises." Vallis exited serenely.

A while later, Corporal Vallis looked round the door. He shook his head, looking at all Mardenifol's writings. "The noon bell has sounded from the fane. You're supposed to be meeting the Drouhin."

Mardenifol leapt up. "Thank you, Corporal! Make sure nobody touches anything in here, please. I'll be back shortly."

The Bruelan Embassy

A gentle breeze trembled glossy leaves from two trees planted in enormous copper pots either side of the main door to the Bruelan embassy. The roots bulged on the surface of the soil like hibernating pythons and could be seen coiling lower where one pot had cracked almost its full height. Nearly invisible, Imber was lounging in the dappled shade, waiting for the Drouhin. He slouched forward when Kalainen and Yanni appeared.

"Did a quick check by lamplight for tracks in and around the residence, just on the off chance that Traid's men had miraculously failed to trample them. Repeated the task after dawn in better light."

"Anything?"

"By the time the muddy boots of the Watch had 'investigated' and sealed the area except for the legion of family, servants and hangers-on, not much. Found these." Imber held his hand out and carefully tipped a few shards of glass into Kalainen's palm. The shards were thin, clear and curved.

"Where?"

"Here. Where the Shaddimur guards were killed."

"Hm," murmured Kalainen, sniffing the pieces of glass and holding one up to the light. "Where are the bodies? Surely they haven't moved them before I've seen them?"

"They said something about piles of corpses outside the door not being consistent with the dignity of an embassy. Got a point. They even sluiced down the bloodstains."

Kalainen gave a nod of resignation. "Any of Traid's Watchmen still here?"

"Couple."

Kalainen nodded. "The sort that are best for standing for long periods rather than, say, asking searching questions and looking for solutions, I suspect. Still, no doubt they will do their best to order off inquisitive gossips and stray goats."

Imber shrugged. "There's a Sergeant Rown. Knows what he's doing."

"I'll talk to him. Anything else to go on?"

"Found a chalk picture of the Dancing Goddess behind an unused shutter while checking a number of ways to sneak in. None show signs of use. Killer could've been let in, but likely went straight through the front door - assuming that an outside agency came in. Could just as well be an inside agent coming out through it, knifing the guards and going back in."

"Anything contradict someone within the embassy killing the inner and outer guards and then murdering Sarrepo and Telas? Pity," he said when Imber shrugged. "Yanni, talk to the staff; kitchen girls, maids, anyone. See what you can pick up. Oh, and if you found who cleared up the broken glass, that would be great." He turned to Imber. "Where's Quern?"

"The two Shaddimur guards were Larno and Timmis. When they were off duty, two other Shaddimur men, Morl and Shandir, took their place. Quern's gone to talk to them."

"Good. Imber, have a nose round. See if you can find any eyewitnesses. Maybe something about these guards. Any general opinions on the embassy policies old and new. Perhaps your Neer connections may have some ideas on merchants dealing with Bruel? Meet up with us and Quern at the Silver Hart at noon. Right, I'll see the bodies and talk to Rown."

Inside was an atrium with white walls and a floor tiled in black and white. There were tables against two walls, both topped with vases of flowers in red and orange. A sergeant from the Watch was having an intense conversation with a subordinate and a member of the embassy staff, who kept bobbing into a curtsey. Kalainen was just heading towards them when an inner door swung wide and a tall man emerged. He had a fringe of hair like a muffler for his ears and a stately stride as he marched towards the main door where they were standing. Kalainen took in the Bruelan livery and smiled as the tall man approached.

"You must be..." he began.

"Not just now, sir," said the man, contriving to appear deferential as he swept past and opened the main door.

A small deputation from the Allecandan embassy meandered in, murmuring words of condolence and sympathy. They were greeted by the tall man, who escorted them into a reception room. In the overheard, delicately-turned phrases, Kalainen understood that they were unsure of to whom they should have been paying their respects. The tall man advised them by neatly agreeing with an unvoiced suggestion that Gwyan would be considered acting ambassador for the time being. None of the Allecandans seemed even aware that there were other people in the atrium.

The Watchman escorted the maid away as Sergeant Rown turned towards Kalainen and Imber. The Sergeant had a thin face with intelligent eyes, a sprawling wedge of hair and a nose as sharp as an awl.

"This is all right, is it?" asked Kalainen sharply. "Isn't this a murder scene? Aren't these people visiting the suspects?"

"And what would you have me do?" retorted Rown. "Ignore the fact that this is Bruelan sovereign territory where we trespass by their kind permission? Kick this group out, insulting Allecando? Slur the remaining diplomats from Bruel by saying we suspect them of murdering their own? I can do my best to ensure Shaddimur is isolated whatever happens with Tarlenia if that's what you think would be best?"

"I didn't..." began Kalainen hotly, but then his tone dropped back to his customary drawl. "I spoke hastily. What I think is that Traid has left a very good and politically astute man in charge here. It just isn't going to make it any easier to get to the bottom of this."

"Captain Traid said you would be helpful." Rown's tones were carefully neutral.

"Did he really?"

The sergeant's thin lips quirked into a smile. "He actually said you'd ask a lot of daft questions, get under everyone's feet, then produce the killer from a box and claim all the credit."

"Sounds more like him," chuckled the Drouhin. "Let's start with a few daft questions. Who reported the deaths? To whom? When? Did they say who found the bodies?"

"Steady on. The deaths were reported in wild shrieks by maids of the embassy staff. The inside guards were found first, about an hour before dawn."

"Could I examine the bodies, then perhaps you could show me where they all fell?"

"Time's tight. I suppose I can show you the bodies and introduce you to the living. Let's talk as we go. Sarrepo, the ambassador, and Telas, his brother, are both laid out in the rooms where they were killed. The two guards hired by Bruel have been put in a spare room upstairs. The outside guards, Larno and Timmis, are here, on a table in the butler's pantry." Rown opened a door and gestured Kalainen inside. "Ever seen two men killed like that?"

The Drouhin looked at the two bodies. They had the same injury. A blade had been pushed behind the trachea and the carotid arteries had been cut.

"Not humans. It's a way to slaughter a trussed animal."

Rown looked at the Drouhin, his sharp little nose whiffling for the next snippet. Kalainen produced the slivers of glass.

"We found these by the door. They could have been drinking."

"From glasses like that? And how much wine do you think they'd drunk - while on duty?"

"I don't know. But Madam Vermoil has been killed. Perhaps there was more to their drink than wine. We're looking into that as well. I'll let you know if we turn anything up."

Rown regarded Kalainen with his lips pursed and eyes narrowed for a moment. "Traid also said that anything you found, you'd keep to yourself. We drink from different tankards, but piss in the same pot, eh?"

"You've met a Drouhin before?"

"No. But what I heard about you made my head hurt."

Kalainen snorted amusement as he did a swift check on the guards, noting how they were still slightly warm but had stiffened, assessing the livid stains where the blood pooled in their tissues. "If they were moved some hours after being killed, they are in a similar position now," he murmured. "Rough guess suggests they died two or three hours before they were found."

"That dead time of night when people sleep soundest," said Rown.

"Fits. Any of the others any different?"

"You check, but I would've said they were all killed at a similar time. The killer seemed to know exactly where to go and how to do it. Suggests it was an inside job."

The Drouhin looked sharply at the Sergeant. "Could be. We suspect the other murders were done after extensive research by a spy. Imber found her mark behind out of the shutters."

"Interesting to know. Those were the spies briefly apprehended by the Watch?"

"One of them, yes. Now, these two guards..."

"Long-term night-shift workers at the embassy."

"Long term meaning that they were trusted in the post – and also that they were a known part of the system and could have been suborned."

Rown sighed. "You've played the game."

"My man Quern has gone to talk to Morl and Shandir, the lads who stood in for them on occasions."

"Yes? I sent a Watchman to investigate them. Larno was a known gambler. Maybe he owed too much to the wrong sort. And Timmis is not long married. Threats to his wife could easily have bought his cooperation."

While they talked, they hurried through the embassy, Kalainen's drawl had a musing tone but his eyes missed little. He listened to the creaks of the floorboards, the groan of an opening door; all the noises that were normally lost in the day but should have given away the intruder in the silence of the night.

"These other two guards were not killed in the same way," said Rown, "but I don't think either of them knew the attacker was there. Do you see any evidence of a fight? Don't think they ever drew blades. One was killed as he came into a room, perhaps by someone behind the door. I guess someone grabbed him from behind, one hand round his mouth, and cut his throat. The second guard came up these stairs, turned the corner, and received a sword thrust right under the chin. Was the killer invisible?"

"Remember the spy. She was really good. The killer knew exactly where the guards were going to be and where he could wait unseen."

"He?"

"That was all we gleaned from the spies before they were lost."

"Not much."

"At least the first of those killings was messy and close up. If the killing was an inside job, someone in the embassy was covered in blood. There should be clothes, evidence of washing, maybe scraps in a fire somewhere."

Kalainen spotted the grimace of chagrin on Rown's face, but the sergeant merely said, "I'll look myself in a moment."

"Your guesses for the deaths look sound. And I agree, similar time of death." Kalainen looked at the belted coats and doublets they both wore, now stained dark. "Were these Gallendians?"

"Yes, both of them."

"Why did Bruel hire Gallendians?"

Rown rubbed the back of his neck and sighed. "I don't know. Likely Bruel had more money than spare troops. The man who could definitely tell us is dead. What I do know is the fact they are from Gallendia adds another whole layer of complexity to the political side." While he talked, Rown led Kalainen towards the master bedroom, their footsteps clacking on the smooth wooden floor. Something crunched under Rown's boot and a little red grit scratched the polish. Flecks and small smears of blood showed they were following the trail of the killer.

"At least it doesn't look as though the Gallendians were involved."

"Unless they let in their killer," said Rown darkly.

"Maybe. Doesn't feel right, though, does it?"

"This is what Traid fears. Doesn't matter what's right. One wrong word; the Gallendians were bought by Shaddimur, the Gallendians failed to protect Bruel. Suddenly we have another state to offend. There's always potential friction between the different peoples. It can explode into violence very easily. Come on, we must keep moving."

Sarrepo was in the master bedroom, a clean blanket spread up to his chin. It did not mask the stench. The material was stuck to the body with drying blood. Kalainen peeled it back, bits of gut and tissue pulling away from the body and plopping back. Two flies droned away in meandering flight, yellow blobs of eggs already laid. Fingerprints of blood on Sarrepo's mouth and chin suggested someone had clamped a hand over his face while thrusting a blade up from his belly under his ribs and thrashing around like stirring porridge. There was a ghastly mess of bowels and blood and filth which even Rown turned away from.

"That's odd," murmured the Drouhin. He lifted one of Sarrepo's blood-smeared hands. "If you look carefully, he used to have two rings on this hand. One of his rings has been removed - but just one. If there is one item of real value taken, that's the signature of our killer!"

Rown's face was twisted either with annoyance or nausea from the reek. "Could be," he said gruffly. "Hurry along now. I've just time to show you Telas."

Kalainen tipped water from a ewer and washed his hands in a basin. "Assuming the maids haven't replenished the water, the killer didn't wash. Going to be quite a sight by now."

"Nobody saw him," said Rown through clamped teeth. "I've said I'll check for clothes washing or disposal."

"Who have we got left in the embassy?" asked Kalainen, following the sergeant out of the master bedroom. They saw blood spots on the floor in several places, but there was no thought that the killer had been injured.

"There's a fair list of staff members, cooks, maids, butlers and the like. Most of them are running about like headless chickens at the moment. I'm sure you'd like an entire list of anyone with access to the embassy and full background details on all of them. We don't have the time. If you find something pointing at someone specific, we'll see what we can do."

"I understand, Rown. So, who do we have of note?"

"There's Gwyan. Telas's son and Sarrepo's nephew."

"Been staying here long?"

"Lives here. Frequently away on long trips, though; trading and diplomatic, apparently."

"Has he been to Tarlenia?" When Rown just shrugged, Kalainen asked, "And with Sarrepo and Telas dead, does he take over as ambassador? Convenient. A good motive - if he wanted to be ambassador. Tell me, Rown, what changes will there be if Gwyan is made ambassador?"

"I think he is in favour of the treaty between Shaddimur and Bruel just as Sarrepo was. But he's a trader. Maybe he had worked out some deal that will cascade gold if the treaty fails – or even if Tarlenia invaded."

"That's a lot of supposition."

"True. But if necessary, it could turn out to be the case."

"You'd make him look guilty?"

"If it could stop a war, save my city, I'd make it look like you assassinated them all." When Kalainen didn't speak, Rown changed topic. "Also present is Esferle, a woman from O-Ram. She and Gwyan aren't married but they seem a couple."

"I know little of O-Ram."

"Well, I know precisely nothing. Gwyan met this woman on a trading mission and they hit it off. She's quite a girl. Common knowledge that they met when she won a camel race and a tent-pegging competition on the same day. Perfectly capable of killing a few guards, I think."

"Why would she do that?"

"If Gwyan wins, she wins. Who knows what O-Ram wants?"

"Have they been together long?"

Rown shrugged another answer. "Many months, at least."

"Has Gwyan changed in that time; habits or views?"

The sergeant stopped abruptly and faced Kalainen. "I have no idea. I've never had occasion to study the background of all transitory migrants. If you think I'm floundering here, so are you."

Kalainen smiled at him. "You're right. The highest fruit is picked by the birds – but sometimes the monkey climbs the tree. Let's keep climbing."

Rown was about to reply when his shoulders slumped and he gave a soft chuckle instead. "I see what Traid means. Anyway, this is Telas's room, and I don't think the monkey will like this."

"By the bell of Mirrin's Tower – wanted to make sure they were dead, didn't he? Place looks like a slaughterhouse. Very nearly severed the head with one, no, two blows. Then stabbed Telas through the mouth. Or perhaps the stab came between two decapitating blows."

"What conceivable difference does it make?" said Rown, turning from the bed. Blood had fountained over the wall. There were streaks and smears of red everywhere.

"To Telas, none whatever. I'm trying to build a picture. These deaths all look to have been caused by a pointed, straight blade with both sides sharpened. One killer, or two with similar weapons? I look for left and right-handed strikes. This could mean left and right-handed killers, or an ambidextrous killer or a killer so adept that they thrust either way with equal force depending on the opening available to them."

"Have you learned anything?"

"Six dead and not much to go on. There isn't a way of assessing fighting style."

"Come on, back downstairs." They clumped off towards a back

stairway. Before they reached it, Rown said, "You've gone quiet. What are you thinking?"

"It's an awfully long way from Sarrepo's room to Telas's."

"Different wing. So?"

"It's difficult to move quietly on these hard floors. It took time and must have considerably increased the risk, however good the inside information. Why kill Telas?"

The stairs were narrow and uneven with a fusty air. Rown took them gingerly, as though a knee pained him. "I suppose Telas would have been ambassador. Puts young Gwyan right up there, doesn't it?" he said at last.

"Would the ambassadorship really be worth killing your own father? What would have been different if Telas had been ambassador? If he would have continued Sarrepo's policies, was it important to take out both of them?"

They emerged into a small parlour. There were two women sitting at a table, cleaning cutlery with rags. Their conversation snapped off as they took in Rown's uniform and they looked up with comically guilty faces, eyes bulging. Rown glared at them for a moment, then flapped a hand at them.

"Give us a moment, will you?" As soon as they had hurried out like flustered hens, he turned back to Kalainen. "It has to be something political, surely. Gwyan certainly looks set to benefit and this would seem to include Esferle as well. We're now dealing with relationships between the cities. It is probably better that Esferle is from O-Ram rather than another of the Seven but I'm no expert beyond the bounds of Shaddimur. Doubtless Aldarilen the Loremaster would enjoy demonstrating his vast knowledge. Do you want to talk to him?"

"Not particularly. He just wants me to pin the blame on anyone providing Shaddimur can duck any responsibility. You seem pretty well informed on the seven cities."

Rown chuckled drily. "Well, maybe some in Bruel want to throw their hand in with Tarlenia. If an invasion is going to happen and they are going to lose, always some that want to be on the winning side. Any of these people could be a Tarlenian stooge."

"Sergeant, we think all the other killings of notables have been done by one person. We can't prove it yet. But what a great play it would be to have this murder done by someone else – and have us discover that. Put Tarlenia in the clear, wouldn't it?"

"If they're as devious as you are, we're in a lot of trouble. This could be your killer, or someone pretending to be him or not. If we find a Tarlenian without proof, they'll deny it and we're no further forward. If it's a local man, it supports the Tarlenian story of a plot in Shaddimur. And if it's someone from another state, Shaddimur alienates them and we are close to some fool starting a pogrom and the city tearing itself apart. My head aches just thinking about it. I'll tell you straight, Drouhin; I'm with Aldarilen on this. If I could manufacture evidence on anyone," he looked apologetically at Kalainen, "On anyone at all, to save the city, I'd do it in a heartbeat."

Kalainen gave a rueful smile, putting his hand on the Sergeant's shoulder. "For all the right reasons. But it means the evidence we find has to be solid. You were telling me of the remaining personnel."

"I appreciate that the best assassin would likely be someone completely minor and invisible, but if it were someone masquerading as a flunkey, they would be long gone. I've taken an inventory of staff and they're all still here. The only other significant figure is Serian. Don't know whether they'd call him a major-domo or a factor or a butler but he is head of the staff. Seems shrewd and intelligent but he's sealed tighter than a lead coffin and gives precisely nothing away. He's been here for about twenty years."

"You don't trust him?"

Rown grunted. "It's not that. Distrusting Serian would be like kicking over a statue of the Lady. He's not obsequious but he wears deference like icy armour. I feel like a piece of dirt he has to send a maid to sweep up. I'd like to kick his toe just to see if he reacts, but picture him as a killer, after twenty years and with nothing apparently to gain? Can't do it."

"Thanks. I'll need to talk to them all, separately, if you can arrange it. Just another thought; money is ever a great motivator. Will Gwyan inherit anything else from Sarrepo or Telas?"

"Good question. No doubt you can ask. I'll set up your interviews."

"Thanks again. Then I'll have to meet my team at the Silver Hart."

"Wish I were doing the same," muttered Rown on his way out.

Standing contemplatively, Kalainen gazed into the embassy garden. Neatly tended beds of white armeria and dianthus; low hedges of oleander, an arch flowing with passion flowers; a seat in a nook to catch the evening sun. It could look delightful, or it could look like a place designed for quiet intrigue with nowhere for eavesdroppers or assassins to hide.

A discrete faux cough behind him made Kalainen jump. Serian posed as a statue of rectitude behind him.

"I understand you have local authority investigating this murder, sir. A modicum of straightening was performed before I was able to advise the staff to desist as evidence might be lost. I apologise if this impedes your work."

"Straightening? Moving the bodies and washing the scene?"

"Exactly so, sir."

Looking up into Serian's imperturbable face, Kalainen could read nothing at all. Did the inscrutability mask something? He decided to try to wrong foot the major-domo.

"A single ring was missing from the ambassador's hand!"

"Yes, sir."

192 ~ ACM PRIOR

That produced the reaction in Kalainen that he had being trying to provoke in Serian. "What do you know of the ring?"

"It was the ambassadorial signet."

Kalainen nodded to himself. "Of course. Just the sort of thing the killer would remove."

"Naturally, I took the ring, sir."

"You took it? Where is it now, Serian?"

"As Gwyan is acting ambassador, I considered it best that he had it. I gave it to him."

"Ah. Hm, yes. Why were the inside guards Gallendian?"

"That would be a decision for the ambassador. Naturally you would not expect him to include me in such deliberations."

"No, no, but you might have heard....? No. Well, is anything else missing?

"Not that I am aware of as yet, sir."

"Was Sarrepo a wealthy man?"

"I am hardly privy to the ambassador's private finances, sir."

Kalainen was tapping his fingers together, his lips becoming pursed, but he tried to match Serian's unvarying tones. "If Telas had not been killed, would the ambassadorship have passed to him?"

"I imagine that is likely."

"So how would things have changed with him in charge?"

Serian's lips thinned slightly, in what Kalainen was beginning to interpret as a wild show of emotion. "It is not my place to offer opinion, sir. All other things being equal, there would have been more parties in the embassy and a rather higher bill at the vintners."

"What about major policy decisions?"

"I couldn't possibly comment. Perhaps he could have been more easily influenced."

"Yes, I see. Would he have been a good ambassador, do you think?"

"It's really not for me to say, sir." There was a silence with

Kalainen just looking at Serian until he continued, "I expect he would have been swiftly replaced with someone more dedicated to the diplomatic life."

"Serian, who might benefit from his death?"

Serian raised his eyebrows but offered no further comment.

Rown appeared, grinning at Kalainen's discomfiture. "Acting ambassador Gwyan awaits in the day room. You don't have long. Let me know what you can later."

The Silver Hart

'Kalainen, Yanni and Imber were sitting at a table in the Silver Hart's snug. While Kalainen and Imber talked in low tones, Yanni was looking nervously at an enormous mastiff which stared back at her.

"Don't worry," said Kalainen, "I'm sure it's quite safe."

"No doubt it conkin' well is. What about me?"

Kalainen smiled reassuringly. "It'll be fine with normal patrons," he said, holding out a hand towards the dog. The mastiff's ears went down and it began to curl its lip. "But perhaps we'll just leave it alone."

Three people clattered into the Silver Hart, dressed in long robes with stylised elongated figures stitched into the dark fabric. They were chattering in sharp accents, one giving a honking little laugh. The dog padded across towards them, herding them towards the bar like flustered deer. Yanni relaxed but Imber still watched the dog silently, eyelids half-lowered.

Kalainen appeared to approve the louder background noise. "How did your nose round town go," he asked quietly.

Imber eventually dragged his eyes from the mastiff and turned to the Drouhin. "What first?"

"Gwyan."

"Commonly said to be in favour of the Shaddimur / Bruel treaty. Bit odd; he's a trader but spends a lot of time not doing anything. Then suddenly does a huge deal. No specific commodity. Just seems to wait and pounce in a big way when he finds something."

"Meaning what?"

"Probably good information network."

"Spies? Like Tertius Orbis and Kari Witchet?"

"Maybe."

"You don't think his connections through the embassies would be enough?"

Imber shrugged. "Possibly. He's also had dealings with Tarlenia."

"Interesting. What about Esferle?"

Imber shook his head. "She's from O-Ram. Nobody knows anything."

"Hm. I suppose a quick scout round for eye-witnesses came up blank?"

"Nothing, and no plants set by anyone for disinformation either. Plenty of gossips, all sniffing for nuggets to reinforce their own bigotry, in whatever direction."

"Nothing from local street girls?"

"This is the embassy district!"

"No beggars, urchins, late night revellers? Someone must have seen something! We may have a killer wandering about covered in blood from earhole to breakfast and suddenly the city's deserted!"

Imber made no reply but waved a hand gently to suggest Kalainen kept his voice lower. The Drouhin smeared a hand over his head and sighed.

"What about the ambassador?"

"Sarrepo's been a long-term ambassador. He's overseen the gradual rapprochement between the two city states from standard distrust to this near treaty. Good reputation for honesty and sincerity, maintained through the old regime and under the new queen. No hint of him doing anything underhand."

"And Telas?"

"Everyone likes Telas. Telas liked good food, wine and a party."

"Women?"

"Liked women in general. Didn't get entangled, no word of lechery."

"But what does he do? What's he good at?"

"Can sink a flask of wine while ordering a second. Brilliant with people. The man everyone wants at a party. Great raconteur, sings a rollicking song, plays endless games with cards and coins. He's a magician at making things disappear, finding them again."

"Could be a cover for information gathering. Maybe he was working with Gwyan, they could have fallen out?"

Imber made a doubtful face. "If that's a cover, it's superb. He never talks about trade or politics but he knows everyone's name and remembers their families. And he doesn't seem to fall out with anyone. Just likes people." Envy seemed to lift Imber's tone.

"So why kill him?" The silence round the table waited for new ideas. Kalainen sighed more volcanically than before. "To sort this mess, I need something from the background, relationships, opinions and personal problems of Gwyan and Telas. Perhaps you can find some merchant from Bruel who had dealings with them. Some émigré from Bruel who knows of a scurrilous past. Who knows, Telas may have gambled too badly – or too well – in some disreputable haunt..."

"Never played for money."

Kalainen threw himself back in his chair with a groan just as

Quern came into the Silver Hart. The big man dropped into a spare chair with a huge yawn and scratched his beard. He grinned a hello and poured himself a mug of beer from the jug on the table. Yawning again, he drew a teardrop shape over the beer. He touched the surface and dotted the foam on his forehead before taking a long draught.

"Why do you do that, Quern?" asked Yanni.

Quern looked at her sidelong and sighed. "It's me Mam, really. If I didn't show my respect to the Lady, she'd still give me a clout!"

"Why doesn't everyone then?"

"We all hear the same bell, but we pray to different gods," put in Kalainen.

Quern made a face, then grinned and flicked froth at Yanni, who giggled. "What gem have you gleaned then, Scrappy?"

"Nothing. But they all know something we don't. Something awful."

"Any idea what?"

"None. But something bad."

Waving at a pot boy for a pie for Quern, Kalainen said, "I think you're right. You get back into it and find it, Yanni. Find it! Don't give me a spoon when the pie is gone. Quern, tell me you learned something useful this morning."

"Oh yes. Um." Quern took another pull at the beer, then sat up straight and squared his shoulders. "The two guards from Shaddimur were Larno and Timmis. They've been doing the nightwork at the Bruelan embassy for years; worked a full shift without a break, if you can call sitting and nattering like two old ladies working. They were expected to take their own food with them to work. The two I spoke to, Morl and Shandir, reckoned the guarding was a soft billet and wanted to do more. Easy money. They did say one interesting thing. Some weeks ago, there was a spell of bad weather. A girl, Dessia, started bringing out a posset of wine each night. Of course, the Shaddimur boys suspiciously thought it was some trick to catch them drinking at their post and they refused. Then first one, then both enjoyed the drink. Larno told Morl about it, so then he and Timmis just wolfed it down when it arrived. It became an accepted ritual.

"I managed to track down Dessia. Sweet-natured little thing, pretty dimples. Anyway, she was given the drink by some man and paid a helm a night to take it out. I asked for a description and she said she didn't know, really. I asked if he had a Tarlenian accent and she said she didn't know really, maybe. Would have said the same if I'd asked if he was blue. Still, she did say he was frightening and she thought he might have had oiled hair. She was told the posset was a gift from the embassy. She never thought to ask why it didn't come from the embassy kitchens."

"So, you went to see Dessia, and that was the end of the morning, was it?"

"Well, it took time to winkle out the details, you know?"

"No doubt it did. Maybe Dessia wasn't very bright, but she might well have been bright enough to know that the flow of helms would stop if she asked questions. It's evidence of a long-term strategy. Anything else?"

"Morl mentioned that Larno gambled a bit."

"Yes, we know."

"Going past, so scouted his lodgings," put in Imber. "Found a lustrous pearl worth perhaps fifty ryals and around half that in coinage. Doubt he's in debt."

"Perhaps he was caught cheating?" Kalainen wondered. "Did you talk to Timmis's wife?"

As Imber shook his head, Quern said, "Timmis had a w...? No, no, haven't got to her yet."

"Nothing on the indoor guards? They were Gallendians. Could have been sleeping agents of Tarlenia, posing as loyal guards only to turn on the Bruelen ambassador at the right time. If they are blamed, xenophobia will run riot."

"But they're dead!"

"So they can't argue the point. Sleeping agents could become a risk and be disposed of. Makes things even more polarised."

Quern put his hands on his head and pretended to pull out his hair. "Aaahh! Just give me someone to clout. This goes round and round and we get nowhere!"

At that moment, Mardenifol came in at the lope. He had to go through all his thought processes and activities while Kalainen nodded and made approving noises. Eventually it occurred to Mardenifol that everyone else was eating pie and saying nothing.

"How are you getting on at the embassy?"

"We're amassing an ever bigger pile of questions and accrue suspects by the hour. On the plus side, Imber found a few slivers of broken glass." Kalainen was listlessly shovelling bits of pastry into his mouth.

Mardenifol frowned thoughtfully. "Where from?"

"About where the outside guards fell."

"That could be it," cried Mardenifol, rummaging in his pack. "That's proof enough! Show me! I've got glass from the broken jars. Compare this with your glass and when they match it'll prove the murders are linked!" He unfolded some bits of one of Madam Vermoil's jars from a rag. "There! They are...."

"Totally different," said Yanni. "Yours are thick and a bit cloudy. These bits are thinner and clear as air."

"Furthermore, yours still have a scent of herbs and soil," said Kalainen, putting them to his nose. "Perhaps I imagine it, but I think to detect a fugitive hint of wine from these. The glass we found is high quality. The sort of thing that might grace an ambassador's table rather than a guard's refectory. The curve and make would be consistent with a good wine glass. We have asked around with the staff. Nobody admits to seeing any glass there nor clearing it up. Perhaps a maid broke a glass and fears to get into trouble if this is known."

"Must be Dessia's glasses," Quern said, "but she didn't mention anything breaking. Perhaps I should go back..."

"Hmf. Well, I still suspect someone was concocting, if not a poison, at least some potion of debilitation. I must get back to my ingredients and stuff soon." Mardenifol stabbed into his pie and smiled happily as a rich sauce bled out, steaming a waft of garlic and rosemary.

After a while of steady eating, Quern waved his beer mug round thoughtfully. "If Mard's right and the two Shaddimur guards were drugged into a stupor – which fits with the way they were killed – why kill them at all?"

"They must have known something," suggested Mardenifol. "Killing them must be something of a risk. Must have been a delay when the killer could've been spotted; and after all, dead and bloody guards would rouse a quicker alarm than two sleepers. Must be a good reason!"

"True. Perhaps he wanted two fewer people onto him if the alarm were raised."

"They never twitched," said Kalainen. "The killer pushed a blade behind the windpipe and cut the carotid arteries. They bled out like trussed goats. Is there a potion that can do that?"

"Maybe the killer's just a conkin' bastard what liked doing it," said Yanni.

Kalainen snorted softly even as he waved an admonitory finger at Yanni for her language. "Hm. Whoever it is, I don't think we're going to get along."

"Mard told me about clerics what can speak with the dead," Yanni said round a mouthful. "Why not just call up Sarrepo's shade and ask him who yerked him?"

Imber froze motionless, his hooded eyes darkening. Quern sat up straighter, brows drawing down into a frown, beard bristling. As his mouth opened, the Drouhin half-lifted a hand for peace and spoke in his quiet drawl.

"I have also heard many seers, mediums and necromancers say they can speak with the departed. A few problems with that. First, necromancy in all its forms, most definitely including summoning back the shades of the dead, is considered an evil desecration in Shaddimur. Even if such a rite were performed, I've been told that being dead gives people a very different perspective on things and any answers they give tend to be tangential at best. On top of that, from what we can tell, both Telas and Sarrepo were killed in their beds and they probably don't have the least idea who wielded the blade. But in the end, it doesn't make any difference, does it? Because even if Sarrepo told us exactly who he'd been killed by, it still couldn't be used as evidence, and even if it could that would put the Queen of Shaddimur on the side of necromancy which would be one of the few things to guarantee making the situation worse."

His frustration was so clear from his rising tone that Imber spoke to ease the tension. "What've you got on the suspects from the embassy?"

Kalainen pushed his trencher away with exaggerated care. "I suppose Gwyan leads the field. He's stepped into the ambassador's shoes, at least for now, which gives him some power. He is a trader between the cities and may have some larger plan for enrichment. Could also be Esferle, a woman from O-Ram."

"You've spoken to them? What did you think?"

Kalainen watched a foursome of bureaucrats from Correbaran enter, sombre-faced, their eyes flicking round the snug as though fearing lurking devils. "Gwyan wore rich clothes," he said. "But he's young and fit and his hands are used to hard work. He gains access to everything in the Embassy and takes over as the Ambassador manqué. If he wanted this position or some item badly enough, he was well placed and though he pretends no great military skill, how much would he need to strike down unsuspecting people? A likely suspect, likelier still to be set-up as a scapegoat by Rown and Aldarilen. He's self-controlled and dignified; possibly a mask for grief. Could it be a mask for a cold-hearted murderer who has killed his own father and uncle? I can't see it. He seems mostly concerned about his own city but also worries about the effect all this will have on Esferle. He told me that Telas would never have been made ambassador, his father being the most likeable man but thoroughly unsuitable for the role. He is, or was, a keen party man and raconteur, a wonder with his tricks but he had neither political nous nor ambition.

"When I asked about what he or Bruel could gain, Gwyan suggested bitterly that I should be asking what Shaddimur would gain from the death. He implied there were some in Shaddimur who did not want the alliance with Bruel, and who would sooner let Bruel fall before Tarlenia rather than risk their own city. He said they might even kill for that. And we know he's right.

"Esferle at least seems very upset. She is a strapping lass and fit - she used to race camels and was a champion tent-pegger but doesn't visibly carry any weapons. She thinks 'they' will think Gwyan did it for some ambition or try to pin it on her just because she's from O-Ram. She said Sarrepo and Telas were both kind to her and it just wasn't fair.

"Overall, they make an unlikely pair but they do seem more than fond of each other. They met eight months ago when Gwyan was considering trade arrangements by ship to O-Ram."

"I heard Gwyan's a merchant of daring and skill," put in Imber. "Recently turned down a lucrative deal to provide material for the Tarlenian military machine. Met Esferle on a trading mission to O-Ram and now hopes to set up a deal trading with O-Ram through

Shaddimur. The deal with Bruel is essential for this given their deeper port and keeled ships."

"Could be a front but more likely true," conceded Kalainen. "They plan to marry but haven't done so. Whether their partnership would lead them to performing some dire act in concert either through ambition or coercion, well, that's harder to say. I can see why Esferle is quite open in her worries about xenophobia blaming her, evidence or not."

"Did you ask whether anything had been stolen?"

"I did. Both looked completely blank. Gwyan icily observed that taking a full inventory of the embassy had not been his first priority. Don't blame him."

"Don't think it's them, do you?" asked Imber.

"No. If Gwyan can be properly arraigned, that will suffice for Aldarilen - but it's wrong. They don't fit the pattern. Similarly, if it were me, I'd have got an assassin to do the killing this time while I provided myself with a perfect alibi. I cannot get it to feel right. This killer is someone who's showing off, proving they can do what they like. They aren't going to delegate the last and most important murder to someone else."

"So, is it our killer, or someone different?"

"There are two problems with it being our man. First, something has always been stolen. This time there doesn't seem to be anything missing. Second, the manner of the deaths; Telas and Sarrepo were both messily butchered. No other killing has been like that. Our killer has taken life with economy and precision. Everything he's done has been measured. Why were these killings so brutal? Not normally the way it's been done by our man."

"So if it was him, why would he do that, then? Surely you aren't asking a question when you don't know the answer!" Quern teased, forcing the Drouhin to focus his intellect.

Kalainen frowned down at the table, his voice slowed. "Either this is a different killer, or he wanted it to look like a different killer ... no." Kalainen suddenly looked up, eyes sparkling like lamps. "No, what does everyone do in those two ghastly rooms, those splattered and reeking scenes of carnage?"

"Take one look at the corpses and get out as quick as conkin' possible."

"Exactly. It's so awful, you aren't looking at anything else. I've only had a brief glimpse, but there is something else to find, something we've missed so far. Something he didn't want us to see. Come on!" Kalainen was on his feet, hissing instructions. "Keep on Madam Vermoil, Mard. Yanni, ferret out what the embassy staff know that we don't. Quern, talk to any Watchmen but we may need your strength on site. Imber, with me." And he was gone.

Return to the Bruelan Embassy

As they hurried back towards the Bruelan embassy, Kalainen was muttering with his head down.

"The guards were dispatched with the ruthless efficiency we've come to expect from our killer. We guess that Sarrepo and Telas have been killed in such a brutal way because it draws all attention and stops us looking further in those rooms. But this still leaves us with the big question; the crux to this puzzle. Why kill Telas? Why?" He paused in the street to look round his companions and catch his breath. "It's a circuitous route through the building, with inevitable risk, to kill Telas. He knew how to do it, thanks to Tertius Orbis, but this doesn't appear to make any sense." Kalainen set off again at a quick walk, still puffing a commentary. "We can't find anything that would have – or would not have – happened had Telas been ambassador. We only hear that he might never have been ambassador anyway, and had he been, it would have been very temporary."

"Maybe the killer just didn't like him," said Quern, his giant legs untired by the pace. "Or he was jealous of Telas's easy popularity."

"Perhaps, although we've never seen a shred of personal feelings before. But there are two puzzles: why is nothing missing, why kill Telas? Suppose Telas had what the killer wanted to steal? Ambassador Sarrepo was killed to further Tarlenian plans, but then our killer can't find what he wants when he ransacks the room. So he goes to Sarrepo's brother's room and finds – or at least searches - there. Telas is killed because Telas had whatever he wanted?"

The Drouhin paused by the pot-bound trees outside the embassy, turning to Quern. "Talk to any Watchmen you can but stay handy. Eyes open." He glanced at Imber. "Telas's room first. Work your magic!"

Kalainen and Imber hastened to Telas's room, the Drouhin still talking, mostly to himself. "If this follows the pattern, there will be something stolen. If Telas had what was wanted, it explains why he was killed. But am I asking the impossible? Can even you find something that isn't there? How do you find out what's missing after it's been taken?"

"You noticed the ambassadorial signet was gone by a mark on the finger and smeared blood. Everything leaves a mark. Maybe a patch of wood slightly less bleached by the sun, a bit of wall discoloured in a square, a curl of decoration that has never seen the maid's duster suddenly exposed."

There were two windows in Telas's room, one to the left of the bed and one on the right-hand wall from where they stood by the door, opposite the foot of the bed. The floor of polished wooden boards was made homely with a goatskin by the bed and a woven rug from O-Ram which looked new, the swirls of red and blue vibrant and unfaded. Kalainen wondered if it had been a present from Esferle. Everything was spotted and splashed with blood. Imber stood at a corner of the bed and stared at the floor, just absorbing the smudges and blots where feet had scuffed blood and printed marks. Then he moved slowly round the room, hoping a different slant of light might show up a new mark, a tiny depression in a rug.

"How can you hope to see anything useful after we've been in here before, the Watch have blundered about and half the staff have been cleaning, wailing or gawping?"

"Since the bloodbath, only one person has been into Telas's dressing room. Probably Rown. Cursory look, no more. Only place anyone could have searched is this table by the bed – might have just been looking at the body." Imber looked along the surface of the table for dust marks. He eased open a small drawer in the table and spent a few moments staring at the contents; a rumpled handkerchief, a striker, spare belts, a battered silver box of pins and brooches, a length of gold chain, a hair brush, a small tub of unlabelled cream with an astringent aroma and a bottle of scent. Everywhere, Imber checked for secret drawers or loose panels. When Imber had finished studying the floor, Kalainen moved slowly round the room. He picked up a few beads of red stone and stared at them in sudden horror.

"Imber?"

"I know. Trouble."

At that moment, Rown looked in and called the Drouhin over with a jerk of his head. He looked grim.

"Sent a man down to the harbour. He spoke to Lengan Perse, owner of the *Dainty Belle*. Sharp enough in his way. He talked of a Tarlenian cog doing a regular trade run, and if it's on schedule, should be in tomorrow."

"Tomorrow!"

"Yes. My man checked the records with the harbour master and

Lengan's right. You've got lots of good questions, but we don't have the manpower and we certainly don't have the time to deal with background checks on minor flunkeys. It's no good looking at me like that; right or wrong, I have to do something before the Tarlenian ambassadorial group leaves. Tomorrow. I have to arrest Gwyan. Then there'll be no need for the Tarlenian to leave."

"That is not going to work. Not now, Rown. You'd better see these."

The Sergeant came in with a wary look. "What?"

Kalainen held out a hand. Three beads shivered in his palm; carnelian, coral and agate. Rown looked up, trying to hide the fear in his face.

"Just a few beads. What of them?"

"Everyone knew the Cape of the Avatar was torn after the tournament. You know it's made of beads just like this. Look over here." Kalainen pointed out another bead on the floor. There was a blob of blood on it. "What does that mean to you?"

"The beads were here before the blood. Nothing to do with the murder, then."

"Good luck convincing anyone of that when they have bloody beads from the Avatar's Cape in the murdered man's bedroom. But it's worse than that. All the blood sprayed about in this room splashes when it hits walls and floors. You can tell from the splash which way the blood was moving. Not this drop. It is perfectly even all round. It fell straight down onto the bead. Someone deliberately dripped blood on this bead. Where it would be found. I'm sure these are not beads from the Cape. But they look as though they are. And they're right here, covered in Sarrepo's blood."

"Balgrim's bloody beard. If this gets out..."

"It's already out."

"No!"

"Rown, how many people have been in here, opening drapes, laying out the body?"

"I don't know. Could be a dozen."

"There are beads everywhere. What chance that nobody spotted even one when they were starting to clean. Yanni said the staff were abuzz with some secret. Want to guess what those two women were discussing when we went down the back stairs?"

"They've set Shen up! Lady's tears – this is a conkin' disaster!"

Kalainen's slow smile was sad. Rown was prepared to fake evidence to help his city but was shocked someone else would do the same, and do it better with advance planning. "You have some circumstantial evidence to implicate Gwyan. They have much better circumstantial evidence it was Shen. Makes it a lot harder to prove it was someone else."

"Ghulsk, we're conked. I've got to get word to Traid. Shaddimur's going to explode." Rown spun away and hurried down the corridor. His boot sent a bead ricocheting across the boards, punctuating his oaths as he went.

"Rown," Kalainen called after him. "I asked Aldarilen to see if there was any way the Loremasters could stall a ship. If he can do it, now would be good." The sergeant waved an arm in acknowledgement but said no more.

The Drouhin was gazing down the corridor after Rown, lost in thought until Imber tapped him on the shoulder.

"I'm not the best tracker but no evidence of searching here."

Kalainen chewed his lip. "He came straight from Sarrepo to here. We said he'd know how to from Tertius Orbis. But he wouldn't have bothered with that information unless he planned to kill Telas. So I was wrong; he intended to do it all along. Not because of something he couldn't find in Sarrepo's room. Why did he kill Telas?"

Imber shrugged. "Search Sarrepo's room?"

The Drouhin nodded and they plodded back to the ambassador's chamber, their failure making the way seem further, occasional red beads mocking them as they went. Serian was waiting for them, standing guard.

"Sir, the gentleman from the Shaddimur watch has insisted I speak to you before the body is moved, as the current ambassador has now instructed. The ambassador believes you have had adequate opportunity to study the scene and further delay now is disrespectful to the departed and the whole city of Bruel."

"Your generous cooperation has been an inspiration to all dealings between the city states. Perhaps you could give us a few moments more, then please make such arrangements as are appropriate."

The butler inclined his head and glided away, leaving them alone. Inside the bedroom, the stench from the gutted corpse was becoming much harder to ignore, even with the windows open. There was no evidence of any searching, let alone random ransacking. Still, Imber went through all his checks again with quiet imperturbability. Kalainen stood tossing a bloodstone bead from hand to hand while his mind whirled backward and forward over the evidence. He ignored a rising susurrus from staff waiting outside the door, low murmurs swelling into audible remarks about how some people had proper work to do and how difficult such labours were made by the thoughtlessness and disrespect of others. Finally, Imber moved to a small chest of drawers. "Here," he said.

"Here what?"

"So many footprints in here. Everyone has trodden in blood to some degree. All leave prints."

"There's a bloody path from the door to the bed even I can spot. Then footprints go in every direction in the room!"

"Yes. They are all going somewhere; to the bed, the doors, the windows. But see here." Imber pointed to the merest hint of a line. "See?"

"See what, my friend?"

"That is the outside of a boot print. It isn't part of a stride, it isn't going anywhere. Whoever made that print stood here facing these drawers. Standing, not crouching. Now... Look here," Imber indicated a minuscule brown smear that might have been blood on the underside of a drawer handle. "This is the one."

He eased open the drawer. It contained two pressed linen handkerchiefs and a small sachet of lavender.

"Nothing there," said Kalainen. "Has something been removed?"

Imber shook his head. "What do you notice about the lock?"

"Hm. Keyhole is undamaged, no scratches, no sign of use. Looks ordinary brass lock. I wonder if it was locked when the killer came?"

Imber shook his head again. He ran a finger along the upper side of the drawer frame in the chest. "No recess. It never locks. The keyhole's blind. Don't need a key for this one." Imber's long finger pressed down on what looked like the lock. It sank slightly. There was a click and the bottom of the drawer sprang open revealing a compartment. Inside was a thin box, a little bigger than his palm, covered in a ribbed material. After a glance at the Drouhin, Imber opened the box to reveal a cushioned pad with a deep indentation where something the size of an eglantine blossom had been removed.

"Far as I can see, only thing that was touched. Knew exactly where to go, didn't he? Tertius Orbis earned her money. Why didn't he take the box? Quicker and leaves no evidence?"

"When we know what it is, we'll know. My guess is that he either used it or wore it. It's all about pride, remember."

Slipping the box into a pocket, Kalainen watched as Imber reset the drawer panel, and replaced everything as it had been. As Imber pushed the drawer closed, he turned to Kalainen. "So, he knew what he wanted and exactly where it was. He killed Sarrepo first and stole a specific item. Then Telas."

"Yes, he knew where to go. But back to the same question: why kill Telas?"

"Because of *what* he stole?"

"Yes. We're getting somewhere. Need to know what this was. Perhaps Gwyan or Serian will know." With that, they left the ambassador's room to a troop of staff and funerary clerics, few of whom managed to conceal their horror at the sights and gut-wrenching reek.

When they were shown in to see Gwyan, the new ambassador was with Esferle in an office. Esferle was sitting awkwardly on a sofa as if she had just dropped onto it. Her hair was long and thick, piled into a dark brown mound, but some tresses had escaped and cascaded round her neck. Gwyan faced the door. He was thin but had wide shoulders. His beard was neatly trimmed and his eyes were bright, but they had a panicked air. Kalainen's glance picked out the corner of a pack kicked behind a chair. In an otherwise neat room, a couple of desk drawers were not quite closed. Kalainen noticed that Gwyan now wore an arming sword and winced.

"What?" Gwyan sounded on the verge of violence.

"Unfortunate choice of blade; it's the same sort that was used to kill the ambassador, your father, and all the others last night."

"Ah yes, the Shaddimur snoop gathers mythical evidence to hang us both," Gwyan snapped, one hand falling to the hilt as he moved towards the Drouhin.

"You are alert to the situation and expect Rown to arrest you. I assure you that will not happen. You need not flee."

Gwyan paused, exchanged a glance with Esferle, then looked back at Kalainen. There was no trust in his face but he didn't do anything as the Drouhin hooked a chair and sat down. Behind him Imber lounged unremarked against the door.

"You're collecting items you consider vital and plan to leave before you are arrested. There's no need to try. Fresh Gallendian guards will arrive. Morl and Shandir of Shaddimur will resume your protection tonight."

"My confidence in protection is not high. And how can you convince me we will not be arrested?"

"Because you didn't do it."

Gwyan barked a bitter laugh.

"Because whoever did it left beads apparently from the Cape of the Avatar of Sunsunni all over the embassy to frame Shen."

"Shen could have done it."

"Perhaps – but he didn't."

"Arresting me will cover that up as well."

"It won't. Too many people know of the beads. It would just look as if we were trying to frame you to clear Shen and so prove Shaddimur's guilt. But I think I know who murdered your father and uncle."

"And you can't prove it to sceptics which leaves me with a trumped-up motive, the means dangling at my side here and all the opportunity I could want. I am not convinced of your sincerity, still less of your ability to help me." When the Drouhin remained quiet, Gwyan looked at him. Slowly a frown deepened across his face. At the same time, Imber stood up straighter near the door, also staring at Kalainen. "You think you can!"

"It's possible. May I ask some questions?" When Gwyan lifted an eyebrow, he took out the box and said, "This was in a secret compartment in a drawer in Sarrepo's room. It is empty. Do you know what was in it?"

"By the Sacred Text, how did you find that?"

"That's not important. There have been many murders in Shaddimur recently, all of prominent citizens. In each case, something valuable has been stolen. But just one item. Does whatever was in this box meet that criterion?"

Something seemed to drain from Gwyan and his lean form crumpled into a chair like a falling drape. "I had no idea where that was. But that box can only have held the Feyhan Star." Seeing blank looks, Gwyan continued, "An almost unique high honour, bestowed on my uncle after a very successful diplomatic mission to Caronile in Belmenia."

Kalainen nodded. "Thank you. Can you describe it?"

The ambassador shrugged. "I've hardly ever seen it. Not for years, anyway. It was made by Feyhan, the foremost jeweller of Bruel. Enamelled petals encased in silver round a pearl centre. Some runes, I think. The whole thing seemed to shine with lilac light."

Kalainen shot away on a different tack. "Your father Telas, he was quite the man for party tricks."

"He was frivolous and carefree." Gwyan's tone left it unclear whether he despised this or envied it. "He made coins disappear and reappear in someone's beard. Flicked his fingers to make cards vanish and then unerringly found them in some gasping woman's shawl."

"Would he have performed his tricks at a top-level diplomatic function with other ambassadors present?"

"Would and did. He had no sense of dignity nor propriety. Nothing pleased him more than borrowing some diamond-heavy brooch from the staidest person present and have it vanish before their eyes. He'd track it across the room and pluck it from a soup tureen before he handed it back and left them studying the gems suspiciously as though he'd have purloined the real ones."

"Could he have found the Feyhan Star?"

Gwyan gaped at the Drouhin and answered with heat. "It wasn't real! My father called himself a magician, yes, but he wasn't a sorcerer! Telas was not the sort of man to hurt himself for power, or anything else for that matter."

"You're sure?"

"If he'd made the Star disappear, I'm sure he'd have found it. He did exactly that often enough. But he never did anything useful. If he lost a key, it was lost. He couldn't utter some cantrip and find it again."

Kalainen sat back with a wry smile. "I'm afraid his little trick with women's trinkets cost him his life."

"I don't understand you," Gwyan said mulishly.

"I do," put in Esferle quietly. "If Telas were alive, the killer thought he'd be able to find the Feyhan Star – which means he could identify the killer."

Gwyan became more strident. "But all you're telling me is that the killer is further ahead of us. He spotted a slim possibility that Telas could find the Star and he killed him. So we've lost my father, butchered mercilessly in his bed, and we can't find the Star – which we couldn't anyway - so we can't find the killer."

Kalainen looked sympathetically at the ambassador. "It's better that I don't tell you. A Tarlenian ship will probably arrive in Shaddimur tomorrow. The Tarlenians will leave, urging many other diplomats from the other cities to do the same. Will you give us this one night?"

"I suppose you think you can trot round to Aldarilen of the Loremasters so he can find it. I know something of these magicians, and I can tell you he'll say my vague recollections are insufficient and he needs to know the object intimately before he can find it and then only if he is practically close enough to smell it!"

"I'd assumed the same," said Kalainen softly.

"What do you need?" Esferle said after a pause, her hands scrunching the brocade fabric of the sofa. "And what can we do?"

"If Rown, Traid or someone from me calls you to bear witness, please go with them and send word to any reliable contacts in as many other embassies as you can."

Gwyan and Esferle exchanged a look.

218 - ACM PRIOR

"All right," said Gwyan. "I don't know what you're thinking of doing. But you'd better be right. I'll say no more."

"Thank you, Ambassador." Kalainen rose immediately and left with Imber a moon shadow behind him.

They were back at Coromal, Quern and Yanni having been sent to collect Mardenifol from the Herbiary. Kalainen and Imber sat with their heads almost touching across the table, speaking very quietly.

"I don't see it yet. We can't ask Aldarilen to find anything – all we have is an empty box and a vague description of the Feyhan Star."

"It's our murderer, Imber. All the places were robbed of some item. Telas found things."

"He found cards in pockets, made rings disappear and pulled them out of someone's ear. He is not a loremaster."

"I think the killer had seen Telas find some jewel at some ambassadorial soirée and had no idea how he'd done it. He couldn't take the chance of Telas finding the Star."

"Bit late now, he's dead and Aldarilen, the best of the Loremasters, can't do it. I'm still missing your point."

"The killer couldn't risk the Feyhan Star being found."

"He could have sold it on before Telas was awake, then it would be the buyer's problem to move it out of range of some spell to locate it."

Kalainen grinned in excitement, steepling his fingers beside his face. "So clearly that isn't true. We knew the places had been robbed, a single thing of great importance or value was taken. But you nosed about time and again for someone selling."

Imber nodded. There had been nothing.

"Which led us to imagine they were stolen to order which was why nobody was trying to sell them. We've assumed the items would have been swiftly moved to their new destinations. If some magician could find them, that would be the buyer's lookout. But suppose they aren't sold on."

"Why steal them?" Imber looked offended.

"Because it was the murder that mattered. The item was just a trophy, a memento for the killer to keep."

Imber shook his head slowly. "Other items could have been traced too. Why this one particularly?"

"This is the first item where one of the people who knew it well enough professed to be a magician. The killer thought Telas could find it by magic. So, it matters where it is found. And if it matters, we have to find it."

Imber remained silent, so Kalainen continued.

"We've climbed the knotted rope to the top and are left with a single explanation. There has been an important role for the Tarlenian with the oily hair. There has been a bigger role for the spy, Tertius Orbis. But that leaves us with the killer himself. One man, a superb swordsman with money and power. The Tarlenian who ran Tertius. We know from the affair of the tournament amulet that it went all the way up to ambassador Guzarin. We know he has a reputation as a peerless swordsman. Remember him saying that Astelin, the Tarlenian warrior in the tournament, wasn't the best in Tarlenia? It's him. Guzarin."

Silent, Imber looked at the Drouhin through hooded eyes.

"We need proof. There is no help from the Loremasters. The Watch cannot storm an embassy. We're going to have to do this the old way."

"You want me to break into the Tarlenian embassy – and find something even if I don't know what it is?"

"Not quite that bad. Going to be ten or a dozen items – from these murders that we know about."

Imber was silent for a moment. "That's a lot of trophies. Unless this is the only one he's kept."

"The spider always spins the same pattern."

"Going to be a big cache then."

"Exactly. And if he is keeping whatever he stole from Sarrepo's room, he thought Telas might be able to find it, which would incriminate him. It means he's still got it. I suppose with one item they could say we planted it. But all of them? If they're in the Tarlenian embassy, that would be our proof incontrovertible. We've got to find them."

"You're telling me to search the Tarlenian embassy?"

"No. I'm asking you. Can you break into the Tarlenian embassy and find all the stolen items?"

"Maybe possible if there are several things to find. There are better infiltration experts. Certainly one."

Kalainen looked at Imber for a while, then pursed his lips. "Tertius Orbis? Which is harder, breaking into the embassy, or finding Tertius Orbis, who may well be dead, and then persuading her to go into the embassy to do what we want – tonight?"

Imber raised his eyebrows, his wide mouth turning down at the corners.

"Would she do it?"

"Might depend how hard they tried to kill her, or whether they broke her out and freed her."

"Traid picked up some of the escaped prisoners. He said they were trying to kill her. Somehow, she freed herself and all the other prisoners and the whole thing developed into a running battle. There were several dead but she wasn't found. Could we trust her either way?"

Imber gave a small shrug which was not positive.

"I concede we did not part on friendly terms. We would be relying on her hatred of the Tarlenians after they cheated her out of the money and tried to kill her."

"Strong motive."

"But would she help us?"

"Double-cross us in a heartbeat if it was to her advantage."

"Would it be possible for you to go in together?"

Imber shook his head fractionally. "No. We both work alone. An extra person, however skilled, adds hugely to the risk. Sometimes there's only one place to hide."

"Is there anyone else, other than Tertius?"

"Wouldn't trust any of them. Only Tertius has the motivation."

"But?"

"She wouldn't trust us not to hand her back to Traid. If she did it, she'd probably try and leave one item for Traid and leg it with anything valuable she could carry."

"All assuming she is alive, and still in Shaddimur, and in a fit physical and mental state to do it."

"Another thing, the Tarlenians just tried to kill her. Just business. You out-thought and out-smarted her. Might hate you more than them."

"You need to change your definition of business." Kalainen thought for a moment. "Not going to work, is it?" He sighed, looking at Imber's head shaking. "And no word of Chelidor? Still wandering? We're on our own."

Quern came in with Yanni, bolting the door behind them. "Traid's right," rumbled the big man. "Rough out there. Fights breaking out, the Watch going in hard. Not nice."

"Where's Mard?"

"Mard? Thought he'd be back here. Herbiary was dark and locked up. No message or anything. Just assumed Vallis had knocked off the for the night and Mard would be here. If he's not..."

The Hind

After their lunch at the Silver Hart, Mardenifol collected a pie and a jar of small beer, then returned to the Herbiary. On the way, he bought supplies from a shop selling parchment, paper and inks, cheap reed pens and sticks of charcoal, ground and mixed with olive oil and formed into crayons. When he returned to Madam Vermoil's Herbiary, Corporal Vallis gave him a salute, the vigour of which might have been amplified by the sight of the pie and beer that Mardenifol gave him.

Mardenifol settled down with the herbal, ticking off ingredients, making lists and poking through shelves of decoctions and infusions. The lists were long with many crossings out and Mardenifol was near the end of the herbal when Vallis came back into the apothecary's shop. The old man stood watching him while he sorted jars and drew lines through his list of ingredients with a rapidly di-

minishing crayon. At length, the Watchman coughed by way of pre-
amble.

"I have interviewed the proprietors of the adjacent premises."

"Yes, I've also spoken to them."

"The lady of the chandler's was unable to further my enquiries.
However, the purveyor of cakes, fine cakes too," he patted his belly
appreciatively, "said that she thought she heard raised voices ema-
nating from here, but was not aware of anyone coming from the
Herbiary and passing her establishment. I conclude that the killer
decamped past the chandlers."

"Very good, Vallis. Likely true. And worth considering," said
Mardenifol. He couldn't see where this was leading but didn't want
to hurt the old man's feelings.

"During these proceedings," continued Vallis, "I repeatedly observed a woman I believed to be performing some handicraft in the
residential properties opposite."

Vallis paused for so long that Mardenifol was clearly supposed to
say something, but he couldn't think what. "Well done," he tried at
length.

The Corporal looked at him, blinking tears from his sagging eyelids. "I understood, of course, that her position gave her a view of the
Herbiary and she could see anyone coming in and out of Vermoil's
apothecary, particularly if they passed the chandler."

"Ah! Your old skills haven't deserted you! Who did she see?" Mardenifol had put down his crayon and was staring at the Watchman.

Vallis waved a hand as though patting an invisible dog. He
sucked thoughtfully at his teeth and continued at his own pace
rather than careering wildly to the conclusion.

"I made further enquiries with the lady of the cake stall. She informed me that Mistress Memlin is a respected lace-maker and that
her sedentary situation and inquisitive nature made her acquainted
with all the regulars at any of these emporia."

"I'm sure she didn't quite say that," muttered Mardenifol. "But who did she see? Have you talked to Memlin?"

Vallis frowned with his lower lip stuck out. "The demands of warding these premises have precluded me doing so thus far."

"Perhaps now...no, wait. I'll go." Mardenifol scampered out. He spotted an open window, an oblong of sunlight draped across a pudgy hand and a ruffle of material. He trotted across the street and knocked at a bare wooden door and called out for Mistress Memlin.

"You'll 'ave to do the door yourself. Me feet's bad."

Mardenifol shoved the door open and found himself in a room that performed all functions but bed chamber. By a stove, copper pans were stacked neatly against a wall coloured a myriad pale shades of damp and dirt. A shelf held beakers and plates in the brown glaze favoured by local potters and mirrored in the kitchen at Coromal. A boy was sitting at a plank table with his back to Mardenifol. He didn't turn but remained absorbed in his work. Mardenifol peered over the boy's shoulder to see he was painting eggs. A little row of finished eggs glistened with colour; a coiling dragon, a winding road climbing a hill wreathed in mist, a hovering sunbird facing a languid butterfly.

"Those are wonderful," began Mardenifol, hoping to make a good impression.

As soon as the boy was spoken to, he wrapped his head in his arms and shook wildly, while making a thin, wailing noise.

Mardenifol leapt back. "Oh, no, I'm sorry!"

At that, the boy suddenly smashed the egg he was working on and fled away, leaving a spreading stain of moss-green paint on the table. Mardenifol pushed a rag into the spilt paint and lifted the crushed shell, now showing the sad remains of a frog by a pool. He turned helplessly to an old woman in shapeless garments of earthy hues. Her face might once have been elegant but now her features all seemed to have melted slightly and slipped down her face.

She sighed, pausing her needlework. "Don't fret none. He'll be all right betimes. Just let him be."

"I'm so sorry. I didn't mean..."

"I know. I seed you coming from the Herbiary."

"Ah. Well, it was that I wanted to talk to you about."

"Of course it was. I seed you there with old Vallis. He used to visit Vermoil a time or two, I can tell you!"

"I gather you see quite a bit of what happens?"

"I likes to watch the comings and goings. What with me feet being that bad, I don't get out so much meself, but I likes watching the doing of others."

"Did you see...?"

"Well," began Memlin, resting her crabbed hands on a drift of lace, "I were that upset when Sissy Flet came a-running from the Herbiary. I knew it were something terrible bad. Then shouting for the Watch, she were, crying murder an' all! Of course, Sissy were in the apothecary reg'lar, what with the terrible trouble she has with..."

"Indeed, indeed, but did you see who went in before Sissy Flet?"

The old woman's lips primped as her tale was cut short, but she rallied. "Of course, I can't be sure that I sees everyone what goes in and out. However," Mistress Memlin adjusted her own lace cap and leaned closer to Mardenifol, "There was a man what entered the apothecary's shop. I wondered what his trouble might be. He looked well enough but you can't always tell, can you? He were there for a while too, what usually means Madam Vermoil was making up a remedy for him. Of course, it could have been something for someone else but he didn't look the sort for running errands. Then he came out and went off past the chandler's walking awful fast."

"Mistress Memlin, do you know who he was?"

"I don't recall seeing him at all before, no."

"What do you remember about him?"

Memlin looked up, consulting her memory. "Well, he was just ordinary-looking, really."

"Ordinary," sighed Mardenifol. "You don't remember what he was wearing?"

"Oh yes. Not a smock nor work clothes. Neither a tunic nor fancy hose like some of the folk what came to the apothecary. Easier with the womenfolk, you know. I always remembers the cut of a dress and partic'lar any lace..."

"But what was he wearing?" Mardenifol knew his voice was becoming shrill and forced himself into composure.

"Well now, I don't rightly know how to say. Leathers; you know, sort of armour, but not made of metal. He had a sword an' all. Actually, when I first seed him, I thought he had a helmet on, but he never."

"A helmet? Why would you think that?"

"It were the sun shining off his head. I thought he had a shiny helmet, but when he moved further, I could see his hair was oiled."

"Was it now? Mistress Memlin, I think you have been of great help to the Drouhin of Shaddimur and the City Watch. Please accept a coin for your trouble – and perhaps another for some more paint and eggs. I'm so sorry for upsetting your boy."

"Oh, he's not mine. I just watches him. He likes it here on account of it being quiet. Normally."

"Yes. Well, I'm really sorry. Perhaps you could say that to him? And if you think of anything more, just call Vallis over." With that, Mardenifol was gone, bounding back to the Herbiary. He dashed into the workroom, signalling Vallis to follow him.

"She saw the oily-haired Tarlenian! He cropped up at Strammon's and Tessavian's! We have to find him."

"Hm. I remember someone of the sort."

"You know him? Who is he? Where can we find him?"

But Vallis merely hummed a few more times, then resumed his

post outside, staring into the past, or perhaps just staring. Mardenifol made an exasperated noise and returned to complete his list. There was little more to do. The list he had made of all the possible ingredients from Madam Vermoil's herbal was long indeed. Still, including the four jars from the garden, he had found most of them somewhere in the shop. Some of the recipes had called for fresh herbs or components. He had to discount those as they would have come from the garden or foraging trips. But even beyond that, he had ransacked every corner of the apothecary's shop and there was no trace of eight ingredients.

Eysyl, henbane and lettuce juice were often mentioned but nowhere to be found. White poppy juice, sumac and mandrake occurred a few times in the herbal but not on the shelves. Hemlock was mentioned for chest complaints and the easing of pain and there was but a single mention of the gall of a barrow swine. Mardenifol had no idea what distinguished a barrow swine from any other pig, but wrote it as he found it.

He tucked the little list of eight items into his purse and headed out past Vallis. The Watchman was sitting on a tub of flowers, his legs stretched out and his back to the wall. His diligence had waned as the afternoon sun warmed him.

"I have to go back to Longyle. I'll return here as soon as I can. Don't let anyone in to see what I've been doing."

"I remain at my post, vigilant and alert," droned Vallis. His red-rimmed eyes wallowed round to look at Mardenifol. "Have no fear, I ease the ache in my back; no more."

Mardenifol opened his mouth to say something, but spotted an empty rickshaw and waved it over.

Longyle was running leaves though a tiny mangle when Mardenifol entered. He hardly turned his massive head but his eyes glinted towards the door. "You still on assignment?"

"I am. Do you want further testoons?" Mardenifol felt his response was rather daring and he was pleased his voice had stayed normal.

Longyle sighed through his nose. "And what is it this time?"

"Same question as before, but a different list of ingredients."

Longyle collected a last drop of sap, then shambled over behind his counter. He took the list from Mardenifol and consulted it, lips drawn down into a half-moon. He read it a couple of times, then lowered the list.

"Are you sure about all these?" he rumbled mildly.

"No. There may be one or two extras in there, possibly one or two missing."

"I see. You want me to make this up for you?" There was an edge to Longyle's voice as he stood looking down.

"No. I just need to know what it would make."

"That's good. If I made this, my shop, my liberty and probably my fingers would all be taken. What it would make is as much woe as the blood of a succubus. I have only once tried to manufacture this, strictly for the Physician's Guild, under a licence provided by the Loremasters and countersigned by the royal seal."

"Is it some sort of poison?"

"No. This is dwale, the distilled essence of sleep. Give a man just a little of this; you can cut his beating heart from his chest and he will remain still as a sausage."

"Yes. Of course." Mard looked up suddenly at the big apothecary. "Do you think it likely Madam Vermoil would have refused to make this for someone."

"Not likely. Certain."

"Thank you. Out of interest, how accurate was the list?"

"Never heard of anyone using sumac in dwale." Longyle shrugged. "Probably wouldn't hurt."

Mardenifol paid for the consultation, but turned at the door.

"Master Longyle, you knew the recipe instantly. Have you been asked to make this recently?"

Longyle dug a finger in his ear, making a disgusted face. "I have. And you're going to ask by whom and I would normally tell you anything like that is confidential."

"Normally?"

"Normally. He had no good intent, that I know. He was a soulburned Tarlenian by his accent. Hard man, probably military. His hair was oiled and held in a ring. Bit bigger than average perhaps."

"No scars or tattoos, rings or insignia?"

Longyle shrugged a negative. "He looked dangerous and wore a blade I suspect has seen much use."

"No name then?"

"He didn't tell me, but someone called to him when he came in. I thought it sounded like Hogfen or Pigpen as you'd expect for a Tarlenian. I was going to ask if he wanted something for a stye but, er..." Longyle raised a bushy eyebrow.

"Not one for a joke, then." Mardenifol did his best to conceal his amazement that Longyle would consider anything amusing.

"No. Anyway, I flatly refused to consider making anything for him. There were two other customers in here at the time and I ignored him to deal with them. I was glad when he left."

"Do you think either of the other customers knew the Tarlenian?"

After a moment's consideration, Longyle replied. "No. I think not."

"Well, they may have saved your life. Thank you, Master Longyle." Mardenifol strode out, his head held high. He could barely believe his own success and marched off imagining Kalainen explaining to Lord Berrin how his son had found the Tarlenian villain.

It was dark when Mardenifol reached the Herbiary again. Corporal Vallis had retired inside and had made himself tea. The old man leaned on the counter and inhaled the vapour as he listened to Mardenifol's tale.

"Just what I thought. Used to know a Tarlenian like that; took just a moment to call him to mind. Always watching him but never caught him in anything. I know he was a villain. Used to drink in the Curls district. The Hind, perhaps, or Marret's, maybe The Yellow Lamp. You might find him there. Name of, hm, Hygven, that's it."

Mardenifol stared at the old Watchman, then leapt to his feet. "Sergeant Vallis, you are a wonder!" Then he was bounding away, ignoring the old man's cautionary observations about the Curls.

Mardenifol shoved open the door into The Hind. Someone had scrawled an unsubtle image of a backside over the picture of a deer on the sign. The Hindquarters seemed a better name to Mardenifol. Still, he wasn't worried about being robbed any more. All his money had miraculously vanished together with his purse in Marret's. The Hind was full of the workers and shirkers from the Curls. Mardenifol slunk through them hoping to spot Hygven in some shadowy corner. The place stank of beer and sweat. In a room full of hessian and filthy smocks, his fine-weave clothes and leather boots marked him out instantly. The Tarlenian accents he hoped to overhear in some clandestine confession were less foreign here than his tones, ingrained at Lord Berrin's table. Still, people seemed bemused rather than unfriendly. He felt disappointed fingers touching the cut strings of his lost purse as he pushed through a knot of locals.

A face appeared in front of him beneath a gleam from oiled hair. The eyes locked on his made his stomach lurch worse than the ruts of Jumblegut Lane. Hygven's grin was feral.

"Oh dear, little inquisitive puppy is right out of his quarter. Time to answer a few questions for me."

Mardenifol went windmilling backwards, blundering through the labourers and artisans, only stopping when he crashed into a wall. His dreams of success burst on the dagger of reality. He had imagined spotting Hygven at a distance, perhaps bringing in the Watch and shouting 'Arrest that man' in heroic tones. He had never prepared for this face to face encounter and his terror blotted thought from his mind. Hygven swaggered after him, hand on the well-used hilt of a sword. Mardenifol's head jerked all ways, searching the clumps of locals in the tavern. They were ordinary folk having a drink at the end of a day, just looking for some conviviality before heading home. Hygven was wearing leather armour and was probably an accomplished swordsman. Why would anyone here intercede on behalf of an unknown youth faced with an armed man? Hygven seemed to guess his thoughts.

"No friends for you here, puppy. Just you. Start by telling me who you're working for."

Mardenifol tore his gaze away from Hygven's sneering face, that callused hand on the sword. Gulping wildly, he thrust the fear down, trying to think. Hygven could have killed him already. But even if they were being pointedly ignored, they were in a crowded place and it was a dangerous time for Tarlenians.

"I challenge ..." Mardenifol squeaked. He tried again, more loudly. "I challenge you to a drinking contest. The winner gets his questions answered. Loser pays for the drinks."

Mardenifol watched Hygven's eyes slide left and right. Several patrons were looking towards them now with hooded curiosity. Having been in complete control, Hygven now turned back to Mardenifol with a measuring stare. They were of about equal height, but Hygven was twenty hard years older and weighed half as much again. Hygven smirked and Mardenifol realised the Tarlenian had been following him for a while and knew he had been asking around on his own. Hygven barked a laugh and moved forwards.

"This may work even better! Trying to draw it out 'til help

comes? There won't be any. Or make it so you don't feel the blade? Well, you've got balls, puppy. I accept. Wine or beer?"

"Brandy, I think," said Mardenifol, sliding sideways and collapsing onto a stool at a table with his back against the wall.

"Brandy. You're a fool. You'll drink enough to kill yourself before you're drunk enough to know you've lost."

"Aren't you glad it'll save you the trouble?"

"Not really. Lord Berrin's boy squealing at my feet? A memory to treasure there." Hygven's hard eyes bored into Mardenifol. His smile was cruel as he waved a sardonic invitation to continue.

Mardenifol sat with his adam's apple bobbing like a cork in a weir, but his voice was steadier now. He nodded to the innkeeper, who had marched over with a cudgel.

"Here's the challenge. We each pour for ourselves. We take equal measures of brandy and water. We pour the measures into this glass beaker and drink. You don't get to see me pour."

Hygven's eyes narrowed. "So long as the spirit goes in the beaker, I don't care. Fine. Do it."

"Oh, one little thing, if the brandy floats entirely on top of the water, the other person has to drink it."

"It doesn't, you milksop!"

"Then you don't have to be afraid."

"Afraid! Be very careful of your words, boy."

"Then you accept? If the brandy floats on the water, the other person drinks. If it does not, the pourer drinks." He had to raise his voice over the muttering of watchers and the innkeeper swearing resignedly.

"What are you playing?" Hygven's glance sidled round the room, the dozen people now crowding round them. Some knew him. His usual belligerent stare at the boy hadn't cowed the brat as much as he hoped. He bit his lip, eyes skating over the locals again. Hygven seemed to brush the nagging worry aside. "It doesn't take the absence of a staff for me to know you're no wizard. And you've no skill with sleight of hand. Bah, I accept! Now get me the first measure before I die of thirst!" Hygven waited until an earthenware jar of brandy, a leather jug of water and two tin cups had been procured. He poured a brimming measure of spirit and tipped it into the beaker. He tossed in a cup of water and held the glass beaker up the lamplight, admiring the perfectly mixed colour. Raising the beaker to his face, he inhaled deeply, grinning maliciously at Mardenifol. "Now we start! To your Lordship," he toasted, then drained the beaker in two long swallows then placed it lightly in front of the boy. The grin widened. "I think one of those will be all you can take, puppy. Your turn."

"They are small measures," said Mardenifol, trying to conceal his horror at the size of the tin cup, "but I suppose it'll have to do." He took the beaker into his lap, while Hygven jeered at him.

"Make sure you fill that brandy cup. I'm watching. That beaker must be just as full as mine. No spilling now!"

Mardenifol filled both cups to the top and gently poured the two measures into the beaker.

"You take a leak into it, boy, and I'll cut it off and feed it to you!"

Ignoring a few people chuckling and clearly enjoying the nob getting ragged, Mardenifol sat up and placed the beaker before him. The brandy and the water were divided into two perfectly distinct layers. He held it up so everyone could see. People began to crane closer, shouting to friends to draw them over.

"Well, that's a surprise. You have to drink that one." Mardenifol placed the beaker before Hygven. The rattle tap of the beaker on the table caused by his shaking hand was not lost on the Tarlenian.

There were gasps and laughs all round the table as they saw the brandy floating on the water. Someone clapped. People further back leaned forwards and bobbed on tiptoe, talking, asking questions.

Hygven looked from the glass to Mardenifol and back again,

frowning suspiciously. "What've you done?" he snapped out. "That's not brandy."

"You'll find it is. Bet was you've got to drink it if it floated. So drink that."

Hygven took the glass and gave it a very different sniff from the last time. He sipped it suspiciously, making an involuntary face as the neat spirit seared his lips. He put a thick finger into the beaker and swirled the brandy into the water. Ignoring jibes from grinning locals, he swallowed the drink.

"How d'you do that, puppy?"

"Could try praying while you pour," smiled Mardenifol.

"Your mouth'll earn you a smack, boy. Which first? Water first, yes?"

"Up to you. You might be surprised."

Hygven picked up the water, narrowing his eyes as he looked at the boy, wanting to choke the trick out of him. Hygven suddenly changed his mind, tipped the measure of brandy into the glass and trickled the water down the side. He held up the glass of mixed brandy and water.

"This is conkin' ghulsk!"

"You accepted the challenge. Giving up already?"

"Not a chance." Hygven gulped the drink and glared across the table. "Let's see if you can do that again."

Mardenifol shrugged, hunched over the beaker and picked up the measures. The taproom was much quieter now, people leaning closer. This time, even if he couldn't see what Mardenifol was doing in his lap, Hygven was watching like a wolf following a straying lamb. He sneered when Mardenifol held up the perfectly separated drink for all to see before placing it on the table in front of Hygven.

"Yes, very clever, but that's your last time. Water first, eh? I've got you now, boy."

The Tarlenian stirred the drink and put it to his lips, his eyes closed. When the beaker was empty, he breathed deeply a few times. Then he filled both cups again, concentrating hard not to spill them. He settled himself, then tipped the water into the beaker. His tongue came out slightly as he tipped the brandy. It swirled down into the glass where it mixed with the water.

"Did you pour in the centre, or let it go down the side? Perhaps you have to pour really carefully," said Mardenifol mildly.

"Do you?" said Hygven, forcing the drink down. "I think I've got a new plan."

He drew his sword and laid it on the table next to him. He watched Mardenifol's eyes as they were drawn to the blade, saw the adam's apple dipping up and down. His grin was lupine as he leaned across the table, breath sour beneath the brandy, while the boy pressed back against the wall. The bravo thrust his face closer to Mardenifol. "I'll stick you with this, make you tremble and shiver so you can't pour into the beaker, still less carefully, you sniveller!"

Even as he said it, a heavy hand lifted his sword off the table. Hygven spun round and half-rose, a snarl on his face, threats spilling from his lips. The man holding the sword gave a grin. He had a massive chest and a bigger belly. He smelled of beer, goats and piss from the tannery. But his other hand pressed down on Hygven's shoulder like a velvet anvil.

"Took a bet, mate. No sense getting nasty. Best see it through, eh?"

Hygven belched brandy fumes at the tanner. He shoved up against the hand, reaching to his scabbard, and found himself still sitting down. When he squinted back at the table, there was a separated beaker of brandy and water on it. He looked at his hand, empty of sword. Then found the drink in it. He drank.

Mardenifol was worried. Hygven might topple unconscious, he might vomit which Mardenifol thought might excite the sympathy of the fellow drinkers – not knowing the usual crowd at the Hind –

or he could get thrown out by the landlord. He might still manage to get to his feet and flounder away into the night.

"What I want to know," he said slowly, "is whether you cleaned your blade properly or whether it still bears traces of Madam Vermoil's blood."

"Always clean it," slurred Hygven. He slopped brandy towards a cup, a tin island in a spreading sea of brandy.

"Don't spill too much or the money you took from her cash box won't be enough to pay for it."

Hygven ignored this altogether. The big tanner was frowning thoughtfully at Hygven's blade in his hand.

"You kill Madam Vermoil?" he asked in a low voice.

"Not my fault! All she had to do was make the conkin' stuff. Stupid bitch. Got what was comin'. 'S all." Hygven was pouring with all his concentration, his face screwed up and his tongue poking out.

"Saw my missus through 'er birthing and weren't easy. And you killed 'er?"

But Hygven was staring at the beaker. There was a hazy graduation between brandy and water. There was definitely more brandy on top. He held it up.

"Ha! There! Drin' that, then, yes!"

The tanner shook Hygven, shouting, "You killed Madam Vermoil!"

Half the mixture slopped onto the table, the other half mixed evenly. Hgyven gave almost a sob as he looked at his ruined efforts. Rage suddenly reddened his face.

"Same way I'll kill you," he roared. He tried to spring up, but only managed to half-rise, staggering backwards as he swung a drunken punch into the solid belly behind him. The tanner made to clout Hygven on the head with the pommel of the sword but missed. The blade skated over the leathers on the Tarlenian's shoulder and kissed his cheek with red lips.

"No, no, no!" called the innkeeper, hurrying over with the cudgel raised.

"Call the Watch, call the Watch!" cried Mardenifol, wringing out his damp sleeve, but nobody was listening. Hygven swung a chair in a wild arc, hitting a woman on the arm. But then the man from the tannery punched him on the ear, he dropped the chair and trapped his feet in its legs. Within a few seconds, the Tarlenian was down, and the kicking had started.

Then someone was shouting about Tarlenian pigs, and a group of Gallendian teamsters didn't like the way the locals were picking on foreigners and the tanner had a grudge against the innkeeper which he settled with the aid of a chair leg and a huge woman from Allecando thought her husband had been sucker punched by a man in a cape and pulled him backwards by his hair over her knee and expertly elbowed him in the crotch and then one of the serving maids was shouting at Mardenifol that he started it and went to hit him in the face with a jug of beer.

Mardenifol was squashed against the wall, half-stunned by the explosion of roars and screams and thumps, gaping at the carnage round him and cringing when a clay bottle smashed near his head. He looked up stupidly as the maid swung the beer jug back just as a pudgy hand clamped on his arm.

He heard a voice saying, "You'll come with me," and a burly form dragged him sideways. The table seemed to leap up before the maid and the beer jug cracked against it with a soggy thud. Then his arm was wrenched behind his back, another hand gripped him by the shoulder and he was unable to resist as he was expertly threaded through the brawl to the nearest exit.

In the street, there were one or two running towards the Hind with motley weapons and gleeful expressions, a few others running from the melee and several more paused in relative safety by door and windows, yelling abuse and encouragement. Mardenifol felt his arm yanked straight.

"Sir, it would be expeditious to proceed to a more salubrious area," wheezed a voice.

"Vallis? Lessan's Tears, Vallis!"

"Yes, sir. I felt I could relax my vigil at the Herbiary once night had fallen. The place is locked securely against vagabonds. I wondered if you might need some assistance. The folk of the Curls tend to the rumbustious. Perhaps we might progress a little slower, sir," puffed the Corporal. "We must maintain dignity."

The Tarlenian Embassy

In Coromal, Kalainen buckled on a sword for the first time since Yanni had known him. They had completed a plan to search for Mardenifol, leaving Yanni at the house, getting her to agree on the basis she was to co-ordinate the teams and breathing sighs of relief that she would not be attempting to quell riots with her stiletto, when Mardenifol knocked at the door, accompanied by Corporal Vallis.

Granted permission to stay, Vallis pushed a chair close beside the range, settled back with his hands clasped over his paunch, and closed his eyes while Mardenifol gave a more honest account of his doings than he had envisaged before being rescued by the Corporal.

"Great work, Mardenifol," approved Kalainen. "You did brilliantly to work all that out. We've been a bit worried – and would have been a lot more so had we known where you'd gone!"

"Well, no, it was a bit awkward and stuff. I know I should have left word but I was so determined to prove myself. It would have ended badly without Corporal Vallis," said Mardenifol, nodding towards the drowsy watchman.

"Prove yourself you have. But brandy doesn't float on water," put in Quern. "We have to see how you did that?"

There was a chorus of assent, with Kalainen fetching a bottle of spirits and a glass. They crowded round the table, Mardenifol grinning but flushing scarlet at the praise and attention. He half filled the glass with water, then dipped his sleeve in the glass to touch the surface of the water and poured in the spirits through the material. When he removed his sleeve, the spirits were floating perfectly on the water. They roared their approval, Quern pausing to scoop up the glass and drain the contents. He laughed at the protests and confirmed it was definitely spirits.

When they had settled again, Kalainen explained his deductions that it had to be the Tarlenian ambassador personally responsible and how he could be proven guilty. Mardenifol said that at least events at the Tarlenian Embassy would not be complicated by the arrival of Hygven, provoking a throaty chuckle from Vallis that sounded like a snoring pigeon.

Imber was grimmer and more silent than ever. Quern clouted him on the shoulder to try to cheer him up.

"Up to you, then! How about a quick trot round an embassy?"

Imber's eyes slid sideways to the big warrior for a moment, then back to the table. "All the embassies are locked down tighter than oysters and this is the Tarlenian. Worst of the lot. And there's no time for reconnaissance or planning."

"Thought they were all brash fighter types. None of your sneaky, well, you know, subtle stuff."

"True. Just brash solid bolts on the inside and little room for subtlety. People have tried before. No way in. Sometimes they've been caught and handed back to the authorities in the mornings. Not pretty. Every young rogue from the Neers dreams of a big haul from an embassy. Of course, everyone knows they're stuffed with gold and jewels and magical treasures from the world over." Imber's tone poked fun at the naievety of youth. "You've been in embassies. They do have wealth, but what are you going to do? Creep out dragging a wall-sized tapestry from Old Harrugan or a marble plinth dating back to the first Emperor?"

"If I could get in, I could open a window for Imber later..."

"Not there Yanni. Tarlenian embassy only employs Tarlenians. They all know each other and how would you get in at night in the first place?"

"We're out of time. We can't organise a delivery or a works' team. We have this night, no more. No time for reconnaissance or preparation."

"Can we arrange a deputation from a different embassy such as Hethrin or Correbaran? Join the delegation and slip away... No."

"We should get over there and break a few heads!" said Quern, thumping one hand into the other.

"Hm, if this swordsman's as good as he seems, it might be my head that gets broken."

"Well, get a full detachment of the Watch to burst in with us," urged Quern.

"I am duty-bound to mention that the Tarlenian embassy is their sovereign territory, Such an action would be tantamount to an armed invasion of Tarlenia itself," said Vallis. "The Watch will not, can not, do it without evidence."

"And if we're wrong, or the trophies are kept elsewhere, or we can't find them? Total disaster. We must make sure that the trophies are there first."

"While it is beyond the law to break in... do you remember old Kedu?" Vallis rumbled from the range. "He was obsessed by the Tarlenian embassy."

"Kedu Lapurra?" asked Imber, raising an eyebrow. "Heard of him. Dropped out of sight years back."

Mardenifol perked up suddenly. "Perhaps he found his way in to a mound of gold and stuff and retired..."

"He suffered too many injuries to carry on."

"Oh. Well, doesn't sound as if he got in."

"No."

"So why mention him?" asked Mardenifol.

"Because he did endless reconnaissance and floor plans change little. If you needed background information on the layout, he'd be worth talking to. And I happen to know he lives in his son's shop. Sells jackets and smocks, hard-wearing rather than fancy. Not far from where I live."

"You know him then? Would he talk to us?"

Vallis opened a bleary eye and sighed. "We often meet up to chase beer round a table. In the end, it turned out that I have more in common with a habitual thief than most of the population I defended from such. And if he thought you might damage the Tarlenians, he will help."

"What turned him against the Tarlenians?"

"Their traps broke him. He retires to bed early, so if you want to talk to him, we should go."

Kalainen was already on his feet. "Good. Go now, take Quern and straight back here as soon as you can."

"Got half an idea," said Mardenifol, jumping up. "Something I need to make."

"Me and all," chirped Yanni. "We've limes and dill and prawns. Mistress Lasith showed me how to make stuffed pancakes!"

Throwing up his hands, Kalainen bolted the door behind Vallis, Quern and Imber, then headed into his workroom.

They moved through dark streets as quickly as Vallis could manage, Quern chafing at the pace, Imber wishing to be on the rooftops.

The air vibrated with an ugly hum of distant chants like the noise of bees warning before defending their hive. Once they heard a sharp crack which might have been a door slamming – or being kicked open. When they reached the shop, Vallis pounded on the door until a strained voice asked who was there.

"Evening, Tor. It's Vallis. Need a word with Kedu."

"All right then," the voice continued over the sound of a bolt being drawn. "He's at table but..." Light bulged out from a small lantern. When it daubed the three outside, Tor might have shut the door again, but one of Quern's hands was on the leading edge and it moved inexorably open.

"Don't be concerned, Tor. They accompany me on secondment to the Watch." Vallis moved confidently into the back, where a palely unhealthy man was hunched over a bowl of broad beans and coddled eggs. Only a couple of stumpy fingers remained on Kedu's right hand, he was blind in one eye with burn scars across his cheek and brow. Seeing the number of visitors, Kedu pulled the bowl closer to himself and hunched over it, stuffing beans past a scrappy beard with a wedge of stale bread. An aura of sour defeat hung over him as though the air weighed heavily upon him like an invisible ghoul. However, when Quern clumped a flagon of red wine on the boards, he brightened. After a moment, he pushed a jar of olives towards them and they sat. Tor brought over some battered mugs. He left a candle burning on the table, a stuttering yellow flame trickling a thin line of soot upwards. Tor removed his father's empty bowl, then disappeared back into the shop with the lantern.

After a few desultory remarks during which wine was poured and no introductions made, Kedu turned to Imber, the candlelight reflecting a shrewd glitter in his remaining eye.

"If you're talking to me, you want to hit the Tarlenian embassy. When?"

"Information is that the Tarlenian staff are moving out tomorrow. Plan is to hit tomorrow night when most are gone and the few staff remaining will be celebrating their freedom from the nobs."

Kedu gave half a nod. "Maybe. But getting in is still hard."

"You manage it?"

"Yes, I got in. Went in as part of a team hanging drapes. Another time I swept their chimneys. Never had a moment without a watcher. At night, no. But I've seen the layout of the place. I know a thing or two. Which I could tell you."

Quern barked a laugh, his beard bristling, but Imber spoke first.

"Happy to leave a few coins. If it's worth it."

Kedu snorted. "Save you looking like this."

Imber stared back at him, his gaze hooded and flat. He gave a single nod.

It was sufficient for the old man, who sat back, his shadow heaving across the dingy wall behind him. "What d'you know of the Tarlenian embassy?"

"Three storeys, solid building set back behind a sombre garden of high hedges and statuary urns as tall as a man can reach."

The old man gave a joyless grin, his face twisting unevenly. "I thought you'd have noticed them. Reckon you could slip inside them, eh?"

Imber said nothing. There was no need.

"Yes. There was always rumours, talk of miners hired to dig tunnels way back. I was convinced there was a secret passage from one of the urns into the embassy."

"Aha! A secret way in!" Quern clapped his hands enthusiastically.

Kedu leaned forward, his wavering shadow rearing over them to eavesdrop. "I was convinced. And I found a tiny hatch at the bottom of the second urn on the left. If you try to open it, the whole bottom hinges open. It drops you into a shaft beneath it, straight down. But I didn't fall. Spread-eagled across the urn, I worked myself up and out. Then I hung a rope and climbed down that. I made it more than half the way down before my breath started to come in ragged gasps and the strength drained from my arms. Something noxious in the air, invisible, odourless and deadly. But somehow I pulled myself higher and clung on until I had enough strength to creep out."

"A dead end then," said Quern.

"Oh, I am not one to give up so easily." The old man pulled at his mug of wine as though trying to restore his strength after the climb, holding it in his left hand, the maimed hand hidden on his lap. "I thought the strange gases might burn or even explode. Despite the risk of it being spotted, I lowered a closed lantern down the shaft. As it neared the bottom, it went out as though smothered by the black coils of a soulsnake. Before it did, I thought to see a deeper shadow at one side as though there were a passage heading towards the embassy. I had to know. I fashioned a long tube of the finest leather stitched round a spiral of wire. Days later, I climbed down again, breathing in through that, out through my nose. Handspan after handspan lower, never knowing if the gases would eat my skin, whether the tube would fail – or be found and stoppered by an unseen thumb. There was little light, so little light, for no torch or lantern survived in that lifeless air. Was there a soulsnake, or worse? I could not see."

"Lady's Light," breathed Quern, "What did you find? Was there a passage?"

The single eye turned to the warrior. "What did I find? Bodies. I stumbled on corpses. I blundered towards the passage with my arms out like a blind man, fearing to walk into the eternal embrace of a soulsnake. But there was no passage. There was just an alcove, designed to look like one. But by then, the leaching air was drinking my strength. I felt twice my normal weight. Lungs hauling at the tube like a blacksmith's bellows, I only just managed to drag myself out. It was said back then that I could climb a strand of hair, and I could barely heave myself up a knotted rope."

"Could there have been another hidden passage?"

Kedu shook his head. "What would be the point with that gas? No, it was just a trap. I thought that if that urn was a trap, it was further proof that one of the other urns concealed a secret tunnel, a hidden route in and out of the embassy. I was sure there was a way in. But the tale, like my fingers, is shortened. I tried every single urn. Most were blank. In others, I disarmed traps. I dodged pitfalls and wormed my way past snares that would have killed a lesser man. My obsession developed; I could not leave it alone. I, the finest burglar in Shaddimur, I must be the one to break the Tarlenian embassy. But a tiny mistake here, the inevitable error there, the slip that always comes when you taunt death once too often. Slowly, those traps broke me. By fire and acid and wire and blade they broke me. I was wrong. There is nothing more there than pits and snares and death."

"What would be the point of that?"

"They don't like thieves."

"Are you sure there are no..." began Quern.

"Yes, I'm sure." Kedu thrust his face and the shattered wreck of his right hand towards Quern. "They did this for a laugh. They poured gold into buying delvers and trappers just for amusement." He turned to Imber. "Listen to me now. There is no way in by the urns."

"All right. Is there another way?"

"There's always another way. The doors are bolted so there are no locks to pick. The windows have internal shutters and the bars have clips so they cannot be lifted from outside."

"Internal?" queried Quern. "Thought they would have used external ones to protect their precious glass windows. Could be a few rocks tossed tonight."

Kedu twitched his shoulders. "Internal shutters don't warp in the sun and are easier to seal. They don't care about glass. In hot weather, if the shutters are opened, guards stand nearby. Normally,

I'd say you'd be better to find a way in during the day and hide out, although I never managed it. The chimneys are too constricted. Similarly, the sewer is impossible."

"The other way?"

"I'd say the place is impregnable."

Quern was rising, looming over the old man like a tsunami, but Imber put out a hand to quell the tide, his eyes never leaving Kedu.

The old man gave half a chuckle. "Not so stupid. Maybe not so young. But you came here wanting a miracle. This isn't some old wine-merchant's house with a barrel-ramp to a bricked-up cellar that no-one remembers but me. Listen, the Tarlenians built it and the strongest building is proof against the best of us. And this one's on high alert."

Imber was frowning now, trying to penetrate to Kedu's meaning. Beside him, Quern sat back and folded his arms crossly while Vallis sipped his wine with his eyes almost closed and a slight smile on his face.

"But," said Kedu, "but it's always on high alert and the defence is run by people. Just average military foot-sloggers. Mostly young. They always get sloppy, take shortcuts."

Imber nodded slowly, eyes turned inwards. Kedu watched him carefully, then said, "Bad luck that you have to go in at night. Bad luck that you have no time for preparation – for tonight. Well, you must trust to luck, or make your own."

The old Neer struggled to his feet and limped to a cupboard. He took out a new candle, lit it from the guttering stub on the table and pushed it into the molten puddle. The new candle burned with a pure white light. Quern looked at it in surprise.

"That looks like one of the votive candles from the Lady's Fane!"

"Remarkable coincidence. Still, I'm sure the Lady would approve of shedding light into every darkness."

"Well, yes, I suppose..."

Kedu turned to Imber, something like supplication in his eye. "I was fixated on those urns. By the time I was cured of that, I couldn't break into a rabbit hutch. Now, I will tell you what I know of the place. Then you must bring me something from the embassy."

Quern and Vallis were both asleep by the time Imber and Kedu had finished talking over the embassy building, the layout, the numbers of guards and their duties. The old man moved Imber's bag of coins to one side and banged his empty mug on the table, causing Quern to leap up drawing a sword and Vallis to half-open his eyes.

"Come on, I should be in bed. Away with you, now."

"Did he really do all that stuff in lightless tunnels under the urns?" Quern asked softly as they headed back to Coromal.

Imber just nodded. The city felt more on edge than ever, even a lack of sound seemed poised, teetering on the edge of violence. The whole place felt like one enormous ambush ready to spring. His eyes scanned the rooftops, the hollow ends of streets, black recesses in the shadowy darkness of the night but his mind wandered the pattern of the building the old man had described.

"Lady! I thought I knew something of courage. I couldn't do that. Never." The big fighter shook his head, resting one hand on the comforting grip of his sword. "He didn't know a single person who got in then?"

"One."

"Suppose that's something. Any chance of using the same route?"

"She managed to get a wire over one of the shutter bars and cut it. Tarlenians tossed her body into the street for the Watch in the morning. Apparently they'd tied her to a chair and systematically broken all her bones. That's how they treat all the ones they catch."

"Oh." Quern walked on quietly for a moment. "This Kedu: professional morale-raiser, is he?"

Vallis gave a soft snuffle of amusement but Imber's expression was clamped shut in the dark, shrouded in silence.

"Well, if there are no secret tunnels, how are you going to get in?"

"I don't know!" Imber rounded on him. For a moment he held his hands out like spades in an odd gesture of desperation, but then just turned and walked on towards Coromal.

Quern looked after him, face creased in thought. He was so used to Imber's competence that he had not considered what was being asked of the man; break into one of the securest buildings in Shaddimur while it was on high alert, guarded by an incomparable swordsman, and find a set of unknown objects hidden who knew where. And if he failed, there would be war between the city states. Perhaps more importantly to Imber, he would be tied to a chair and have all his bones broken. Quern suddenly made a wide-eyed expression, shrugged and caught up.

A group of half-a-dozen people burst out of a side street in front of them. They were talking in the loud voices of men who were soaring on the winds of adrenaline and alcohol.

"Local accents," noted Quern. "Shaddimur men, should be all right."

When they were close enough for the charcoal night to resolve the shapes into men, one of them pointed at Vallis. "Look, there's one little Watchman!" The group headed rapidly towards them.

One of them asked Quern, "Hey, is he taking you in, man?"

"There was three of 'em a moment ago," said another, the voice slowed by doubt.

"Conkin' Watch! We was set on by conkin' Tarlenians. Your mates from the Watch came in on their side! Whose conkin' city is this, eh? EH?"

Vallis stepped forward to face them; ignoring his sword, he wagged a finger at them. "Steady lads. We don't want this to turn nasty, do we? You don't want to be on the streets tonight. Best just head back homewards, don't you think? Look after your families."

One of the men waved vaguely at Quern. "Back off, big fellow. You do not want to be part of this."

"You are so wrong there." Perhaps if the light had been better, Quern's grin would have caused them to consider the pleasures of home and hearth in a positive light.

"There were three of them. I'm sure there was."

"Yeah? One must've ran off."

"If you won't get out of the way, you get what's coming. Come on, Leshy," a heavy man waved at one of his colleagues and they rushed forward together.

Stepping in front of Vallis, Quern swayed away from the stocky man's charge but left a leg for him to trip over. As he stumbled, Quern straight-armed Leshy under the chin, dropping him on the spot. Quern grabbed the first man as he struggled to his feet, lifted him and flung him rolling back to his comrades in a flurry of squawks and cries.

There was a pause while Leshy struggled to his knees groaning, shaking his head, and the stocky man was helped back to his feet.

"If that's the way you want it..." The men began to spread round Quern and Vallis. One of them fumbled a long knife from his belt.

There was a faint whistle and a 'pok' noise. The knife-wielder yelled in pain and doubled up, clutching his ear. Imber's voice slithered through the darkness, it was difficult to say where from. Somewhere high.

"Blades down. That was a stone. Crossbow bolt next." There was an ominous click from somewhere above them.

Vallis's bleary eyes looked round them. He shook his head sadly. "Easy now, boys. There may be serious trouble ahead and Shaddimur will need every able-bodied man. You do want to be an able-bodied man, don't you? Your city may need you."

There was a shuffling quiet when the only sound other than the scrape of boots was an unnerving chuckling growl from Quern.

"Yes. Well. Got to be ready for the big one, haven't we? If they invade... You know. City defence and all. Suppose there's no sense scrapping amongst ourselves."

The man still holding his ear rounded on his group. "We're not backing down from one Watchman!"

"What's got into you, Talpa? You picked the fight with those Tarlies earlier. You want a stone in your other ear or a bolt in your backside, you go ahead."

Talpa glared maliciously at Vallis but said nothing. Someone else mumbled, "Watch were just breaking up the fight, really. I reckon, maybe."

"On your way, then, lads," said Vallis, looking thoughtfully towards Talpa. As they shuffled away, Leshy was supported between two others and waggling rubbery legs around as though he had no knees. Vallis stared after them, then ambled on towards Coromal.

For a moment, Quern watched them go looking like a toddler whose friends have all just been called inside. He turned as Imber appeared beside him and they caught up with Vallis in a few strides. After a while, Quern gave a sniff of approbation. "Lot of Watchmen would have started with the sword. There would have been death."

"Perhaps. I can't see so much in this dark now. But Talpa, that's a worry, that is a worry." Vallis hitched his trousers up and bumbled gently forwards.

In Coromal, Kalainen sighted down his sword as though afraid it might be bent and began rubbing furiously at areas of rust. He had much work to do. Mardenifol was sitting at the table. He had a small clay bottle in his hand, the lid coated with wax. His fingers trembled as he aimlessly rotated it while talking to Kalainen, his voice high and shaky.

"I don't understand this relentless evil. Why are the Tarlenians so determined to attack?"

"Money."

"I thought they were rich! They daub gold about like a farmer's wife feeding ducks."

"The gold of plunder." Kalainen sighed and put down the sword. Talking might keep Mardenifol's mind off his fear. "Their economy is hollow and dying. They have no port and the overland routes are arduous and slow. They face high duties on anything they move through another city state to their port facilities which makes their goods expensive. The laden camel wins no races. They have to use their military strength to acquire a port to save themselves. How far would you go?"

Mardenifol nodded glumly. "Yes, I suppose if the alternative is the starvation of your people, collapse of government and anarchy, I would go a long way. You mean they have no choice?"

"They have the consequence of old choices. Tarlenia used to manage fine. They have rich mines, excel in metal work. They have rare commodities from the forests; fungi, fruit, meat, rare woods and furs. Then they acquired a cavalry unit to augment their small armed force and discovered stealing material from their neighbours was easier than growing or making it. The military machine grew. The men needed paying, training and equipment. But with fewer people working land and mines and so on, that funding could only be acquired with more raiding. Taxes rose but the home economy cannot support a large military without plunder. The situation spirals."

"Couldn't they have put the money into infrastructure or road-building? Supported their other businesses?"

"They didn't. So now they have what looks like a solution; acquire a port, enrich yourself with the wealth of an entire city."

"That would work for them."

Kalainen shrugged. "No, only in the short term. Given their culture, the money would go into the army, which would get bigger. Before long, they would need to gobble up another city state. Currently, the people are unhappy in Tarlenia. They have high taxes and few goods in the shops. So, the Tarlenian rulers start a war, blaming the other side, of course. That draws their people together, distracts them from domestic issues. It's easy to hate people you don't know."

"So Tarlenia has a large army it can't afford. Large armies only have one application. War is inevitable!"

"I hope not. The Tarlenian plan was to ruin the treaty. If that is ratified, the combined cities are too strong for Tarlenia to attack and Tarlenian aggression will be doomed to fail."

"Given a large enough army and a good general, history suggests they could still pick the cities off piecemeal."

"You're thinking back to the old days of Kalcos the Second. His armies dwarfed the little militias round the Seven Cities. The Tarlenians are strong enough to take Bruel – which would mean the Seven Cities were reduced to their original number. But they certainly can't do it if Bruel is reinforced by Gallendian ships, while the Shaddimur militia attack the Tarlenian right flank, forces from Hethrin and Allecando harry their left and Correbaran and Palemin harrass their homeland. That is why all the effort to block the treaty. They won't attack if they can't win."

"They might if they have no other option. Shouldn't we leave them a way out?"

Kalainen stopped rubbing at rust and looked at Mardenifol. "Something in those books of yours after all. If the army doesn't get paid, some splinter groups may take up independent raiding. And other units will take employment as guards against them. However, don't forget this is Shekkem – where towers grown from ancient stones are raised and razed again. There are ruins of old civilisations all over the place. Remember Yanni hearing about Captain Maiban going off on an expedition? The cheapest place to hire armed guards is going to be Tarlenia. They can make a business of it, maybe even challenge the biggest ruin of them all, the lost city Siuda Reyes."

"I've heard of that, I think. What was it?"

"The City of the Magi. Back when magic was more powerful, there was a city dominated by sorcerers of unbelievable strength. The story is that they managed to create talismans enabling them to cast spells without feeling the pain. But something went wrong and the city itself fell in colossal ruin and its site is lost. Treasure hunters have sought it ever since."

"I've got to learn more of that!" said Mardenifol.

Kalainen shrugged. "Well, even from lesser sites, once the gold trickles back into Tarlenia in private hands, entrepreneurs and businesses will follow to peel it off them. The economy can be rebalanced. And the Tarlenian military will be dispersed among the cities. But," Kalainen returned to the rusty weapon, "but if all the ambassadors quit Shaddimur amidst tales of intrigue, there is no treaty. Mutual mistrust will stop the rulers of any city denuding their own centres of troops and Tarlenia will take Bruel – or Shaddimur itself."

At that moment, there was a bang on the knocker and Kalainen leapt up to unbolt the door for Quern, Imber and Vallis. While Quern and Vallis headed for the kitchen, the big fighter sniffing enthusiastically at the tang of limes, Imber swung himself up into his little eyrie. When he came back down, he said, "Someone's been trying Coromal's defences."

"Serious?"

"No. But interesting."

"Passing thieves or spies?"

"Or assassins?" put in Mardenifol.

Imber shrugged.

Then there was a crackle as Yanni tipped batter onto a skillet for the first of the pancakes, provoking a drift towards the table, an easy space made for Vallis. Mardenifol brought a jug of water from the cistern and fetched clay drinking pots. Kalainen opened a hoarded flask and poured wine the colour of reed stems in winter sun. He watched as Imber sketched the vital areas of the embassy as he had gleaned them from Kedu - the state rooms, guards' mess hall, the ambassador's study - and nodded carefully, assimilating the details. Quern was smacking his lips, scooping up a piping hot pancake and trying to eat it without burning his mouth, big teeth bared. Imber shook his head in disbelief and smiled at Yanni. She grinned back and danced back to the range to pour more batter.

But when there was no more than a smear of oil on the plate, there was a silence and a sombre toast to the evening ahead.

"Need to go. Do as much reconnoitring as I can. Going to have to make my own luck, so better give it as long as possible." Imber rose soundlessly, floating towards the door like a billow of smoke. Quern noticed his wine was barely touched and slid it surreptitiously towards himself.

"Did Kedu tell you how many guards there might be?"

"They rely on keeping people out. Used to be just two guards. Four when the tension rose. Maybe up to six for their last night. But there's Ambassador Guzarin, somewhere."

A blunt truth uncomfortable to them all.

"We don't have a better plan," said Kalainen at last. "Imber, I've arranged that we'll move to the Bruelan embassy, set up there. Close as we can get. If you find anything, get back there as quick as possible. Timing is going to be everything."

"Imber wait," called Mardenifol. "There's a dead bird outside you can take, jackdaw, I think. It's seething with maggots. I saw it earlier and it gave me an idea."

When Imber paused and looked at him with one eyebrow raised, Mardenifol continued, "It smells pretty bad. I thought you might be able to use it."

"Sounds a bit far gone for towing him up to the rooftop, Mard," said Quern.

"He could, you know, drop it down a chimney?"

While Imber gave a mild shrug, Kalainen observed that it was the wrong time of year for nesting birds.

"The bird is dead. Could have lodged up there for ages – if anyone thinks about it."

"Mard, what on earth for?"

Mardenifol waved the little tightly-sealed bottle. "Made this from sulphur and stuff. Really stinks! Don't get any on you – or hiding is really not going to be an option. Might empty a room for you!"

Quern grabbed the bottle and pretended to read a label. "Mardenifol's Concentrated Essence of Dowager's Fart. Yes, the commercial possibilities are huge."

Despite the laughter, Mardenifol looked hurt. Imber squeezed his shoulder and took the bottle.

"Thanks, Mard. Where's the bird?"

After Imber had left, Yanni bolted the door behind him, then stood in the doorway to the kitchen with her hands on her hips.

"Who's on overwatch?" There was a significant quiet. "There's nobody on overwatch? He always does it for everyone else. Who's he got to rely on, if not us?"

"Imber's the best there is at overwatch. If one of us goes blundering about, we'll likely to be spotted and make his inside job impossible."

"You can't just leave him on his own!" she declared resolutely, glaring at them.

"You have to trust him. We're moving as close as we can. Can you check all the devices are set, Yanni? Imber would want Coromal to be safe. As soon as you're done, make sure you have everything you need and we'll go to the embassy. We'll stick together."

"He's on his own out there!"

"And who do you think could get the drop on Imber at night in his own city?"

Yanni paused for a moment, then nodded decisively. "I'll see to the traps." Kalainen watched her go, concern creasing his face.

They padded over streets of earth and stone towards the embassy district. Kalainen allowed no lanterns and had Quern lead the way, looming more massively than ever with a thick gambeson wrapped round him. His hand frequently dropped to the pommel of his sword. Yanni was beside him, having swiftly demonstrated that she had the keenest eyes in the dark. That established, she promoted herself to group lookout and nearly dislocated her neck trying to cover all directions. Thinking of Imber, she remembered to check the overhanging roofs for lurking silhouettes, which left her walking like a poorly controlled marionette. Vallis shambled serenely along beside Mardenifol and Kalainen brought up the rear. The wind darted out of alleyways, flapping at Kalainen's cloak, blowing a white noise that would prevent them hearing anything softly creeping closer behind them and the Drouhin looked back more often than forwards.

As they crossed into the Embassy district, Yanni dropped back with such an air of nonchalance that Kalainen knew what was coming. She drifted closer to him and murmured, "Somebody following us. Seen them a few times now."

"I thought I saw something once," Kalainen sounded apologetic. "But it looked more like a lost child to me. We don't have time to stop and help them now and we're almost at the embassy. This should be a fairly safe area, unless some fools decide to burn the Tarlenians out or something."

Yanni turned her head to regard the Drouhin with disappointment. He didn't think it was his poor eyesight that caused it but just as he started to ask, she said,

"Well, we'd best hurry then," and scuttled back to the front with Quern.

Kalainen scowled after her, then looked behind again. Was

that...? No. For a moment, he thought, but it was nothing. At least, nothing getting closer to them. And if there were some agent trying to follow them, what of it? It would hardly matter now.

Straddling one alarm wire, Imber rested easily, balanced over a lead-lined valley in the Tarlenian embassy roof. He had cut a second wire out of his way, maintaining tension by tying it to an iron wedge forced between two tiles. He didn't like leaving any trace of his passage, but he might have to move a lot quicker on his way back and it had been necessary. Even in the dim night, Imber could see the slight bump in the lead that marked a pressure plate. In his experience, an easily spotted trap often meant a much more cunningly hidden one nearby. He moved another handspan forwards, testing, checking.

Assessing every tile, watching for bits of moss loosened by an unwary boot, avoiding a drift of house leeks that looked unnaturally placed, it took him over an hour to reach the chimney, memorising each footstep for the way back. He reached up the stack, managed to get his fingers over the lip and pulled himself smoothly onto the top of the chimney. There were four flues, all sooty from use. Faint light seeped up three of them. Imber recalled what Kedu had said; the most eastern flue led to the guards' mess hall. Looking down, Imber could make out a disc of hearth below him. There would be a fire in the winter but it now lay swept and empty. The flues were scarcely wide enough to take his arm, there was no possibility of anyone climbing down them. Imber could hear no sound of voices but the wind stroked his ears, whispering of waves and swishing branches. He tried pressing the side of his head over the flue, one hand clamped over the other ear. Still nothing.

There were a few bits of rusted wire over the top of the chimney, no doubt to deter birds from nest-building. He pushed a blade through the wires guarding the chimney top and paused. If he had put them here, he would have had at least one of them wired to an alarm or trap. It was too dark for perfect visual assessment, but his fingers tested the tension in each one. He then used the knife to ease the gap wider until the bird would fit through. He listened again, but there was still no sound louder than the soughing of the wind. Edging round so the wind blew on his side, he opened Mardenifol's little bottle. A foetid sewage stench clawed at him, dragging bile into his throat. For a moment, he turned away, swallowing hard, his face curled in disgust. Then he dabbed a thick liquid onto the maggoty bird.

He hoped the rotten jackdaw wouldn't snag on the way down. Imber shrugged. Trust to luck or make your own. He carefully wrapped the wings round the heaving body, posted the bird through the gap head first and dropped it. There was a rustling noise, a trickle of soot, and it was gone.

Before it landed in the grate, Imber was lowering himself down the side of the chimney. Not hurrying but moving swiftly and methodically on his pre-determined route, Imber reached the edge of the roof just over the window to the guards' mess hall on the second floor. Even before he arrived, he heard oaths and groans from the hall. He had counted eight seconds before there was a noise of a door bursting open.

"Balgrim's balls, what a stench! Even for you, Karth, that's a bad one. You soiled yourself?"

"Not me! Some bird died in the chimney and it's fallen down. Conkin' maggots all over the place."

"Get rid of it, you donkey dropping, before I see my supper again."

"Well how? Want me to burn it?"

"Oh, burning feathers, yes, that'd add to it nicely. Chuck it out the bleeding window, all the maggots and all. Make it the gardener's problem in the morning. And if this place still smells like an armadillo's arsehole in the morning, Karth, you're cleaning it. And don't you even think of leaving the room while the window's open unless you want to personally debate the matter with the ambassador. Got that? Henno, check the roof anyway. Never know. Something may have knocked it down."

"None of the wires sprung. Half the alarms go off if a squirrel farts up there."

"I said, check anyway. Look hard, look well and make sure. By the Saint, what a stink! Need an alarm for Karth's farts in here."

A door shut. There was a clang, then a couple of scraping noises. A window opened with a whine from dry hinges. Karth leant out, sucking gratefully at fresh air. Invisible above him, Imber perched, immobile as a gargoyle. A whiff of sickly taint seeped upwards. Then Karth disappeared. Imber counted seconds until he reappeared a moment later, holding the bird by one wing tip. Karth gently swung it, then sent it arcing away, spalling maggots, dropping into darkness as it left the light from the room. A few more breaths.

"Get you little bleeders swept up before I have to hunt all over the bleeding room..." Karth was muttering.

Imber leaned down from the roof. Karth was on his knees by the fireplace, coaxing maggots into his palm. There was the sound of a hatch opening somewhere behind Imber, but he swung silently down and into the room. A moment later, Karth hurried back to the window, tossing out a wriggling handful of stench. He sniffed at his hand and groaned. Karth looked suddenly at the door, but there was nothing there.

Imber looked along the passage. Watch lanterns dotted the corridor, bronze glows behind smoky glass. A count of eight. That would put the guard captain and the others in one of these rooms. One door to a bedroom or dormitory was not quite shut. Sounds of movement. Why here? Were they guarding a bedroom? Was that where the trophies were hidden? It didn't feel right. There were voices. Imber couldn't hear the words, but there was a soft rumble like someone reassuring a waking sleeper. Perhaps a staff dormitory. Footsteps approached the door and Imber hurried past. A little further on the right, a bare wood door with a simple catch was ajar. More footsteps came down a wooden stair behind the plank door. Imber hopped sideways and padded softly down a small stairway. He caught a glimpse of boots on the stair; Henno's voice reporting that the roof was clear as the guard Captain came from the bed chamber with the open door. Imber guessed they were making a steady sweep of the embassy.

Going down, Imber passed a door exiting to the first floor but thought to hear something behind it, perhaps the other pair of guards, and continued down. At the foot of the stairs, he opened a latch on another rough wooden door and peered into a kitchen. On his left, beyond an archway, was a large open fireplace with a bread oven on one side and a whole series of hooks and racks he assumed were for cooking. The fire was banked and dim but provided some light. There was a girl curled up asleep on a ratty blanket on the hearth. He slipped into the kitchen and relatched the door. To his right was a window, the shutters barred with iron. There was another shuttered window on the opposite wall. He had reckoned on the window nearest the fire being the most frequently opened when they were cooking and thus perhaps the easiest and quietest for him to open, but he had not anticipated the girl. A draught of air might wake her, as might the least sound. He needed quick exit points but this was too risky.

Sidling noiselessly through the open archway, Imber found himself in a scullery. There was a window behind a stone basin. Kneeling on the edge of the basin, Imber lifted the shutter bar with no more noise than a rat scratching its whiskers. He unlatched the window and tested it, then pulled it home and pushed the shutter back into place. As he went to ease himself back down, he had to avoid glass

264 ~ ACM PRIOR

jars on a draining board beside the basin. He stared at them for a moment, then took one back into the kitchen. The jar had been carefully washed. There was no visible mark from a label, but he was quite sure that the jars were the ones taken from Madam Vermoil's apothecary. He replaced the jar on the draining board and looked more carefully round the scullery. Nothing seemed out of place. Back in the kitchen, the girl slept on. With furious concentration, Imber scanned the room. On a shelf of the dresser, a fold of paper was shoved between two plates. Silent as a reflection, Imber eased the paper from the dresser and slowly unfolded it. Holding it up to the light of the fire, he could see line drawings of a rosette of leaves, then a fan of seeds, a long root with upright leaves. A neat hand wrote of parsnips and the dangers of the sap. He was about to leave it as something to do with kitchens but checked the back of the page. He felt a coldness spreading from his gut as he read.

"*Dwale. A potion to make a man sleep through any injury: take one ladle of the gall of a barrow swine for a man, and for a woman of a gilt, one ladle of hemlock juice, one ladle of mandrake. (weaker variants may be made with wild neep or white bryony if mandrake is not to be found), one ladle of lettuce juice, one ladle of white poppy, one ladle of henbane, and one ladle of eysyl. Mix and boil momently. Store in a well-sealed glass vessel. Put one ladle into a jug of wine and mix well.*"

The jars and the missing page from the herbal. Imber wondered whether they would be evidence enough. They might be enough to prove the Tarlenians had been involved in the killings at the Bruelan embassy. Although of course the Tarlenians would say he had planted the evidence. Still, it was all adding up to a picture where the denials would look increasingly thin. If only he could find the trophies... Imber looked back to the girl. She was sleeping, the artless pose more convincing than any pretence. It might be better to leave the paper for others to find in verifying company but the thought of the recipe becoming widely available was ghastly. He tucked the page inside his jerkin and was gone with no more noise than smoke rolling against a wall.

He drifted through into the ground floor reception and meeting rooms of the embassy. The watch lanterns here were towers of silver with filigreed panels of delicately coloured glass. They shed sufficient light for the regular guard patrols to move through. Imber was at once grateful for the light even as he regretted the exposure.

He could not just wander around the embassy in vague hope. The guard captain and Henno were clearly conducting a slow sweep of the building. Karth had been alone in the mess hall and may still be there. That left at least one, and possibly three, more guards somewhere, lurking or searching. And Guzarin himself, of course. Between them, Kalainen and he had thought the most likely rooms for the trophies would be the Ambassador's study on the first floor or the Ambassador's bed chamber, a grand affair on the second floor, according to Kedu. Obviously, there could be any number of other options, even a part of the cellar of which they knew nothing. But Guzarin's tenure had not been long and it seemed unlikely that major renovations would have been undertaken in that time. Imber tried to persuade himself it was logic that decided him to try the study first. The overriding fear of meeting Guzarin alone might have had more to do with it. At least he was not opening random doors; Kedu's mapping meant he knew exactly where to go.

Behind him, he heard the door to the kitchen open, lantern light waking reds and golds in the drapes of the reception room. Voices. He couldn't hear what they were saying – demanding tea from the kitchen girl? If so, it would be helpful to know how many ... but he could not wait and this might be the opportunity to search the study.

Imber watched the main staircase. A wide flight with delicate banisters led to a small landing with a display cabinet. A lantern above it spilled light towards some wall hanging, perhaps a flag. The stairs split at the landing and two flights fluted up to the first floor.

It would be impossible to pass the landing and remain invisible to anyone watching from above. Imber could not help thinking of all the ways he would defend the stairs. It was not the Tarlenian way, but they might leave someone on watch. His eyes measured carefully, then he moved. The banister ended in a volute, a whorl of wood that made a fine foothold. Imber leapt lightly onto the left-hand one and sprang up. His fingers caught the edge of the first-floor landing and he eased himself up to peek over. He paused, motionless with his right foot resting on the sloping banister of the stairs. Search the shadows as he might, he could see nothing to alarm him. A susurration from his clothing, a creak from strained wood, and he had swarmed up, rolled over the banister and onto the landing. He slid into the shadow of a gaming table, and waited, listening. It seemed to him suddenly that the house was listening back just as hard.

There was a corridor to his left towards the ambassador's study, a woven rug along it deadened his footfalls still further – and would similarly mask anyone else's. He stepped quickly to the first door and stood with a sense of unease, frowning at a hairline of light beneath the solid panelled door. There was a brass escutcheon. Imber ran his fingers over the keyhole. Hardly any light shone through, suggesting the key was in the lock on the inside. He pressed an ear to the heavy wood; a minatory silence pressed back. It did nothing to banish the feeling that someone else was there.

Imber went on to the second door which Kedu had told him led into a small library with a connecting door to the study. He slid to the floor but there was no line of bright light. There was another lock on the door similar to the one into the study, but this time there was no key. He checked for any visible traps or wires, then tested the door. The lock held. Imber ran his fingers over it like a

blind man touching a familiar face. Head bowed, he flicked a glance
either way up the corridor, then eased tools from a pouch and bent
to work. Moments later, he slipped into the library beside the Ambassador's study and shut the door behind him. There were three
watch lanterns spaced through the room. Their soft light showed a
book-lined chamber with a small writing desk with pens and inks.
There were two leather chairs, a small table between them had a lac-
quered tray on it with a half-full decanter and two glasses. Imber
stepped swiftly to the angled bay window and unbarred the shutters. He peeled one back, unlatched the window and pushed it open.
Carefully looking all round, he leant out far enough to check the
study windows. They were sealed. He eased himself back into the library and pulled the window almost closed. The window had cushioned seats set into it as a comfortable spot for reading. He tucked
the shutter bar under the long cushion and pushed the shutter back
into place.

Sweat was beginning to prickle onto his skin as he moved to the
connecting door between the study and the library. He could hear
nothing. But the warning feeling came more strongly still. It was
time to leave. The silence of the house seemed normal – but it was
the same as moving through a room with a sleeper. By the noise of
their breathing, you knew they were asleep. When that noise suddenly changed, however much they lay there, pretending uncon-
sciousness, you knew the pretence. So it was in the embassy. Had
he triggered some alarm? Had someone noticed the missing page
from the herbal? Something magical? It didn't matter. Something
was awake.

He stood before the door, fingers resting lightly on the carved
panels, his forehead touching the wood. A clear image came to him
of someone standing on the other side of the door, mirroring his
posture, listening for him.

Of course, it would be Guzarin. He knew with cold certainty

that the trophies were somewhere in the study, and the ambassador was with them, just waiting for him to try this door, the only possible way into the study. Guzarin precisely understood the importance of the trophies, which was why he had killed Telas. He would not depute anyone else to ward them until they were shipped away with him back to Tarlenia. And with mounting terror, Imber knew Guzarin was aware of him.

Yanni

The Bruelan embassy was awash with arguments, disclaimers and cavils. A noble from Palemin posed with his head turned sideways, nose elevated, a cloak drawn up to his chin, while a compatriot swirled about with much arm-waving and expostulations before a stolid trio from Correbaran, frowning in grim rejection. Gwyan was barking comments, clearly losing patience with a couple from Allecando. The man wore a circular hat, baggy trousers and a tight jacket with silver toggles. His voice grew higher and louder by the minute while the woman chirped "Of course!" and "How could it be otherwise?" after each sentence. Her own robe was a gorgeously patterned material in green and black, long enough to swirl about her feet. To Gwyan's side, Esferle was talking to a severe-faced woman from Hethrin, judging by her black and white costume, topped by a black hat with a red tassel. Although she seemed thin, her breasts and stomach sagged, her hips were wide and there were rolls of fat on her neck that made it seems as if she were peeping over a pile of buns.

"It was an affront when Bruel threw off the sheltering arm of Hethrin," the woman asserted. "Declaring independence! Really, Bruel only has itself to blame. Of course, were Bruel to accept the sovereignty of Hethrin, the full might of our forces would naturally be available…"

"Surely at the very least you can see that if Tarlenia take Bruel, that will be the end of your hopes of reunification?" Esferle, spoke with a clenched mouth, her eyes flashing. She towered over the Hethrin woman. Her well of reasonableness was near exhausted and phase two looked likely to involve her fingers round the Hethrin woman's throat. The same prospect may have occurred to the Hethrin diplomat, as her eyes were rolling round the room looking for allies. She tried a placatory tone.

"Of course, we would be happy to come to an accommodation with any party…"

"An 'accommodation'? What accommodation could you come to with Tarlenia?" Esferle loomed closer.

Serian drifted round making tiny comments about propriety and probity which everyone ignored. Mardenifol and Kalainen were debating points of law and permissible actions with Rown and a lawyer from Shaddimur with a high forehead and an even higher sense of self-importance. The lawyer held a finger up as though testing the wind and declaimed in a nasal voice.

"Irresponsible action is both provocative and deplorable. The distrainment or sequestration of goods can be neither countenanced nor condoned by inaction where such confiscation has not been both deemed appropriate and sanctioned by due process of law employing protocols established by the Seven Cities Convention."

"Load of twaddle," muttered Quern. "Tarlenia's nearly won if this is the best we can do." He raised his eyebrows at Yanni and headed towards the kitchen in a meaningful way. Quern was sweating in the heavy gambeson and was hoping some beer might be undefended.

Yanni pulled at Mardenifol's sleeve, looking up at the lawyer, and whispered, "Is he not letting us do anything? We have to raid the Tarly embassy, don't we? Who's he to stop that? Is he very rich or something?" Even with her spiky hair plastered down she would only just pass as a kitchen girl but the fierce disdain curling her small mouth into a horseshoe of dislike would not have disgraced a duchess.

"He'd be rich all right, if self-esteem were gold," grinned Mardenifol. The lawyer clearly overheard and became even more stiffly formal. Kalainen flashed a look at Mardenifol and turned back to the lawyer, trying not to let exasperation colour his quiet drawl.

Nobody else paid the least attention to Yanni, except Serian, who tried to flap her away from the reception rooms. She was dusted to the front door, where two armoured guards grudgingly opened the door to let her out, still without noticing her at all, or breaking off from their conversation about Hulvia, apparently some silken-haired girl with a backside to die for. Yanni stood under one of the trees and glared out across Shaddimur. Light flared unevenly and there was the stink of smoke in the air – and not just the familiar clawing of woodsmoke. This was more bitter, hinting at cloth or hair, perhaps flesh... Yanni shuddered. Looking round, she saw nothing but tight-shuttered windows, clam shells closed in insular defence. No help anywhere for anyone else. And somewhere out there was Imber. On his own with nobody to watch his back as he had stood watch for so many others. The Tarlenian Embassy, she mused. It was not that far. Yanni slunk into the shadows and sloped off towards Imber. She glanced round to see if anyone had missed her from the Bruelan embassy, but it was as closed and shut as all the others. Just for a moment, she thought she saw a small shape dart back into the cover of the building. The old terrors leapt at her, the fear of snaring hands, brutal adults... but no! Yanni knew she must not let that start or she would start running and never stop until her heart burst. And surely that shape – had she even seen it? – surely it was too low to have been a man. If it had been there, and there was nothing now, perhaps it was just a dog. Perhaps.

She turned resolutely towards the Tarlenian embassy, forcing herself to use the darkest shadows to hide rather than fearing them. If she started checking for pursuers, she knew her fear level would block her thinking. What would Imber do? Of course, he would be up on the rooftops. But then he knew the high paths as well as he knew the streets below; knew where he could walk silently; where the tiles were thin and crazed with age, shattering at a touch; the easy places to hop from one building to another rooftop; the valleys between pitches that ended in sheer chimneys. In the dark, she would either fall, lose her way or alert every house resident from here to Kathos with her blunderings. Perhaps the only way would be to find a house opposite the embassy and climb that.

In the meantime, she must become part of the night. Be the predator, become the most feared thing in the dark, not the prey. She scowled into the night and touched the hilt of the stiletto. The bravado was a thin veneer, but for the moment, it held.

She remembered Kalainen saying that when bulls fight, it is the grass that gets torn. She felt like an ant in the grass now. Whichever group of chanting men found her, the result would be the same. But the ant kept on walking.

It wasn't far, although it seemed a crawl the length of the Long Wyrm to Yanni. There was too much noise, a rhythmic clashing of metal, shouting, a flicker of orange light to the south, booms and the clanking of alarm bells. But nothing too close. The embassy district had so far avoided attention.

Finally, she was outside the tall hedges that masked the Tarlenian embassy. There was a building opposite of two storeys. It had a brooding feel of weightness about it, but the roof would give a fair vantage over the hedge toward the taller embassy.

Yanni lay on her side between ornamental grasses, her heartbeat gradually slowing to merely twice its normal rate. The two guards conducting a sweep of the gardens had passed almost within touching distance of her, but their talk had been of the eddies of smoke, the pulses of rioting sound and how they compared in volume with the cries of the youngest child of one of them. Having heard the rumbling growl of a dog in the building, Yanni was terrified that it would be padding alongside them, unerring nose ignoring her simple concealment but there was no sign of it outside, yet. Her attempts to climb the building had been a failure. Imber always seemed to find a convenient lintel or a scented climber with funnel-shaped flowers and stems like a ladder. She had tried three different places but found no way to cling on and pull herself up and the only plant she had tried climbing had such brutal thorns she looked as though she had been plucking wild cats. She had just fallen off the wall when she had heard the guards' voices and barely had time to dive into the grass clumps. Now the footfalls were fading but her fear of the dog remained. She would be all right on the roof but could see no way to get there. Even had she made it to the second storey, getting onto the gabled roof might well be beyond her. She had to retreat.

Back in the road, she looked at the hedge, solid as a wall. She rolled into the base of it and found she could get behind the dense exterior. Inside was a black mass of thick stems and trunks. She began to worm her way not through but up. She kept thinking she was trapped, but she wiggled and pulled and made slow progress. Then there was a sudden pain like a burn on her hand. She squeezed her hand shut, clamping her mouth at the same time to stop crying out. She could feel the blood welling and dripping down. That was not a thorn.

When she could, she felt up gingerly until she reached something that was not plant; a wire. For a moment, she panicked, thinking she had tripped an alarm and would be caught. But then she stopped. There couldn't be an alarm attached to a wire. It would go off every time the wind blew. Hunting for them, she found many wires laced through the hedge. Thick wires to reinforce the hedge and block penetration, thin wires to slice flesh. But most of them were on the embassy side of the trunks and didn't stop her climbing upwards.

She had to stay still for a while when she heard a group hurrying past on the road, although she almost chuckled at the thought of what they might think if they saw the hedge shivering in the darkness, ready to spew out some monster at them. Then she thought that although if she had been on the road, she would have been running with her legs blurring like a wheel, it is quite possible that they would have just poked the wobbly bit of the hedge with a spear or two. She stayed still.

Eventually, she managed to worm her head above the level of the hedge, fingers slimed with blood and sticky with sweet-smelling sap. She was pretty sure her head would be invisible amongst the sprigs, waving in the breeze. She looked round briefly, then stared at the blank face of the embassy, behind the lines of huge urns waiting like pitcher plants for crawling thieves. She scanned the rooftop time and again. There was light etching the shutters in some rooms, but there was no sign of Imber.

For a while she watched with just the occasional dimming of light behind one shutter to be replaced by a similar faint flaring elsewhere to keep her attention. She kept looking for Imber's silhouette on the rooftop, only seeing it when her watering eyes gave brief life to a chimney.

She spotted a hint of light on the side of the house at a ground floor window where all had been black. She watched in confusion, then saw a flicker of reflected light suggesting a window had opened. It almost closed again and then the dull gleam faded into blackness. Perhaps a shutter reclosed. Was someone in an almost unlighted room throwing something from a window? Then she couldn't help a grin. That window had been left as an escape route. Imber was inside! It hadn't been impossible for him after all. And she was on overwatch. She gave a tight grin and glared forward more fiercely than ever, determined to miss nothing.

She forgot about the larger matters in Shaddimur, so immersed was she in trying to envisage the silent struggles within that too silent house. But there was still the occasional drift of light from one room to another, just faint lines of white creeping round shutters behind the dark windows.

Then another window opened in the middle storey. A room which showed but a dim light. For a moment, Yanni even thought to see a movement, a figure leaning out to assess the next room, the only room that had been lit all the time she had been there. Once again, the window was pulled to, but Yanni had no doubt that a second escape route had been set. She had to force herself not to wriggle in delight and set the whole hedge to shaking. Imber was unstoppable. He was in, and they would have the proof they needed. She waited, hoping, expecting Imber to appear. The wait went on.

Suddenly there was a shaft of almost searing light as the shutter was opened in the lighted room. The window opened and a man leaned out, looking towards Imber's last escape route. As she frowned at it in worry, another window opened and someone else's head poked out. The first man made some arm gestures and the second head withdrew. The first man also disappeared briefly but returned with a crossbow. He rested easily in the window, the cross-bow pointed towards Imber's window.

Now there were lights appearing everywhere. They seemed to be converging on where Imber must be. Yanni stuffed her fist into her mouth, watching in horror. She couldn't think how to help. Could she scream? Would anyone hear except the man with the crossbow?

Could she not scream? She watched impotently, willing Imber to appear, gracefully leap from the window and vanish into the sheltering night, terrified that he would appear and be shot with the crossbow. She found she was praying to the Lady. Then suddenly there were shouts; lights showed in Imber's room. The crossbow man aimed carefully and waited. She prayed to see Imber, she prayed not to see him.

Then it all went very quiet. The man with the crossbow lowered the weapon, slid back into his room and closed the shutters. Imber was taken.

For a moment, Yanni could not move, gazing sightlessly at darkness. Then she slid down, flowing through the branches like congealing wax. She fell to the ground, hardly able to think. But Imber was taken, she was on overwatch and she would get help. He would not, could not be left for the Tarlenians to toss out another broken body in the morning.

Mechanically, she climbed to her feet and turned towards the Bruelan embassy. A fat hand clouted her on the ear and knocked her down again. She tried to scrabble away but someone heavy trod on her leg.

"What you doing in this nobs' district? Thought you was on a job, 'iding like that. Summat to do with all that noise, I bet? But you ain't got no bags of loot. Still, you staying in with rich people now. We tried to get into your place but it's done up tighter than a crab. You're going to tell us how we get in."

"Flour-duff!"

"Pleased to see your old friends, eh? Now you're wearing such pretty threads and living in a fine 'ouse and all, knew you'd want to share."

"You never shared anything in your whole life."

"No? Well, I never 'ad much. But we'll share with you now."

"Not now, Flour-duff. I got to go."

"To see more of your ambastadoor friends? What's wrong with your old mates from Meiling, hey? We want in to your lovely new 'ome. Maybe it's all empty, hey? Maybe we can wait there for you while you're eating sugar tarts and swigging wine here, hey?"

Climbing back to her feet, Yanni looked round at the four of them. Leggy looked round-eyed and scared. She knew he didn't want to be here. She could run past him and might escape but Flour-duff would take it out on him. Perhaps they would back off if she drew the stiletto. But then either Flour-duff would take it off her or she would stab someone. Moffy she knew little and Hoob had only just appeared when she left. Anyone new was probably the most dangerous if he was keen to impress Flour-duff.

"Flour-duff, it's a bad night..."

"Yeah, just what I was saying. Bad night, I said. Best be in somewhere safe. Of course, our old friend Yanni's tucked in somewhere safe. How do we get in, Yanni? You must 'ave a way."

"I can't. You can't. Have to get someone inside to unbolt it."

Hoob smacked her from behind and she staggered to her knees.

"You said you wouldn't" wailed Leggy, as Yanni struggled up again. Moffy gave a nervous laugh, but kept looking into the shadows all round them, fear bulking heavily like a black storm cloud.

"Yeah," said Flour-duff, knocking Yanni down again. "We said we wouldn't, but we said our friend Yanni would 'elp us, what with being our friend. If she is a friend, course she'd tell us. An' if she isn't, it don't matter, do it? So, little friend Yanni, you're going to tell me how we can get in to Coromal, hey?"

Yanni staggered up again. She turned to the new boy. "Don't you do that again." But she had turned away from Flour-duff and the big girl punched her in the side below her ribs. Yanni doubled up, wheezing.

"So ... tell ... us ... how ..." Flour-duff was saying in a sing-song voice, slapping Yanni's head with each word.

"Enough!" shouted Yanni, forcing herself erect. Looking at the ferocity in her eyes, even Flour-duff stepped back. "You know what, Flour-duff, you go on like this and I will tell you, oh yes. But the traps at Coromal were set by Imber. You know Imber, Flour-duff? You want to pit yourself against Imber? If you touch those traps, you'll end up counting fingers and wondering why the number is so low even you can do it."

Hoob raised his fist and moved towards Yanni but she turned on him. "I've told you, you don't do that again. You think you can find me? Well done. But I can find you. In the dark. Any time I want."

"You can't scare the four of us," retorted Flour-duff. "When you're done being clever, who's the one bleeding here? You were born in the dirt, and you never escape the dirt, Yanni."

"You won't coz it's in your soul, Flour-duff. Everything you do just roots you in the gutter. And you'll keep all your friends in the dirt with you. There are ways out. You could work. You may not have the brains to do anything else but Leggy has. Moffy's smarter than you. Reckon he is too," she said, jerking a thumb at the boy she hardly knew. "That's what you're frightened of, isn't it? They're all going to see that you're going nowhere and without them you have nothing at all. If you think there's a future for picking on someone smaller when you are four to one, life's never going to get better."

"Going to get worse for you," snorted Flour-duff, raising a thick hand.

"No. You're still picking on someone with nothing. You think that's a clever plan? You think that is bright leadership? Not enough, Flour-duff, and they know it. Don't you? Eh?" Yanni glared at Hoob and Moffy, but they were backing away, looking at each other.

"I'm warning you..." began Flour-duff.

"Or what? You going to hit me again? Picking on one of your own, just rats fighting in the gutter. It won't help, will it? I've got nothing for you to take. And now they know it. You've brought them all out on this night, for nothing. Never could have gained you anything. Run back to Meiling, Flour-duff. Maybe they'll let you stay with them, maybe not. But there is nothing for you here, now or ever."

And then they were all backing away from her gleaming eyes and her words that hit harder than Flour-duff's fists. Hoob was watching Flour-duff in a measuring way. Leggy smiled at Yanni but she was too busy glaring at Flour-duff to notice. Then there was the noise of a door opening and squad of men came out from a house, spears just visible in the dimness of the night. They marched swiftly towards the youngsters. When Yanni was watching them, Flour-duff picked up a stone and threw it into her. As Yanni gave a cry and fell again, Flour-duff called, "I win, Yanni. I lead here. You're nothing and you're still in the dirt."

Then the Meiling Square group whirred away like startled pigeons, but the armed group moved swiftly by, ignoring Yanni crouching in the dark street. As they passed, she could see a woman in robes in the middle of the group. It was too dark to make out much more and she was in too much pain to care.

For all her aches, Imber was in trouble and she was on overwatch. She limped off towards the Bruelan embassy. She hurt too much to slink along in the shadows. Cursing Flour-duff almost every step, she trudged forward, pressing her filthy blouse over her hand where blood still oozed from the cut on the wire in the hedge. Her whole head felt as though it was swelling up like a gas-bloated corpse but she would not stop.

She finally marched up to the Bruelan embassy door and pounded on it with her good hand. After a moment, there was a click from some spyhole.

"Go away, girl. You can't come in here," came a voice.

"It's Yanni. Let me in quickly."

"Just push off before someone chucks a chamberpot at you."

Yanni groaned. Of course they didn't know who she was. They hadn't taken any notice of her and paid less attention to her name than to the croaking of a toad. She gave the door a ferocious kick.

"Then ask Gwyan, you conkin' tadpole turd!"

"I don't know you, so clear off, you little brat!"

"You don't know me? Well, I know you and if you want to have any hope of seeing Hulvia's arse again in this life, you had better open this door now or she can tie her silken hair round your..."

"All right, all right, what in Balgrim's name do you..." one of the guards opened the door slightly and looked out worriedly.

"GET KALAINEN!" shouted Yanni, running straight through him before he could react. "Quern! Kalainen! Mard!"

Yanni's entrance hardly added much to the bedlam in the embassy, but Kalainen broke off and came straight to her.

"Your face, Yanni! What's happened?"

"They've taken Imber!"

Kalainen stopped short. "Are you sure?" He seemed to sag as responsibility hammered guilt onto his shoulders.

"I saw the lights home in on his position, I heard the shouting. They got him."

Kalainen turned to look at Quern. The big man had already dropped a half-eaten chicken leg on Serian's tray, ignoring the horrified look on the major domo's face, and had a hand on Mardenifol's shoulder, guiding him over. The warrior had light sparkling in his eyes.

"We go!"

"We can't! We'd never get in! It was tough enough for Imber!" Mardenifol was still not sure what was happening.

"We'll get in somehow. Subtlety's over. You'd be surprised what enough violence can achieve with a door or window," growled Quern. "Wish I had a hammer."

"You must stay here, Yanni. The embassay will have someone treat you..."

"No! I'm not Ruffin. I choose this. You don't know how to get in. There's a way," said Yanni urgently. "Imber left an escape route - a window unfastened! Come on!"

As they left, they passed Vallis dozing near the front door. Kalainen grabbed the old watchman's arm.

"Vallis! Persuade Rown somehow. Raise the embassies, get the Watch, whatever you can..."

Vallis held up a lugubrious hand. "I cannot do that and the Watch cannot act until there is solid and incontrovertible evidence to incriminate the ambassador."

Kalainen looked at him aghast, "I cannot say that!"

Vallis gave a bleary blink. "Say what?"

"That we've definitely found evidence!" Kalainen shouted in his exasperation with the apparently slow wits of the Corporal.

"I hear you. Definitely found evidence." Vallis shambled heavily away into the hurly-burly of the reception rooms.

Guzarin

Then they were back in the street, jogging towards the Tarlenian embassy, Kalainen grim, Quern oozing enthusiasm. Mardenifol was still puffing worries.

"Surely we must wait for the Watch? I mean, this is sort of their thing, isn't it?"

"They've taken Imber, Mard." Yanni was leading the group, trying to drag them faster by force of will.

"And the four of us are going to attack an Embassy? What exactly are we going to do?"

"We can get in!"

"And then what? They've got professional guards. With real spears and stuff. And the best swordsman..."

"Mard, we're a man down," Quern rumbled. "We do whatever we have to do."

"He may be dead!"

"And he may not be."

When they reached the embassy, there was no hesitation. Yanni

just waved them to follow her and they ran to the window she had
seen open on the side of the house, feeling obvious as bulls in a bird
cage. The window was wide open. Yanni was in too much of a hurry
to notice. She leaned through and pushed on the shutter. To her
huge relief, it swung back. Quern moved her aside, then squeezed
himself through the window. He fell into a basin, but rolled and
landed on his feet. Mard was already climbing in behind him. In the
quiet of the night, they sounded like a delivery of barrels. Quern
helped Kalainen through, then picked up Yanni and placed her beside him.

They moved quickly through an arch into a kitchen. A fire was
burning low and gave some light. The girl was just sitting up as they
came in. She blinked at them wide-eyed. Kalainen smiled kindly at
her. He put his fingers to his lips and made a gentle shushing noise.

The girl's eyes widened further, she drew one breath and gave an
almighty scream. She then curled up with her arms over her head,
still screaming in terror.

"Stay together. Find Imber," shouted Kalainen over the din and
they hurried forwards.

Imber backed away from the connecting door to the Ambassador's study from the library. He could feel them waiting for him.
More than one? Or just Guzarin? It didn't matter. Covert entry was
impossible while it was so guarded. However, the occupants didn't
seem to be doing anything immediate. Imber guessed Guzarin had a
similar feeling to him, the indefinable knowledge that he was here,
somewhere. But the ambassador would not leave the study on a
vague presentiment. Perhaps he would only come out if he were sure
of catching his interloper. But if he were sure, how could Imber not
be caught?

Biting his lip, Imber turned back into the library. He took a
wooden ruler from the desk. He filled one of the glasses from the de-

canter, sniffed it and gave appreciative tilt to his head, recognising fine spirits. He put the glass on one end of the ruler, then balanced a book on the other end over the edge of the table. He put the remaining glass on top of the decanter and placed the whole thing on the floor below the book. He could burn off the brandy to lighten the glass, but he could not risk a fire. That might well smoke the ambassador from his den, but it also might permanently destroy all the evidence and offer proof of Shaddimur working against Tarlenia. Imber took a drape and gently dangled it in the beaker. The drape slowly began to wick away the fluid, lightening the beaker. But by then, Imber was gone.

With the vague hope of setting up some distraction, Imber worked towards the Ambassador's bedchamber. He passed a second pair of guards on their slow sweep of the house. The message that the embassy had been penetrated had clearly not reached them yet. It seemed probable that they would check in with Guzarin when they passed the study. After that, they would be more alert. For now, Kedu was right. They looked, but they did not see. Although they were splendidly predictable as they worked through the rooms, Imber did not permit any complacency in his approach. One unlucky glance could ruin everything. As the Drouhin would say, even the blind singer catches a coin occasionally.

Moments later, Imber faced the door to the Ambassador's chambers. Lamps burned inside and shed a thin glow beneath the door. Imber guessed that there was someone inside here too, waiting for him just as Guzarin waited in the study. Perhaps another guard, perhaps a trusty servant. At least they had a light on which would make a little light out in the passage invisible to them. Imber took a taper from a pocket and lit it at one of the watch lanterns. In the clear white light, he examined the lock. His shoulders slumped wearily. There was no mistaking Nyrudin's work. The finest picker of locks was also the finest locksmith in Shaddimur, famed for his intricate mechanisms. Imber wondered if Nyrudin had been involved in the traps beneath the urns. He shook his head. No, not unless they had some sort of hold over him. Perhaps they had, for this was undoubtedly a lock by Nyrudin and it might take him a long while to pick it and who knew what would happen when he tried. The front plate looked easy to remove, but what traps would be triggered if that happened? The lock was new. Very new indeed. The plate was of brass, unmarked by the usual dints and scratches about the keyhole. However, Imber's fingers detected two marks incised into the brass on the underside of the lock. In confusion, he bent and peered up at them. They were quite clear. The first was a rune for a trap with a line through it. The second was the rune for an alarm. But could this be a double bluff? For a moment, he sat back on his haunches in thought.

Then there was a soft thump and the noise of breaking glass from downstairs. There was little time left. He swiftly opened the shuttered window at the end of the passage, then returned to the lock. Offering a brief prayer, he undid the front plate and gradually pulled it clear, hunting for wires or releasing springs. Nothing seemed to happen. He stared into the mechanism in amazement. Beautifully made, it was nonetheless so simple it could have been picked by a child, or at least by some children Imber knew. The only addition was a pin tensioned by a leaf of metal. When unlocked, the pin would move and the sprung leaf would pull a wire, presumably setting off some form of alarm somewhere.

Suddenly there were roars and shouts reverberating round the house. Imber jumped, sure that he had been fooled by the lock and had set off a more subtle alarm, but the shouts came from the library area. With desperate haste, Imber grabbed a ball of fine twine from another pocket. The twine was coiled round a hollow core with a loop of cord through it. Ignoring the stamping and wild yells, Imber tied one end of the fine twine round the top of the pin, put the thick cord in his mouth, and allowed the twine to unroll as he backed down the corridor and out of the window.

However urgent the need for hurry, Imber moved slowly, digging his soft boots into the stone for grip, testing each handhold as he steadily drifted round the wall of the house towards the library. He heard the slam of shutters before he reached them. But even as he neared the library window, he could hear voices. There was no mistaking that of Ambassador Guzarin.

"So you're telling me that nobody could possibly have got in on your watch but there is someone in the house?"

"Sir, the window..."

"What of it?"

"The shutter bar was missing. We found it under the cushion, sir." Imber recognised the voice of the guard captain, but the tone was very different now.

There was a long ominous silence before Guzarin's voice came again. "You failed to notice the window was unbarred on your sweep? Hm. Now you're suggesting that someone inside my embassy is in league with our enemies. One of our own bought or coerced to let some villain inside? For all their fabled honour, these Shaddimur dogs stoop to any trick. But I will learn who has betrayed us and neither they nor their families can expect any mercy. Treachery will be rewarded. As will incompetence, Bazzard."

There was a crunching noise from broken glass, a riffling of pages. Guzarin's voice came again, musing with studied calm. "Did our unwanted visitor stop to bolster his education while sipping my brandy?"

"Sir, it is possible some items may have been knocked over by us. We came in hard."

"And how did our mystery guest get past you then?"

There was a pause. "They must have escaped before we got here, sir, probably through the window. They won't get in again."

"You think they left, taking time to pull the shutter home perfectly while clinging to a wall? No. You will assume our thief is in the embassy. I expect them found. Now."

"Shall I leave the window. Sir?"

"Obviously bar it again. It is more likely to slow them than us, and will at least prevent further ingress."

"Yes, sir."

"And if it is that soul-burned Tertius Orbis, your failure to kill one girl locked in a cell will be looked at again, Bazzard."

Imber heard the shutter bar being tamped back into place. He gave a tiny shrug and gently pulled on the twine. Unheard, a little pin released a leaf spring in Nyrudin's lock and the twine popped off the top of the pin.

A chime sounded from the ambassador's study.

Guzarin's voice was a tight, half-whisper. "They're working on the upper door! We've got them. You know the drill. Move!"

Imber flowed down the side of the building like a flake of black snow. He darted round the side of the embassy and pulled open the window to the scullery. Silent as a cat, he leapt through. Pushing the shutter back into place behind him, he sped through the kitchen like a moth. He ran through the reception rooms, up the stairs and on to the ambassador's study. The door was unlocked. Loosening a knife, he slipped inside. The study was empty. He locked the door behind him with the key in the lock. That might give him an early warning if Guzarin returned. He didn't know how long he would have. It might be very little time indeed and this was his one chance.

He first glanced at the shutters, hoping to open them as an escape route. However, they were not only closed and barred, but the bar was clamped in place with a heavy lock. No time to pick it now.

Imber stood still, taking in everything in the room. It was spacious, elegantly but sparsely furnished. There were many paintings; some portraits of severe men in dark clothes but mostly landscapes

Imber did not recognise, probably places in Tarlenia, and one of Shaddimur's old Moon Palace glistening on the island in the bay. The room was dominated by a large desk. A small fireplace with a raised grate was clean and empty. A bowl of orange flowers with a faint scent was on one side of the mantlepiece. Imber wondered briefly if all the trophy items could be hidden in plain sight, something like the bowl, disguised with a few drips of paint, then his thought was jarred by the sight of an ominous chair with straps. He forced himself to focus. The floor was wooden boards, decorated with beast skins and pelts, and the walls were covered with white panelled wood. Beneath the picture of the moon palace, almost hidden beneath a deer skin on the floor, there was an old scratch mark which described a perfect arc. It was almost polished out now but it showed Imber where a hidden door had created it long ago, opening across some small stone. At that moment, the silence of the house was shattered again by a scream, this time a woman's. The screaming went on, more noises building. Imber's concentration was such that he barely heard them, only registering the brief thought that it might work to his advantage if the defenders were now looking in two places, neither of which contained him.

He stepped smoothly towards the picture, looking for dusty marks, the greasy taint of fingers. A touch ... *there* ... a gentle pull, and the hidden panel swung open.

Here was Guzarin's trophy cabinet. There were rows of pegs, neatly numbered. Some of the pegs had legends written beside them. Most had little objects dangling from them. A swift glance took them in; a silver ring of three snakes each biting the tail of another, a small silver blade with an onyx handle, a miniature helmet with golden letters round the casque, an earring with an enormous green stone, a lacquer brooch in the shape of a spade, a dagger made from a vast serrated tooth, the stole of Roeseus made of bullion thread,

290 - ACM PRIOR

a cockade of sandgrouse feathers, a golden nib holder with a spiral pattern of silver chased into it and a silver globe on a shelf.

He gave a brief nod to himself. He slipped the spade brooch into a pocket for evidence, closed the cabinet, and hurried away. Once out through the library window, all he had to do was report to Kalainen and get the whole Watch here as soon as possible. Imber softly opened the door to the library and stepped back with Guzarin's sword at his neck. The ambassador was breathing hard.

"You came close. But the moment those fools burst in, I knew this was the only place in the embassy that matters. Without them, you might have made it, even if your accomplice at the upper door died. But as it is.... Take a seat."

Imber could only comply. The ambassador glided into the room with a bent-kneed crabbing gait, his torso and the sword perfectly level. He motioned a guard forward, who strapped Imber into the chair while the ambassador stood poised with the blade. As soon as the straps were tightened and checked, Guzarin said,

"Go and help the others kill those idiots then get back here." He turned away from Imber, sheathing his sword. "Obviously you found my cabinet, or you would not have been leaving. I don't know how you could but that is not important now. But I would very much like to know who opened the shutters and the window for you."

As Imber remained silent, Guzarin opened the cabinet again, admiring his trophies.

"I find myself reluctantly impressed with a thief. I think perhaps your knife might make a fitting addition to my collection." He removed Imber's knife from his belt, then after a sudden whim, checked Imber's sleeves and removed a further knife from each sleeve.

"Tricky, tricky, tricky. And my spade brooch?" When Imber gave a small nod to his pocket, Guzarin retrieved the brooch and checked it carefully. He rehung it on its peg. "Now that is going to cost you, for I loathe theft. But you were closer to success than all the rest. I really thought it was impossible. Nothing to say? You could even be Imber the Silent, now that would be something. Still nothing? Perhaps you are." He sighed. "No matter. You will not be silent long. Candidly, I am not one for all this breaking of bones, but previous incumbents of the ambassadorship have felt it appropriate and, on some matters, I am a stickler for tradition."

Guzarin collected the poker from beside the fire. He tapped Imber on the head and then the hand with it.

"What shall it be? Teeth first, or fingers?" He rested the poker against the chair and smiled nastily. Taking a cord, he tied it to the butt of one of Imber's knives, then knotted a small loop in the other end. He slipped the loop over the point of the knife and carefully hung the knife on a peg in the cabinet.

"So many beautiful things," he crooned to himself, running his fingers over his prizes. He took out the ring of interlocking snakes. "You know this ring is supposed to ward against poison, however inflicted. If we had a little more time, I would place it upon your finger, pour poison down your throat and have you stung by a scorpion and bitten by a snake. If you lived, you would at least have performed a useful function." He took out the pale blade. "This is a holy dagger of Ameroth, the trembling force within it can be used to reverse the most malefic of spells – but only once, so we won't be wasting that on you either." Guzarin rehung the blade and lifted the silver globe, inscribed with strange patterns. "But this, this is a mystery. Someone carved this with skill and care – but to what end? What do these shapes represent?"

He put the globe down on the desk as they heard footsteps approaching. "My men return. I daresay they can wield the poker, it's about all they're fit for. Actually, Henno has quite a proficiency with it. You may think you are not going to tell me who let you in, but of course you will."

On the ground floor, Kalainen, Mardenifol and Yanni piled after Quern, almost fleeing the screaming woman in the kitchen. As Quern burst into the reception room, two men were running towards him, blades drawn. The first was almost upon them as Quern reached for his sword.

"No, no! Leave that in its scabbard and maybe you won't get hurt!"

"All right. But I can't say the same." Quern's boot smashed into the lead guard's wrist. Astonishingly, the guard managed to keep some grip on his sword, but the next instant, Quern had one hand clamped round the guard's neck and the other pinioning the wrist of his sword hand. Driving forwards, Quern shoved the guard back into his colleague. Trying not to skewer his friend, the second guard fell back against the wall, Quern unleashed his strength and used the first guard as a club, tossing him about as though he were a scarecrow. Now Quern was bellowing wordlessly, thumping one man into the other, one crashing thud after another. After a while, the bellowing stopped. Quern lowered the first guard on top of the second and neither moved very much. Quern made a few harrumphing noises, straightened his gambeson and drew his sword, trying to ignore Mardenifol's wide-eyed horror.

As he looked forward, Karth and another guard were coming in. The unknown guard took one look at his fallen comrades and immediately ran at Quern, howling with rage. He lifted his sword overhead as he made a final leap, intending to crush through any defence with a mighty blow. With surprising speed, Quern bounded forward to meet him, his own sword spearing into the guard's chest. There was the noise of fighting rams as their bodies crashed together. Quern remained braced on his feet. The guard bounced away and fell lifelessly to the floor. Quern put a foot on the man's chest and yanked his sword free.

Karth made a strange ahh noise like a shop keeper considering a small discount and was backing away from them when Bazzard and Henno came careering down the stairs. The guard captain swiftly sized up the situation.

"Karth..." he growled. "Forget the old man and the children. Three of us take down that warrior."

Quern wasn't one for adopting defensive positions, nor would he allow them to plan to overwhelm him. He just ran at Henno, Karth's retreat making him the nearest enemy. Kalainen moved to one side, trying to block any one from reaching Mardenifol or Yanni without going through him. Mardenifol stayed carefully behind the Drouhin. Yanni, however, ran in every direction. She hurled anything that came to hand irrespective of weight or value and the guards operated under a rain of dishes, decanters and decorations. After a while, Mardenifol took down a watch lantern and waited for an opening, his shaking hands rattling the door and slopping oil from the reservoir.

Bazzard managed to reach Henno so that they faced Quern together, Karth tried to fence round to cut at the big man's legs but Kalainen attacked him and kept him distracted and Yanni scored a fine hit with a bust of Zardeem II, opening a cut over his right eye.

Even with Karth fully occupied, Quern still faced two seasoned opponents. These two had fought beside each other before and had the advantage of height from the stairs.

"This doesn't end well for you," warned Bazzard. "Quit while you can!"

But while they clearly imagined one of them engaging Quern while the other enjoyed a free attack, Quern didn't co-operate with the plan. His style was a wild and sustained flurry of blows; boot, fist or blade. It looked almost frenzied, but somehow Quern was always balanced as though his moves were planned. His fights rarely went on very long. Bazzard managed to slash a cut across Quern's chest that did no more than leave a deep wound in the gambeson. After that, the guards' confidence rapidly dwindled into a grunting defence. Then Quern's blade sliced into Bazzard's right arm and the guard's sword clattered away. As Henno darted forward at Quern's flank, Quern met him with a kick in the solar plexus that sent Henno flying through bannisters exploding like a blown dandelion head to land in a heap. Mardenifol wasn't sure whether Henno was writhing around trying to get up rather than just trying to breathe and threw the lantern at him. Other than a soft tink, this produced no discernable effect. Then Yanni whacked Henno clumsily but quite effectively with a hardwood chair.

With Bazzard slumped against the left-hand bannisters trying to stem the rush of blood from his arm, Quern leaped towards Karth. With a squeal, Karth dropped his sword and fell on his knees, screaming for mercy.

Kalainen held out a restraining arm but it wasn't needed. Quern kicked Karth's sword away and was leaning over the Tarlenian like an avalanche waiting to happen.

"I... I... Please..." Karth was trembling, his eyes rolling between Bazzard and Quern.

Kalainen understood the reason for his distress. Neither Bazzard nor the Ambassador would forgive his surrender. "Leave by the front door now. You can leave it open behind you."

"I will. I promise. I'll go, I'll go, please. Please."

Karth ran to the door opposite the stairs. Still gibbering pleas, he wrestled the bolts, half-looking over his shoulder for an attack. Finally, he hauled the door open. Yanni flung a small bowl of dried rose petals after him. He shrieked as it bounced behind him and fled into the darkness, the petals drifting down like blood spots behind him.

Just as Guzarin was saying, "My men return. I daresay they can wield the poker, it's about all they're fit for," Imber was turning his head to listen to the footsteps, his ear cocked. The study door handle rattled briefly, then hurrying steps moved to the library. Guzarin's words dribbled away, then, in a tone of mild interest, he said, "Apparently not my men." He drew a main gauche with his left hand and flicked the blade. He held the dagger to his ear, listening to the ring of the steel, and smiled. He drew his arming sword with his right hand and waited, at ease and relaxed.

The library door banged open with nobody visible. Then Quern leapt forward, Kalainen at his heels. Guzarin graciously motioned them in with the sword.

Kalainen was surprised the ambassador was not standing with his blade to Imber's throat. He crabbed into the room suspiciously, his sword held forward.

"Ah, the long-nosed prying Drouhin himself. If I'd had a fraction more time, you and I would have met before now. I am very pleased to see you before I leave."

"I don't think you will leave," grated Quern.

"You have no power to stop me." The ambassador spoke lightly, as though at a social function. Guzarin waved the dagger at Yanni suddenly. "No, no, little girl. Leave our friend in the chair. I now have a duty I will now have to perform myself with him."

Guzarin seemed almost to float round the room, both blades held forwards. Quern moved in step, always facing the ambassador, his single sword ready, beard a-bristle as he focused on the Tarlenian.

"Please call your other friend to join us from upstairs. The little reptile, Tertius Orbis? Ah, I see in your face there is no-one else. How did.... No matter. Very well." The Tarlenian reached out and pushed the door with the point of his long blade. The door swung back and closed with a solid clunk.

"And now, all the people who know of my little trinkets are right here in this room. How terribly convenient, for me." Guzarin gave a little laugh. He set down the main gauche, reached back and opened the secret cabinet.

"Your thief found it, seems only fair that you get a brief look. Wonderful things," Guzarin purred. "I know all about them; their histories, their powers! Their previous owners did not appreciate them."

But none of them took their eyes from the ambassador. He shrugged, uncaring, and picked up the main gauche again.

"It is the collector who kills the butterfly," murmured Kalainen.

"Only the dead butterfly can be displayed." Guzarin laughed at his own wit. "Shaddimur's finest minds and warriors? You are pygmies beside me. Pygmies!"

"Sitting on each other's shoulders, three pygmies see further than the giant."

Guzarin seemed to be trying to find a suitable rejoinder, but then he shrugged. "Spit roast pygmy, then." At the same moment, he and Quern lunged together and disappeared in a maelstrom of flickering swords. Kalainen searched for an opening but the action was too fast for him and he was more likely to get in Quern's way.

Quern attacked with the same maniacal speed he had shown on the stairs. Sometimes a boot, sometimes a slash or thrust, a punch, they came at the Tarlenian seemingly at random in an unceasing rain. For a moment, Kalainen thought Quern's mighty strength and frenetic style might beat through Guzarin's defence. But the Ambassador flowed round the blows like a fly dodging a carthorse. Unorthodox but brilliant, Guzarin used the arming sword to block or parry and each time he did, the wicked dagger flicked out, cutting deep, punching holes. Guzarin was better even than Astelin of Tarlenia, perhaps better than Shen. Kalainen then realised what Quern had known before he had attacked. He could not win. Kalainen needed to help, but the combat was too fast-moving; manoeuvre

as he might, Guzarin never gave him the least opening. Suddenly
Quern was hopelessly off-balance. The main gauche thrust into his
leg, Guzarin's elbow struck him on the back of the head and he
crashed down beside the desk. As he fell, Guzarin's sword lunged
out, striking straight into Kalainen's chest. Kalainen's sword was still
coming up into guard and he only had time for a surprised expression before he collapsed over backwards.

"And so it is over." Guzarin sounded almost bored. Then he
watched with a detached interest as Kalainen crawled back up,
coughing. He waved the little blade in a mocking salute.

"Well, that is a surprise; the Drouhin has chain mail. You do not
have to die here, you know? I could use you. We do things by force
of arms but we are not blind to the value of intelligence. How much
gold would it take, Drouhin?"

"A fox believes everyone eats hens," Kalainen said, his slow drawl
eked out by dragging gasps. Behind him, Quern hauled himself back
to his feet, leaving bloody handprints on the desk, dark drips mar-
ring the silver of the patterned globe.

Guzarin sighed. "I am the finest swordsman in Tarlenia – which
is to say in the Seven Cities. I do not boast, I merely state. You have
no power to hurt me and you throw a good offer back in my face.
Even if you do not want to live, there are ways you do not want to
die. Trust me on that. But the way you die is the last choice you
have."

Quern's attack was blindingly fast. He launched himself off the
desk directly at Guzarin, his huge strength carving a blow that
should have beaten through the best defence. Somehow the Tarlenian swayed out of the way so skilfully it looked as though the
blade had passed right through him. The counterstroke was almost
too easy. Guzarin's sword drove straight into Quern's chest, punching through the thick gambeson with a hideous tearing noise, the
main gauche thrust upwards on the other side just below Quern's

ribs. But the big man's momentum could not be stopped by any force, his bulk clattering into the Tarlenian. The sword strike had just been a distraction. With a wordless bellow, Quern swung his left fist, clutching the silver globe. The heavy trophy should have crushed Guzarin's skull. Almost impossibly, Guzarin nearly managed to evade the blow. But only nearly, and with Quern's full weight behind it, the globe smashed him on the side of his face even as he jerked away. His cheek bone shattered, the right eye burst in a smear over the remains of his nose. Partly as a result of the power of Quern's arm and partly his own leap backwards, Guzarin went flying over the desk leaving a spray of blood, his feet waving as he crashed onto his back.

Quern collapsed back in a sitting position against the desk, the two swords still stuck through his chest. He made a gurgling noise that was almost a laugh. "You're lucky ... that didn't hurt ... at all, then! Eh?"

Guzarin was floundering back to his feet, the perfect poise broken. Blood was pouring down the right side of his face and he was yelling, more in outrage that it could have happened than in pain.

Mardenifol raced to Imber to try to unbuckle the heavy straps. Guzarin saw him, but both his weapons were buried in Quern. Even as the ambassador staggered towards a sabre displayed on the wall, there was a wild screech as Yanni leapt on his back from his blind side. Reeling and bellowing as she gouged for his good eye, Guzarin grabbed her and bodily hurled her across the room to crumple into a small table in a shower of fragments.

The Tarlenian turned back to the wall, his legs half-flopping, and wrenched down the sabre. He tossed the scabbard away and forced himself into a fighting stance, hitching awkwardly at his shoulder.

"I will cripple and blind every one of you," he snarled. His eye blazed madly as he moved clumsily towards Imber and Mardenifol. Mardenifol's thin fingers had failed to loosen any of the straps and now his eyes widened in terror, mouth stretched into a crescent of fear. But even as he cringed away from the Tarlenian, he yanked a knife from Imber's neck sheath and sawed wildly at the tough leather.

Before Guzarin reached them, Kalainen moved into the way, his rust-spotted sword held forward.

"And you are suddenly going to announce you were First Sword in Caronile, are you?" The words bubbled out of the ambassador, distorted by his wrecked face, thickened with loathing. Guzarin coughed and swallowed painfully, glaring at the Drouhin.

"No. I was a common soldier, once."

"You cannot face me," said Guzarin.

"Beat you, perhaps not. But face you I will." Kalainen's soft drawl was as steady as the sword point.

"The great man of peace reaches for a sword," Guzarin sneered. His head jerked round, the eye rolling madly, as he tried to look all round him.

"When he must. My students have taught me it is better to face death and die than run away and live."

"Die first, then." Guzarin rotated his shoulder uncomfortably again, snarling like a bear. Then he attacked. But his usual fluidity had deserted him as he dragged at breaths. His moves were slowed as though demonstrating the correct positions to a novice. He grunted with each slash of the heavy sabre.

Despite that, Kalainen could only defend desperately. He looked for an opening, but there was none through Guzarin's flawless technique. He could only beat away each attack, never able to risk a counterstroke through that deadly maze of steel. But every clash of blades ticked another second for Mardenifol.

Guzarin stopped again, his arms hanging as though the sabre was too heavy to lift. His features were contorted with effort as he wheezed, his one eye afire with rage. Suddenly he coughed and spat a lump of bloody phlegm on the floor. As he looked at it in confusion, Kalainen lunged.

Still too slow. Reflexively, Guzarin's sword whipped up, parrying with such force that sparks flew from the Drouhin's blade as it went spinning from his grip. Kalainen fell awkwardly, twisting sideways towards Imber's chair to avoid Guzarin's return stroke that nearly caught him, biting into the floor like an axe. Guzarin took half a step after the Drouhin, then lifted his shoulder again, his body twisting. He raised his elbow, slowly lifting his arm and his head wobbled down to look beneath it. Nestling in the hollow of his armpit was the hilt of Yanni's stiletto. As he stared at it uncomprehendingly, there was a sudden blur and the butt of Imber's throwing knife appeared a handspan lower.

Guzarin grunted, then roared as he turned to Imber, who had one arm now free. Then Kalainen rose up and smacked down the poker with a blow like a farmhand trying to swat a rat. The poker broke Guzarin's hand at the wrist. The Tarlenian ambassador toppled slowly to his knees and stayed there. He felt round and picked up the sabre with his left hand and began feebly trying to push himself upright with the blade, digging a few splinters from the floor.

Completely ignoring the fallen ambassador, Kalainen ran to Quern. The big warrior was sitting immobile against the desk, staring at the kneeling ambassador with a look of satisfaction. Kalainen dropped to his knees, feeling for the hilts of the two blades.

"Dead when they come out," murmured Quern. "Dead anyway." He blinked slowly and exhaled in a way that might have been a laugh. "Worth it."

Yanni crawled over to him from where Guzarin had tossed her. She made no sound but tears were pouring down her cheeks. She dropped her face on his leg, her fingers clutching into the material of his breeches.

Quern moved a massive hand to her shoulder. He spoke softly

with a voice getting deeper and slower. "Don' cry, Yann. What I was born for. You were always ... the toughest of us." He tried to look down at her. His eyes closed. They did not open again.

There was the confused noise of many voices coming up the stairs. Imber, now released from the chair, collected his knives except for the one buried in Guzarin. As he clipped the two wrist knives back into place, he looked thoughtfully at the ambassador's desk. A sand shaker of dark wood had been knocked onto its side. The Tarlenian crest was inlaid into it in gold. Kedu would appreciate that. Imber popped it in a pocket to take to the old rogue. He unlocked the study door and opened it, allowing the swelling din to wash in like a tide. Then he slipped away through the library.

A large detachment of dignitaries, led by Gwyan and Sergeant Rown, began to push their way into the study, looking around with distaste or distrust. Many were exclaiming with affected horror, squabbling for advantage like vultures round a carcase.

Rown came straight over to Kalainen. "I brought a healer," he said. "In case, you know. I thought."

Kalainen raised a desolate face to the Watch Sergeant. He nodded. "Too late for Quern. Would not have helped. Best see to the ambassador."

The diplomats were shown the cabinet with its trophies. Vallis stood beside the cabinet, refusing to allow anyone to touch the items. One minor noble perhaps hoped to ingratiate himself with his superiors, or perhaps to acquire valuables for himself.

"Stand aside, fellow! I know where many of these trinkets belong and will return them."

"The provenance of the items is known to the Watch. All items will be returned shortly when no longer required as evidence."

"Out of my way, I say. I tolerate no nonsense from flunkies, I can tell you!"

"Indeed, sir," said Vallis, his watery eyes swivelling round to stare directly at the Shaddimur noble. "We of the Watch are almost fully occupied dealing with one ambassador bleeding out on the floor here. But only almost."

The noble flapped his mouth at Vallis, then suddenly turned, calling to an imaginary friend, "I say, we've found the Holy Dagger of Ameroth. Isn't it marvellous?" He hurried away.

Vallis gazed placidly over the heads of the assembled diplomats, with perhaps the tiniest smile.

"Drouhin! The Feyhan Star is not here!" The cloaked man from Palemin turned from studying the secret cabinet and gave an accusing stare at Kalainen. Rown had obviously explained Kalainen's deductions and the man acted as if this one glaring absence undermined the whole story.

Kalainen paused for a moment, then waved towards Guzarin where he lay on the floor, pale and sweating under the ministrations of the healer, who was mopping and tutting in a professional way. Guzarin's tunic had been opened, his undershirt cut away. The Feyhan Star was on a chain about his neck. It seemed to shine with a gentle lilac light.

Rown moved forward to remove the jewel from the ambassador's throat. When he tried, Guzarin roused to swipe at him weakly.

"No! It's mine now. Mine!"

When Rown tried again to remove the Star, Guzarin ignored the protestations of the healer and surged up, his remaining eye staring glassily over the silenced group from the shocking mask of his face.

"Out!" he roared. "Nobody touches this. Nobody but I could take it." The words came out in a slurred bellow. His arms jerked wildly as though he leapt upon them with both his blades. "I ... kill..." he gasped suddenly, stiffened horribly and fell.

Rown and the healer caught him as he went down, but he only twitched a couple of times, and died. They laid him on the floor and stepped away.

There was a profound silence as the diplomats from seven cities regarded the fallen Tarlenian. His last words echoed round the crowded study, branding the listeners with the knowledge that here was the killer who had stalked Shaddimur. Then there was a slight scuffle as Yanni pushed through the crowd. She held one arm across her chest but used the other elbow with some skill and little consideration for the august dignitaries. She slid past the healer who was wringing his hands ineffectually.

She kicked Guzarin's arm out of the way, bent down and wrenched her stiletto from his armpit with a ghastly sucking noise that made most of the diplomats recoil, wincing.

"Well, I'm having this back," she said, and wiped it on a clean bit of Guzarin's undershirt. Then she pulled the Feyhan Star free of him, letting his head fall back onto the boards with a thud like dropping a cabbage. "You don't kill, you die. Conkin' pile of ghulsk," she said, making the assembled company recoil still further, and spat on the ambassador.

Turning round, she lifted Sergeant Rown's arm as he stood stiff with horror and hung the jewel on it.

Rown croaked, "Some ... respect..."

Suddenly seeming to notice everyone staring at her, Yanni stopped.

"Where it's due, Sergeant," she said sweetly. Then she shrugged, turned back and gave Guzarin's body a walloping kick somewhere that would have softened the blow of being dead.

Epilogue

Mardenifol admitted Captain Traid to Coromal with his usual courtly bow. The Captain growled something and waved his hand in a way that could have been a gesture of dismissal or perhaps the sketchiest of salutes. He clumped into the kitchen, pulled a pack off his shoulders and dumped it on the floor with a leaden rattle, then dropped himself heavily into a chair. He looked round almost nervously.

"Kaller... hmm. Where's that ... you know."

"Yanni?"

"That girl, yes. Where's she?" Traid seemed to think Yanni might leap out at him brandishing stilettoes at any moment.

"She accepted a post as a cook."

Traid brightened a little at her absence. "Down at the Iron Eye? Oh. I suppose that means no tea?" He slumped back in his usual depression.

Kalainen chuckled. "Not the Iron Eye. She's working at the Bruelan embassy for Gwyan and Esferle."

"They've let her near an embassy? After that squawking from the
nobility? Lady's sake, she spat on an ambassador! Kicked his corpse
in the cullions and called him a ..." For a moment, Traid almost
grinned. The half-grin fell away and he shot an accusatory look at
the Drouhin. "You've got ears at the heart of an embassy!"

"I'm sure she'll be a model of rectitude."

"Hah! Not that girl. She's got a taste for meddling, I know the
type."

"It's a good appointment for all of them. Yanni didn't want to
stay here after what happened. Now, I think we could run to a beer,
assuming you've come with payment."

Traid snorted. "Probably should run to the finest brandy." His
brows drew together as the irritation he always felt around Kalainen
grew. "Although I have no idea what the reward is, except this." He
drew a heavy box out of the pack on the floor and clunked it on the
table. "It's locked," he added.

"And the key?"

"I am instructed to say that the key is in the box. It comes with
the compliments of Master Nyrudin, the Queen's locksmith."

Kalainen laughed and pushed the box aside. "Well, I think I know
someone who may be able to help with that."

Traid looked glummer than ever. "It was a terrible night. We
managed to more or less keep things under control but there were
fires to fight, fights to f... break up. My lads were heroes, not that
they'll get praise or chests of gold."

"Quern died."

Traid shifted uncomfortably. "Well, I suppose you did your bit.
A good man, Quern. I'm still not clear how Sarrepo was murdered."

Kalainen poured beer into three mugs as Mardenifol joined
them. Traid was about to say something but stopped. He gave an ap-

praising look at the lad. The boy had come through a lot. Quite well, considering. And he was Lord Berrin's son. "You need a shave," he said gruffly. "Come on then, what happened?"

"The Tarlenian's sent Guzarin here as the Ambassador. His task was to weaken Shaddimur by killing those who would lead the defence. He hired a spy, Tertius Orbis, to scout the properties of victims. Then he chose to keep a memento of each murder. For the murder of Sarrepo, the Breulan ambassador, Guzarin first sent Hygven to collect a sleeping draught from Madam Vermoil, the apothecary. She refused to treat with him and an argument developed in which Vermoil was killed. Hygven robbed the petty cash to make it look like a burglary, tore the page for dwale from her book and took all the ingredients he needed.

"To confuse the issue, Hygven tipped the contents of several other random jars into a pile behind the counter and threw the empty vessels into the herb garden. The dwale decoction was created in the Tarlenian embassy kitchen, where we found the jars and the recipe.

"As the weather cooled, a girl, Dessia, was paid to take a wine posset to the guards every night. On this night, the posset was spiked with dwale and the guards slept.

"With the guards incapacitated, it was a simple matter for Guzarin to slip within and despatch guards and Sarrepo. With four guards and the comings and goings of embassy staff, they didn't even lock their main door. To add to his collection, Guzarin stole the Feyhan Star, a family jewel like a large pearl in a silver flower.

"Guzarin then searched out Telas and killed him in his bed. Necessary because Telas played party tricks finding coins and pretended to be a magician. Was he good enough to cast a spell to locate the Feyhan Star? Likely not, but it was a risk Guzarin decided he could not take. No other loremaster could locate it, not having studied the Feyhan Star. We found the Star round the ambassador's neck."

"Proof enough, given the whole trophy cabinet full of things stolen from every murder victim and the good ambassador's final words."

"Before representatives from every city."

Traid drank more beer, then nodded. "It'll do. Our methods are..."

When Traid broke off, Kalainen put in, "We have different forks, but eat from the same plate."

Traid sighed volcanically and rose. "Why couldn't a loremaster find any of the other items, then?"

Kalainen shrugged. "The Feyhan Star was the only item taken from someone known to be a magician. Loremaster Aldarilen said he would have to know a specific item in great detail before he could find it. Have you ever known a loremaster find anything? Most of the ones I know can barely find their way to the privy. Aldarilen pointed out that the Star was the only trophy not kept in the cabinet and suggested that the cabinet might be magically shielded."

"That would no doubt account for it." Traid turned at the door. "I suppose you've heard Chelidor has wandered back to Shaddimur? I heard he had a message for you. It'd better not be trouble."

Kalainen nodded. "Be good to see him. He's missed all the excitement."

"Well, just make sure he doesn't stir up a lot more. I'm holding you responsible." Traid smoothed his whiskers and headed out into the rain.

Mardenifol bowed him out, then sat down by Kalainen. For a while, they both stared at the range, lost in their own thoughts. Mardenifol rubbed the thin point of his chin between the thumb and fingers of his left hand as though hoping a fetching goatee had developed.

"I've been thinking. You want to go back to Drouhin. I could come with you, visit the place. It'd be an adventure."

A sad smile touched Kalainen's face. "You know I can't go with Ruffin so ill."

"He's getting better. Yanni said she and Imber will watch over him for a bit. We could go."

"Yanni suggested I went?"

"Yanni doesn't want you to go. She wants you to come back."

"No, it's kind, but you don't want to leave Shaddimur, nor all your family and your experiments."

"No, well," began Mardenifol, thinking leaving his family would cause fewer pangs all round than the other two, "But it wouldn't be for long, would it? I mean, how far away is Drouhin?" When there was no answer, Mardenifol pressed on. "How long would it take to get there? Kalainen?"

When he finally spoke, Kalainen's voice was desolate. "I don't know."

"You don't know? Just roughly? Is that because of the war zone round Tarlenia? We could visit Allecando, they make the best glassware there. Alembics and retorts and stuff. Or is it south? I mean, we'd follow the coast road through Gallendia, wouldn't we? Which way is it? Kalainen, when were you last there?"

Kalainen's voice cracked with a pain so deep it stuck Mardenifol silent. "I remember a beautiful town of roses and balconies washed with the smell of the sea. The great bell of Mirrin's Tower suffusing the air. Racing and yelling and leaping down rickety steps with friends. I remember the smell of drying fish and singing and the festival of cakes. Then images of fleeing with my mother. We'd been visiting, perhaps it was her family. I don't know. Never made it back. Pounding hooves, fire. Then being on my own, always trying to get away, get further from Drouhin. The further I went, the less sure I was of where I'd been. Now I need to go back but Drouhin is lost, as lost as Siuda Reyes. Nobody's heard of Drouhin anymore, nobody's met anyone from Drouhin. Perhaps I am the very last. Even the great city of wizardry Siuda Reyes was destroyed. But Drouhin was a hidden town in a cleft in the rock. Perhaps it survives still, the call from Mirrin's Tower still ringing down the evening? Chelidor has been looking."

"Looking for Drouhin?"

"For Drouhin. For anyone from Drouhin. For anyone who has even heard of the little town in the chine."

"By the Lady, I never thought... But now Chelidor has a message for you!"

"He's back." Kalainen looked up, eyes sparkling, the old grin dimpling his cheeks. "And yes, yes he does."

The End of the Drouhin of Shaddimur.

Other stories in the Power of Pain series:

The Riddle of the Seer.

In a land where magic is shaped from pain, who would be a sorcerer?

Attics hide many things of the past. There Jebbin finds a spell book and discovers he has the rare talent of magic. But nothing is free and spells are created from pain. Jebbin winces, but the pain is not yet so important. For a country lad, the world seems to beckon with wonders. That naivety leads to jail where he meets a sinister magician prepared to mortify his own flesh for power.

Jebbin is joined by a blunt wrestler and a bard as adept at reading people as at crafting songs. In a vibrant world of intrigue and danger, he needs all his wits and magic to decipher the Riddle of the Seer amid the teeming colours of Lana Fair. Finally, he must learn the true Power of Pain.

Exciting, inventive and occasionally hilarious, the Riddle of the Seer blends magic and realism in a classic quest.

The Maker of Warriors.

Someone is practising arts best left to rot...

The Maker of Warriors is melding steel with flesh to create peerless fighters. The wrestler Bolan seeks revenge on the creator of the giant who killed his friend in the catacombs below Rokepike Castle. He needs the help of the magician Jebbin. Only the Thieves Guild have the network to find the sorcerer. Unfortunately, they have also sworn to kill Jebbin to end the threat of the Mage without a Staff, and they have paid the assassins to kill Bolan.

Bolan's failure to follow Algolian rules forces him to flee across the country with a renegade captain, pursued by the army, Rhabdos of the Hazel staff, and the thieves before he can even think of reaching the Maker himself on the island of Torl.

A story of loyalty, courage and love, the Maker of Warriors is the fast-paced sequel to the Riddle of the Seer. Both are complete and self-contained novels in the Power of Pain series.

CPSIA information can be obtained
at www.ICGtesting.com
Printed in the USA
BVHW041943100820
585960BV00013B/800